ALSO BY JOHN CLARKSON

THE JAMES BECK NOVELS
Among Thieves
Bronx Requiem
Death Comes Due

THE ONE SERIES
And Justice for One
One Way Out
One Man's Law

New Lots
Reed's Promise

TRIBES

JOHN CLARKSON

Tribes
Copyright @2023 by John Clarkson
All rights reserved.

This is a work of fiction. All the characters, organizations, and events portrayed in this novel are either products of the author's imagination or used fictitiously.

No part of this publication may be reproduced, distributed or transmitted in any form or by any means, including photocopying, recording, or other electronic or mechanical methods without the prior written permission of the publisher, except in the case of brief quotations embodied in critical reviews and certain other noncommercial uses permitted by copyright laws.

First Edition published 2023 by John Clarkson Inc.
www.johnclarkson.com
ISBN 978-1-7356335-2-7   softcover
ISBN 978-1-7356335-3-4   e-book

Subject of this book:
Crime – Fiction
Ex-convicts – Fiction
Class war – Fiction
White Supremacy – Fiction
Upstate Rural New York – Fiction

Cover and interior design: Design for Writers

For the divided

1

Somewhere in the back of his mind James Beck knew that drinking alone outside at night in December wasn't the best thing he could be doing. Particularly at an isolated hangout in upstate New York patronized by blue collar working types, half of them members of a rural gang referred to as the Kin. Beck was familiar with the type – lots of beards, tattoos, and threatening glares. They reminded him of white Aryan gang members he'd run across during his eight years in New York State prisons. The Kin boys annoyed Beck, but they didn't intimidate him. He either ignored them or stared back, daring them to say something.

Beck's size and demeanor, salt-and-pepper Covid beard, and dark hair grown past his collar made him look like someone best left alone. Particularly hunkered down in an Adirondack chair with his black knit cap pulled low and his dark Burberry quilted coat zipped up. And perhaps some of the Kin boys knew an ex-con when they saw one. Even in the half-light of the firepits scattered around the Field.

The locals called it the Field because that's what it was. An empty field in the Catskills bushwhacked out of overgrown farmland, surrounded on three sides by a scrub forest and on the fourth by a rundown red barn set back about twenty yards from a dirt road. Behind the barn, steel rings contained fires that didn't provide much warmth against the wintry night air but did have an evolutionary power to be comforting.

The Field had its advantages. It stayed open as long as people wanted to drink. It was only two miles from Beck's house via back roads, so there was little chance of getting nailed for a DUI before he arrived home to a spacious house on twenty-seven acres. Also, the Field didn't have much competition. After years of Covid, legit bars opened only three or four days a week; none of them stayed open late.

The two brothers who ran the Field, George and Vic Myer, didn't bother with closing hours, a liquor license, permits, health codes, or filing tax returns. They did make sure to keep the peace so the state police and county sheriffs could continue acting as if the Field didn't exist. If a disturbance broke out, George and Vic would emerge from their dilapidated red barn carrying baseball bats, intent on turning unruly patrons into piñatas. It put a quick end to trouble. Beck figured that if George and Vic relied on baseball bats, it meant the locals knew enough to leave their guns at home or at least in their pickup trucks.

On balance, the Field worked for Beck the few times a month he was in the mood for it. Sitting outside by a fire sipping Irish whiskey helped Beck ignore the toll that living alone in a rural area had taken on him. Leaving Brooklyn had seemed logical. Covid, the gentrification of the fringe Red Hook neighborhood, and the desecration of his home by a maniac who had set fire to it as part of a gruesome war waged against Beck and his tight-knit crew of ex-cons were all good reasons to move upstate. But the months and years of isolation had diminished Beck's already small tolerance for anyone trying to impose their will on him.

There were times when sitting back in a weather-beaten Adirondack chair, sipping good Irish whiskey, followed by a swallow of Guinness, and glancing up at a black winter sky bristling with billions of gleaming stars, made James Beck feel as if all was right with the world. Even though it wasn't.

2

Andy Miller stood in the shadows watching Beck. Andy didn't know Beck's name. He knew him by his drink order – a double Redbreast Irish whiskey in a four-ounce tumbler when they had it, Jameson when they didn't. Guinness chaser in a 14.2-ounce can. Miller carried drinks from the barn to customers scattered around the Field, along with enough free chicken wings and chili to keep the drinkers drinking.

Andy had been waiting to see if the bearded guy wanted another round. He usually nursed one round but sometimes ordered a second. Miller kept track because Mr. Redbreast was a good tipper. Then Andy saw Irene Allen step into the firelight surrounding Mr. Redbreast. The odds on a second round went up.

Irene approached Beck with her usual conspiratorial smile. She was one person at the Field Beck enjoyed seeing. He liked Irene's looks and manner. Country cute, good humored, and a trim body, all of which went well with her who-gives-a-shit personality. And Irene never stayed long enough to wear out her welcome. She liked to move around, hit and run, visit with anybody and everybody, flirt, crack wise, and find out the latest scuttlebutt.

Beck pegged Irene as mid-thirties. Around five-four. Maybe a hundred-ten pounds. She dressed like a tomboy and seemed impervious to the cold. This night she wore a snug fitting thermal top under a brown plaid flannel shirt and a half-open canvas Carhartt barn jacket. Tight jeans showed off her legs and ass. No hat covered her tousled, short, dark hair.

Beck knew that Irene worked in construction. He was sure that underneath the layers of clothing, there wasn't enough body fat on Irene Allen to hide her lean muscles. Beck didn't dwell on what Irene would look like without clothes. She deserved her privacy, particularly around the Field. Few women patronized the Field, and none of them came alone. Irene Allen always came to the Field by herself; another reason Beck liked her.

She stomped toward Beck in her Red Wing work boots, holding a bottle of Lagunitas IPA in her right hand. She straddled Beck's left leg and sat down on his thigh. Beck didn't react. Even though Irene presented as lesbian, she always flirted with Beck, although not quite this blatantly. He could feel her pubic bone pressing into his leg. It distracted him so much that before he knew it, Irene leaned over and snatched his small tumbler of Redbreast with her free hand. She took a generous sip, chasing it with her ale, and put his glass back on the arm of the Adirondack chair.

Beck grabbed the remains of his whiskey. Irene smiled and said, "Jeezus, I'm horny tonight."

"And thirsty."

In response Irene tipped her bottle of ale at Beck and took another swig.

"Don't you have a girlfriend waiting somewhere for you?"

"Friendzzzz. I can't find any of 'em." She bounced a little on Beck and said, "I can make do with a man if I have to. How are you in bed, Irish? Any good?"

"Absolutely life-changing. Now get off me and pull up a chair. You're too heavy."

"Bullshit." Irene gave it one more bounce and pushed off Beck, swinging her leg over like she was dismounting a horse. Irene stepped into the shadows and reappeared dragging a yellow Crosely lawn chair mottled with rust. She set the flower-shaped metal chair on Beck's left next to his glass of Redbreast which was now empty. She stared at the empty glass.

Beck said, "You want one?"

"Thought you'd never ask."

As if on cue, Andy Miller came out of the shadows, smiling.

Beck held up his empty glass and said, "I'll take another."

Andy bobbed his head as he listened to Beck's drink order. He never looked directly at whoever was speaking. Beck wondered if that was because Miller couldn't see very well. He wore glasses with lenses so thick they made the frames slide down his nose.

"And a Guinness?"

"No. Just the whiskey."

Irene leaned over and gave Beck a look. "Aaand?"

"And a Redbreast for Irene."

"A double," said Irene.

Andy nodded and gave them a thumbs-up.

As Miller disappeared into the shadows, Irene said, "I have a theory why he always wears them shitbag, worn-out Dickie coveralls."

"To hide his bowlegs?"

"You got it, man. That and how skinny he is. Like bag of bones skinny."

Beck nodded.

"I like that fucker," said Irene. "The help at this shithole comes and goes, but Andy hangs in. The assholes around here rag him about being an inbred retard, but he works hard and never complains."

Beck said, "Inbred?"

Irene waved a hand dismissively. "He comes from people been here a long time. Generations. Hill people. You know, kissin' cousins and all that bullshit."

Beck nodded, thinking about Andy's bowlegs, bad eyesight, and apparent mental deficits.

Miller emerged out of the shadows with the drinks on a small tray. He handed Irene her drink.

She smiled. "Thanks, sweetie."

Miller placed Beck's whiskey on the arm of his chair and scooped up the empty glass. Beck handed him a folded fifty-dollar bill and thanked Andy.

Irene caught the bill's denomination in the firelight but didn't say anything. She liked this guy she called Irish. She didn't know his name, what he did for work, or where he lived. Clearly, he had money. He tipped well, dressed well, and drove an expensive two-year-old black GMC Denali Sierra. But he wasn't interested in people knowing he had money. Or knowing anything about him, for that matter. Unlike the assholes who wanted everyone to know they had enough money to buy the expensive trucks and SUVs they drove to the Field because they were part of the Kin.

Irene had slept with a few women, but more out of curiosity than sexual preference. She wasn't gay. She projected that image mostly so that the men at the Field wouldn't hit on her. That didn't include the bearded stranger who drank expensive Irish whiskey, had a sense of humor, and knew how to tip hard-working people.

Irene took another sip of her whiskey and said to Beck, "Hey, Irish, anybody ever tell you that you don't talk much?"

"Not really. What have you got to say for yourself tonight?"

"Not much. Although I saw something interesting a few minutes ago."

"What?"

Irene dropped her voice. "Before I came looking for you, I went to see if your truck was in the parking area. I saw three guys having an argument. One of them is mid-level Kin leader named Lund. Oscar Lund. Longish gray hair. Gut hanging over his damn pants. He doesn't come here often. One of the other two was a meatball asshole named Hamm Elrod. The third guy was Joey Collins. It was mostly Hamm Elrod doing all the bitching. Lund was trying to squash it."

"What's so interesting about that?"

"Nothing much. The interesting part is that Hamm Elrod and Joey Collins shouldn't be anywhere near each other. Hamm Elrod is Kin muscle. A knuckle-dragger whose go-to move is a fist in your face. Joey Collins is like Kin aristocracy. A lot of high-up leaders came out of his family."

"You seem to know a lot about the Kin."

"I grew up around here. People are always talking about the Kin."

Irene jumped up and finished her whiskey.

"I want to mingle. You gonna be here for a while?"

Beck looked at his drink and lifted his can of Guinness to gauge how much was left.

"A bit."

Beck watched Irene disappear into the shadows. He took a sip of his Redbreast. Suddenly, he didn't feel like finishing the booze. A sense of unease came over him. He'd been telling himself there were plenty of locals at the Field who weren't part of the Kin. The guy who'd told him about the Field worked on his property and had nothing to do with the Kin. But there were enough Kin assholes around the Field to cause trouble he didn't need to be around. He checked his watch. Nearly midnight. The fire near him had burned down to embers. Time to go home.

Just as Beck leaned forward to push himself out of his Adirondack chair, voices approaching from the shadows stopped him. Three men emerged into the firelight off to his left. The three Irene had talked about. It wasn't hard to figure out who was who. Oscar Lund looked like a hundred other guys he'd seen in the area. Maybe bigger than most, but typical. Beefy, wearing a camouflage vest, sweat-stained Carhartt ball cap, jeans, and boots. He was talking to a fireplug of a man walking next to him who had to be Hamm Elrod. His hair was cropped so short he looked bald. Elrod moved and sounded like a disgruntled dive bar bouncer who'd been in too many fights. He wore baggy jeans that hadn't seen the inside of a washing machine in a long time, a fake sheepskin jacket patched with a piece of duct tape on the right shoulder seam over a dirty t-shirt, and Walmart boots. That left Joey Collins. Younger. Saying nothing. His corduroy pants and down coat looked clean and relatively new. He walked behind the other two like he didn't want to be with them.

Lund tried to keep his voice down, but he had a smoker's rasp that made it easy to hear him as they came parallel to Beck.

"Goddammit, Hamm, I'm done talkin' about it. You knocked that fucking geezer down so hard I heard his skull hit the asphalt from fifty feet away."

"What was I supposed to do? Pretty boy Joey was nowhere to be seen."

Lund started to say something, stopped himself, and said, "Quit arguing with me. I'm done talking about it."

Beck sat back waiting for them to pass by. As they walked past him, he spotted the gun holstered at Oscar's hip. Oscar Lund's down vest didn't quite cover it.

Apparently, the brothers' ban on guns at the Field didn't apply to Kin leaders.

As they walked past the firepit, the bald bruiser picked up a piece of firewood from a pile nearby and tossed it onto the fire, sending smoke and sparks in the air that wafted in Beck's direction. Beck waved away the smoke catching Hamm Elrod's attention. Elrod turned and sneered at Beck. "What's the matter, princess? Smoke get in your eyes?"

Beck's eyes narrowed. He kept his mouth shut and tamped down the anger that flared in his gut, but there was no way he could leave now and let some fat asshole think he'd driven him off.

Beck checked his watch. 12:13 a.m. Suddenly, the cold seemed to penetrate into him. He finished his whiskey and chased it with the remains of his Guinness, keeping an eye on Elrod to see if he was going to become the focus for Fatboy's bad mood. The three of them stood on the other side of the fire. Elrod kept glancing back at Beck with hostile glares. Beck knew nothing good would come from letting this guy get away with that shit, but he decided walking over and breaking his nose wasn't worth the trouble.

Beck watched the three of them. Lund was doing the talking. He pictured what would happen if he told Elrod to go fuck himself. Beck figured he would bull rush him and try for a roundhouse right aimed at his head. The bruiser was shorter and heavier. Ducking under the punch would be difficult. The move would be to step right and lean away from the punch. When the punch missed, pivot left and deliver a short, hard right hook as the bull staggered past him. Aim for the jaw, just under the ear. The pivot would have to be fast. The counterpunch faster. Beck knew he'd be lucky to take him out with one shot, but if he connected, he'd break the fucker's jaw and knock him out. And probably break a couple of his knuckles. Then there were the other two, one with a gun. He'd have to take down all three before they could react. Very difficult. Nearly impossible with a broken hand. The hell with it.

Hamm Elrod stopped glaring at Beck when Lund reached out and backhanded Elrod's shoulder to get his attention. Lund spoke slowly. Beck could hear most of what he said.

"All right, you two, you got it done, but not how you should have. There could be blowback but screw it. Won't be nuthin' we haven't dealt with before." The bruiser started to say something, but Lund raised a hand and said, "No. Zip it, Hamm. We sent a message. It's done. We'll talk in a day or two when things settle down. For now, I want you both to hang out until the place thins out so people will remember seeing you. First round is on me. But don't overdo it. Just goddamn relax. We're done."

Joey Collins said, "Yes, sir."

Elrod nodded and kept his mouth shut.

Oscar said, "Okay." He turned and walked in the direction of the barn to pay for the first round of drinks. Elrod and Collins grabbed two chairs and sat down opposite Beck on the other side of the fire.

Interesting, thought Beck. *They'd hurt an old man and now they're here to establish an alibi.*

Andy Miller had been waiting for Oscar Lund to leave. Now he stepped into the firelight, a scarecrow in his stained Dickie coveralls, nodding. Andy bounced up and down on the balls of his feet, ready to take their drink order.

The bruiser ignored Andy. He turned to Collins, still pissed off about what happened.

"Fuckwit. Would've been no problem if you'da been where you were supposed to be."

Joey Collins snapped back, "When are you going to get it? He was already out of the van helping those guys load up. It was so damn simple. All you had to do was wait for him to…"

"Shut it. Like Oscar said, we'll go into it later. I know you think you got status, pal, but you had a chance to prove you've got some balls and you blew it. Trust me, I ain't takin' all the blame. Right now I need a fucking drink." He looked up at Andy, still waiting. "Gimme a Scotch. Double. No ice."

Collins said, "Beer."

As Andy Miller turned to fetch the drinks, the bald asshole lifted his foot and booted Andy in the ass.

"And make it quick, retard."

Beck saw Andy wince. He was too thin to take the blow. He moved away from the pair awkwardly, trying not to show how much the kick hurt.

Beck's anger and disgust ignited breathtakingly fast. Fucking lowlifes. He had no business being here. Whatever fondness he had for drinking under the stars at the Field evaporated. As he was about to leave, Irene dropped down onto the chair next to Beck.

She said to Beck, "Did you see that?"

"Yeah, I saw it."

"Goddamn Elrod is such an asshole. The word is they were on some kind of holdup or something and went wrong. My money says the fuckup was Hamm Elrod."

"How do you know all this?"

"I got my sources around this dump."

Beck shrugged, put his empty glass on the chair arm next to the Guinness can, and was about to stand up when he saw the bald bruiser storming in their direction heading for Irene.

He pointed a finger at Irene and yelled, "You got a big fucking mouth, you little dyke bitch!"

Elrod was surprisingly fast for a short-legged thug. Before Beck rose fully out of his chair, Elrod made it past him, reaching for Irene who jumped off her chair, but not before Elrod grabbed the front of her barn jacket intending to slam her onto the ground. Irene pulled a three-and-a-half-inch stainless steel push dagger from her belt buckle and punched the tip of the blade into Elrod's forearm. Elrod howled and let go of her. Irene backpedaled and fell. Infuriated, embarrassed, Elrod lost whatever control he had. He moved toward Irene intent on stomping her. He didn't care about her knife or anything else, including Beck. Big mistake.

Beck took one long step and slammed his right forearm into Elrod's chest with all his two-hundred-fifteen pounds behind the blow, the impact made more powerful by the momentum Beck had generated with his lunge forward. The blow knocked Elrod away from Irene, turned him toward Beck, and made him raise his arms. That opened him to Beck's left hook, delivered from a crouch, with all the power of Beck's hips, legs, and shoulder, aimed just below Elrod's bottom right rib. A body killer. A perfect liver shot.

The blow made a popping thud followed by Elrod's painful grunt. Elrod dropped to his knees, then down onto his forearms, paralyzed by excruciating pain. Beck didn't waste another second on Elrod. He turned to check on Irene. She was still on the ground, still holding the knife, motionless, stunned by what Beck had done.

Beck looked back at the young guy to make sure he wasn't going to draw a weapon or get into the fight. Joey Collins stood by his chair, hands down, confused at how quickly Hamm Elrod had been rendered helpless.

Beck helped Irene to her feet. Hamm Elrod tried to stand up. Beck ignored him and put his arm around Irene's shoulders, gently but firmly steering her away from the scene.

"Time to go. Put the knife away." Irene turned to look at Hamm Elrod, who'd dropped back onto his hands. Beck said to her, "C'mon. It's over."

Irene slipped the knife back into her belt buckle.

From behind them Hamm yelled, "Keep walking, faggot. Next time ain't going to be no bitch to get in the way so you could sucker punch me!"

Beck was one second away from turning around and pounding Hamm Elrod's face into pulp when he saw the Myer brothers emerging from the back of the barn carrying their baseball bats. He realized he'd never seen them. Both were big. One of them was huge.

Irene saw George and Vic, too.

She said, "Shit. Hurry up. They'll come after you when they see what you did to Hamm."

Beck let go of Irene and walked next to her, heading quickly toward the parking area on the left side of the barn. He kept an eye on the brothers. He figured it would take them a few moments to find out what had happened. He wanted to be gone by then. He and Irene made it into the shadows and increased their pace.

"Where's your car?"

"We just passed it. That beat-to-shit Ford Focus." Beck stopped, not anxious to turn back. Irene decided for him. "Forget it. I'll come back and get it later. I'd rather stick with you if you don't mind. I don't want to get caught on the road if they come after me. I'm about a half-hour from home. How far is your place?"

"Five minutes. Let's go."

3

They were silent until Beck said, "Here we are."

He turned onto a gravel driveway that ran about fifty yards before it angled left, revealing a two-story, 2,500-square-foot white colonial with a red front door. A covered walkway on the right side of the main house led to a guest house which at one time had been a stable.

Beck parked his GMC in a space cleared of snow on the left side of the house. A curving waist-high wall of split firewood set the parking area off from the surrounding grounds. Discreet lights flanking the front door and mounted above a side entrance illuminated the area.

As Irene jumped down out of the truck she said, "Nice house. How much land you got here?"

"Twenty-seven acres. About five of it cleared."

Irene asked, "When did you get it?"

"Couple of years ago."

They entered the house through a side door that opened onto a mudroom. A green bench ran along one wall facing a rack of brass hooks. Irene sat down on the bench, pulled off her Red Wing boots, and hung her barn jacket on a hook. Beck did the same with his ankle-high black Timberlands and Burberry down jacket. He wore a black cashmere sweater that kept him warm at the Field. Irene walked into the kitchen ahead of him.

With her Carhartt jacket off, Irene looked even more diminutive in her oversized plaid shirt.

"How old is this place?"

Beck said, "I think they built the original part of the house around 1860. There's been sections added on and renovations done over the years."

Irene pointed to the overhead beams that ran along the kitchen ceiling.

"Those beams are original. Chopped out with an ax."

"Yes."

"The kitchen is new."

"Everything you see was done before I bought the place."

Irene asked, "Is there a bathroom on this floor?"

Beck pointed the way, and Irene walked out of the kitchen. He grabbed a bottle of seltzer from his refrigerator and two water glasses from his dishwasher. He took down two rocks glasses from a cabinet above the counter and a bottle of Midleton Irish whiskey. He placed everything on a large, free-standing, rectangular worktable that had been custom-built for the kitchen. There were two matching stools on one side of the table.

He heard a toilet flush as Irene emerged from the downstairs bathroom. She entered the kitchen with a smile.

"Your house is about a hundred times nicer than my hovel."

Beck said, "A hundred times?"

"At least." Irene sat down on one of the stools opposite where Beck was standing and said, "Are you pouring?"

"Yes." Beck poured two fingers of the whiskey in each glass and asked, "What do you want to chase it with?"

Irene slugged down half the whiskey. "I'm fine. This is great." She held up the rocks glass. "What is this?"

"About three hundred dollars a bottle."

"Show off."

"I've got to live up to my image."

"Don't worry, your image is just fine."

Beck sipped his Midleton then asked, "You okay?"

"Yeah. Sort of. Stuff like that doesn't usually happen to me."

"But you carry that knife just in case."

"I've been carrying a weapon since I was young. That was the first time I ever had to use one."

"Hopefully the last."

"Yeah, well, my little push knife wouldn't have stopped Hamm Elrod from stomping the crap out of me. It's a good thing you were there."

"Yes."

"Hopefully Vic and George would've stopped him before he killed me."

Beck tipped his head slightly, not agreeing or disagreeing. And not saying anything about the damage Hamm Elrod could have done before anyone stopped him. Beck had seen grown men broken, beaten, forever changed in seconds. One punch or one slash of a knife could do terrible damage.

"Tell me more about this Kin outfit. Who are they?"

"Mostly a bunch of Deliverance assholes living around here who are proud of being ignorant and angry. QAnon morons, dead-end Trumpists, white supremacists, Christian fundamentalists, racists, you know, basically white men who believe they have the right to do pretty much whatever the hell they want."

"What's around here mean?"

"Well, as far as the Kin goes, they're mostly in the three surrounding counties and a couple of areas across the river. A lot of 'em live in fairly isolated places. Up in the foothills of nearby mountain regions."

"What are they into?"

"Drugs, for sure. If it's a crime, the Kin are behind it."

"How big are they?"

"I don't really know. In the gang or militia or whatever they call it, I'd say a couple of hundred. But they got a lot of supporters." Irene leaned forward, her forearms on the worktable. "What you gotta understand is – the Kin controls a lot of what goes on around here. They go back a long way. There's a lot of local people who support them and endorse their white supremacy bullshit."

Beck nodded, not all that surprised.

"The Kin makes make a lot of noise about defending property rights, gun rights, family values, their right to keep their kids uneducated, and male dominion over women. You ever hear the white supremacy mission statement?"

"No."

Irene raised her right hand and recited, "We must secure the existence of our people and a future for white children." Then she turned her hand around and extended her middle finger. "The Kin boys believe they were here before anybody else and act like they got first dibs on everything."

"So much for the Mohicans and Iroquois and Lenape."

"Yeah, right."

Beck asked, "So why do you hang out at the Field? It doesn't sound like you'd want to have anything to do with those guys."

Irene finished her whiskey. "I don't know. I guess I'm stubborn. Why shouldn't I be able to go where I want? I go back a couple of generations myself. And what the hell, there are a lot of people who hang out at the Field who aren't in the Kin."

Beck nodded but didn't say anything.

Irene said, "Although I doubt I'll be going back there any time soon."

"That's probably smart."

Irene paused and then asked, "You think there's going to be repercussions? I just kind of poked that fat fuck to get him off me. Maybe it'll blow over."

"The problem isn't the knife."

"What then?"

"The humiliation. For guys like that the embarrassment is worse than a knife wound."

Irene grew quiet. "Yeah. I can see that."

Beck leaned on the counter to get down to eye level with Irene.

"Usually it depends on the bosses in the organization. Do you know how much control they have over their people?"

"I'd say they have a lot. Everything is in levels. There's district leaders like Oscar Lund. Then the leaders of the main groups. Then the top guy that nobody hardly sees or knows about. You hear his name, Camdyn Dent, but that's it. He's the supreme leader. Head honcho. Grand master. Whatever."

Beck stood up straight and took another sip of his whiskey.

"Well, I would say going after a small woman doesn't make the Kin look good. Most crews I know wouldn't endorse that."

"True. But there's another part."

"What?"

Irene said, "You stepping in. You're an outsider. The Kin has a thing about outsiders. Worse, you're an outsider who doesn't take shit from anybody. Which you demonstrated tonight. You put that fat fucker Hamm Elrod down hard. They might want to, you know, teach you a lesson."

Beck nodded. Listening but not saying anything.

Irene lifted her glass for more Midleton. "Just a splash."

Beck poured. Irene took a sip. She said, "What the hell, it might blow over. I don't think Hamm Elrod has a lot of fans. And it doesn't help that Joey Collins was there."

"Why is that?"

"A lot of high-up Kin leaders came from the Collins family. Probably even at the top level, although that kind of information is kept totally secret. Point being, what happened wasn't good for the Kin image, and Joey Collins was there. And he didn't do anything to stop it."

Beck said, "I guess we'll see."

Irene sipped more whiskey and slid off the stool, too restless to keep sitting. It reminded Beck of how she never stayed in one place for long.

"By the way, Irish, what's your name? You never told me."

"Beck. First name James."

"What's that? German?"

"Maybe. I heard my father's relatives emigrated from England. My mother's people were Scottish. Or Irish. I'm not sure."

"Based on your choice of whiskey, I'd say Irish."

"Maybe. Your first name is Irene. What's your last name?"

"Allen. Irene Allen." She reached across the worktable. Beck's reach was long enough to meet hers. They shook. Irene's hand was small, but she had a good grip, and the palm of her hand was not soft. It was the hand of a working woman.

"Pleased to meet you, James Beck."

Beck nodded and drained the rest of the whiskey in his glass. He didn't want any more alcohol. And he didn't believe that Irene Allen thought everything might blow over.

Beck turned and put the empty glasses in the sink. He turned back to Irene. "You want to go back and get your car?"

"Not really. Honestly, I'd rather stay away from there tonight. And I've had a little too much booze to drive home. My house isn't that close."

"You're welcome to stay here."

Irene smiled, opened her eyes wide, and waggled her eyebrows. "Finally! You picked up on my clever plot to get into your bed." Irene thought that would get a smile out of Beck, but it didn't. "Jeezus, don't look so serious. I can see the idea isn't sending you into a frenzy of passion."

"No, it's not that. I just thought…"

"I was gay?"

"Yes."

"Well, I've slept with a few women, and I know I kind of look like it, but it's mostly an act I put on so those mutants at the Field don't bother me."

"Oh."

"Hey, I'd rather they called me a dyke bitch than hit on me all the time."

Beck said, "I get it."

"I'll tell you what I want more than sex."

"What?"

"I'd die for a long, hot shower. I can get barely five minutes of hot water in my house. I smell like smoke from those firepits. I wouldn't mind washing my clothes, too. I guarantee your washer and dryer are better than mine."

"How do you know?"

"Because I don't have either one. Gimme twenty minutes, one of your clean t-shirts, a blanket, and put me up on a couch. I can sleep anywhere."

"I have a spare bedroom."

Irene smirked and said, "Right. What was I thinking?"

That did get a smile from Beck.

He led the way upstairs. As they passed a small closet in the hallway, he picked out a bath towel for Irene and walked her to the bathroom. He opened the door and switched on the lights.

Irene stopped at the entrance and let out a laugh.

"Holy shit, this is a bit much."

Beck said, "I didn't build the house."

"Like you don't think this is great."

Irene stood looking at a double vanity with matching mirrors and sinks. There was a built-in marble bathtub on one side of the room and a walk-in shower on the other. To the left of the door stood a settee and above it a shelf made out of polished mahogany set into the wall. At one time the shelf held a makeup mirror and cosmetics.

Beck stepped into the bathroom and laid Irene's bath towel on the settee. Irene walked in and started undressing. By the time he turned to leave, Irene had already taken off her flannel shirt and slipped out of her jeans. She pulled off her thermal top. Standing in a sports bra and blue cotton panties she said, "Hey, where're you going?"

Beck hesitated.

Irene spread her arms wide and said, "Are you telling me you don't want to see me naked? I want to see you naked. Come on, take a shower with me. You have to show me how to use all the handles and levers and shit. I don't want to break anything."

Beck smiled. Of course he wanted to see her naked. More than that, he wanted to get close to her. Between the forced loneliness of his pandemic months and the booze and the swirl of danger, Beck found himself in the mood to go along with this feisty, reckless woman.

He pulled off his black jeans and dropped them on a chair set next to the sinks. Irene had the rest of her clothes off before Beck unbuttoned his shirt. She looked even better naked than Beck had imagined. She had the proportions of a model but on a smaller scale. Nice shoulders, small waist and narrow hips, teardrop breasts unaffected by gravity, and the sleek, toned muscles of a woman accustomed to physical work.

She opened the glass door of the walk-in shower and stood waiting for Beck.

"Hurry up."

Beck stripped down and stepped into the shower behind Irene, taking a quick look at her perfect ass. The space was large enough to easily accommodate both of them. He reached over Irene and turned on the shower. Irene leaned back into Beck until the water warmed up. There was a second showerhead on a handheld wand affixed to the wall.

Irene moved under the warm spray and picked up a large bar of Molton Brown bath soap from a ledge recessed into the wall. She pulled Beck under the shower spray and began soaping his chest, shoulders, and arms.

Her efforts seemed improbably kind and considerate. As if Beck were the guest and deserved all of her interest. She attended to him without guile or inhibition. She worked on every part of his body, examining the knife scars on his left forearm he'd incurred in prison. Looked closely at the different skin texture on a rectangular section of his left buttock where surgeons had harvested skin grafts for third-degree burns on his ankle and calf.

She massaged him as she lathered the rich soap. She said nothing, working calmly and happily.

Beck enjoyed it but also found it a bit difficult to be so compliant. And then she rinsed him off with the handheld spray and moved him away so she could get under the warm, plentiful stream of hot water.

She handed Beck the bar of soap. It was her turn now, and Beck was happy to oblige her. Beck slid the luxurious soap over her hard, compact body and worked up a cleansing, soothing lather, all made more pleasurable by how she seemed to enjoy Beck's big hands gently working the soap over her, particularly her shoulders and back.

Irene slipped away from Beck to grab a cylindrical bottle of purple shampoo. She poured a bit on her short dark hair and worked the shampoo into a lather.

"I like the scent. What is it?"

"Beats me."

Beck shampooed his hair and beard, while Irene talked about his size, his muscles, and asked him how much he weighed. Beck mumbled an answer as he stepped under the shower to rinse off. Irene joined him, trying to bump him out of her way. Beck was immovable. He finally stepped back and let Irene have access to the shower spray. When Irene finished, she stepped forward, held her arms wide, and said, "Ta-da!"

That's when Beck noticed a delicate script tattoo running underneath her left breast: *How You Do Anything, Is How You Do Everything.*

That saying seemed to fit Irene Allen. Beck wasn't sure what it all meant or what Irene Allen was really all about. Or the Kin. He was sure, however, that he wouldn't be digging out bedding for the guest bedroom.

4

Abel Proctor couldn't believe that someone was stupid enough or reckless enough to murder Joey Collins. He'd been with the Cumberland County Sheriff's Department for nineteen years, the last five on the Bureau of Investigations, the last two years of those five as the Senior Investigator in charge of three other deputies, and even though murders were rare in the county, most of them were easily solved because most were understandable. Not this one.

The call from Vic Myer had awakened Proctor at two-forty-five. The Bureau Investigator on the midnight-to-eight shift, Russell Hibbard, arrived at the Field first. Russell, a plodding and diligent deputy, had followed Proctor's orders – *close down the Field. Don't touch the body. Wait for me.*

When Proctor arrived, he drove around the sheriff's patrol car blocking access to the parking area. Hibbard positioned his truck so that his headlights illuminated the scene. George Myer had done the same with his truck, a big Ford F-350. The body lay near the split wood fence that bordered an empty field about ten yards north of the parking area. George and Vic Myer, Andy Miller, and Hibbard stood near the corpse of Joey Collins. Proctor had stopped twenty feet from the body. Even at that distance, he could see the blood staining the snow under the corpse, an announcement in gore that everything Abel Proctor had spent years protecting was now in jeopardy.

A light snow had been falling, blown around by frigid gusts of wind. Proctor approached the scene, trying to button up his wool coat. Proctor was sixty-two, still strong, hair turning gray, both knees on their way to replacements.

Proctor nodded to Russell Hibbard and the Myer brothers near the body. Andy Miller stood off to the side.

As Proctor pulled on nitrile gloves, he asked, "Who found him?"

George Myer said, "I did."

"How?"

"He and Hamm Elrod had been hanging out. Hamm said Collins went to take a piss and never came back."

"So?"

Vic chimed in. "Hamm said he went looking for Collins. Saw that his truck was here but couldn't find him."

Proctor looked to his right and saw Collins's Chevy Silverado. He pointed to it.

"That's Joey's?"

"Yeah."

"Who owns that Ford?"

Vic said, "That girl, Irene."

"Irene who?"

The Myer brothers answered with shrugs.

Proctor looked at Andy Miller. "You know her?"

Andy nodded. "She drinks IPA. She left with the guy who drinks Redbreast."

"You know their names?"

Andy said, "I know the girl's name is Irene."

Proctor gave up and turned back to Vic Myer. "Okay, so Elrod told you he was looking for Collins, saw his truck, and then said what?"

"Told us if we saw Collins, tell him Elrod went home and Joey should go fuck himself."

"What was he pissed off about?"

George said, "They had some sort of argument."

"About what?"

George gave Proctor a shrug that said he either didn't want to talk about it or didn't know.

Proctor asked, "So when did Hamm talk to you?"

George said, "Around one. Thereabouts."

"And you went looking for Collins?"

Vic broke in, "Yes. A little while after that. Around one-thirty. We didn't jump up and go looking for him right away."

"So, you both found him?"

Vic said, "No. Just George. I was looking elsewhere."

Proctor nodded but didn't follow up on that. He said, "Where's Hamm?"

Vic said, "Home I assume."

Proctor's anger flared. They should have kept Elrod here until they found Collins. Then again, they probably didn't know as much as he did about why Hamm and Collins were arguing. Proctor had been monitoring calls into the sheriff's department when the church van hijacking was going down. He knew the driver of the van had ended up in the hospital with a broken nose and a grade-four concussion. He pictured Elrod blaming Collins. And Collins not inclined to take shit from Hamm Elrod.

Proctor took out a Maglite from his coat pocket and aimed the beam near the fence and around the body. Any boot prints left four hours ago would be long gone with this wind and light snowfall.

"So what did you do after you found the body?"

"We had Andy watch over it and sent everybody home. There were only four guys here by then. We didn't tell anybody anything."

Proctor said, "When did you call it in?"

"After the last truck pulled out. Around two."

Proctor nodded, took out his notebook, and wrote for a minute. He looked up and turned to Russell Hibbard.

"Russ, call the coroner and see when he expects to arrive. Then call into the office. Get a couple of deputies to go out and find

Hamm Elrod. Wake his ass up. Bring him into the office and hold him there for questioning."

Russell Hibbard nodded and wrote down the orders in his notebook. Proctor watched him, biting his tongue. He wanted to yell at Hibbard to stop taking fucking notes and do what he said. Most everything about Hibbard annoyed Proctor. He was a goddamn bureau investigator, but he still chose to wear the standard-issue gray deputy sheriff's winter coat. He ate right and didn't drink. Ran twenty-five miles a week, even in winter. His wife Sheila was soft-spoken and worked at the public school where their daughter attended. Proctor had been married eleven years when his wife died of a cerebral aneurysm. Right up until the day she died, Martha had never stopped nagging him about the extra thirty pounds he carried. Martha had miscarried three times before they gave up on having children. His life was everything Russell Hibbard's wasn't. Proctor was just about to bark at Hibbard when he stopped taking notes and asked, "Anything else?"

"No."

Proctor turned his attention to the body. He'd been avoiding it. Maybe because once he looked closely, there would be no denying the reality. He motioned for Vic and George to move back.

Joey Collins lay face down. Blood covered a wide area around the head and shoulders because the frozen ground hadn't absorbed much of it. The blood had frozen into dark red slush.

Proctor slipped on a pair of blue booties so he wouldn't leave shoe prints. He crouched down, wincing at the pain it caused his knees. He shined his Maglite on Joey Collins's right hand. He carefully turned over the hand. There was blood on the fingers and palm, mixed with snow and dirt. Same on the left hand.

Proctor shifted around and aimed the beam at Collins's head. The left side of Joey's face lay on the ground, stuck in place by the freezing blood. Proctor leaned closer, conceding to getting the knees of his pants wet and dirty. He saw a deep gash on the right side of Collins's neck. The cut started under the right ear, continued toward the middle of the throat, then disappeared under the section of the neck facing the ground.

Proctor assumed the wound continued around to the other side. Someone had slashed Joey Collins's neck from ear to ear. Somebody in a rage would have done that.

Proctor heard the crunch of tires approaching. He looked up to see Joseph Montgomery arriving in his van. Montgomery was the coroner. Had been for as long as Proctor had been with the sheriff's department. Montgomery owned the largest funeral home in the county. Knew the procedure. He would set up work lights. Take pictures. Supervise the removal of the body. Transport the remains to his funeral home and notify the state police that the county would need an autopsy.

Proctor struggled to stand upright, using the opportunity to press his right hand into a portion of the freezing blood on the ground. Nobody noticed what he did. All eyes had turned to watch Montgomery slowly get out of his van.

Proctor got to his feet and slipped off his gloves, turning them inside out as he did so. He quickly stuffed them into the inside pocket of his coat.

Vic Myer turned to Proctor and said, "Let's talk in the barn, Abel. Too goddamn cold out here."

Proctor said, "Okay. Let me check with Mr. Montgomery. I'll meet you inside."

Proctor knew that once he and the Myer brothers were alone, he'd hear more about what had happened at the Field. Hopefully, enough so that he'd be ready to make his most important phone call. The one to Camdyn Dent, supreme leader of the Kin.

5

Irene woke bundled underneath Beck's duvet, alone in his king-size bed. If someone had walked into the half-light of the bedroom with the shades still down, they wouldn't have known she was in the bed.

Irene sat up and looked around. Where was the big guy? She felt uncomfortable being alone in a dark room in a strange house, naked.

She climbed out from under the covers, steeling herself against the chilly air in the bedroom, and hurried into the bathroom. She couldn't resist another shower.

When she came out, wrapped in a towel, she heard Beck in the kitchen. She went into the laundry room to put her clothes in the dryer, but they were already in. The big guy must've taken them out of the washing machine when he woke up. She opened the dryer door and checked the clothes. They were mostly dry, but her jeans were damp.

She went to the top of the stairs and yelled, "Hey Irish, thanks for putting my clothes in the dryer. You got something I can wear for a while?"

Beck yelled back, "There's a robe in my closet."

Irene found a terry cloth robe, but it was ridiculously large on her, extending past her feet. She picked out a corduroy shirt instead that reached her knees. She went back into the hallway and yelled, "Hey! You got any socks I can wear?"

Beck yelled back, "Hang on!"

He came upstairs and opened the top drawer in his dresser. He picked out a pair of thick wool socks and tossed them to her. He'd fetched the socks himself because he didn't want her to see the 9-millimeter Browning Hi-Power semi-auto in the back of the drawer.

Beck turned around in time to catch a glimpse of Irene perched at the end of his bed, lifting her leg to slip on one of the socks he'd given her. She said, "Stop peeking, man. You saw enough of me last night," but she continued putting on the socks.

"There wasn't as much light."

Beck admired Irene's bare leg and the bottom of her thigh. Her skin looked smooth and flawless. There was a richness to her skin tone that made him wonder about her heritage.

Beck said, "There's coffee downstairs on the counter."

Irene finished putting on the other sock and said, "Thanks for putting my clothes in the dryer. How much time did you spend fondling my underwear?"

"Five minutes."

Beck headed downstairs while Irene finished dressing. He hadn't fooled with her underwear, but he had looked at the contents of her pockets on top of the washing machine: a card wallet, cell phone, keys, a crumpled KN95 face mask, a fold of thirty-two dollars, and her belt with the concealed knife in the buckle.

He'd flipped open the small wallet. There was nothing in it but her New York State driver's license, vehicle insurance card, and registration. She looked younger in the picture. Her hair was longer. On impulse, Beck had pulled out the license and taken a picture of it with his cell phone. He put it back and closed the wallet.

Before he left, he'd picked up her belt with the knife concealed in the buckle. The round belt buckle featured the image of a skull. The knife slid out from the right side of the buckle. About half the buckle formed the handle of the push dagger. The buckle had nothing to do with holding the web belt in place. The belt adjusted by itself, and the buckle clipped on.

When Irene came downstairs, she sat in the same stool at the free-standing worktable where she'd been drinking Beck's Midleton whisky.

Beck gathered his breakfast plate and coffee mug still on the worktable and a book propped open against a small pile of other books.

Beck asked, "Coffee?"

"Yes, please."

"Milk or sugar?"

"Black."

He said, "You hungry? Want breakfast?"

"I'm starving. Last night was quite a workout."

"I have ham and eggs. Yogurt and fruit."

"Ham and eggs. Sunny side up. With toast, if you have bread. Please."

"Got some nice wholegrain."

Irene checked the digital readout on the coffee maker. 7:17 a.m.

Irene asked, "What time did you get up?"

"About an hour ago."

"You usually get up so early?"

Beck said, "Pretty much. How'd you sleep?"

"Like the dead. You wore me out. How'd you sleep?"

"Fine."

When Beck didn't elaborate, Irene said, "All right, dammit, I gave you like three hints. Did you enjoy sleeping with me or not?"

"Absolutely. You take up hardly any room, and you don't snore."

"All right, fuck you, forget it."

Beck stopped what he was doing and turned around to face Irene.

She said, "What?"

"Sometimes words are inadequate."

"That's usually what we go by. Words. Although I know you don't use many."

Beck nodded. He started to say something, then stopped. Then he said, "Unforgettable."

Irene lifted her chin and said, "Go on."

Beck looked up, then at Irene, and said, "My hope is that you were as pleased as I was."

Irene still wouldn't let him off the hook. "Well, how pleased were you?"

"Very."

"Okay then."

Irene drank her coffee and watched Beck prepare her breakfast and pour himself more coffee. After a while, she said, "Weird night, though, huh?"

"I suppose."

"I don't usually do that sort of thing."

"Go home with a stranger or stab people?"

"Both. And you're not that much of a stranger, Irish. I've talked to you before."

"You didn't know my name until last night."

"Oh yeah, your name."

Beck said, "You better remember my name, or you're not getting any ham and eggs."

Irene quickly said, "James. James, James, James. But you didn't tell me your last name, did you?" Beck stared at her deadpan. Irene said, "Oh wait, you did. B-something."

Beck continued staring.

"Black. Wait, it wasn't a color. Boyd. Brick. Oh, wait, Beck. Yeah, James Beck."

"Very funny."

"And mine?"

Beck didn't bother kidding around. "Allen." He set her breakfast plate in front of her. "What's your day like, Irene Allen? When should we get your car?"

Irene looked at the time displayed on the microwave. "Well, I'm not sure we have time. Do you think you could drive me to work?"

"Yes, but how would you get home after from there?"

Irene nodded. "Oh yeah. Right. Good point."

"What kind of work do you do?"

"Construction. I'm an electrician."

"Are you licensed?"

"No. You don't need a license around here. Cities like Albany and Troy have license requirements. I got a general contractor's license that covers me. I work under a licensed electrician, so I could apply and take the licensing test at some point, but I haven't gotten around to it. What about you, Irish? Where do you get all your money?"

"I live a simple lifestyle."

"Yeah, sure. Real simple." Irene gestured with her fork. "Living in this place, wearing the clothes you wear, driving a sixty-thousand-dollar truck."

"I've been successful with investing."

"Really? Are you like a hedge fund guy or something?"

"No, I'm not a hedge fund guy. Why are you so interested in my money?"

"Isn't it obvious? I want to marry you, Irish."

Beck couldn't help himself. He smiled first, then he laughed. It felt strange. He hadn't laughed out loud in a long time.

Irene said, "You're right. It's none of my business."

"Well, just know that I worked for whatever I have." Beck checked his watch. "Your clothes should be dry by now. I'll clean up here. Get dressed, and we'll go get your car."

On the drive to the Field, Beck and Irene settled into a silence that became awkward. Irene had been so talkative before, Beck wondered if she were having second thoughts about their night together. Beck had enjoyed being with her, but now he started thinking about the circumstances. He'd taken Irene home because she was afraid that Elrod or some of his buddies from the Kin might come after her. One thing had led to another, and they'd slept together. He didn't regret sleeping with Irene. He'd never slept with a woman so intent on having fun with it all. Reveling in her body. And yet, she had a way of making him feel a bit uneasy. Maybe because he just wasn't accustomed to being around a woman. Certainly not a woman like Irene Allen.

And then those thoughts evaporated as Beck approached the Field and saw flashing red and blue lights.

Irene sat up straight and peered out the windshield. "Shit."

Beck slowed down as he came parallel to the red barn. Yellow crime scene tape stretched from the corner of the barn over to a split rail fence bordering the parking area where Irene had left her Ford Focus. A New York State police car and a county sheriff's car were parked nose to nose, blocking the way into the parking area.

Irene said, "Uh, I think we should get the hell out of here. Forget about my car."

A deputy sheriff stood near the yellow caution tape. A state trooper standing on the dirt road waved Beck to a stop. Beck complied and powered down his window.

The trooper looked at Beck and said, "Where you headed?"

"Work."

He looked past Beck at Irene sitting back in her seat, eyes straight ahead.

The trooper waved Beck on and said, "Have a good day."

As Beck pulled away, Irene said, "Jeesuz, what do you think happened?"

"Nothing good. I'll drive you to work."

"Yeah. Okay. I'll figure out a way to get home."

Beck didn't bother to point out Irene would need her car once she got home. He was too preoccupied with the law enforcement presence at the Field.

Irene said, "You think that might be connected to what happened with Hamm Elrod?"

Beck thought for a moment and said, "You think anybody at the Field would call law enforcement because of that?"

"I guess not."

Beck approached the intersection where the dirt road met a paved road. He stopped and asked Irene, "Which way to your job?"

"Left."

Beck made the turn, thinking about what might have happened at the Field after they left, and if the police might come looking for them. The answer came quickly. Beck saw a sheriff's patrol car appear in his rearview mirror.

6

After four cups of stale coffee, Abel Proctor had reached his limit. He'd worked non-stop until dawn dealing with the coroner, negotiating with a state police sergeant for jurisdiction, and talking to Vic, George, and Andy Miller.

When he met with the state police sergeant, Proctor didn't let on that there was no way he was going to let the State Police take over the investigation. Being first on the scene gave him a strong hand. He also knew that the troopers had ignored the illegal operations at the Field for months and had no incentive to get involved now. So he wasn't surprised when the sergeant conceded jurisdiction to the county and gave Proctor the usual offer to provide any necessary assistance.

Proctor spent most of his time talking to the brothers. He didn't bother with the mentally challenged Andy Miller. The Myers filled in the information about Hamm Elrod and Joey Collins arriving with Oscar Lund. About Elrod going after Irene Allen because of her big mouth and getting put down by a stranger in about two seconds. None of which had much to do with Joey Collins.

Vic and Proctor went over everything with big brother George mostly listening.

Proctor said, "I have to put Hamm Elrod at the top of my list, but I don't see him doing that to Joey Collins."

Vic Myer shrugged and said, "You get the right mix of anger, booze, and stupidity and just about anything can happen."

Proctor nodded. He still didn't think Hamm Elrod had it in

him to slice open Joey Collins's throat. He did, however, think that he could build a case against Elrod. There was motive. A woman had further humiliated Hamm. A stranger had kicked his ass. Hamm was already pissed off about Joey's behavior at the robbery. Probably got more pissed off because Collins didn't back him up in the fight with an outsider. Also, Elrod was the last to see Collins alive. And he'd left the scene. That was all Abel Proctor needed because right now he cared more about pleasing Camdyn Dent than solving the crime. The leader of the Kin would not tolerate the savage murder of Joey Collins. He would want progress. Proctor's first priority was to convince Dent he had the situation in hand. The last thing Proctor needed was for Dent to call in the head enforcer of the Kin, a psychopath named Emmett Devereaux.

Proctor decided he had enough to call Dent. It meant going through a secret protocol. First, Proctor sent a text message to an answering service that changed its phone number every month. The service relayed his text to Dent. It took Camdyn Dent ten minutes to call Proctor from a burner phone. Longer than usual. Dent had been sleeping at 5:13 a.m. when he received Proctor's text.

The supreme leader of the Kin didn't bother with pleasantries. He said, "Talk." Proctor did for almost three uninterrupted minutes. Dent said, "Understood. Get this resolved quickly, Abel. Stay in control of it."

Dent ended the call. Proctor left the barn to find Russell Hibbard who had been spending time talking to Andy Miller, trying to nail down who else had been at the Field that night. Andy worked outside so had most likely seen everyone who had been at the Field. Andy knew at least the first names of all the regulars. Unfortunately, he didn't know the name of the stranger who had put Elrod on his knees. He did give Hibbard a description of the stranger's truck – a black GMC Denali. Later, when Hibbard saw a black GMC Denali pass by the Field, he quickly found Abel

Proctor and gave him the information. Proctor jumped into a patrol car and raced after Beck.

Beck accelerated a bit as he watched the sheriff's department car following him. The patrol car matched his speed.

Irene said, "You think he's coming after us?"

"Yes."

As if to confirm Beck's answer, the patrol car's rooftop light bar turned on.

Beck didn't slow down or accelerate. As he drove around a bend in the road, Irene powered down her window and side-armed something out of the truck.

The movement caught Beck's eye.

"What was that?"

"My knife."

The wail of a siren pierced the air. Beck checked his rearview mirror. The patrol came around the bend speeding toward them. Beck flicked on his turn signal but didn't pull over and stop. He wanted to get as far away as possible from where Irene had ditched the knife. He took his foot off the accelerator but did not brake. He changed his turn signal to emergency flashers and eased over to the right side of the road. The snow piled up by plows made it difficult to find a clear space. Beck pulled over as far as he could and stopped with two wheels on the asphalt. The patrol car pulled in fifteen feet behind him, siren off, lightbar still flashing. The two wheels on the driver's side of the sheriff's car were also on the road.

Beck quickly went through a list in his head. He had no weapons. His driver's license, a credit card, and a fold of money were in his front pocket held by a money clip. The registration and inspection stickers for the truck were up to date. He saw a man dressed in a suit, tie, and dark wool car coat pull himself out of a county sheriff's patrol car. Not a deputy sheriff in uniform. Some kind of detective or investigator. The man's tie was down below the open top button of his shirt. His winter coat unbuttoned. Everything about him looked uncomfortable and annoyed.

Irene turned around and said, "Now what?"

"Say as little as possible. Don't answer questions. Don't ask questions. And don't argue."

He powered down the window just as Abel Proctor was about to rap on it.

Beck looked at the heavy-set man. His eyes were red rimmed. He looked like he had been up all night and as if Beck were the one responsible for his misery.

Proctor said, "License and registration."

Beck didn't say anything. He dug in his pocket for his license, found his registration in the center console, and handed them to Proctor. The cold December morning air whipped into the cab of the GMC making everything more uncomfortable.

Proctor read the license and registration. He leaned over and looked at Irene. He told Beck, "Stay here."

Beck powered up the window and used his side view mirror to watch Proctor climb into his patrol car.

Irene said, "What's he doing?"

"Checking to see if my license is suspended or if I have warrants."

"Warrants?"

"That's what they do."

"Why did he stop us?"

"No point guessing."

Beck didn't want to answer Irene's questions. He wanted to keep his eye on the guy in the sheriff's patrol car to see if he got on his radio.

Irene said, "So now what?"

"We wait." Beck watched his rear view mirror. "Here he comes. If he asks, give him your name and address. Nothing else."

As Proctor came closer, Beck powered down the window again.

Proctor handed Beck back his license and registration. He asked, "Mr. Beck, do you currently reside at that address?"

Beck answered, "Yes."

Proctor leaned past Beck and said, "Miss, can you show me some ID?"

Irene wanted to ask why. Wanted to ask what was going on, but she followed Beck's advice. She took her driver's license from her wallet and handed it to Beck, who handed it to Proctor.

Proctor looked at Irene's license and took a picture of it with his phone. He handed it back to Irene via Beck.

Proctor asked, "You currently live at that address, Miss?"

"Yes."

It seemed to Irene like this was over. Beck knew it wasn't.

"Sir, turn off the engine, and please step out. You, too, Miss. I need to talk to you both. I don't want to stand out on the road like this."

Proctor turned and walked toward the rear of the truck, where the patrol car protected them from traffic. Beck took note that the detective had pushed back his coat and suit jacket so that he could rest his hand on the butt of the gun holstered at his right hip.

Just before he got out of the truck, Beck said to Irene, "Don't put your hands in your pockets. Keep your hands visible. Both of them."

"Jesus, what the fuck? We didn't do anything."

"That doesn't matter. It never has. And we did do something. You stabbed somebody, and I assaulted him."

Beck stepped out before Irene could respond.

All three gathered behind the rear of the GMC. Beck and Irene stood with their backs to the truck, facing Abel Proctor. Now that Proctor could see their hands, he took his hand off his gun and let his suit jacket and coat cover the weapon.

"My name is Abel Proctor. I'm an investigator with the county sheriff's department."

Irene looked at Beck, waiting for him to respond. Beck didn't even nod.

Proctor looked at Irene and said, "Ms. Allen, do you own a dark blue Ford Focus?"

Before Beck could stop her, Irene blurted out, "Yes. What's this all about? What's going on?"

Proctor stared at Irene, giving her a look that said *I'm cold, tired, and hungry.* "Let me ask the questions. You were at the Field last night, weren't you?"

Before she could answer, Beck touched her forearm and said, "We both were at the Field last night. I take it you're investigating a crime."

Proctor turned to Beck. He stared at him. Beck stared back without expression. They stood about four feet apart.

Finally, Proctor said, "You're not from around here, are you?"

Beck didn't answer. Proctor nodded. "Like I said, you're not from around here. Keep quiet while I do my job."

Beck's anger and focus ticked up a level.

Proctor turned to Irene.

"Why did you leave your car at the Field last night?"

Before Irene could answer, Beck took a small step forward and said, "No."

Proctor turned back to Beck. His face hardened. He pulled his jacket back and placed his hand on his gun.

"What?"

"I said no. That's not the way it's going to work, Officer. We'll be happy to answer your questions with a lawyer present."

Proctor lifted his chin and narrowed his eyes. "What the hell is wrong with you? You really want to go that route?"

Beck ignored Proctor's question. He leaned over to look at Proctor's patrol car.

"You don't have a dashcam in that patrol car, do you?"

"What's that supposed to mean?"

Beck ignored the question even though he was fully aware of what his question meant. It meant that he and Irene Allen were in danger. They were on an isolated road being stopped for a crime serious enough to bring out state and local law enforcement. The man standing in front of him was pissed off, tired, and clearly looking to make an arrest. Beck knew if he landed in a county jail his record of arrest for the murder of an NYPD detective and incarceration would be discovered. Once that happened, he'd be at the mercy of a system without any knowledge of county law enforcement procedure, no connections, hours away from the only lawyer he trusted, Phineas Dunleavy. The risk to even a law-abiding citizen was significant. The risk to an ex-con was off the charts.

And based on what Irene told him about the Kin's influence with law enforcement, Beck could see himself arrested and blamed for whatever had happened at the Field. His guess was that Hamm Elrod had somehow ended up dead or seriously injured, and this two-bit county investigator was going to arrest him for it. Or maybe just shoot him and frame him for it.

Beck said, "You should call your supervising officer. Get him on the scene."

Proctor reacted the way Beck thought he would, barely in control of his emotions.

"What the fuck did you just say to me?"

"You heard what I said."

"I don't know who the hell you think you are, asshole, but you do not give orders to me." Proctor swept his coat and suit jacket back and put his right hand on his gun. "Both of you, turn around. Hands on the top of that tailgate."

Beck didn't move. He motioned for Irene to stay put.

"Are you detaining us for questioning?"

Proctor raised his voice. "Turn around."

"Are you arresting us?"

"I said, turn around!"

Irene kept looking back and forth. She didn't dare move now.

Beck never broke eye contact with Proctor. He said, "No. We're not turning around until you tell us what's going on. If we need a lawyer, we need to know what to tell him."

Abel Proctor took a deep breath and stood up straight. He slowly pulled his gun out of his holster.

Beck nodded slightly. He'd goaded the investigator into showing his true character. So be it. Better to deal with this bozo here and now.

Beck slowly raised his hands. He knew he was too far away to disarm the man, but not by much. He watched Proctor carefully. Proctor held his gun down by his right leg. Beck wanted him to raise the gun, to bring the weapon within reach. He hoped the cop would raise the gun slowly. That would give him time to close the distance, grab the chamber of the gun with his left hand so it wouldn't fire, and push the gun aside so it wouldn't be pointing at him or Irene.

Beck concentrated on the gun. Ignoring everything – Irene, the cold, the wind, the exhaust pluming from the Denali's tailpipe behind him. The gun was a Glock. There was a double pull on the Glock's trigger. A slight pull to release the safety, a full pull to fire a shot. Beck knew he had enough time to get his left hand on the gun. This was an angry man who'd been up all night. He'd never react to Beck's move in time. Once he had the gun under control, it would take a split second to snap his forehead into the investigator's face. Shatter his nose, pull the Glock free, take the cop's feet out from under him.

Beck shifted his weight making sure not to edge forward, waiting for the investigator to point the gun at him.

The shift in stance caught Proctor's attention. For a split second, he was confused. And then reality hit Abel Proctor like a slap in the face. The man standing in front of him wasn't just another rich, arrogant asshole threatening him with a lawyer. Proctor looked at Beck's eyes. He saw no fear in those eyes even though the guy was standing in front of a deputy sheriff with a gun. Beck looked like a large, powerful animal ready to strike.

Proctor instinctively took a step backward. He felt his bowels loosen. He said, "What the fuck are you doing?"

Suddenly, Irene yelled, "Hey!"

Proctor looked at her. Beck did, too, now that he was too far away to reach Proctor's gun.

Irene stepped toward Proctor with her arms extended, hands balled into fists turned upward. "You want to arrest someone, arrest me. I don't give a fuck. I didn't do anything."

Beck had to clear his throat and refocus.

Proctor looked back and forth at Irene and Beck. He stepped to his left in front of Irene and away from Beck.

She stepped closer to Proctor. "Come on. Arrest me. That's what you want to do. So do it."

Proctor realized he had been barely breathing. The only thing he was sure he wanted to do was holster his gun and stay away from the big, bearded, crazy bastard standing in front of him. He had a picture of the asshole's license. He didn't need it. He wasn't going to forget the name James Beck anytime soon.

Proctor holstered his gun and took out a pair of handcuffs from a leather case attached to his belt. He'd arrest the woman. Irene Allen. She was the better choice anyhow. Clearly, Beck was a hard case who wouldn't say a word without a lawyer. He knew he could get more out of the woman. He had plenty of time to take care of James Beck. Teach him what a mistake he had made. Teach him a lesson he'd never goddamn forget and then arrest him.

Proctor told Irene to turn around. He pointed at Beck, "You get in your truck."

Beck took a few steps toward the front of the truck and stopped.

Proctor took a deep breath. He felt drained. He had to concentrate on what he was doing. "Hands behind your back."

Proctor cuffed Irene and walked her to his patrol car. Beck kept his distance. Proctor kept a hand on Irene's back and mechanically recited the arrest script.

"Do you have any weapons on you? Anything sharp? Drugs? Needles?"

"No. Do you mind telling me what you're arresting me for?"

"I'm going to check your pockets. Don't move."

Proctor kept his left hand on Irene's shoulder while feeling her pockets with his right hand. He quickly ran his hand over her legs, her back, and stomach. He did not touch her breasts. He turned toward Beck for a moment. "You stay where you are, or I will shoot you."

"Where are you taking her?"

Proctor ignored the question and guided Irene into the back seat. Once she was in the seat, he told her, "I'm arresting you for the murder of Joey Collins," and then he began reciting Miranda rights.

The accusation stunned Beck. Irene seemed too shocked to react. Beck pulled himself together enough to yell at Irene, "I'll get a lawyer to you as soon as possible! Don't say anything until he gets there."

Proctor closed the car door and got into the driver's seat. He watched Beck until he had the car in gear and pulled out onto the road, his anger rising, his light bar still flashing.

7

Beck sat in his truck, still parked at the side of the road, and punched the speed dial for Phineas Dunleavy's personal phone number. Dunleavy answered on the third ring.

"James, how are you, lad?"

"Could be better." Beck turned up the heat in the truck.

"How much better? Is it serious?"

"Probably."

"Probably?"

"A woman I slept with last night was arrested for murder just now."

Phineas paused for a moment. Even coming from James Beck, it took a moment for him to digest that sentence.

"You said, last night?"

"Yes."

"At your home upstate?"

"Yes."

"Was she with you at the time of the murder?"

"It seems so."

"Which was when?"

"I'm assuming sometime between twelve-thirty and six."

Phineas made a noncommittal sound, then said, "So you're her alibi."

"Yes."

"We need to get her a lawyer. This has to be handled correctly."

"Yes."

"I take it you're somewhat romantically involved?"

Beck thought about that for a moment. Whatever the involvement was, it didn't seem romantic. Sexually involved, yes. Emotionally involved? He supposed.

Beck said, "I don't know about romantically, but we're involved. I promised her I'd get her a lawyer."

Phineas said, "All right, understood. When did she get arrested?"

"Three minutes ago."

"You were there?"

"Yes."

"You can fill me in on the reasons later. We have to handle this carefully. If she's going to use you as an alibi, the DA will try to dirty you up."

Beck said, "By making me an accomplice."

"Or an accessory or a co-conspirator to the murder. And, of course, by using your background. There are several paths they can take. I'm sure you told her not to say anything without a lawyer present."

"I did."

"Will she listen to you?"

"I hope so."

"Do you know when they plan to arraign her?"

"No. I don't know how things work up here."

"All right, James, we have to move quickly. The longer she's in custody without a lawyer, the more risk she'll break down and try to defend herself."

"Agreed. I don't know much about this woman, but I do know she's a wild card."

"Okay, let's concentrate on her first. If they come after you, we'll deal with it, but let's not get ahead of ourselves. We've got to get someone to cover her. What's her name?"

"Irene Allen."

"And she lives where?"

"Nearby."

"In Cumberland County?"

"Yes."

"I heard about a criminal defense lawyer in your area. Trying to remember his name. Used to be a prosecutor in the Brooklyn DA's office. Fled up to the northern region during the pandemic when criminal trials came to a halt down here. I think his family had a house up there. I don't know what he's doing now."

Beck pictured Phineas flipping through his address book while he talked. Phineas was old school.

"Might be retired. I've never worked with him, but I assume he's competent enough to make sure his client keeps her mouth shut and navigate the arraignment. Ah, here it is. Morelli. His name is Peter Morelli. I'll have him call you. Where are you?"

"About ten minutes from my house."

"Do you know anything about the murder victim?"

"Nothing."

"Any contact with him?"

"Not directly. We were at the location where he was murdered. We left before the murder."

"Where is that?"

"An illegal drinking hole near my place."

"All right. Details later. Go home. If you don't hear from Morelli soon, call me back."

"I will."

Phineas said, "In the meantime, do you have any information about this woman?"

"I have a picture of her driver's license."

"I won't ask why you have that."

"Call it spur of the moment due diligence."

"You might want to call our good friend Mr. Liebowitz and have him start looking into her. He's faster and better at that than I am."

"Good idea. I'll let you know when I hear from Morelli."

"Right. Talk to Morelli. If you don't like the cut of his jib, we'll find somebody else. Keep me informed."

"Will do."

"I don't know what's going on up there, James, but watch yourself."

"I don't know either, but I'm goddamn going to find out."

"Assume they'll try to arrest you next. You'll want to avoid that."

Phineas ended the call. Beck stayed parked off the side of the road while he texted a picture of Irene's driver's license and a note to Alex Liebowitz. His text said: *Find out everything you can about this woman. She claims to have a contractor's license in Cumberland Cty, NY. Will explain later.*

Beck headed for home, thinking about Irene's driver's license. She was thirty-two years old. Not so much younger than him. Her picture on the license gave the impression she had been annoyed about being photographed. That seemed in character.

By the time he pulled into his driveway, Beck's phone signaled that he had a text. Peter Morelli asking for his address. Beck waited until he was in the house before he texted back his address. The response came quickly. *Will be at yr hse within an hour. My understanding is that you are taking responsibility for fees. PM.*

Well, at least Morelli got to the point.

Beck checked his watch. 10:55 a.m. There was something he knew he had to do before Morelli arrived, but he couldn't quite bring himself to do it.

8

Irene sat handcuffed in the back of the patrol car, listening to Abel Proctor talking on his two-way radio.

"Russ, you still at the Field?"

"Yes, sir."

"I'm heading over to the station with a suspect. It's Irene Allen. Make sure you impound her car and have forensics tow it in. Any word on Elrod?"

"I sent two deputies over to his place."

"Let me know what they find."

"Will do."

Irene shifted in the backseat of the patrol car, trying to find a comfortable position with her hands cuffed behind her back thinking it would be a long time before she saw her car. If that wasn't bad enough, Proctor made a U-turn and headed back toward where he'd stopped Beck. What the hell was he doing? She got the answer when he slowed down and peered out the passenger side window of the patrol car.

Proctor stopped suddenly just before the curve in the road near a birch tree bent low from ice and snow. He pulled the patrol car to the side of the road and turned toward Irene in the backseat.

"You know how long I've been doing this job?"

"No."

"Long enough to know that guilty people like you try to get rid of incriminating evidence when they're being followed by law enforcement."

Irene didn't know what to say, so she took Beck's advice and said nothing.

"It's right about here, isn't it? Near that birch tree."

Proctor waited for a response. He didn't get one.

"You know, I'm tired, I'm hungry, my damn stomach aches from too much coffee. I don't want to be tramping around in the snow and muck looking for what you tossed out of that truck. You make it easier for me to find it; I'll take that into consideration."

Irene suddenly understood how tempting it was to try to get on the good side of someone arresting you. And how much saying nothing was the better option. And how glad she was that she had taken off the other half of the belt buckle and stuck it under the seat in Beck's truck.

Proctor kept staring at her. Rather than try to keep up a poker face, Irene turned away and looked out the car window.

Proctor said, "All right. Have it your way. It's just going to make things worse for you."

She watched as Proctor got out and looked for her punch dagger. He surprised her with how patient he was. He found a tree branch and pointed it at the ground as he walked, not to turn over the snow and leaves but to guide his eye. He walked back and forth methodically. At one point, Irene thought he might give up. Mark the area and send back a team to search more thoroughly. Irene tried to remember how far she'd thrown the knife. And then she found out, not far. Proctor located the knife about five yards past the drainage ditch that paralleled the road.

He returned with the small knife in an evidence bag he'd taken from the glove compartment of the patrol car. He sat behind the wheel, saying nothing. No gloating or berating her. From the back seat, it looked like he took something from the side pocket of his car coat and put it in with the knife. He then carefully placed the evidence bag with both items in his coat pocket.

Irene tried to tell herself that the knife wasn't a big problem. She'd used the knife in self-defense against Hamm Elrod. She had an alibi for Joey Collins. She certainly had no reason to kill him. Beck had money for a lawyer. None of that lessened her anxiety.

Proctor drove off, heading now toward Belleville. He said nothing until he walked into the sheriff's department headquarters holding Irene's right arm.

He told the deputy on duty, "Process this woman. Put her in a holding cell."

The deputy sheriff on duty looked back and forth from Proctor to Irene, then said, "The charge?"

"Murder."

The deputy's eyes widened.

Proctor said, "Details to come," and headed to his cubicle. He didn't need to report last night's events to Sheriff Richard Ciccone's schedule because he was at a meeting with the local school board regarding security in schools. Ciccone's job was equal parts politics and law enforcement, which made dealing with him dicey. Particularly when it came to anything involving the Kin. This gave Proctor a chance to palm the job off on Ciccone's undersheriff, Bruno Cole. Bruno had been around longer than Ciccone and knew more about the Kin. He was more adept at walking the line between tolerating the Kin and keeping their influence inside the department in check.

Proctor stopped by Cole's office and gave him a truncated version of the Joey Collins murder, and what had transpired in the last nine hours. Bruno listened without interruption. He sat behind his desk, white-haired, avuncular, wearing civilian clothes, surrounded by plaques, certificates, and a load of law enforcement paraphernalia.

Proctor said nothing about finding Irene's knife. He watched Bruno carefully for his reactions. There were none. Bruno Cole had a good poker face.

Cole asked, "So we have jurisdiction?"

"Yes?"

"How strong are you on your suspects?"

"Can't say for sure yet. Hamm Elrod is on my list, too. I'm covering every possibility."

Bruno nodded. Putting it together. This was Kin business. Proctor had quickly identified suspects. That would keep Camdyn Dent and the other Kin leaders at bay. For now, that bought Proctor time. And if Proctor was lucky, he might actually solve the case. If not, he'd probably have someone they could at least prosecute.

"I'll call Grotowski. He'll want to handle this personally."

Proctor preferred to call the County District Attorney himself. But he let it go because he wanted Cole to deal with the Sheriff.

Proctor nodded and said, "Okay. But we don't want an arraignment until tomorrow. No rush."

Bruno caught the use of the word *we*. He would make sure to distance himself from Proctor's suspects and this case. He could not see any good coming out of something so closely related to the Kin.

Cole said, "Grotowski won't rush this. He'll want something solid before he arraigns."

"Right. You going to fill in Ciccone?"

"I assume you'll be busy pursuing this while it's hot."

"Yes."

"Okay. I'll fill in the Sheriff."

And with that, Proctor left Bruno Cole's office.

When he arrived at his cubicle in the investigation unit's section of headquarters, he saw Russ Hibbard waiting at his desk.

Proctor didn't waste time. "What's the word on Elrod?"

"We have him in a holding cell."

"Good. Was he home?'

"Yep. In that trailer where he lives with his mother. You ever see that old hag?"

"Once. She looks like an older version of Hamm with more hair, fewer teeth, and bigger tits. She's been on opioids for years. Between the junkie mother and her dying dog, you wouldn't want to spend any time in that trailer."

Hibbard grimaced at the thought.

Proctor said, "We now have another suspect in custody. And a possible accomplice. Good work noticing that truck."

"Thanks."

"We got to jump on this fast."

"Sure."

"It's going to be coffee and grabbing whatever sleep you can for the next couple of days."

"I know."

Proctor sat at his desk. Files, papers, notebooks, and general clutter covered the desktop. He took out his phone and pulled up the pictures of Beck's driver's license and truck registration. He sent the images to one of the printers nearby as he spoke to Hibbard.

"I want you to run down information on someone named James Beck. Start with New York State Uniform Crime Reporting and the U.S. Department of Justice National Instant Criminal Background Check System. I can just about guarantee you this son of a bitch has some sort of criminal history. Keep going with whatever you find in those records until you tap out."

Hibbard had been making notes.

"I sent a copy of his driver's license and vehicle registration to the printer."

"Okay."

"Keep in touch with me."

"I will."

Proctor said, "Go to it."

Hibbard jumped up and headed for the printer.

As soon as Hibbard walked out of his cubicle, Proctor pulled out a burner phone from the top drawer in his desk and sent a text to Oscar Lund. *Set up yr shed 4 an interrogation. B thr in a half hr.*

9

Beck opened his front door to a man looking up at him. Beck recognized that look. It was an expression that said – *you've done something bad enough to involve law enforcement and now I have to find out how bad and what I have to do about it and how much can I charge for it.*

The lawyer, Peter Morelli, extended his hand accompanied by a forced smile. Beck accepted the firm handshake along with the lawyer's silent accusation.

"James Beck?"

"That's me."

"I'm Peter Morelli. Phineas Dunleavy says you need a lawyer."

"For a friend."

"Right, right. A woman you met."

Beck took note of that. Not a woman you know. Not a friend of yours. A woman you met. A stranger you shouldn't have had anything to do with.

Beck ushered Morelli into his house. The lawyer looked like a typical member of the upstate professional class. His suit was off-the-rack, his shirt white, his regimental striped tie innocuous. He wore a wool Orvis driving coat. Half-boots with waterproof bottoms suitable for the mud and snow. All pro forma and practical. His car was a three-year-old, tan Subaru Outback, practically the official car of upstate folks with a few bucks. Despite the cold, Morelli wasn't wearing a hat. His salt-and-pepper hair had grown long enough to cover the tops of his ears, perhaps the result of less frequent trips to the barber due to Covid.

As Morelli took off his coat he asked Beck, "Would you be more comfortable if I wear a mask?"

"I take it you're healthy. Been vaxxed and boosted and all that."

"Yes. And infected once. I've got plenty of antibodies."

"Same here, except I've had it twice. No need for masks, but thanks for asking."

Morelli slipped off his boots and handed Beck his coat. Even Morelli's thick wool socks looked practical. They stood in the hallway that led to Beck's kitchen. Flanking the hallway on both sides were two rooms, mirror images of each other. One was a formal dining room. The other a sitting room. Beck put Morelli's coat in a small closet near the front door and led him into the sitting room where he had a fire burning.

"Phineas said you were in the Brooklyn DA's office."

"Yes. Went to the other side about six years ago."

"What brought you up north? The pandemic?"

"Pretty much. And the fact that criminal jury trials dropped to just about zero." Morelli shrugged, conceding to the reality. "Wasn't my first choice. Spent years building my business down there."

Beck motioned for Morelli to take a seat on one of the matching couches that flanked the fireplace. Beck sat on the couch across from him.

Morelli continued, "I have connections up here, too. My family's had a ski house near Winholm for a long time. I'm in the process of making it a more permanent place."

"How's that working out?"

Morelli gave Beck a crooked smile. "Slowly. How about you? How'd you end up in these parts?"

"Covid. Issues with where I was living. A friend of mine recommended the area."

Morelli waited for more details, but they weren't coming. He looked around the sitting room and across the hall to the dining room. "Nice place. Did you buy it?"

"Yes. Shortly before prices went nuts."

"Good for you." Morelli opened his briefcase and extracted a legal pad and pen. "So, fill me in on this arrest."

Beck gave Morelli the details. He didn't leave anything out except how close he'd come to relieving Abel Proctor of his gun. He spoke quickly without elaborating.

Morelli sat on the edge of the couch leaning forward, nodding, and taking notes.

"So, you think they recognized your truck when you went to get your friend's car and came after you."

"Yes."

"Because you and your friend were at that drinking place last night."

"Yes."

"Can you tell me a little more about that place?"

"It's called the Field. That's exactly what it is. An empty field behind a falling-down barn. On a back road. I guess it started as an alternative to traditional bars and stayed that way. Everything is outside, although I think one or two people drink in the barn occasionally. It's a bit clandestine. Mostly local people a little rough around the edges. And a good number of men who apparently belong to some sort of rural gang called the Kin. People keep to themselves. There are firepits scattered around. People gather around them in small groups."

Morelli nodded as he wrote on his pad. "How did you hear about the Field?"

"The guy who maintained this property for the previous owner told me about it."

Morelli nodded again and changed direction. "What do you know about the murder victim, if anything?"

"The guy who arrested Irene Allen said his name was Joey Collins."

"You said he was a sheriff's investigator?"

"Yes."

"Did you catch his name?"

"Abel Proctor. Early fifties. Carrying about thirty extra pounds. Six feet. Dark hair."

Morelli nodded. "I know Abel Proctor. He's the senior guy on their Bureau of Investigation. It's like their detective division. But it's only four deputies. Proctor and three others. So, about Joey Collins, do you know him at all? Anything about him?"

"Only what Irene Allen told me."

"Which was?"

"He comes from a family connected to that group called the Kin. You know anything about them?"

"Some. Not much. They're secretive. I'm still considered an outsider, so I don't have any inside information. As far as I know, I haven't represented any of them. The general scuttlebutt is they've been in this area a long time. Whatever crime goes on around here, they seem to be part of it. There's a bit of an outlaw ethic among a certain part of the population around here. Supposedly it dates back hundreds of years to the problems between tenants who rented land from wealthy landowners like the Livingstons, the Van Rensselaers. They resented the economic and political subservience. There were violent rent strikes. I don't think that resentment ever completely died out."

"I hear the Kin has a thing about white supremacy."

"Yes, that seems to be getting more traction these days. The local version has an Aryan superior race element for sure. There was actually a summer camp for Nazi youth near Winholm before the war."

"Really?"

"Yes. Nineteen thirty-seven. In those days people up here were openly anti-Semitic. You had resorts and boarding houses that said 'No Hebrews Taken' in their ads. When they forced 'em to stop that, they switched to saying, 'Churches nearby' instead."

Beck said, "How many locals are associated with the Kin?"

Morelli shook his head. "I honestly don't know. There are large pockets of conservative people around here, Mr. Beck."

"You know anything about the leadership structure?"

"Not really. Although I sense they're pretty well organized, like most right-wing groups."

Beck asked, "Do you know anything about Camdyn Dent?"

Morelli paused and looked up from his legal pad. "I've heard the name. He's supposed to be the top dog. I don't know anything about him."

Beck nodded. Morelli confirmed what Irene had told him, but not much more.

"So, what do you see happening with my friend?"

"Well, first of all, this is a murder case, so there'll be a good deal of heat on it. I don't think there's been a murder in this county for at least two years. And trust me, law enforcement will know about the connection between Joey Collins and the Kin. That will increase the attention paid."

"Why?"

"The sheriff's department will want to solve the case before the Kin takes matters into their own hands."

"Meaning?"

Morelli shrugged. "I can't say for sure. I assume the Kin will want to find out who did it and take revenge."

"How?"

Morelli's expression changed. "I'm sure there are a number of ways the Kin could cause trouble."

Before Beck could follow up on that, Morelli asked, "What's your friend's relationship with the Kin?"

"I don't think she has any relationship with the Kin other than growing up around here. If anything, it's not positive."

"So why does she frequent the Field?"

Beck thought about why Morelli was asking that. He decided because he might need an answer for her defense.

"I asked her that. She said she has friends who go there who aren't Kin people. And she said she grew up here and feels she has the right to go wherever she wants. And there's the practical reality. There aren't many places open late where you can have a drink and socialize."

"You say her opinion about the Kin isn't positive. What has she said?"

"Pretty much what you have. Listen, I wouldn't have a positive opinion about any group with members like Hamm Elrod who came at her like he was going to do serious damage to her. But they didn't arrest her for that. They arrested her for killing someone she has no motive to kill. More important, as I told you, I don't see how she could have. We left that place together. And when we left, Joey Collins was alive. She was with me the rest of the night until we went back to get her car, and the sheriff's investigator arrested her."

Morelli nodded and looked at his legal pad. "And you left when?"

"About twelve-thirty."

"And returned?"

"Around eight."

"Right. And Elrod attacked her – why?"

"Not sure. He overheard something she said. Or I said."

"Which was?"

"I don't recall." Beck leaned forward. "That's not an evasion. I really don't. But be clear about this, Mr. Morelli, nothing we could have said justified his attack."

"Yes. Agreed. But the more I know the better. I'm worried about two things."

"What?"

"They have leverage on her because she stabbed Elrod. They will use that leverage to get whatever information they can."

"And that is why I'm hiring you. It's your job to make sure she says absolutely nothing to the sheriffs."

"Agreed. One last thing?"

"What?"

"Do you mind if I ask how much you had to drink last night?"

"I don't mind you asking me anything if it helps you get Irene Allen out of jail."

"Well, frankly, it's about helping you."

"I'm not the issue."

"But you will be, Mr. Beck. I assume Dunleavy pointed out that the DA would try to nullify her alibi by making you an accomplice."

"Yes."

"I just want to make it clear that I don't want to get Irene Allen out of this by putting you in trouble."

Beck leaned forward.

"Listen to me carefully. I'm not going to deny she was with me at the time of the murder. If it implicates me, I'll deal with it."

Morelli didn't agree or disagree. He simply nodded.

"As far as how much I drank last night, frankly not all that much." Beck looked at his watch and said, "Are you ready to meet with her now?"

Morelli studied Beck for a moment. Beck waited. Morelli finally said, "Yes. Yes. I am. You and I need to do a little paperwork. Then I'll get over to the sheriff's and make sure she knows what's going to happen and that they can't question her without me being present."

"Any chance you can get her released?"

"No. She's in the process now. I don't think the arraignment will happen until tomorrow afternoon. And they could easily hold her for a maximum forty-eight hours."

"Why?"

"So they can get as much information about her involvement as possible. Mr. Beck, the sheriff, judges, DAs are all elected officials. Despite all the downstate liberals filtering in, the locals still have the votes. And you don't get elected in this county unless you're tough on crime. I think they'll keep her in jail until they decide whether or not they have enough to indict her."

"They won't let her make bail when they arraign her?"

"Very unlikely on a murder charge. And even if they do, the bail will be substantial."

"I'll cover it. And your fees."

"Good to know, but let's not get ahead of ourselves. Like you said, right now she needs to know she has representation. We'll find out more at the arraignment. I've got to convince the DA that he doesn't have a case here and decide not to charge her. Let's take this step by step."

"All right."

"And please remember, we'll still have to deal with her using a knife…"

Beck interrupted. "I know, I know. First, get in to see her, Mr. Morelli."

"Yes, agreed. Just know that anything and everything that happened last night will be investigated because a murder was committed."

"Understood."

"By the way, do you know what happened to that knife?"

Beck paused before he said, "No." He wasn't sure why he'd decided to tell Morelli a half-truth. Mostly because he wanted Morelli to leave and meet with Irene. Partly because Morelli was turning out to be like most lawyers. Bring up every possible problem and lay out reasons he might not be able to solve them. Both of which would result in a higher fee.

Morelli persisted. "I assume it's not in this house."

"Correct."

"All right. Hopefully, nobody will show up with a search warrant anytime soon." Morelli gave Beck a look. Beck took it to mean that he'd better go through his house and get rid of anything incriminating.

"One more thing, and don't get mad at me for taking more time."

"What?"

"I wouldn't be surprised if Abel Proctor isn't working up to arresting you, too. You might want to make yourself scarce."

Beck nodded. He had to concede Morelli had made a good point.

Beck said, "How soon do you think he'd get an arrest warrant?"

Morelli looked at his watch. "By end of day. But as you know, they'll most likely come for you in the middle of the night. So, you have some time."

"Right."

"Let's get the paperwork done. I need you to sign a retainer agreement. I've filled it out as you retaining me to represent Irene Allen. But it won't go into effect until she signs it. My retainer fee is seventy-five-hundred dollars." Morelli pulled out an agreement from his briefcase. "As soon as you sign this, I'll get over there and talk to Ms. Allen. I'm assuming she won't have any objection to me representing her."

"Just tell her I sent you, and I'm paying you."

Beck signed the agreement with a cursory glance and signed two copies.

"I'll get you a check."

"Fine."

Beck went to the small office he'd set up off the kitchen and grabbed a checkbook. He had money in various accounts that one of the ex-cons in his tight-knit circle, Alex Liebowitz, had set up. One of the accounts held over three million dollars, all of it carefully laundered and taxed appropriately, four-hundred thousand of it in cash.

When Beck returned to the sitting room, Morelli had packed up his briefcase and was standing in front of the fireplace. The logs had burned down to flickers of flame and a pile of glowing embers.

Beck asked, "Who do I make it out to?"

"Morelli Law LLC."

The lawyer handed him a business card he had been holding. Beck's copy of the retainer agreement was on the couch.

Beck wrote the check and handed it to Peter Morelli. He slipped it into the breast pocket of his suit jacket.

Morelli looked up at Beck. He was six inches shorter than Beck and fifty-five pounds lighter.

"One question, Mr. Beck."

"James is fine."

"James, I'm curious. Why didn't that sheriff's investigator arrest you, too?"

Beck's expression hardened a bit as he remembered facing down the investigator.

He gave Morelli a slight shrug and said, "I think he had his hands full. He was alone. And I made it clear I wouldn't be answering any questions without a lawyer. Like you said. He probably figured he could bring me in later."

"Right. You have any questions for me?"

Beck said, "Not at the moment."

Morelli picked up his briefcase and headed for the front door. Beck walked with him and stood while Morelli put on his coat and shoes. Morelli told Beck he'd let him know the results of his meeting with Irene Allen and that he intended to speak to the DA as soon as possible.

Beck nodded, but he wasn't listening. He had counted on Peter Morelli ushering Irene through an arraignment, entering a plea of not guilty, and getting her released on recognizance or bail. After that he'd get Phineas on the case. But Morelli had been clear that Irene would not make bail at her arraignment, which might not happen for forty-eight hours.

Morelli had made it clear that Beck was an outsider in a rural area with a law-and-order district attorney and a sheriff's department that would be going all out to investigate a murder because the victim belonged to a family with standing in a crime group called the Kin – a rural, white-supremacist, underground militia who Irene warned would likely want to make him pay for putting one of their thugs on his knees. And most likely for also being at the Field shortly before someone killed Joey Collins.

The smart move would be to disappear. Beck had money and resources to go anywhere in the world and stay for as long as he wanted. But he couldn't bring himself to leave Irene Allen fending for herself. And at his core, James Beck didn't believe running was the way to solve a problem.

Beck knew the only way to solve this mess was to find out who killed Joey Collins and prove it before the Kin killed him or Abel Proctor arrested him.

Beck also knew there was zero chance he could do it alone.

He closed the door after Morelli left and walked into his sitting room. Beck had a call to make. The phone seemed to ring a long time before Manny Guzman answered.

"James."

"Manolito, how's the hand?" As if that were the reason he had called. Still avoiding it.

"Good enough. How are you, hermano?"

Beck blurted out the words. "Got a problem." Now there would be no turning back.

Manny said, "How bad a problem?"

"Don't know yet. Bad enough to reach out."

"That's what you're supposed to do."

"Doesn't make it any easier."

"It shouldn't be hard, James. We don't look out for ourselves, we're dead. Simple as that."

"After the last time…"

"That's over, man."

Beck said, "Not completely."

"Yeah, I know. My hand, your lungs. The shit that happened to Demarco and Ciro. So what? Why'd you call? What's going on? You're two seconds from insulting me, James."

Beck finally said, "Can you come up north?"

Manny said, "How long does it take to drive to where you are?"

"Three hours, give or take."

"Got it. Hang on, James. The big guy came over about an hour ago. He's about to grab the phone from me. Fill him in while I pack."

Beck heard Ciro Baldassare in the background telling Manny to give him the phone. He knew his next call would have been to Ciro anyhow. Not letting the fearsome mafioso know about his troubles would have been an insult. Not something Beck would ever contemplate doing to his friend and ally.

"Jimmy!"

"Ciro."

"What's up? You got trouble in the neighborhood?"

Beck smiled. Everything was urban to Ciro Baldassare.

"Looks like it."

"All right. Fuck it. I'll bring Manny up there."

That was typical Ciro Baldassare.

Beck said, "Bring shoes that work on something other than concrete."

"Hey, don't worry about it. I went deer hunting once with my cousin. I know the score."

"Good."

"Jimmy."

"What?"

"It's past time."

Beck didn't have to ask what Ciro meant by past time.

"I know."

"Where will we find you?"

"I'll text you an address."

"You need anything from down here?"

Beck didn't have to ask what *anything* meant. He knew that despite the risk, neither Ciro Baldassare nor Manny Guzman would go anywhere without their guns, even on the long drive upstate. A Smith & Wesson .45 semi-auto for Ciro and two revolvers for Manny – a five-shot Charter Arms .44 Bulldog Special and whatever long-barrel .38 revolver he favored these days. Probably a Taurus 82.

"I'm good. What are you driving?"

"Cadillac CT-Five, goombah. It's got all-wheel drive, man. It's okay in the snow and shit."

"If you bring anything extra, make sure there's someplace to conceal it in your car. Try not to speed. State troopers are always patrolling the Thruway."

"Okay, Mom, don't worry. How long we going to be up there?"

"I'm hoping forty-eight hours."

"You got room for us, or should we get a motel or something?"

"You'll stay here."

"Sounds good." Ciro laughed and said, "Hey, keep a fucking light on for us," and hung up.

Beck knew that if Ciro and Manny were coming, so would Demarco Jones. It didn't matter that Beck only needed Manny right now. That's the way it worked with Beck's crew.

He dialed Demarco Jones. Demarco lived alone in his upstate house having broken off the relationship with the man who introduced him to the Hudson Valley. The call went straight to voicemail. He left a message telling Demarco when he expected Manny and Ciro. He'd figured out their arrival time, knowing that Ciro would need to go back to his place in Staten Island to pack.

Beck suddenly had plenty to do. Find sheets and bedding for the spare bedrooms. Get the heat going in the guesthouse. Make a run for food.

Suddenly, a wave of exhilaration swept over Beck. The months of isolation weighing on him for so long evaporated. Even though Beck and his men stayed in touch by phone, the disconnect had never abated. Now they would all be together. His friends. His partners. His crew. Men who had helped each other survive in a world that had ostracized them and taken every opportunity to kill them off or send them to prison.

But in the next second, the sense of dread that always lived somewhere inside James Beck crept in and replaced his elation. The feeling started at the base of his skull and rose into his brain, darkening his mood and draining away his joy. Beck told himself this wouldn't be like the last time. But he couldn't convince himself of that. Beck felt another cycle of violence pulling him in. He could still run. Get out of this redneck, bullshit, white supremacist backwoods ass-end of the world. Forget about Irene Allen. Make believe none of this had anything to do with him.

Yeah, well, fuck that.

10

Proctor grabbed the keys to his truck, a red 2011 Nissan Frontier with 127,185 miles on it. He walked downstairs to the holding cell where Hibbard had placed Hamm Elrod. He was the only one in the cell, splayed out on a bench, head back, snoring like a hog in the grips of sleep apnea. Proctor kicked the bars and yelled, "Hey!"

Elrod woke with a start. It took him a while to realize where he was. He rubbed his face and stood up. Proctor unlocked the cell door. He stood holding a Ziploc bag holding Elrod's wallet, keys, phone, and $22.18.

"Follow me. Don't say anything."

When Proctor reached the parking lot, he pointed to his truck and told Elrod to get in. Hamm almost asked where they were going but didn't.

The drive took twenty minutes. Proctor cracked the window on Elrod's side to let out the annoying body odor and smell of booze. Proctor glanced over at Elrod. He looked like he'd slept in his clothes. Probably went home and dropped into bed. Proctor recalled the one time he'd been in that trailer. The place reeked of body odor, old dog, cooking smells, dirty clothes, and general funk. By the time they pulled up to Oscar Lund's corrugated steel storage shed, Proctor had the window on his side open, too.

The shed was 30' x 40' and should have been torn down and recycled years ago. Rust stains covered the corrugated roof. Moss and mildew layered the sides. Gray rotting plywood covered the only window. Someone had spray painted the outline of a door in orange DayGlo next to the window but never got around to cutting out the section.

Once they were out of the truck, Proctor told Elrod to walk around the far corner of the shed, where they entered through a metal door crudely attached to hinges bolted onto the corrugated steel. Inside Oscar Lund sat on a wooden stool next to a worktable, his back against the table. Hamm looked at Lund but kept his mouth shut. Proctor was surprised to see a glowing, four-tube fluorescent light hanging from the ceiling. Somehow Lund had supplied electricity to the shed. Probably by running five hundred feet of outdoor extension cord from his house. Enough for light, but not enough to run a space heater. There was no difference between the temperature inside and out.

Lund had turned over a rusty metal milk crate in the middle of a ten-foot square area he'd cleared of junk. He'd also set up a wooden rocking chair about six feet in front of the crate. Two of the spindles were missing from the back of the rocker, and the caning in the seat was coming apart.

Lund pointed to the crate and told Elrod, "Sit."

Proctor sat in the rocking chair opposite Elrod, on the front edge of the seat so the chair wouldn't rock. He took out his Glock 21, chambered a round, laid his right forearm on the arm of the chair, and pointed the gun at Hamm Elrod.

Elrod couldn't keep his mouth shut any longer.

"What the hell is all this!"

Proctor answered with quiet intensity, speaking slowly. "Hamm, do not talk until I tell you to. I swear to God, the first goddamn second I hear anything from you I think is bullshit, I will shoot you. Believe me. You will not leave this place alive unless I hear the truth from you. I have no time for anything else, and neither do you." Proctor stared at Hamm, daring him to say something. He didn't.

Oscar Lund sat on his stool, an elbow resting on his worktable, watching without expression. There were tools on the worktable

Oscar intended to use on Hamm Elrod if the truculent bastard pissed him off any more than he already had. Lund had already heard about Joey Collins getting his throat slit. And the fight Hamm got into. Lund knew he was in the shit just by being at the Field the same night somebody killed Joey Collins. If Hamm Elrod had killed Collins, Lund knew the Kin would kill him for leaving Collins with Elrod. He dragged a small sledgehammer across the table next to a heavy-duty straight-blade pry bar that looked like a giant screwdriver. Oscar Lund planned to pound the screwdriver into Elrod's kneecap if he heard any shit from him.

Proctor turned away from Elrod and asked Lund, "Did you talk to Vic?"

"Yep. He told me what happened. Gave us the green light to do what we need to do. He said it's up to us. He said he doesn't want Devereaux to get involved."

Proctor grimaced. "God help us if it gets to that."

Hamm Elrod looked back and forth. The mention of Devereaux suddenly made it difficult for him to breathe. The stories of Emmett Devereaux torturing, mutilating, and killing people were horrifying. His mouth went dry. He had to clear his throat to mutter, "Hold on now. What the hell is going on?"

Proctor hadn't teed up Oscar Lund to say or do anything except confirm he had checked with Vic Myer. According to the Kin's structure, Lund was under Vic Myer, who was in charge of the Kin's militia. As was Hamm Elrod. The Kin militia were the active members who ran the distribution of drugs, collected dues, took care of the Kin's day-to-day business. Proctor was responsible for taking care of law enforcement efforts involving the Kin. To monitor every interaction. Sometimes that meant covering up crimes or steering investigations so they wouldn't produce arrests. Sometimes it meant going forward and convicting selected Kin members to limit the damage.

Emmett Devereaux occupied the role of enforcer. Only Camdyn Dent could unleash Devereaux.

Proctor didn't mind that Lund had invoked Devereaux. It would make questioning Hamm Elrod easier. Proctor turned his attention back to Elrod.

"I hope to God above, Hamm, that you really don't know what this is about."

"I don't. Unless you're talking about that asshole who sucker punched me."

"It isn't about that. Last night, somebody killed Joey Collins. Cut his throat from ear to ear and left him to bleed out at the Field."

Proctor saw the confusion on Elrod's face. Was it genuine?

"Where?"

"At the Field, Hamm. You were the last person with him before he died. You, Hamm."

Elrod opened his mouth to speak. Proctor held up a hand to stop him.

"Wait. Don't say anything yet. I want you to start from when Joey picked you up and tell me every goddamn thing that happened between you two until the last moment you were with him. Talk slowly. Think carefully. Don't leave out one fucking thing."

Proctor watched how fear concentrated the mind of Hamm Elrod. His usual bluster and belligerence nearly disappeared. Elrod looked deflated. Proctor could see that Hamm figured they were going to blame him for the death of Joey Collins no matter what he said. And that was fine with Abel Proctor. It took the bluster and belligerence out of Elrod. He spoke as if he were resigned to his fate and had decided to tell the truth because he didn't have the energy to make anything up.

When Elrod finished, Proctor nodded. Most of what Elrod said conformed with what he already knew from Lund and the Myer brothers.

"Sounds like you were pretty pissed off at Collins for what happened with the hijacking and because he didn't back you up in that fight."

"I was. But not enough to kill him for chrissake. I'm not that stupid."

Elrod slumped on the metal milk crate, his belly hanging over his pants, his duct-taped coat open. The crate held his weight but sitting on it was painful.

Oscar Lund spoke up. "Which direction did he go to take a piss?"

Elrod shrugged. "I don't know. I didn't notice."

"How long did you wait for Collins to come back?"

Another shrug. "Long enough to figure he'd just gone and left me there. He was my ride home. Figured it was something he'd do. I told Vic and George that Collins was missing and got a ride home from Denny Raab."

Proctor said, "Why'd you bother telling Vic and George?"

Elrod shrugged. "I don't know."

"Yes you do. Don't bullshit me."

Elrod's voice rose. "Because I wanted Vic to know what an asshole he was. Everybody thought I was the asshole that night. But I didn't leave anybody high and dry."

Lund asked, "What time did you leave with Raab?"

"I don't fucking know. Twelve-thirty, one?"

Proctor said, "And you didn't see Joey's truck when you left?"

"No. Denny was waiting for me in his car near the barn. I just got in and went home. I didn't see no truck. And I didn't kill Joey Collins."

"What did you do from the time Collins left you until you got that ride home?"

"Nothing."

"No," said Proctor. "You did something. You sat there getting pissed off about that guy who knocked you on your ass. And about Irene Allen, too. You sat there thinking about what you wanted to do to Joey Collins because he didn't back you up. Maybe he even razzed you about getting your ass kicked and left you to find a ride home. You were fucking furious at him, weren't you?"

Elrod looked up and made eye contact with Proctor. His usual anger and bluster suddenly returned.

"Yeah. I was pissed off. And more pissed off on the ride home. And more pissed off trying to fall asleep in my stinking trailer. But I didn't fucking kill Joey Collins!"

Proctor put his gun back in the holster. He stood up and motioned for Oscar Lund to follow him outside.

Lund closed the door behind them and said, "So?"

Proctor frowned and shook his head. "He's a suspect for sure. He had motive. He had opportunity. But I don't think he killed Collins."

"Why not?"

"He's not that good of an actor. He was pissed off at Joey Collins, but I think he was a hell of a lot more pissed off at Irene Allen and the guy who put him on his knees. Those two humiliated him."

Lund nodded, thinking about that.

"So, what do you want to do?"

"Help me use all that hate inside Hamm to get something done. Listen, I can't hardly see straight. I've got to go home and sleep." Proctor pulled out the Ziploc bag with Elrod's belongings from his pocket and handed it to Lund. "Get Hamm and two more militia hard boys who can help you put the hurt on the guy who punched out Hamm. I want the four of you to give him a beating he won't forget, but don't put him in the hospital. After you soften him up, I'm going to arrest him."

"For what?"

"I'll explain later. I want it done tonight. Around seven-thirty. Can you get it set up by six?"

"I think so. Where do we find this guy?"

Proctor pulled out his phone and showed Lund the picture he'd taken of Beck's driver's license. Lund squinted at the image and said, "Yeah, that's the guy. I recognize him. Hamm was giving him shit just after we got there. That's his address?"

"Yes. Meet me at our usual spot at six. We'll pick it up there."

Lund said, "Okay." He didn't ask questions. Proctor ranked higher than him. Whatever he was planning, Lund knew it had Camdyn Dent's blessing. It had nothing to do with him. He figured Abel wanted to teach this guy Beck a lesson for beating down a member of the Kin and arrest him for killing Joey Collins. He didn't know how Proctor would make that stick and he didn't care.

11

Lund watched Proctor drive off. He checked his watch. Nearing two o'clock. He had to hustle before he met Proctor at six. He couldn't stop thinking about Emmett Devereaux. He had a feeling that Dent had already given Devereaux orders to organize his men, mostly hill people, mostly living over in the Taghkanics. Throwbacks. Hard, primitive, superstitious men. Led by the worst of the worst, Emmett Devereaux. Criminals born and bred, their roots going back to the sixteen-hundreds when they'd first arrived and started intermarrying with the native population.

Lund figured that Camdyn Dent would blame Hamm Elrod for Joey Collins even if Elrod hadn't killed him. When Devereaux finished with Elrod, he'd burn what was left of him, shovel the ashes into a box, and toss it into the Vosburgh Swamp. Lund knew that would put him dangerously close to being next on Devereaux's list. He hoped Proctor would be able to direct the Kin leader's wrath onto James Beck, whoever the hell he was.

Lund stepped back into the storage shed. Hamm Elrod hadn't moved off his milk crate.

"So, what's the verdict, Oscar? You gonna put a bullet in my head?"

"Hell no. Proctor don't think you did it. He figures you told him the truth."

Elrod stood up. "For real or are you bullshitting me to get me off guard?"

"For real." Lund pulled out the Ziploc bag with Elrod's possessions from the pocket of his down vest and tossed it to Elrod. "Come on. Proctor wants you in on a job tonight."

Elrod caught the plastic bag and said, "What is it?"

Lund could see that Elrod was still suspicious. They both knew men who'd been told to come out on a job and ended up dead.

"You and a few of the boys are going to teach that outsider who put the hurt on you that he made the biggest mistake of his life."

Hamm Elrod's demeanor changed completely.

"How? When?"

Lund said, "I don't know the details yet. C'mon, I'll take you home so you can clean up and get your car."

The ride to Elrod's trailer took twenty minutes. Fifteen trailer homes sat parallel to each other along an access road that curved in from the county highway. Most of the homes were beyond bad shape. Hamm Elrod's was at the end of the line.

Lund told Elrod, "Wash up and put on clean clothes. I'll be out here calling the others. Don't bring any guns or weapons with you. We don't want the guy dead. Proctor has plans for him."

Hamm nodded and said, "All right." But he was lying. He intended to kill Beck the first chance he got.

"And Hamm…"

"What?"

"No need to tell your mother what's happening."

"Hell, she wouldn't remember anyhow."

It took seven phone calls to get two other men for the Beck job. He finished the last call just as Hamm approached his Jeep wearing a black t-shirt, Wrangler jeans held up with red suspenders, and the same fake sheepskin jacket with the duct tape on the shoulder seam.

When Elrod came to the driver's side, Lund opened the window and said, "Take your ride and follow me."

"Where we going?"

"You know that diner outside of Coleville?"

"Yeah."

"We're meeting there."

"With who?"

Lund didn't appreciate Hamm Elrod asking him questions, but he decided to humor him.

"J.T. and Reid Vander."

Hamm nodded as if he approved. He said, "Those are good boys."

Lund said, "They'll do."

J.T. Stott was a confirmed white supremacist who made sure everyone knew it. He had so many white supremacist tattoos that he'd lost count. They included iron crosses, swastikas, symbolic numbers, SS lightning bolts, gothic lettering for CWB initials (Crazy White Boy), Mein Herr, and Heisst Treue and an Odin's Cross on his back. J.T. Stott was the one you brought along to intimidate people. He was six foot five and big. Big muscles, big bones, big close-cropped head. Stott moved slowly. Methodically. He was tough to take down. Once Stott got his hands on someone, severe damage was inevitable.

Reid Vander was a dangerous sneak. Compact, wiry, and fast. Vander's choice of weapon was a knife or razor. Vander did not fight. He did not mix it up. He enjoyed sneaking up on someone or getting close with a relaxed self-effacing smile, then inflicting damage before the victim knew what had happened. He would slap and slash, kick, and then be gone before the blood hit the floor.

Lund checked his watch. Four-thirty. Time to meet and set up the job before he reported back to Abel Proctor at six.

Oscar Lund almost felt sorry for James Beck. If things got out of hand, there wouldn't be enough left of James Beck to arrest. Well, that would be on Abel. He had to know what might happen if these three were unleashed. Lund knew the men respected his district leader rank, if not him personally. They would listen to him, but only to a degree. Hopefully enough so he could prevent them from beating James Beck to death.

12

Ciro Baldassare insisted on doing the driving, which was fine with Manny Guzman. It was Ciro's car, and it gave Manny a chance to nap. Except that Ciro had something to say every ten or fifteen minutes, which forced Manny to rouse himself and respond. Barely. Then slide back to sleep as the miles zipped by.

It occurred to Manny that Ciro Baldassare had become more talkative over the last few months. He wasn't sure why. Maybe because Covid had isolated Ciro more than most. Two of his money-making operations had withered during the pandemic: money laundering through a string of restaurants he controlled and illegal sports betting. Whatever it was, when Ciro said something about upstate New York or asked what could have made Beck reach out for help, Manny responded, even though he didn't have much to say.

When Abel Proctor's alarm sounded at five o'clock, he struggled to wake up. It took a shower and two cups of coffee before he felt almost normal. It reminded Abel of when he worked the midnight-to-eight shift for almost three years. Much longer than he should have because he was one of the few men with no wife or kids. His sleep patterns had been off ever since.

On the drive to his meeting with Oscar Lund, Abel called Russ Hibbard to check on the arrest warrant for Beck. Proctor wanted it by six o'clock, seven at the latest.

"Russ, how's it going on that warrant?"

"I was about to call you. We got it."

"Good. You should grab some sleep. Bunk in one of the cells in the new jail."

"I will."

"I'll come in to pick you up. I want to serve the warrant around seven-thirty."

"Okay."

Proctor cut the call as he turned into an Applebee's parking lot off Route 9. It was 5:57 p.m.

Proctor had considered using a couple of deputies to arrest Beck but decided to keep it to himself and Hibbard. He might keep Hibbard out of it, too. No need for others in the department to see a prisoner in the condition he expected Beck would be in.

Proctor didn't look for Lund's green Jeep Cherokee. He knew that Oscar would park next door in the Wendy's lot and walk over. Neither of them wanted anyone spotting their vehicles together.

Proctor parked at the far end of the Applebee's lot, facing a storage facility about a quarter-mile away. The facility covered sixty-five acres.

Proctor heard a tapping on the passenger side window. He unlocked the door. Oscar climbed into the passenger seat, his weight rocking the Nissan's cab.

Proctor said, "You all set on your end?"

"Yep. J.T., Hamm, and Reid Vander. Vander snuck onto the guy's property. He has eyes on him now."

"His name is Beck."

"Yeah, I know. Beck."

"And?"

"He's home."

"All right, good. Your boys go in at seven-thirty. Make sure they don't beat him too bad. I want him able to walk."

"Understood."

"Hamm is the one you'll have to put a leash on."

"For sure. You want us to be there for the arrest?"

"Just you. I'll come in at about eight."

"Got it. You don't have to say anything, Abel, but I'm assuming you're going to arrest this guy Beck for murdering Joey Collins."

Proctor gave Lund a deadpan stare.

Lund said, "What's your evidence?"

"Don't worry about it, Oscar. I have the evidence I need."

Lund raised his hands. "Okay. Not my business. Forget I asked."

Proctor was about to change the topic and ask Lund details about what happened at the van hijacking. And get Lund's side of the story of what went down at the Field. But he decided against it. He knew the word had come down from on high to use Joey Collins. The supreme leader had decided Collins should get his hands dirty. Get some experience under his belt. Somehow the whole thing had turned into a total disaster. With Oscar Lund in the middle of it. Proctor decided there would be no point in getting Lund's side of events. It would just give Oscar a chance to whine about how none of what happened was his fault and plead with him to intercede with the leaders. Instead, Proctor stared off in the distance at the storage facility. There were seven buildings. The office and indoor storage units were in one large building. East of that were six long buildings lined up parallel to each other offering outdoor storage.

Proctor lifted his chin toward the storage facility. "You know, when I started with the sheriff's department, that place wasn't even there."

Oscar followed Proctor's gaze. "No, I suppose not."

Proctor looked at Lund and said, "When in the hell did people get so much shit, they had to rent somewhere to put it in?"

"I don't know. The shit ain't even made here anymore. China. Mexico. Vietnam. Bangla-frickin'-desh."

"Sixty-five acres of junk packed into storage units. How'd that happen?"

"Fucking liberal bullshit trade policies. Nobody gives a damn about the working man."

Proctor said, "I'll bet half the junk sitting in those units isn't even paid for yet."

"Probably not."

Proctor grunted, wiped his face to dispel his fatigue, and turned toward Oscar Lund. Abel felt the handle of his Glock 21 holstered at his right hip press into his side. He suddenly had an intense desire to pull the gun and shoot a bullet into Oscar Lund's forehead. The feeling came over Proctor like a black wave, disorienting him, making him slightly dizzy. Proctor had to catch his breath. Even though Proctor knew where the deadly impulse came from, the urge to murder Oscar Lund still surprised him. Oscar Lund had fucked up that robbery and compounded the mess by leaving Hamm Elrod and Joey Collins alone together. No matter which way the murder investigation went, odds were that Oscar Lund didn't have much longer to live. Anybody who had anything to do with Joey Collins getting killed would be made to pay. When it came time to cut out the cancer, Camdyn Dent cut deep.

Abel shifted position so that the gun didn't press into him. He wondered how much longer he could stand covering up stupid shit like a botched robbery of donated food that belonged in a dumpster.

Abel Proctor was getting tired of everybody doing whatever they wanted to do without one goddamn thought about the problems they created. Like the dopes who bought so much crap that they had to store it in those units. Why? Because they wanted what they wanted and refused to give the junk away or throw it away because they believed they should have it. They would believe that right up until the day they sold off the crap for back rent on their storage unit. And even that wouldn't stop them from borrowing more money to buy more crap. Everybody wants what they want, even if someone else has to pay the price for it.

Oscar said, "What's the matter?"

Proctor turned back toward Oscar and said, "Nothing."

Proctor looked away from Oscar and turned his attention back to James Beck. Right now, he had the beginnings of a scheme to solve the murder of Joey Collins. Arrest Beck. Hope Beck had handled Irene Allen's knife – maybe when he took her pants off before he fucked her. Then doctor the blade with Joey Collins's blood he'd left on his nitrile glove. That would give him the murder weapon. Framing the two of them would be feasible. The only thing lacking was a motive. He might be able to fudge that by claiming they mistook Joey Collins in the dark for Hamm Elrod. Quite a stretch, but Grotowski might run with it.

If it had been Hamm Elrod who got his throat sliced open, it would be a slam dunk: Beck and the woman came back to the Field and did him in. But it hadn't been Hamm, and Proctor knew he didn't have a clue about who really killed Joey Collins or why.

Whatever. Step one, that asshole James Beck was going to get a beating tonight and be arrested for murder. *At the very least, that arrogant prick is about to learn he made a big mistake when he thought about taking me on.*

Proctor turned away from Lund and started the engine of his Nissan. He was getting cold.

"Okay, Oscar, get it done, and I'll see you at eight."

Lund opened the truck door and stepped out. "All right. Hell, man, all of a sudden, things are gettin' busy."

Proctor said, "That's what happens when all of a sudden somebody gets murdered."

13

Beck looked out the window of his sitting room and saw headlights at the bottom of his driveway. Ciro must've done eighty-five the whole way. He checked his watch. 7:26 p.m. Demarco hadn't even arrived yet from the other side of the river.

Beck opened his front door. He saw a second pair of headlights. Had Demarco, Ciro, and Manny arrived at the same time? Two realizations flashed in Beck's brain. Both pairs of headlights were high off the ground, but only Demarco owned a truck. And his shotgun was upstairs under his bed.

As Beck turned back into his house, he heard something smash open his kitchen door. He kicked his front door shut and broke into a run through the hallway toward the stairway leading to the second floor. Beck veered right and made it up three steps before J.T. Stott burst into the hallway. Stott lunged at Beck. He managed to grab the back of Beck's belt. He pulled Beck off the stairs, lifting him off his feet. Gravity and Stott's strength combined to send Beck flying backward until he hit the wall on the opposite side of the hallway. Beck's right shoulder and arm took most of the impact. He ended up crumpled against the wall, half-sitting, the wind knocked out of him.

Stott lumbered over to him. Beck heard loud sounds at the other end of the hallway. More attackers trying to break open his front door. Stott straddled Beck, bent down to grab Beck's shirt and lift him off the floor. Beck saw the big face coming down at him. Skinhead. Ugly neck tattoos. A face twisted with hate. Beck whipped his left fist, powered by adrenaline and rage, into Stott's nose. Cartilage splintered, and the right side of Stott's nose broke with a crack. The blow knocked J.T. upright and sideways. Stott let go of Beck and covered his nose with both hands. Beck, still sitting, grabbed Stott's belt with his right hand and powered a vicious left uppercut between Stott's legs. The big Nazi let out a shrieking grunt and crumpled to his knees. Beck shoved him aside. Stott keeled over and coiled into a fetal ball, cupping his ruptured testicles. Like a Greco-Roman wrestler, Beck spun out and got to his feet as he heard the frame of his front door splintering. Beck stomped hard on J.T.'s right kidney just below the big man's rib cage. And again, even harder. Stott's grunts weren't loud enough to cover the sound of his floating ribs cracking.

Beck's front door flew open. Beck stomped the heel of his boot into Stott's tailbone, breaking the tip of Stott's coccyx sending crippling waves of pain into Stott's lower back and legs.

Beck turned just in time to duck under an eighteen-inch aluminum fish bat aimed at his head by Oscar Lund. The bat smashed a dent in the wall on Beck's left. Beck stayed in his crouch. As the momentum of the swing brought Lund around, Beck drove two hard left hooks into Lund's ribcage and liver, then he rammed his left shoulder into Lund and drove him back into the two men coming in behind him. Lund fell back, taking down the shorter Hamm Elrod with him. Reid Vander was agile enough to jump out of the way and avoid going down with the two bigger men.

Beck stepped back, shaking his right arm, still numb from hitting the wall. Reid had no room to get around Hamm Elrod and Lund, so he pushed himself off the wall, stepped on Elrod's back, and jumped at Beck, slashing at him with a straight razor. Beck deflected Vander's razor with his left arm, but the blade cut across the bottom edge of Beck's radius bone, slicing him from his wrist to his elbow, cutting off a thin layer of skin and a chunk of flesh at the notch of his elbow. Beck's blood spattered on the hallway wall and floor. Swinging the razor had turned

Vander halfway around and down, leaving him open to a right hook from Beck that hit him on the side of his neck. Vander hit the floor gagging for breath.

Hamm Elrod was back on his feet. Nothing was going to stop him from getting his revenge on James Beck. Before Beck could regain his balance, Elrod bull-rushed him. He rammed into Beck with his big head and shoulder. He grabbed Beck around the waist and ran him back until Beck hit the wall at the end of the hallway cracking a four-foot dent in the plaster. As Beck hit the wall, Elrod's shoulder slammed into Beck's sternum sending all Beck's intercostal nerves into spasm. He could not breathe. The pain was excruciating, but the inability to breathe felt terrifying. Beck refused to panic. He held his breath, got his arms on the back of Elrod's head and thick neck but not in time to stop Elrod from snapping his head up into Beck's chin. The back of Beck's head hit the wall. Everything turned black. Beck still couldn't draw a full breath. He felt himself losing consciousness.

Lund was on his feet now, bent over, listing rightward from the damage caused by Beck's left hooks. He had to shift the fish bat into his left hand. He stepped toward Beck.

Stott had managed to prop himself up on one arm. Vander was on his knees, holding the side of his neck, pulling in ragged breaths, deciding to stay out of the fight and leave it up to Elrod and Lund to take out the stranger. He couldn't believe this one guy had almost taken them all down.

Panic and rage had replaced any desire in Lund to hold back. Whoever the hell James Beck was, this son of a bitch needed to be dealt with once and for all. Now. He yelled at Elrod, "Hold him up! Hold him against the wall!"

Elrod kept all his weight on Beck, pinning him to the wall. He grabbed Beck's left arm and held it against the wall while he shoved his left forearm up into Beck's throat, pinning his head back.

Beck had just finally taken a breath, but now with Elrod's forearm pressing against his throat again, he could barely breathe. His right arm was still free. He tried to punch the base of Elrod's skull to take out the brain stem, but Elrod's head was bent back, and the folds of his fat neck provided too much protection.

Lund raised the fish bat like a tomahawk and tried to crack open Beck's forehead. Beck managed to move his head, but not all the way clear of the bat. The hard aluminum clipped the side of his head and ear and smacked into Beck's trapezius muscle.

The sting of the blow enraged Beck. He lifted a knee into Elrod's stomach, barely moving the ape. Lund reared back to finish Beck off with the bat. J.T. Stott was up on his knees now. He lunged toward Beck and grabbed the leg Beck had used to knee Elrod. Elrod lifted his forearm to push Beck's head tighter against the wall. Beck could barely see where the bat was. He knew the next blow would put him down. He knew if he went down, these men would beat him to death.

And then the bat disappeared.

There were no lights at all illuminating the country road. Not even moonlight. Ciro squinted at the GPS map display. Beck's house seemed close. He hoped the lights were on because he couldn't see shit. And then he came around a bend. He peered through the forest and saw a house illuminated by multiple headlights from trucks and vehicles parked in front.

"What the fuck is this?"

Manny sat up in the front seat. He tried to see past the trees and foliage as Ciro turned into Beck's driveway and accelerated, the Cadillac slipping and sliding on the remains of snow and frozen gravel. They slid to a halt behind the vehicles parked in front of the broken front door.

Manny had his Charter Arms five-shot revolver in his right hand. Ciro grabbed his Smith & Wesson from under the front seat. He popped open his door and hurried out, stiff from sitting behind the wheel for hours. He broke into a hurried limp. Manny hunched over, eyes on the broken door, followed Ciro but off to the right to make it harder for anybody who might shoot at them.

The sight of the broken back door sent Demarco Jones into an explosion of movement, impossibly fast for a man his size. He came through the kitchen and burst into the hallway at a full run, jumped over J.T. Stott, still hanging on to Beck's leg, and grabbed the lethal fish bat held by Oscar Lund as he reared back to smash open Beck's head. Demarco landed on his feet next to Oscar Lund. He twisted the bat out of Lund's hand and rammed the crook of his thumb and forefinger into Lund's throat. He kicked out Lund's left leg, sending him down to the floor.

In two seconds, Demarco took in everything. The big guy who had the bat was on his back, clutching his throat gasping for air. The skinhead hanging onto Beck's leg wasn't a threat. The short bald guy who had Beck pinned to the wall wasn't doing much more than that. The skinny asshole with the straight razor weaved back and forth, swinging a razor at Demarco's eyes, yelling, "C'mon, nigger boy. Come and get it."

Demarco thought, *Nigger boy? What rock did this guy crawl out from?* And then he starting swing the small aluminum bat with force and brutality and accuracy.

The first downward swing broke three of Lund's ribs, adding to the one Beck had cracked with his left hooks. A counterclockwise turn and Demarco whipped the aluminum bat sideways into the back of J.T. Stott's head. A cracking clunk sound told Demarco he'd fractured the tattooed guy's skull.

Elrod still had his left forearm jammed against Beck's throat, pinning him to the wall. With Demarco taking care of the others, Beck only had to concentrate on Elrod. He reached around with his free right hand and worked three fingers between Elrod's left thumb and closed fist. With one sudden, vicious twist, he tore the thumb out of the saddle joint and ruptured both tendons holding the thumb in place.

All the strength went out of Hamm Elrod. He screamed. Beck scraped the edge of his shoe down Elrod's shin and stomped on his foot. He shoved Elrod away from him, came off the wall, grabbed the back of Elrod's thick neck, pivoted, and with all his returning strength, rammed Elrod's head into the wall. The blow knocked out Elrod and ruptured two vertebrae at the top of his spine. Elrod slid down the broken plaster leaving a blood trail. He ended up on the floor, his face pushed against the baseboard. Beck stomped on Elrod's back and ribs until he ran out of breath.

Demarco focused on Vander and the straight razor, waiting for the wiry, swaying weasel to make his move. Demarco knew someone with a blade could always do damage, particularly if he got lucky, but there was enough space between them that Demarco had little doubt that the razor blade wouldn't get past the fish bat.

He heard Beck beating someone behind him, cursing about how he had dared to come into his house.

Vander watched the six-foot-four menacing Black man with a lethal aluminum fish bat. He tried to find an opening. A way to cut him. But the nigger just stood his ground. Hardly moving. And then Demarco smiled at him. That was it. Vander turned to run. Too late. He ran right into Ciro Baldassare's fist.

As strong as Demarco and Beck were, Baldassare was stronger. More powerful. If he had hit Vander with all his strength, he might have killed him. Which was fine with Ciro, but he knew he'd probably break his hand. So, he mostly let Vander run into his fist, giving him a short, hard pop. It was enough to break Vander's nose and send his brain banging into the front and then into the back of his skull. Vander was unconscious before he hit the hallway runner. His head bounced once. Manny stomped on the hand with the straight razor. Twice. Breaking three metacarpal bones at the base of the last three fingers. He didn't bother to kick the razor out of the way.

Everything went quiet except for the forced breathing and groans of pain from the Kin attackers. And Beck catching his breath.

The hallway walls were dented, cracked, and stained with blood. Pictures were broken, askew, or down on the floor. Strangely, a delicate, half-circle table in the middle of the hallway remained intact.

Beck gently checked the side of his head where the bat grazed him.

And then they heard a far-off police siren.

Ciro said, "I see you're making a lot of friends up here, Jimmy."

Beck stood straight, coming down from combat, blood dripped from his arm onto the hallway carpet runner.

"Fuuuck!"

Demarco said, "You think that's state police or county?"

Beck said, "County. Either way, it's not happening. Not today. Let's get the hell out of here."

Ciro said, "I'll buy you some time."

Beck hesitated, then said, "Okay, but don't kill anybody."

"Why not?"

"We don't have time to get rid of the bodies. Meet us behind the house."

Ciro said, "Check," and hurried out.

"Manny, grab a vehicle from out front." Beck looked down at Oscar Lund. "I guess we don't know which one is his."

Manny said, "I'd say it's the Jeep. That's the one parked right in front of your door."

"Okay, is it running?"

"Yep."

"Take it. Come around behind the house." Beck turned to Demarco as he stepped toward the unconscious Oscar Lund. "D, help me drag this lard-ass out of here and get him into the bed of your truck."

"Got any rope or duct tape? We don't want him trying to jump out."

"Assuming I don't throw him out first."

Out front, Manny climbed into Lund's Jeep Cherokee and drove around to the back of Beck's house.

Ciro jumped into the nearest truck, J.T. Stott's fifteen-year-old Dodge Ram. The engine was still running. He drove around the top of the circular driveway and positioned the truck facing out. Ciro killed the headlights. He saw a sheriff's patrol car turn into the driveway entrance, its siren fading but lights still flashing. The patrol car came slowly toward the house. When the car was twenty yards away, Ciro tightened his seatbelt, gripped the steering wheel, and accelerated straight for the patrol car. Ciro didn't give a shit if the cop came at him head-on or turned off. He had a truck. They had a car. Sure enough, the patrol car swerved left. Ciro accelerated, turned into the patrol car, and smacked the back end with the corner of his front bumper. The impact turned the sheriff's department Chevy Impala sideways. The driver's side of the patrol car smashed into the driver's side of the Dodge with a resounding, crunching bang.

Ciro kept his steering wheel jammed to the left, keeping the vehicles plastered together until the patrol car smacked into a tree.

Ciro threw the truck into park, climbed over into the passenger seat, and got out. He left the engine running. Abel Proctor, half-conscious, pawed at the driver's side airbag that had exploded into his face. Ciro headed for his Cadillac, got into his car, and drove around to the back of Beck's house before Abel Proctor even released his seat belt.

Luckily for Russell Hibbard, Proctor had decided to serve the arrest warrant by himself, knowing that Oscar Lund could help him load Beck into his patrol car.

Behind Beck's house, Manny helped Beck and Demarco lift Oscar Lund into the bed of Demarco's truck, an all-black Honda Ridgeline. Ciro pulled his Cadillac in behind Lund's Jeep. Demarco climbed into his truck. Manny into the Jeep.

Beck walked to the Jeep and asked Ciro, "How many deputies were there?"

"One. In one patrol car. I took care of him."

"Can you describe him?"

"No."

"Is he still alive?"

Ciro shrugged. "Probably."

Beck ran into his house. Ciro waited patiently, tapping his thumb on the steering wheel of his Caddy, humming the Sinatra version of *Strangers in the Night*.

Beck came out wearing his quilted, Burberry down coat carrying a Beretta 1301 tactical shotgun in one hand and a sleek, pre-packed backpack in the other. He had bound up his bleeding left arm with a roll of three-inch self-adhesive bandage wrap. Inside the backpack, Beck had everything he needed to get anywhere in the world and set himself up for as long as needed. There was nothing of interest left in the house except the broken and beaten men he'd left in his front hallway.

With Beck finally in Demarco's Honda Ridgeline, Demarco led the way off the property. He drove out the same way he had driven in, on a rough gravel driveway that led over a ridge and down to a paved country road. They were gone before Abel Proctor crawled out of his battered patrol car.

No one in the small convoy knew what exactly would come next. They did, however, have a pretty good idea what James Beck had in mind for the guy bouncing around in the bed of Demarco's truck.

14

Beck bent closer to look at the GPS map display on the screen in Demarco's truck. They were heading south on Route 385 toward the bridge that would take them across the river where they would head south to Demarco's house. Beck looked behind to make sure Manny and Ciro were following. Then he tapped Demarco's arm and pointed to the map display.

"See that road?"

Demarco glanced down and nodded. There was a small line on the map about a half-mile ahead.

"Slow down and watch for it. Looks like it dead-ends somewhere at the north end of Vosburgh Swamp. Hit your turn signal so the guys will follow us."

Thirty seconds later, Demarco turned onto a small clearing that led to a dirt road heading east.

Beck said, "Hold up for a second."

Manny stopped the Jeep close behind Demarco's truck. Ciro pulled his Caddy in behind Manny.

Beck walked to the Jeep and told Manny, "Go around Demarco and take the lead down that road. D will drive behind you. Stop when he flashes his high beams."

"Okay."

Beck walked to Ciro's Cadillac and said, "We're going to head down this road and have a little chat with our friend in the truck bed. Turn around, back into the road, and douse your lights. Make sure nobody comes in after us."

Ciro reached back near his hip, pulled out his Smith & Wesson, and placed it in his lap.

"Got it."

Manny led the way in Lund's Jeep. Demarco drove behind him on the two-track road, bumping and sliding over the rough, unplowed surface. There was enough snow to leave tracks, but Beck didn't care.

After a half-mile Beck said, "This is far enough."

Demarco flashed his lights at the 4Runner, and Manny stopped.

Beck got out and dropped the tailgate on the Ridgeline. He dragged Oscar Lund out of the truck bed and dumped him on the ground. They'd wrapped heavy-duty duct tape around Lund's wrists and ankles. The snow and ice on the ground made it possible for Beck to drag the heavy man around in front of Demarco's truck. He propped Lund up against the rear bumper of the Jeep. He went back and found Lund's fish bat he'd thrown in the truck bed.

Manny watched Beck in his rearview mirror. He saw Beck make a sign to cut the Jeep's engine. Manny got out and joined Beck in the glare of Demarco's LED headlights. Despite his aching windpipe, fear made Lund breathe heavily. Each breath hurt and sent out plumes condensing in the freezing night air.

Beck squatted in front of Oscar Lund. He held the fish bat and lightly tapped it on the front of Lund's head. Even the light tapping made Lund grunt and try to twist away.

Lund raised his bound hands to block another blow, but Beck smacked them aside with the bat and hit him on the head again. Harder.

"You didn't come to my house for any little taps on my head, did you?"

Lund didn't answer.

Beck hit him again.

"No. You were trying to split my head open. Or beat me to death, huh?" Beck's anger rose, but his voice didn't. He hit Lund again. And one more time. Each time a little harder.

"Weren't you? Weren't you?"

Lund yelled, "No! We weren't coming to kill you. Just teach you a lesson."

Beck stopped.

"What lesson?"

"Not to fuck with us."

"Us? Who's us?"

Lund didn't answer.

Beck started again with the small fish bat. Lightly hitting parts of Lund's head that had begun to swell and bruise. Lund twisted and turned, trying to avoid the blows.

Beck asked, "Who's us? The Kin?"

"Yes!"

Beck stopped hitting him. "Who'd I fuck with? That bald asshole at the Field?"

"Yeah."

"What's his name? Hamm something?"

"Hamm Elrod."

"He's in the Kin?"

"Yes."

Beck placed the end of the bat against Lund's left side and pushed it into Lund's broken ribs.

Lund cried out.

Beck said, "You came to my house with three men to beat the hell out of me because of that sorry-ass piece of shit? You're lying. Tell me what's going on, or I'll do what you tried to do to me. I will beat you with this bat until you are permanently crippled or dead."

Beck shoved the bat into Lund's broken ribs. The pain made Lund scream, "Stop it! I'll fucking tell you. And you'll be goddamn sorry you did any of this shit."

Lund began talking. It wasn't so much that he was giving information to Beck as he was threatening him. Demarco had come out of the truck. He stood behind Beck and Manny, leaning back against his truck, arms folded.

Lund went on about how powerful the Kin was. Shouting about districts and regions and hundreds of members. He told Beck he was the leader of a district. He told Beck he was a dead man, and nobody would ever find out what happened to him or where his body parts ended up.

Beck listened to about a minute of Lund's diatribe and then pressed the fat end of the fish bat against Lund's forehead. Lund stopped talking.

"Who was in the sheriff's patrol car?"

"I don't know!"

Beck punched the handle end of the bat down hard on the nerve bundle behind Lund's collar bone near his neck. Lund screamed in pain.

"Who was it? Abel Proctor?"

"Yes."

"He came to arrest me?"

"Yes."

"For what?"

"What do you think? The murder of Joey Collins. He's got evidence against you."

"What evidence?"

"I don't know." Beck raised the bat again. Lund yelled out, "I don't know!"

Beck hit him in the same spot with the fish bat again. "What evidence?"

Lund bellowed, "I don't fucking know! He didn't tell me. Whatever it is, he can take you down anytime he wants. You got half a goddamn brain, you and your buddies would run now. Disappear. You don't belong here anyhow."

Beck stood up and backed off, looking down at Oscar Lund, thinking about what Lund had said. He asked, "Where do I find Camdyn Dent?"

For a moment, Lund paused. The mention of Camdyn Dent surprised him.

"I have no fucking idea. You can beat me all you want but you ain't gonna find out anything about Camdyn Dent from me because I don't know anything. It don't matter anyhow, pal, because he'll find you soon enough."

Beck nodded. He stood up and motioned for Demarco to help him lift Oscar Lund and carry him to the open driver's side door of his Jeep. They stood Lund up against the side of the car and Beck checked Lund's pockets. He found a cell phone and wallet. He dropped the cell phone on the ground and stomped on it until it was in pieces. Then he took Lund's driver's license out of the wallet and put it in his back pocket. He threw the rest of the wallet into the cold, black forest. Beck and Demarco wrestled Lund into the Jeep's driver's seat while Lund croaked about his broken ribs. Beck elbowed Lund back out of his way, leaned over to pull the gear shift into neutral.

Duct tape held Lund's wrists and ankles together. He gripped the top of the steering wheel even though he couldn't turn the locked wheel.

Beck told Lund, "If I ever see you again, I'll kill you."

He slammed the door and led Demarco and Manny to the Honda Ridgeline. They climbed in, Manny taking a seat in the extended cab behind Demarco.

Beck said to Demarco, "Pull up to his bumper and give him a push."

"How far?"

"Until he goes off the road. Try to get a little speed behind it."

Demarco had a heavy-duty bull bar and skid plate covering his grill. He drove up tight against the Jeep and gradually accelerated. He got up to twenty miles per hour before the road veered off to the right. Demarco braked; the anti-lock mechanism made the Honda shudder as they watched the Jeep sail off the road, bouncing and crashing into underbrush until it smashed into the base of an oak tree.

Demarco said, "Hope he hit his head again."

Beck said, "More likely his face against the steering wheel."

15

Back at Beck's house, Abel Proctor had to push aside the patrol car's exploded airbag, climb out the rear passenger door, and slowly make his way to Beck's house. By the time he peered through the broken front door and saw the three bloody, broken men, Beck and the others were long gone.

J.T. Stott sat near the end of the hallway, pitched to one side to keep weight off his broken tail bone. He had thrown up in his lap from the skull fracture caused by the fish bat in the hands of Demarco Jones. Blood seeped from his left ear.

Hamm Elrod laid face down in a pool of blood at the far end of the hallway. A bloody gash on his forehead oozing blood.

Reid Vander was near the front door on one knee, cradling his broken hand, using his sleeve to wipe away the blood dripping from his broken nose.

Proctor looked around. He asked Vander, "Where's Oscar?"

"I don't fucking know. He was gone when I came to."

Vander made it to his feet.

Proctor said, "Who did this to you?"

"The guy who lives here and friends of his who showed up out of nowhere."

"Beck?"

"If that's his name. Who the hell is he? He almost took all of us out before we had him under control. Next thing I know, a big, Black buck appears from the back of the house, and two more through the front door who took me down while I was tryin' to fight off the coon."

Proctor tried to shake off his confusion.

"How long before the others showed up?"

"I don't know. Couple of minutes."

"And four of you couldn't take down Beck before that?"

"We almost had him, and then the others showed up. Ain't you listening to me, Abel? What the fuck did you send us into? Don't you hear what I'm saying? We just about had Beck, or whatever his name is, under control, when three other sons-a-bitches showed up. It was supposed to be one guy!"

Proctor still could not process what Vander was telling him. Vander's yelling at him didn't help. He told Vander, "All right, all right. Calm down."

"Don't fuckin' tell me to calm down, Abel. This shit can't stand. I'm going to Vic about this."

Proctor finally had enough. He yelled, "Shut up! You'll do what you're goddamn told. Anybody speaks to Victor, it'll be me." Proctor went to Hamm Elrod, got down on one knee, and checked for a pulse. He felt Elrod's blood pounding through his carotid artery. He got down on both knees and slowly rolled the heavy man on his side. He didn't want Elrod to suffocate face down in his own blood. He went to Stott. He had never seen the big tattooed rough boy so beaten.

"You all right, J.T.?"

Stott cleared his throat and turned his head to spit out a mouthful of blood and saliva. He was having trouble talking.

"Just trying to move my legs. That guy fucking smashed my balls, and I think he broke my tailbone. Somebody hit me in the head with something."

"All right, take it easy. I'm calling for help. Did you see what happened to Oscar?"

"A big coon showed up and put him down. Like nuthin'. Hit me with Oscar's bat. I wasn't too clear after that. I think they dragged Oscar out of here."

Proctor heard Vander say, "We can't go to no hospital without a cover story."

"Make one up. Say you got into a fight."

"That'll bring up a few questions."

Proctor turned toward Vander. "Which you aren't going to answer."

Reid Vander was still cradling his broken hand. The bridge of his nose was already beginning to swell. The area under both eyes turning blue. He probed the side of his neck where Beck had hit him.

Vander said, "All right, Abel, I can get to the hospital myself. I can still drive. You going to take care of these two?"

"Yes. Which truck is yours?"

Vander said, "The black Dodge Ram. Why?"

"Never mind. Go on. I'll catch up with you later."

Suddenly, Elrod jerked awake with a grunting shout. He tried to sit up and fell over. He tried to feel the back of his neck, but his dislocated thumb stopped him.

Proctor hurried over to Elrod.

"Hamm. Hamm. Calm down. You're okay."

Elrod stared up at Proctor with blank eyes. He didn't know where he was or what had happened. He tried to sit up again. Proctor helped Elrod up so he could lean back against the wall. He put his face close to Elrod's and said, "Hamm, just take it easy. You're hurt. I'm getting help. You hear me?"

Elrod blinked at Proctor. For a moment, anger and confusion flared up. "My head. Can't move my fucking head."

"You're all right, Hamm. Can you move your legs?" Proctor wiped away the blood dripping from Elrod's forehead into his eyes. Elrod turned his feet back and forth.

"Good. Just sit there."

Proctor unclipped his police radio from his belt, then put it back. He couldn't call this in. He couldn't let any deputies or medical personal see this. There was no way to explain it. He'd have to take care of this mess. But how? This thing had spun way out of control. Three of the Kin's toughest taken down and seriously injured. The guy he was going to set up for the Collins murder, gone. According to Vander and Scott, three allies of Beck suddenly involved. Oscar Lund taken. And his patrol car smashed.

All right, Proctor told himself. *First things first. Get these men out of here and into a hospital.* He couldn't call Vic Myer and ask for help. Myer would be furious. He'd demand an explanation that Proctor didn't want to give him. This had to go to Camdyn Dent. Dent would decide which people to send and make it happen. And once Dent heard what had happened, there was no doubt in Abel Proctor's mind that it would be Emmett Devereaux and his people who would step in. So be it. There was no choice. The Kin was now at war.

16

Demarco managed to turn his truck around on the narrow two-track road. It took five careful back-and-forth maneuvers.

When they reached the small clearing at the top of the road, Beck got out of Demarco's truck and climbed into Ciro's Cadillac.

"Anybody pass by?"

"Nope. All quiet."

"Good. Pull over and let Demarco drive out, then follow him. We're going to his place. I'll ride with you and fill you in on what's happening."

"Okay. You left that hump in the woods?"

"Yep."

"Alive?"

"Probably."

Ciro smiled.

Thirty minutes later, Beck and his crew entered Demarco's place, banging through the back door, their weight shaking the floors of the old house as they headed into the kitchen on the main floor.

Demarco's rambling wood frame house sat on a secluded thirty-acre property. There were three floors. A ground floor that housed a utility room and storage space and a small apartment that opened onto a stretch of lawn with a view of the Berkshires in the distance. The first floor held a living room, an open kitchen, and a dining area large enough to hold an oval table that could seat ten. Four bedrooms took up most of the third floor. Demarco hadn't done much to the house except refinish floors, paint the inside with brighter colors, and install new appliances.

Ciro looked around and said to Demarco, "Nice place. Awfully quiet." He leaned over to look out the window above the sink. "Christ, you can't see a damn thing out there."

Demarco said, "They haven't installed any sidewalks or streetlights yet."

"No shit."

Manny checked out the contents of the refrigerator.

Ciro said, "Is there any beer in there, Manny?"

With his head still in the refrigerator, Manny handed Ciro a bottle of Brooklyn Lager, surprised that Demarco had found it this far north.

In another part of the kitchen, Demarco stood picking out first-aid supplies from an open drawer under the long kitchen counter. Beck hung his coat on the back of a chair and sat at the dining table. Ciro sat opposite Beck and drank half the bottle of lager. Beck started unwinding the self-adhesive wrap that covered his forearm from wrist to elbow. The pressure from the wrap had stopped the bleeding, but not before blood had seeped through his shirt.

Demarco came over and sat at the head of the table, setting down his first-aid supplies. He asked Beck, "That slimy little bastard got you with his razor?"

"Yep."

The pain from the razor cut and the fight had hit Beck on the drive to Demarco's house. His head and ear hurt where Lund had clipped him with the bat. His shoulder, sternum, rib cage, and throat all hurt. Beck hesitated. He didn't want to remove his shirt. He did not want to see the wound. He'd had his fill of wounds.

Ciro asked, "You want a beer, James? A shot of something?"

Demarco said, "Hold off on that, James. You'll just feel worse." He turned toward the kitchen. "Manny, give James that quart of orange juice in the fridge. And the ibuprofen on that shelf next to the sink, please."

Manny laid out slices of pizza on a baking pan and took out more bottles of lager from the refrigerator. He turned on the oven and brought the orange juice and painkillers over to Beck.

Beck tapped out six pills and took three long swallows of the orange juice. He wanted a beer and a shot of whiskey, but he knew Demarco was right. The juice would help replace the glucose he'd burned up during the fight. Make him feel less shaky and more alert. The ibuprofen would take the edge off his pain.

Ciro finished off his first bottle of lager. He let out a burp and said, "Shit James, I thought everything was nice and peaceful for you up here?"

"It was. Until last night."

Demarco squirted sanitizing gel on his hands. He worked the gel into his skin until it evaporated. He used blunt-tipped bandage shears to cut through Beck's shirt and carefully peeled off the blood-soaked fabric. He made Beck lean forward so that he could place Beck's arm on a kitchen towel. He carefully poured hydrogen peroxide over the wound, watching it bubble up.

Beck said, "I heard that's not good for healing."

Demarco said, "Probably, but it's the best disinfectant I know if you don't want to scrub the wound."

Ciro said, "Hey, James, that guy you left in the forest..."

"Yeah?"

"You told me he said the cops have evidence you killed somebody."

"Yes."

"Did you?"

"No."

"So, what evidence do you think they have?"

"Bullshit manufactured evidence. By the way, it's either state troopers or county sheriff's deputies up here. Only the larger towns have cops."

"Sheriff's deputies?"

"Yes."

"Do they carry six shooters and ride horses?"

"I don't think so."

Ciro said, "And the sheriffs are in cahoots with what, Nazi peckerwoods? Aryans?"

"Something like that."

Demarco said, "This militia, or whatever it is, they call themselves the Kin?"

"Yes."

Demarco began blotting the dried blood and hydrogen peroxide with a large gauze pad. "You said they've been around here a long time."

Through gritted teeth, Beck said, "Yessss."

Beck knew Ciro and Demarco were asking him questions to distract him while Demarco worked on his arm.

Demarco kept cleaning Beck's wound. When he finished, he aimed a powerful flashlight across Beck's arm and carefully checked the laceration. It was about an inch wide and extended along the bottom of the radius bone from Beck's wrist to his elbow.

Demarco said, "This isn't deep. The blade must've been perpendicular to your arm. There's a cut at the beginning near your wrist and a chunk shaved off at your elbow. Could've been worse."

"Compared to what?"

"Kind of underlines the scars from your prison knife fights."

"Lucky me."

Demarco warmed up a four-by-four-inch hydrocolloid bandage between his hands. "These bandages are pretty good at preventing scars."

"I saw enough of them in the hospital. They put that kind of cover on my burns. They puff up with fluid underneath."

Ciro asked, "What kind of fluid?"

Beck said, "What are you, a fucking med student now? I don't know. It helps the skin heal."

Demarco cut the four-by-four-inch bandage in half to create two four-by-two-inch coverings. He applied them end to end on

Beck's arm. The eight inches weren't long enough to cover the elbow, so he cut a third piece of the hydrocolloid bandage and applied it to the side of Beck's elbow.

While Demarco worked on his arm, Beck checked two texts Peter Morelli had sent him.

Manny came to the table with re-heated pizza and more lager. He had a bottle of Jameson under one arm. He set it down in front of Beck.

Ciro grabbed a slice and another beer.

"This pizza is good. Where'd you get it, D?"

"A place on Route 83 near the Parkway."

"Shit, you can get pizza this good up here; it can't be all bad."

Demarco said, "I'm still waiting for soul food." As he gathered up bloody gauze and bandage wrappings, "So, James, you want to fill us in on how you ended up with four white supremacists trying to beat you into submission so a sheriff's deputy could arrest you for a murder you didn't commit?"

Beck took a swig from the bottle of Jameson, followed by a swallow of Brooklyn Lager. Demarco had summarized the situation concisely.

Beck said, "It was like the old saying about going broke."

Demarco said, "Slowly, then all at once."

"Yes. But mostly all at once. I think sitting up here in the middle of nowhere all these months has dulled my brain. I should have seen it coming."

Manny said, "So what exactly happened?"

Beck spoke with little emotion, almost as if he were talking to himself. He told his crew about the Field. Where it was. Why he'd been there. Meeting Irene Allen. The confrontation with Hamm Elrod. Taking Irene home. The arrest the next morning. How he had been so pissed off, he almost tried to take down the sheriff's department investigator. And what he knew about the Kin.

By the time he finished, he was on his second bottle of Brooklyn lager and third shot of Jameson.

Ciro spoke first. "Sounds like we should have killed those assholes at your house and left the bodies. Sent a goddamn message."

Beck said, "Including that deputy you pinned to a tree?"

"Why not? Only way for this to go now is worse. How many are in this Kin gang?"

Beck shrugged. "From what I hear, too many."

Demarco asked, "What about the woman? What's her deal?"

"Don't know her well enough to say."

Ciro said, "Guess you didn't talk much last night."

"Or this morning," said Beck.

Manny asked, "James, how much of this is going to involve the woman? What's her name? Irene?"

"Yes, Irene." Beck put down the slice of pizza he was about to eat and thought about Irene, relaxed now under the influence of the whiskey and beer. "I can't see letting her take the fall for a murder she didn't commit. And beyond that, I got to get her out of the hands of the sheriff's department before they turn her against me. Not to mention, she stepped in between me and that investigator before I ended up with the whole goddamn sheriff's department after me."

Demarco said, "The lawyer you got her, you think he can get her out?"

"I don't think anybody could get her out. Apparently, nobody makes bail on a murder charge around here."

Demarco said, "So you figure once they turn her, they'll come after you?"

Beck thought for a moment and said, "I have a feeling after last night they'll try to kill me. Charge me with the murder after I'm dead. The woman will say I wasn't with her since it won't matter. They'll add that to whatever they have and convict me. Solves a lot of problems for them."

Manny said, "If they're corrupt enough to fabricate evidence, they don't need to bother making a deal with the woman."

Ciro said, "Yep. Convict her. Send her to prison and have someone kill her inside. Wipes the board clean."

Demarco returned from the table after dumping Beck's bloody sleeve and other material in the kitchen trash can.

Ciro asked, "How long do you think she'll hold up in jail, James?"

"The lawyer texted me earlier. Said he met with her and told her not to say anything unless he's present. Said he's trying to meet with the local DA to see what he can negotiate. If anything."

Manny asked, "I assume she's a civilian."

Beck said, "Far as I know. I don't think she has an arrest record."

Ciro said, "Chicks usually save that info for the second or third date."

Beck smiled and took another sip of whiskey.

Manny said, "How long before they arraign her?"

Beck said, "They have forty-eight hours up here before they have to arraign her. Hopefully, the lawyer is good enough to convince her to hold up until then."

"So what do we do in the next thirty-five hours?"

"Find out who really sliced that poor bastard's throat."

Ciro said, "Jimmy, maybe the move is to get the fuck out of here and head back to our home turf."

"If I do that, the girl will break for sure. And since when the hell did running solve anything? Four assholes think they can come into my house and beat me to the ground? A corrupt sheriff's deputy working with a gang of white supremacy pricks thinks he can frame me for a murder? No. I'm not going anywhere."

Ciro nodded and said, "All right, brother. I'm with you."

Manny asked, "What's the first move?"

Beck turned to Manny. "The first move is to put the OG to work."

Everybody turned to Manny. Beck finished his Brooklyn Lager and pushed away the bottle of Jameson. He sat forward and said, "Okay Manolito, let me run it down for you."

17

The gray, eleven-year-old Toyota 4Runner Demarco had given Manny to drive didn't have GPS, so Manny had to follow the directions on his iPhone. Demarco had installed a holder for the phone that clipped onto the air vent fins to the left of the steering wheel. When Manny glanced at the phone screen, the surgical scars on his left hand caught his eye. There was enough light from the phone to illuminate the thin lines on his skin and cross marks from the dozens of stitches. There was also scar tissue on both sides of his wrist. Manny's left hand wasn't terribly mangled, but it certainly didn't match the right hand. Manny wondered if the two thugs Beck said ran the Field would ask him if he could cook with it. Probably wouldn't even get that far. Even though Beck told him they were always looking for help at the Field, Manny couldn't get his head around walking into a place late at night asking for a job.

Manny shifted in the driver's seat, checked the iPhone screen again, and looked for the turn that was supposedly coming in two-tenths of a mile.

The only light on the unpaved road came from the Toyota's high beams. It felt like he was in the middle of nowhere. Completely isolated. He wondered how Beck dealt with living up here. Clearly, it had affected him more than he realized. At least the four of them were together now. Not under the best of circumstances but fuck it.

Manny raised his damaged hand from the steering wheel, turned it back and forth, opened and closed it. If they asked about his hand, he'd tell them he could cook anything they wanted to serve. Beck said it was usually chicken wings, sausage balls, and sometimes chili. Cheap food they gave away for free so they could keep assholes drinking outside in the middle of fucking winter. He could make that crap with one hand.

Beck didn't know anything about the kitchen. Didn't matter; he'd find out soon enough. More important, Beck told him about the guys who ran the place. Two brothers, named Vic and George Myer. A couple of hard cases running an illegal drinking hole on an old farm. All of that in his favor, because who the hell would want to work there? Especially after some poor bastard got his throat cut at the shithole.

During his years in prison, Manny had seen more men killed by knife wounds than he could remember. And he had lived and dealt with hundreds of Aryan white supremacy types spouting a mix of Bible bullshit and half-ass Nazi nonsense, all wrapped up in stars and stripes or, more often, Confederate stars and bars. So now he'd be dealing with the same shit on the outside.

Manny took his foot off the accelerator as the iPhone voice told him he had reached his destination. And there it was. A rundown red barn with a glimmer of light shining behind it. Manny pulled in and parked near other vehicles on the west side of the red barn. He climbed out of the Toyota into a gust of bitterly cold wind and looked around. Near the road where he'd entered were strips of broken crime scene tape attached to fiberglass poles that fluttered in the frigid wind. Wind strong enough to bend the thin, flexible poles. Behind him there were half a dozen cars parked facing a split rail fence. In front of him he saw the firepits illuminating the patrons of the Field.

Manny hunched against the night air slashing at him. He'd lived through New York winters all his life and never become accustomed to the cold. Maybe it was his Latin blood. Standing outside made it even harder for him to imagine why anybody would drink here, especially after a murder the night before. *What the hell,* Manny thought; maybe that added to the appeal.

Walking from the parking area to the back of the barn gave Manny a better view of the men sitting in mismatched chairs clustered around firepits dotting the empty field. It was too dark to see any of them clearly. And impossible to see anything beyond the firelight.

As he approached the barn, Manny saw a shaded overhead light casting a faint glow, illuminating a pair of double-wide doors. A couple of feet to the right was a standard-size door. Manny pulled open the door and walked into a brightly lit space. He had to blink and wait for a moment for his eyes to adjust. A hundred-foot yellow electric cord crisscrossed the rafters above. Evenly spaced along the cord were utility lights holding 100-watt bulbs. The ample lighting might have been welcoming, but the interior wasn't. Everything looked ramshackle, rundown, and improvised. The back of the barn held four mismatched tables and chairs. Past them was a serving bar made out of a rough-hewn plank of wood holding liquor bottles and glasses. On the floor next to it was a battered sixty-five-quart cooler filled with beer and bags of ice. The kitchen area was a joke. An old Viking stove that hadn't been cleaned in years. A flexible yellow hose running along the floor through a hole in the side of the barn supplied propane to the stove from a two-hundred-gallon propane tank. A sheet of plywood on sawhorses next to the stove supplied counter space. Next to that was a free-standing double sink fed by five-gallon water jugs with spigots attached to the back of the sink. Like the propane line, a drain hose ran from the sink through another hole to the outside.

Another cooler holding food sat under the work counter where hulking George Myer stood slathering sauce from an aluminum bowl onto chicken wings laid out on a heavy-gauge baking sheet.

Another big man Manny presumed was Vic Myer sat talking to a man wearing dark clothes at a two-top table against the wall on the right. Vic faced Manny. The man with his back to Manny didn't bother to turn around. He was much smaller than Vic Myer.

Manny could hardly believe anybody would eat or drink anything served out of this fucked-up, so-called kitchen. He knew he wouldn't. But he also knew that there was a good chance he'd hear something in this small space. Maybe even get the opportunity to strike up a conversation. Which was why Beck had sent him here.

Vic Myer looked up at Manny.

"Hey, you opened the wrong door, pal. Get the fuck out of here."

Manny stood his ground and said, "My name is Eddie. I'm looking for a job as a cook."

Vic looked Manny up and down and said, "Eddie or Eduardo?"

Deadpan, Manny said, "Eddie."

"You want to work *here*?"

Manny looked around and said, "Not really, but I need a job."

That got a maniacal smile from Vic.

"Who told you we needed a cook?"

"A friend of mine said you were always lookin' for help."

"What friend?"

"A guy named Dave. Does lawn work in this area."

Vic nodded his head and said, "Dave Lee?"

"Yeah."

Vic turned toward his brother George still hunched over, slapping sauce on the chicken wings. "Hey George, this guy wants to cook here."

George finished swabbing the last chicken wing, shoved the baking sheet into the oven, and turned around. He wiped his hands on a stained kitchen towel hanging from his belt and stared at Manny without expression.

Manny returned George's stare. Big George lifted his chin at Manny.

"Is that so?"

"You look like you wouldn't mind someone else doing the cooking."

"Is that how I look?"

Manny said, "Maybe you look like that most of the time."

"Yeah, well, you look like a low-life piece of shit ex-con. I can see the prison tats creeping out from the cuffs on your shirt."

Manny said, "Who else do you think would be looking to work nights in a shithole like this?"

Vic laughed at that, but George didn't.

George asked, "How long you been out?"

"A long time."

"You still on parole?"

"Nope."

"Who'd you say told you about this place?"

"A guy who does home repairs and lawn work in the area. How much are you paying?"

"You're jumping the gun, poncho."

"Might as well get to the point."

"What kind of experience you got?"

"Twenty years' worth. Cooked in a bunch of diners in New York…"

George interrupted, "Where in New York?"

"Washington Heights. Then in Kingston. I worked for a catering company in this area that did mostly weddings on weekends. Business was coming back, but it's gone to shit now with the bad economy and new variants."

"What were you in prison for?"

"Gang stuff. When I was younger."

George said, "Fuck, I can't believe we're down to hiring a spic. Next thing, it'll be a nigger." He pulled the kitchen towel off his belt and tossed it on the counter. He turned his back on Manny and went to the sink to wash the sticky barbeque sauce off his hands.

Vic watched George washing his hands. He knew his brother hated being in the kitchen.

Vic said to Manny, "Don't mind my brother. We'll give you a tryout. Kitchen closes around two. You get twenty percent of the tips. Servers split the rest. You should be able to make forty, fifty bucks a shift."

Manny nodded.

A skinny guy wearing coveralls came in with a tray under his arm. Manny pegged him for the one Beck told him to get friendly with. Vic got up to pour drinks.

"You got reliable transportation? I don't want to hear a bunch of shit about your car breaking down."

Manny said, "Yep."

"Okay, I'll guarantee you forty bucks a night if the tips fall short. I buy the food. We serve food as long as people are here. Keeps 'em drinking. There's no menu. You cook what we give you. Make it last. You clean the kitchen, too. We'll see how you do. If it goes okay, I'll guarantee you fifty bucks a shift."

"When do I start?"

"Now. But tonight is a tryout. No pay."

Manny could hardly believe it. Forty maybe fifty bucks for five hours of work in the middle of the night in a cold barn, and he had to try out for free? He wanted to shoot the big fuck in the head, beat on his creepy brother until he found out who the hell killed that poor bastard last night. And leave.

"What time do I start tomorrow?"

"If you pass the tryout?"

"I will."

"Nine o'clock."

George turned around, drying his hands with a piece of paper towel. He pointed at Manny and said, "I hear any lip from you or complaints, I'll throw your ass out of here."

Manny nodded, thinking he'd probably need two bullets to put down big George.

Almost as if he'd read Manny's mind, George said, "You bring any kind of weapon in here, you're done. And the first day you don't show up is your last day. There's no fucking vacations here."

Manny nodded again, kept his coat on, a double-vested gray wool coat he'd had for about twenty years, and went to check on the chicken wings. As he passed by the table where Vic and the other man sat, he looked over. The stranger who hadn't turned around during Manny's conversation with George and Vic turned to look at him now. He was about Manny's height, wiry, dark hair, dark complexion with sharp features. He wore a four-button, black leather vest over an almost black denim shirt. Manny met his eyes, dark and deep set. It took Manny Guzman less than a second to know he was staring into the eyes of a black-hearted killer. Manny didn't dare show any sign of weakness. He met Emmett Devereaux's gaze until the Kin enforcer turned back toward Vic Myer.

Manny Guzman knew that whatever he was going to find out, he had to do it quickly.

18

At 12:37 a.m., Beck's phone rang and vibrated. He was in the ground-floor bedroom in Demarco's house trying to ignore the aching wound on his left forearm, the throbbing in his right shoulder, and the pain on the side of his head so he could sleep. It wasn't working.

The small twin-size bed didn't help.

Beck grabbed the phone on the third ring. The caller ID said GREENPOINT. Alex Liebowitz. Beck had called him earlier and sent him the picture of Irene Allen's driver's license. His conversation with his crew had made it clear to Beck how little he knew about Irene.

Beck answered, "That was fast."

"Were you sleeping?"

"I should be, but I'm not. You got something about Irene Allen?"

"Sort of."

Beck knew Liebowitz could easily veer off into a long explanation about what he had found and how he'd found it. Beck had learned to trust Liebowitz. He didn't need to know how Alex had done it. Just what he had come up with.

Beck said, "So what's the bottom line?"

"The farther down I drilled, the less her story fit together."

"Meaning?"

"After the first couple of layers, it doesn't hold up."

"How so?"

"I started with the driver's license you sent me. It's legit. So is the address on the license. Her name, address, driver's license, social security – all that hangs together. But when I used that information to dive deeper, it taps out. Her credit history only goes back thirty-two months. Same with her residences, her banking information. Social media is non-existent. Warrants, arrest records, liens, relatives, nothing. It's thin."

"So it's a fake identity?"

"Yes. But it's more a genuine identity sitting on top of a hidden identity. Like I said, the driver's license is legit."

"So what do you think is going on, Alex?"

"There could be a lot of reasons someone has an ID like this. It's similar to what they do in witness protection. WITSEC doesn't build extensive backgrounds for their clients."

Beck thought about that for a moment. He knew a criminal when he saw one. Irene Allen didn't have that vibe. It did bring up the other side of the coin.

"What about law enforcement?"

"Possibly. Police forces provide undercover cops with even less. Usually just a driver's license. They leave it up to them to build an identity over time. They don't put you undercover unless you're the type who looks the part and can make up shit about people they know, places they've been. You know, build a persona and act it out. You've been around enough cops, James. What do you think?"

"I don't think it's likely. The local sheriff's department arrested her for murder."

Alex said, "Oops. Well, you never know. It could happen. Wires get crossed. The locals might not know she's law enforcement. Maybe she's working for the state. Maybe she did kill someone. It wouldn't be the first time an undercover cop took out someone."

Beck said, "Except she was with me at the time of the murder."

"Oh. Then why'd they arrest her?"

"I think to frame me."

"Fuck, James, what the hell have you gotten into up there?"

"I'm just finding out. This little bit of news doesn't make it any better."

"Sorry, man. Listen, I'm not ruling out that she built this identity herself. Or, more likely, she paid somebody who isn't a pro to do it. A full package costs thousands. That's probably what's going on."

Beck nodded to himself. He agreed with Liebowitz, but that didn't explain why Irene Allen needed a new identity.

Liebowitz said, "Is there any way you can break her down and find out what her deal is?"

"Not at the moment. She's in jail."

"Is that good or bad for you?"

"In the short run, probably good. It means she has secrets so that points to her keeping her mouth shut. In the long run, bad. Once law enforcement finds out who she really is, it'll probably give them leverage.'"

"Sounds right. Anything else you need?"

"Not at the moment. You going to be around for the next few days?"

"Yep. Call me if you need me."

"I will."

Beck cut the call and dropped back in the bed, feeling more tired and less likely to sleep than ever. He checked the time. 12:55 a.m. No point sleeping now. He should be hearing from Manny soon about what happened at the Field.

19

By 1:30 a.m. Manny Guzman was ready to make a move.

He was at the Field to find out information. But after working two hours in the stinking, freezing barn Manny didn't see that happening. The guy Beck told him might be a source of information wasn't inside the barn long enough to strike up any kind of conversation. The big, sullen cabrón George wasn't going to talk to him. Or that culo Vic, jumping up and down like a bug making drinks, keeping a sly eye on everything, and counting money. And there were no conversations in the barn worth hearing.

Manny definitely had enough of cooking cheap chicken wings with lousy commercial barbeque sauce. He announced to no one in particular, "I'm getting a smoke."

George ignored him. Vic leered at him with his creepy smile and said, "No problemo."

Manny headed outside. He walked away from the entrance and stood under the glow of the rusting gooseneck light mounted above the barn's double doors, breathing in the frigid night air, trying to get the smell of manure and hay out of his nose. He was about to go back inside when Andy Miller appeared out of the dark, loping toward the barn, his empty serving tray under his arm.

Manny said, "Yo, got a sec?"

Andy headed toward Guzman in his usual bowlegged gait. He stopped in front of Manny, shuckling like he was about to recite prayers. In the light, Manny could see Andy better. The disheveled hair, thick glasses, and the stained coveralls. Manny didn't have high hopes this guy would be of much use.

"What's your name, bro?"

"Andy. What's yours?"

Manny almost said his name but then remembered what he'd told Vic and George.

"Eddie. How the fuck can you work in this cold without a hat?"

Andy shrugged. It seemed like he hadn't given it much thought.

Manny asked, "You got a smoke?"

Manny didn't think Andy smoked, but the skinny bastard reached into the front pocket of his coveralls and extracted a crumpled pack of American Spirit cigarettes along with a pink, ninety-cent disposable lighter.

Manny hadn't smoked a cigarette in years, but he took the pack and lighter from Andy. He lit up a cigarette, half-expecting it to help warm him. The first inhale hit his throat and lungs with a weirdly pleasant jolt.

Manny handed the pack and lighter to Andy, who slipped them back into his coveralls. Manny got the impression that Andy carried the cigarettes for customers.

"How long you been workin' here?"

Another shrug from Andy. "I don't know." He squinted, concentrating. "Like maybe eight months."

"This place open all year round?"

Andy nodded.

"Must be better in the summer."

Andy shrugged. "Yeah." Then he said, "Except for the gnats and flies. And the ticks. Gotta spray for the ticks."

Manny nodded.

"Who the fuck wants to sit out in the cold this time of night and drink? I mean, shit, it can't be the free chicken wings."

Andy almost smiled. Or maybe that was his smile. A half-smile followed by another shrug.

Manny nodded. He stared at Andy. That last shrug, the fucking nodding all the time, there was something going on beside the slow-witted reactions. Was it the glasses? They'd slid to the end of his nose. Was he even looking through them? Manny looked closely at Andy Miller's eyes peering over the glasses. Guzman had seen every type of con invented by every type of criminal known. Those eyes didn't belong with the act. Something was going on behind those eyes. Manny Guzman decided he had no more questions for Andy Miller, the half-blind, half-retard scarecrow. Manny shrugged back at Andy, dropped his barely smoked cigarette on a patch of dirty snow, and ground it dead.

"Thanks for the cig."

He headed back inside. Ignoring Andy Miller following close behind him.

Manny kept cooking until one-thirty and then started cleaning up. Once he had a garbage bag filled, he asked Vic, "You got a dumpster or something?"

Vic pointed a thumb over his left shoulder. "Around the side."

As soon as Manny dumped the trash, he pulled out his cell phone. Beck was right. He had two bars on his phone. Beck answered on the first ring.

Manny said, "Not sleeping?"

"Not really."

Manny got right to it.

"We should follow this guy, Andy, when he leaves. Won't be easy in the dark, but..."

Beck heard the urgency in Manny's voice. He didn't waste time asking why Manny wanted Miller followed. He'd find out after they set up the tail. Beck was already picturing how to do it.

"How much time do we have before he leaves?"

"I don't know the routine here. I expect they'll do a last call or something. Drink orders are slowing down. There's no more food. Maybe another forty-five minutes."

Beck was already on his feet. "It's going to be close. We're on the other side of the river. Stay around and find out which direction he goes."

"Sure. I'll kill time cleaning the filthy fucking oven they use."

"Okay. When he leaves, call Demarco, and tell him which way Miller turned. If he turns right, wait a few minutes, and go in the same direction. I doubt if he'll head left. There's not much in that direction, but if he does, you'll have to follow him. He'll probably spot you but stay on him until we catch up to you and we'll figure it from there."

"Got it."

It helped that Demarco Jones was a light sleeper, and that Ciro had left his key fob in the Caddy. They needed two vehicles to track Miller. Demarco would take his truck. Beck Ciro's caddy.

Beck was counting on there being no traffic this time of night, and no sheriff's deputies or state troopers looking out for speeders. They had to get across the river fast enough to cover the first of two intersections where Miller could make a turn about four miles past the bridge, assuming he turned right after leaving the Field. Beck led the way and kept in touch with Demarco over their cell phones.

When Manny left the Field, he called Demarco, knowing Beck didn't want to deal with creating a conference call on his cellphone. Demarco set up the conference call.

"Okay, Manny, James is on too. Did he leave?"

"Not yet. The geek is still in the barn. Probably waiting for his money."

Beck asked, "Where are you?"

"Across the road. I backed into a little clearing where I can still see which way he goes. I'm shut down. He won't spot me. It's dark as fucking ink out here."

"What's he driving?"

"An old Subaru Forester. Black."

Beck said, "Okay. We have a shot. Stay on your phone, Manny. Keep us posted. Demarco and I will try to get to the intersection of three-eighty-six and sixteen. If he goes north, Demarco will follow him. If he goes south, I will. You hang back until we see which way he turns."

"Done."

"Whoever ends up following him will drop off when one of us catches up and takes over so he doesn't get suspicious."

"Yep."

Ten minutes later, Manny's voice came over the conference call.

"He just pulled out."

Beck asked, "Which way did he turn?"

"Right, like you figured."

"His right, not your right."

"Yeah, yeah. My left, his right."

"This is going to be close. Hang back a minute, then follow him."

Beck accelerated to sixty-five on the dark, two-lane road. Demarco stayed close behind.

They took three minutes to get to the first intersection where Miller could turn. When he got there, Beck made a hard left heading south. He fishtailed to a screeching stop, made a one-eighty, pulled over to the edge of the road, and shut down the Caddy. Demarco turned right and did the same. They both had a view of the road going east.

Beck spoke into his phone. "Demarco, I'm down a little south of the intersection. There's no place to pull over. I've got my headlights off. If he goes straight, he won't see me. If he comes south, I'll just block him. You come in behind. We'll deal with him out here."

Demarco said, "Okay. I have more room. I'm sitting between a couple of trees off the side of this road. If he turns north, I don't think he'll see me. I'll pull out and follow him."

"Good. Got it."

"You want to find out where he lives, right? Or do you want to take him down on the open road?"

"Right. I want to find out where he lives. Manny, where are you?"

"Heading toward you. A half mile or so behind him."

"Okay."

Suddenly, after a frantic high-speed drive there was nothing more to say or do. Beck peered through the dark forest on his left trying to spot Miller's headlights coming in his direction. He couldn't see anything. There was no moonlight. No stars. Nothing but black.

Beck checked his watch. 2:36 a.m. They'd made it to the intersection in thirty-eight minutes. Where the fuck was Andy Miller? Did they miss him?

Thirty seconds later, a pair of dim headlights appeared heading toward the intersection. A vehicle the right size and shape paused at the stop sign and rolled straight ahead. If Beck hadn't been paying attention, he would have missed it. He watched the pair of tail lights heading east.

Demarco's voice came over the phones.

"That was him, right?"

Beck said, "Yep. We got him. I'll get behind him. D, you fall in behind me. I'll drive without my lights. If I end up in a ditch, you can pull me out."

Demarco said, "If you end up in a ditch, call a tow truck. I'll pick up the tail."

Beck fired up the Cadillac and followed Miller's tail lights with his headlights off, barely guided by the two red dots floating in the black ahead of him and the faint lines of snow on the shoulders of the road.

When they approached the outskirts of Coleville, Beck watched the black Forester slow down and turn into a Sunoco station. Beck figured this had to be the only station in the area open 24-hours. Andy Miller had been driving to this gas station, not to his home.

Beck slowed down and looked for a place to pullover where he could keep an eye on Miller. He spotted a small motel, closed for the winter, and turned into the motel's lot. He shut down the Caddy and told Demarco and Manny what was going on. Moments later, the dark form of Demarco's Honda Ridgeline rolled pass the Sunoco station continuing southeast.

Demarco's voice came over Beck's phone.

"You think he won't see you parked in that motel lot?"

"Maybe. At this point, I don't really give a shit. One way or another, we're going to have a conversation with Andy Miller."

"Okay. I'll pull over and follow him if he comes this way."

"Good."

Demarco asked, "What's he doing now?"

"He went into the station. I guess to pay for his gas."

"Not using a credit card."

"Nope."

"Let me know when he leaves."

Manny's voice came over the phones, "I'm pulled over north of the station where he can't see me. You think he might come back this way?"

Beck said, "Maybe. If he does, I'll be behind him. You follow me."

"Okay."

Three minutes later, Andy Miller emerged from the store with a small brown bag. He dropped the bag onto the passenger seat of the Subaru Forester and proceeded to gas up the car.

"Interesting," said Beck.

Both Manny and Demarco said, "What?"

"No glasses, a knit cap, and no more bouncy retard walk."

Manny said, "I knew it was an act."

Beck said, "How?"

"His eyes. He don't have stupid eyes."

Demarco said, "Nobody cons the old con."

Beck watched Miller finish gassing up and waited for him to pull out.

"Okay, D, he's headed your way."

"I see him."

"If you can, stay with him until you find out where he lives. Manny, come forward until you see a motel just before a Sunoco station. I'm in the lot. Pull in and we'll follow slowly behind Demarco."

Six minutes later, Demarco said, "I got him. Where are you two?"

Beck checked Ciro's GPS map screen.

"Coming up on Wickham Road."

"Okay, keep going past two roads, then a left on Johnny Cakes Road. When you spot a shed with a light mounted near the peak, pull over. I'll meet you there in a few minutes."

Beck said, "Is Miller's house on that street?"

"Yep. He just walked in."

"Anybody else in the house?"

"Couldn't tell for sure. The house was dark, but someone else could've been in there sleeping."

"Okay."

"What now, James?"

"I'll tell you when we meet."

20

Oscar Lund managed to tear the duct tape off his wrists with his teeth. Then he freed his feet. He shouldered open the car door and fell out. He had to crawl through the forest floor to get to the unplowed dirt road. He almost passed out when he stood up to walk. Every step he took felt like someone was stabbing his side with a long, blunt butcher knife. He couldn't even bend over to catch his breath. His head throbbed. He'd broken his nose against the steering wheel when his Jeep hit the tree. He couldn't stop the bleeding or the swelling, making it even more difficult to breathe.

With every painful step, Lund's determination to kill James Beck grew. No more bullshit. No threats. No words. No nothing from now until the moment he fired all ten of his Glock's .45 caliber bullets into James Beck's bearded face.

Lund's progress was so slow, he feared he would freeze to death before he made it out of the forest. He clenched his teeth, growling and cursing, forcing himself to walk. Each step driven by his hatred.

By the time he reached the paved road, Lund's bleeding nose had swollen enough to cut the blood to a trickle. He could only suck in air through his mouth. He'd taken to pressing his elbows against his broken ribs to keep going. But now the problem was where to go. He had no idea where he was. He checked his watch. Almost one in the morning. Small chance any cars would show up. He had no choice but to pick a direction and walk.

After ten minutes, Lund stopped. He suddenly felt parched. Depleted. And then everything seemed to drop away. All his strength, all the fabric holding him together drained out of him. He could barely feel anything now. Not the cold. Not his broken ribs. His heart began to pound. Was this it? A heart attack? He felt dizzy. Lund knew that if he collapsed now, on this road, in the dead of night in the dead of winter, there would be nothing left for him but death. He looked down at his work boots. It felt as if the boots and the feet inside them were no longer attached to his body.

That was the last conscious thought Oscar Lund had for the next fifty-six minutes. Bright lights and pain caused him to fight his way into consciousness. He felt movement. Then realized he was strapped to a gurney. A light above him was so bright it made him squint. There was something on his face. He tried to reach for it, but his arm wouldn't move. He tried to say something, but it came out muffled. A hand pressed his shoulder, and a face came into view. He heard the words but didn't understand them at first.

Something about being all right. Being on the way to a hospital.

Lund's mind cleared. He looked around. He was in an ambulance. He was not dead. He tried to speak but couldn't. His throat too dry. The oxygen mask too muffling.

He nodded at the paramedic staring down at him. He nodded again hoping it would prompt the paramedic to say more. Lund closed his eyes. Everything came rushing back. None of it mattered except the realization that he was alive. He would survive this. Live to take his revenge.

Lund closed his eyes and retreated into himself. Focusing on what to do now. First, say only that he'd been in a traffic accident. Then say he remembered nothing. Call Abel Proctor. Tell him what happened. Tell him where the Jeep was and make sure he retrieved it. Tell Proctor this had to go to the top. To Camdyn Dent himself. Demand it. The Kin owed him. He had paid his dues. Put in his time. The Kin owed him the death of James Beck.

21

The house turned out to be on Johnny Cake Lane, not Johnny Cakes Road. *Quaint,* thought Beck. Johnny Cake suggested warmth and comfort. This road or lane offered neither. Only a sense of foreboding on a dark, bitter, December night.

Beck drove the Cadillac slowly, checking out the surroundings. Far down the road he saw a light shining weakly over an old wooden shed, just as Demarco had described. There weren't any other houses or structures around. He tried to spot Demarco's truck but didn't see it. The clouds overhead cleared a bit, and a slice of moonlight leaked through, adding dimensions of gray to the darkness.

Manny followed closely behind Beck in the Toyota 4Runner.

Beck looked for a place to pull over near the shed. Suddenly, the Cadillac's headlights reflected off the tail lights on Demarco's Ridgeline parked under a large oak tree. The tree's wide branches had kept a circle of ground under it clear of snow. The Honda Ridgeline wasn't running, and Beck did not see Demarco in the truck.

He maneuvered the Caddy next to the Honda and turned off the engine. Manny pulled the 4Runner next to him and joined Beck in Ciro's car. They sat in the silent darkness, listening to the sheet metal pinging as it cooled in the frigid air.

Neither Beck nor Manny spoke. Beck pulled a Browning Hi-Power semi-automatic from a holster at his right hip. A classic gun. No other gun felt as good in Beck's hand. He released the ambidextrous safety and slid the weapon back into the holster.

A light tap on the right passenger side window broke the silence. Neither Beck nor Manny had seen or heard Demarco Jones approach the car.

Beck released the door locks and Demarco slipped into the back seat along with a gust of freezing air.

Beck half-turned toward Demarco. "So?"

Even sitting in the back seat of the Cadillac, Demarco disappeared in the darkness. He wore a black leather Montcler down jacket and a black Kangol wool hawker hat. His pants were slim cut thin wale charcoal gray corduroy.

"It's a cheap prefab ranch house about sixty feet down the road. There's a gravel area, not a driveway, in front of the house. It's plowed clean. He parked his car there and went inside. There's one house about five hundred yards past his. And the house here on the other side of this shed. Everything else is open fields with corn stalks sticking out over snow and ice, and forest."

Beck asked, "Any dogs?"

"Don't think so. A dog would've heard me. I circled the house on foot."

Manny asked, "We had a dog when I was a kid. He didn't make a sound unless he knew you."

"What?"

"If a stranger or somebody came around, the stupid perro didn't do shit."

Beck asked, "Why not?"

Manny said, "There wasn't nothing in it for him. If it was somebody in the family, he'd bark his ass off and put on a big show."

Demarco asked, "What kind of a dog was it?"

Beck said, "A smart one. We'll assume there's no dog in there. I'm going to knock on the front door and see what happens."

Demarco said, "I'll come in the back while you have his attention at the front door."

Outside, Beck and Manny walked slowly to give Demarco a chance to get into position behind the house.

It wasn't a long walk to the house. But it was cold enough to make it seem long.

Beck and Manny approached the front door. Just to make sure, Beck tried the door handle. Locked. He slipped his Browning out of his holster and stood to the right of the door. Manny had his short-barrel Charter Arms revolver in hand and stood left of the door. Beck leaned over and did a shave-and-a-haircut-two-bits knock on the front door. Friendly. Like a neighbor. He waited a moment, then did it again, a bit louder. No response. He peered in the front window. No movement. No light.

Beck thought he saw a dark shape moving in the house at the far side of the living room. Too big to be Andy Miller, the human scarecrow. Had to be Demarco. He'd found a way in to the house. And then Beck heard a car door opening behind them.

A voice called, "Okay, fellas, drop them guns and raise your hands or I'll try my best to put a bullet in you. I ain't that great a shot, but I don't have to be at this range."

Beck slowly turned. Manny was already facing Andy Miller, who stood behind the open back door of his Subaru pointing a gun at them with a two-handed pistol grip, his wrists resting on the top of the open door.

Beck and Manny still had their guns pointing down. Beck said, "There's two of us and one of you. You might get one shot off, but not a second one."

"You wanna bet?"

"Okay, maybe you'll get a second shot off, but you won't hit anything."

Miller tipped his head toward Manny. "Neither will Mr. Eddie, and the one shot I get off will definitely hit you, Mr. Redbreast. Even before your third guy shoots me."

Beck frowned. Whoever Andy Miller was, he'd gotten the better of them.

Miller said, "Come on, put them guns down. You didn't come here to kill me, did you?"

"No. Came here to find out who you really are."

"Yeah, well…that's not happening until your third guy comes out where I can see him. We'll all put our guns away, go in the house, and talk it over. Come on, it's cold out here. I'm sick of being in the cold."

Beck saw that Andy Miller wasn't wearing glasses. All the head bobbing and other bullshit were gone. He still wore the ratty coveralls, but now he also wore a blue North Face down vest. And a fluorescent orange knit cap. Beck really wanted to talk to this guy.

Beck held up his empty left hand and slowly holstered his Browning with his right. He nodded toward Manny, who reluctantly pocketed his revolver.

Beck said, "Is Andy your real name?"

"Sure."

"Okay, Andy, your turn. Put your gun away. I suppose we fucked this up, but as you mentioned, we still have a third guy. I don't know where he is. You don't know where he is. I guarantee he has you in his sights and will kill you the second you look through those sights to take a shot. It's a standoff. What do you want to do?"

Miller said, "Shit. Promise your guy won't shoot me."

"Cross my heart," said Beck.

"All right. Unload your guns and put 'em away."

All three unloaded their weapons and put them away. Miller slammed the door of the Forester and headed for the house. He still had a slight bob in his bow-legged walk, but nothing like before.

As he approached his house, the front door opened. Demarco stood with his gun pointed at Andy Miller. Miller stopped short and raised his hands. "Hey, your buddy promised."

Beck reached out and gently pushed Demarco's hand down. "Don't shoot him. Yet."

Everybody stepped aside. Miller entered his house. He

switched on lights revealing a sparsely furnished living room. He turned to face Demarco.

"Does he get to keep his gun loaded?"

Beck said, "I guess so."

Miller shrugged and said, "Have a seat. I'm counting on you all having no reason to shoot me."

Demarco kept his Glock in hand, his eye on Miller, and said nothing. Keeping his loaded gun eliminated any reason for a contest to see who could load and fire their guns first.

22

As the pre-dawn light seeped into Oscar Lund's hospital room, Abel Proctor felt his burner phone vibrating. He pulled the phone out of his pocket, already knowing it was from Camdyn Dent. He read the short text: *all of them.*

Proctor erased the text and put the phone in his shirt pocket so he would remember to destroy it as soon as he finished here.

He heard Oscar Lund stirring. Proctor thought it might be the dawn light waking Lund. It wasn't. It was the pain.

Lund hurt so much he didn't notice Proctor sitting beside his hospital bed in the overnight sleeper chair. His broken ribs ached. The bruises on his head throbbed. His back and right hip hurt where he hit the ground when they dumped him out of that truck. And he couldn't fucking breathe because someone had packed his broken nose with gauze. The hydrocodone dripping into his vein didn't have a chance against all that.

Proctor spoke up. "How are you, Oscar?"

The question startled Lund.

"Shit! I didn't see you there. How the hell do you think I am?"

"I think you're plenty fucked up is what I think." Proctor fought with the sleeper-chair lever trying to sit upright. "I talked to your boys at Beck's house. What was left of 'em. They told me their side of what happened. How about you tell me yours?"

Through his pain and discomfort, Lund realized that this wasn't the time to berate Abel Proctor for the disaster at Beck's house. Proctor looked exhausted, uncomfortable, in need of a shower and food.

Lund said, "How do you raise this bed? What's this goddamn thing they have on top of me?"

Proctor reached over the bed rail, picked up the control, and raised the head of the bed. Sitting up made Lund's broken ribs ache more, but he didn't say anything.

Proctor said, "It's a thermal blanket to raise your body temperature. They're pumping warm air into it. You came in with hypothermia. And dehydration. You were lucky, Oscar. A guy out on a service call for a busted furnace saw you collapsed in the middle of the road. Couple more hours, and you'd been a frozen pile of dead meat."

"Shit. What'd they do to my nose?"

"Packed it so it'll stay in place. It's broken. So, what happened to you, Oscar?"

Lund couldn't help himself. "What do you think happened? I got beat to shit. Why'd you send us to Beck's house without warning us?"

"No. What happened after they took you out of Beck's house? I know what happened in the house. You had three of your best and couldn't take out Beck before his friends showed up. He was one guy, for fuck's sake. You brought three."

"You should've warned us he'd might have help."

"How was I supposed to know? It was still four against four. And one of them broke off to drive a damn truck head-on into me and pin me against a tree. Answer my question, Oscar. I need to know what happened when Beck took you out of there. What did he say to you? And what did you say to him?"

Lund tried to calm down. He could feel his blood pounding in his ear. His head felt like it was in a vice. He forced himself to lower his voice.

"Three of them beat me down. Then Beck and this other guy, a big Black bastard the size of an NFL lineman, duct-taped my wrists and ankles. Dragged me out and put me in the bed of a truck. They drove me the hell out to the middle of nowhere, banged a bat on my head, and busted my ribs. Then they put me in my Jeep and shoved it into a fucking tree. And I didn't tell him shit!"

"Just Beck and the other guy?"

"No. Beck, the nigger, and another guy. I think he was a spic, but I couldn't see him too clearly in the dark. There was one other, but I didn't get a good look at him."

"What did Beck ask you?"

"He wanted to know why we came there. I told him to teach him a lesson not to fuck with us. He knew who we were, Abel. He knew about the Kin. He knew Camdyn Dent is the leader. He knew you."

"How'd he know all that?"

"Not from me."

"So, what did you say to him?"

Lund shifted slightly, trying to get more comfortable. And trying to buy time before he answered.

"I told him the Kin was going to take him down for what he and his men did to us and for killing Joey Collins."

"For killing Joey Collins? Why would you say anything about killing Joey Collins?"

"To put the fear of almighty God in him, Abel."

Proctor knew Lund was lying. He regretted telling him the evidence he had against Beck. He wanted to give Oscar hell for telling Beck the Kin would take him down for murdering Collins, but there was no point. It would just make it more difficult to do what he knew he had to do. Proctor knew what *all of them* meant.

Instead, Proctor said, "What did Beck say after you told him all that?"

"Said he wanted to talk to Camdyn Dent."

Proctor thought about that for a moment.

"And how does Beck know about Camdyn Dent?"

"I told you. I don't know."

"What did you say to him when he asked about Camdyn?"

"I told him he didn't know what he was talking about. Told him I didn't know shit about any Camdyn Dent. You want me to guess how Beck knows about Camdyn Dent? I'd say he heard about Camdyn from that little bitch Irene Allen."

Proctor nodded, taking that in.

Lund said, "I don't know who this asshole Beck is, Abel, or what he thinks he can do, but this has gone too damn far. I can't get word to the leader, but you can. I've put in my time. I deserve to say my piece. We can't have outsiders come here and think they can do this to us."

Proctor didn't respond. The last thing he needed was Oscar Lund telling him what to do.

Lund saw the look on Proctor's face. His bluster disappeared. He spoke quietly now. "I'm serious, Abel. We should put those sons of bitches in the ground. Or what do we stand for?"

"You don't have to lecture me, Oscar. You heal up. I'll put it in motion. You'll say your piece, and then we'll do what we're told. Just as we always have. Is that fair?"

Lund nodded. "That's all I'm asking for. The sooner, the better."

Proctor nodded. "When do you get out of here?"

"If they don't let me go today, I'll check myself out."

"Fine." Proctor stood up. "What about your Jeep? I assume it's still out there?"

"Where else would it be? I crawled out of that forest. Where'd that guy find me?"

"On three-eighty-five about a quarter-mile from Matteson Road."

"Then just go down Matteson Road and you'll find my Jeep."

Proctor nodded and said, "Okay. I'll find out when you're going to get discharged. I'll get your Jeep pulled out of there and arrange for somebody to drive you home."

"Okay, Abel. I appreciate it."

"Sure. No matter what, the Kin takes care of its own, right?"

Lund nodded but didn't say anything.

On the way out, Proctor showed his ID to the nurse on duty and asked when they would discharge Lund. He watched her check Lund's chart. He thought the little blonde looked like a high school girl.

The nurse told him, "He's not getting any acute care now. The doctor should sign him out sometime this morning. He'll be ready for discharge around one, two at the latest."

Proctor nodded. "Thanks."

He'd have to work fast. Good. The faster, the better. Just get it done and don't think about it.

23

There were only two places to sit in Andy Miller's living room. A well-used chair upholstered in a synthetic microfiber attempting to look like leather. And a six-foot gray sofa left near a clothing donation bin. Miller had positioned the chair diagonally from the front door and placed the sofa under the only window in the room.

Miller sat in the chair. There was a small table and lamp next to it. Newspapers, books, and magazines covered the table and floor on both sides of the chair. Beck and Demarco sat on the sofa facing Miller. Manny Guzman dragged a chair from the kitchen table and placed it facing Miller.

There was no carpet. Nothing on the walls. No television, radio, or computer. Past the living room was the kitchen with a table for two made out of white pine. Beck turned on a floor lamp next to the sofa.

Miller slipped off his knit cap, kept his down vest on, and said, "So what do you want to know?"

Beck said, "What the hell is a johnny cake? Is it like a pancake?"

Miller smiled. Three tough guys show up at his house with guns, and the first question is about johnny cakes.

"Basically, it's a pancake made out of cornmeal."

"Ever had one?"

"Can't say as I have. They're big in Rhode Island. Never been to Rhode Island."

"How long have you lived around here?"

"All my life."

"When did you figure out we were following you?"

"Trust me, it wasn't hard." Miller had been answering Beck's questions with a slight smile. He dropped the smile and said, "Why'd you follow me?"

"Curious about why you want people to think you're simple-minded when you're not."

"Says who? Mr. Eddie?" Miller looked over at Manny. "By the way, is Eddie your real name?"

Manny didn't answer.

Miller turned back to look at Beck and Demarco.

"Ah, well, Mr. Eddie looks like someone I should be more careful about talking to under a light, up close where he could see me. You ought to be more careful, too, Mr. Redbreast, if you don't want to be seen in a rearview mirror. Even if you turn off your headlights, there's still light from the dashboard. I'll give you credit for keeping these other two fellas out of sight. At least until that truck followed me all the way home. So, what do you fellas want from me?"

Beck said, "I want to know why you're working at the Field."

Miller looked at Beck as if he didn't understand the question. "For money. Why else?"

"You can't find a better way to make a few bucks?"

"No."

"Why not?"

"In case you hadn't noticed, restaurants and bars ain't really made a comeback around here. The Field was the only place that's stayed open day in, day out, no matter what. Plus, I ain't the type to work in a regular restaurant and bar. The Field is steady work and cash money. Winter sucks dick. But I'm used to it."

Beck nodded. "And you don't mind shitheads booting you in the ass while you're trying to make a buck?"

"Yeah, well, fuck Hamm Elrod."

"Is that what's behind your dummy act? Keeps the Kin assholes from getting physical?"

"A bit. Mostly because it gets me bigger tips. Turn up the ol' Stepin Fetchit act. You know, bow and scrape. By the way, Mr. Redbreast, you know my name. You never told me yours."

"James."

"Okay, Mr. James. And that's Mr. Eddie." Miller looked back at Demarco, "And you, sir, what's your name?"

"Mr. Jones."

For a moment, Andy looked like he was going to comment on the name Jones, but instead he asked, "So why are you boys following me home and asking me all these questions? Who are you, Mr. James? And what happened to the side of your head and ear? Not that I had anything to do with it. Just curious."

Beck ignored Miller's questions and said, "Do you know who killed Joey Collins?"

There was a pause. The mood in the small room changed. Miller answered, "Why the hell are you asking me that? I have no idea whatsoever."

"Are you the one who found him?"

"No."

"Who did?"

"Don't really know. All I know is George and Vic were suddenly telling everybody to go home. They told me to stand by the body and make sure nobody got close to it."

"Where was it?"

"A little ways past the parking area. Near that split rail fence. In the dark."

"I hear Joey Collins was from an important Kin family."

"He was. Both sides. Mother and father. Mostly his father's side."

Beck said, "What do you know about Camdyn Dent?"

"Nobody knows much about Camdyn Dent."

"What can you tell me about the Kin?"

Miller waved away the question. "You should ask whoever told you about the Kin and Camdyn Dent. I presume that was Miss Irene."

"I will. I want to know what you know."

Miller sat back in the upholstered chair and crossed his arms. He looked like he was trying to sort out his answer.

"Anybody can tell you what they think they know about the Kin. I truly believe most don't know what they're talking about."

"Why's that?"

"The Kin goes back too far. Information gets jumbled over time."

"What were they originally?"

Miller shrugged. "I wasn't around then."

"What have you heard?"

"The Kin came from real primitive folks. Original settlers in this region. Supposedly married into the native Mahican population. You hear weird shit about them. Bushwackers, mountain dwellers, hill people. Hardly anybody knew about them until state troopers went up there in the late twenties, early thirties."

"Really."

"Yup. The Kin been around since before the war."

"Which war?"

"Revolutionary War. They was stickin' it to the man even back then, my friend. The landowners who bought up most everything around here, the Livingstons, Van Rensselaers, they worked their land with tenant farmers. Treated 'em like chattel. For those folks it was pretty close to being a slave. There was some violent reactions."

"How about now? Who are the Kin now?"

Miller waved a hand. "I don't know. Seems like anybody with a grudge can be part of the Kin. Don't much care. Why the hell are you so interested? And what about Mr. Eddie and Mr. Jones? They just happen to be up here visiting you for the holidays? Who are *you*, for that matter?"

Beck ignored the questions and said, "What do you know about Oscar Lund?"

Miller paused. "How come you're the only one gets to ask questions?"

Beck said, "Because Oscar Lund and three other assholes from the Kin came to my house and tried to beat the shit out of me. As for Mr. Eddie and Mr. Jones, they're friends of mine. Me, I'm just somebody who came up here for a little peace and quiet. So, what do you know about Oscar Lund?"

Miller didn't answer right away. Beck had the impression Miller was evaluating what Beck had told him.

"Oscar Lund is a district leader in the Kin. Mid-level sort of thing."

"You know where I can find him?"

Miller paused again. "Oh, hmmm, his place ain't that easy to find."

"Why?"

"It just ain't."

"Where does he live?"

"Far as I know, he lives near Bolton. Up in the hills, four or five miles from the river. If you want to know more about the Kin, you should go talk to him. He knows more than I do. Knows more about Joey Collins, too. He was the one who brought Joey to the Field that night."

"And you have no idea who would kill him. Or why."

Suddenly Miller stood up and announced, "I already answered that. I been more'n hospitable to you comin' to my place in the middle of the night. You got problems with the Kin, Mr. James, that ain't my fault. Best you deal with it yourself and leave me out of it. I'm going to sleep. If you're lookin' for a place to hideout, this ain't it. Close the door when you leave and turn off these lights."

Demarco glanced at Beck. He wasn't ready to let Andy Miller walk away. Beck responded with an almost imperceptible shake of his head, and Demarco settled back, thinking about throwing Andy Miller against a wall.

Miller walked past the kitchen area toward the back of the house. They heard a door close.

Beck stood up and motioned for the others to leave. They didn't turn out any lights. And didn't talk until they were in the Toyota. Manny fired up the engine to get the car warm.

Demarco asked Beck, "What do you think?"

"I think he's still half acting the fool."

Manny said, "And the question is still why. It ain't just for tips. And it ain't to keep the Kin boys off him. Acting like a dolt can get plenty of attention he doesn't want."

"Why then?" said Demarco.

Manny said, "So they don't notice him hanging around listening and watching."

"And why would he be doing that?"

Manny said, "I don't know. Maybe knowing what the Kin is up to helps him stay out of harm's way."

Beck recalled his conversation with Alex Liebowitz about Irene Allen using a false identity. He said, "You think he might be working undercover for law enforcement? Hanging around criminals in the Kin to pick up information."

Manny said, "His gun looks like police issue."

"How so?"

"It's a Gen 4 Glock with MOS sites. Supposed to be for law enforcement only."

Beck said, "Interesting, but you can get police issue guns from resellers."

Demarco said, "I doubt that guy could pass a police physical. And somebody undercover has to do more than just hang around listening. He has to witness actual crimes. Be involved."

Manny said, "So what's that weird son of a bitch doing?"

There was silence in the car as they thought it over. Darkness hid everything outside except for plumes of exhaust swirling past the car windows.

Demarco broke the silence. "He might've slipped up talking about his Stepin Fetchit act."

Beck said, "How so? It sounds like an accurate description of what he's doing."

"Only because of that damn stupid name. Stepin Fetchit is misleading. It was a stage name for a Black actor named Lincoln

Perry. Perry was a Black man working in Hollywood, in the thirties when there were virtually no Black people in movies, and yet he ended up making millions. Think about that for a second."

Beck waited to hear more from Demarco.

"His character Stepin Fetchit was billed as the laziest man in the world. Lazy, stupid, shiftless. A dimwit. But that laziest man thing was a scam, a con developed during slavery. It was called putting on old massa. Slaves would break shit. Act the fool. Do anything to screw things up until the white massas got so frustrated they ended up doing the work themselves."

Beck said, "Go on."

"Acting the fool made Perry's bosses feel superior. And audiences for that matter. But it was a grift, a con to get the racist movie industry to promote him as someone everyone could look down on, laugh at. All the while he was pocketing more money than any actor in Hollywood."

Manny said, "So where is Andy Miller leading us?"

Beck said, "I think D is right. I think Miller's conning us into helping him do whatever he's trying to do. Me in particular, since he didn't even know you guys existed until tonight."

Manny said, "So, what is he trying to do?"

Beck shrugged. "Make money like Lincoln Perry? If the Kin is doing crime, it involves money. Money is as good a motive as any. Along with power and revenge."

Demarco closed one eye and said, "I wonder."

"What?"

"You think Miller let Manny see through his act on purpose?"

Beck thought about it and nodded, "Maybe. And now I'm wondering if maybe Andy Miller and Irene Allen are working together. She was the one who started the trouble last night. I jumped right in."

Manny said, "So, now the question is – did he push everything forward by killing that guy Collins?"

Beck said, "That would be a hell of a push. But I don't think Irene had anything to do with that. If she did, I can't see her stepping forward to get arrested."

Manny said, "Did she know this Collins guy was dead when she stepped between you and the sheriff's investigator?"

"No. She didn't know that until Proctor had the cuffs on her. She thought she was taking the hit for poking Hamm Elrod with a three-inch knife."

Demarco said, "That makes more sense."

Beck rubbed his face. "Fuck it. We'll never figure this out until we know more about the Kin. I'm tired, my head hurts, let's focus on the one solid thing Miller gave us."

Demarco said, "Talk to that guy we left in the forest."

Beck said, "Yes. Miller said Lund knows all about the Kin. Lund is the one who set up the robbery that went bad. He's the one who brought Joey Collins to the Field that night. Miller might or might not be scheming and conning us, but there's one thing he didn't lie about." Beck reached into his shirt pocket and pulled out Oscar Lund's driver's license. He held it up. "Where Oscar Lund lives. County Route 18, Bolton."

Demarco said, "Well, I hope that loudmouth made it out of that forest before he froze to death."

Beck said, "Time to find out."

24

After adding another three hours of sleep to the time he'd dozed in Lunt's hospital room, Abel Proctor walked into the sheriff's headquarters at eleven-thirty. He'd showered, eaten, and put on fresh clothes. Chief Assistant District Attorney Brian Lawlor was sitting in the chair next to Proctor's desk. The chair's hard seat made Lawlor's ass numb. He'd consumed too much coffee and felt the sting of heartburn coming on. All of which made him more pissed off about not having the information he needed to figure out what he should do at Irene Allen's arraignment, scheduled for one o'clock.

Proctor stepped into his cubicle.

"What the hell, Abel, you're fifteen minutes late."

"Sorry. I was trying to nail down something before we talked."

Proctor didn't tell Lawlor that something was talking to Camdyn Dent on what he wanted done.

Lawlor looked at his watch. "I got a little over an hour before the arraignment."

Proctor said, "I know. I know. Let's talk in one of the interview rooms."

"Why not here?"

Proctor said nothing but pointed to his ear.

Lawlor said, "Ah jeezus, now what?"

He followed Proctor to a windowless room empty except for two steel chairs on opposite sides of a steel table. One of the chairs and the table were bolted to the floor. An eyebolt for handcuffs was welded to the center of the table.

Lawlor said, "I hate this fucking room."

"That's kind of the point," said Proctor. "Unfortunately, I don't think your mood is going to improve any."

"Ah shit. I knew it. You're leaving me high and dry. I knew it."

Proctor sat in the chair bolted to the floor. He waited for Lawlor to sit opposite him.

He said, "It's not all bad."

"Is that supposed to make me feel good?"

Proctor took a deep breath and said, "The state lab didn't finish the testing on the murder weapon."

"Fuck me. Do you know who's presiding today?"

"Judge Geller."

"That's right, Abel, Judge Geller. That ornery old bitch is going to rip me a new one. Every fucking thing she does, she does to make herself look tough. You must have something. You arrested the woman, for chrissake. What have you got?"

"It's thin."

"Thin doesn't help me, Abel. Thin helps her lawyer."

Proctor said, "Who's her lawyer?"

"Peter Morelli. He's an experienced guy. Was an ADA in the Brooklyn office before he moved to the defense side. Came up here full time during Covid. Says she has an alibi."

"I'm not surprised."

"Can you bust it?"

"Better than that. I can implicate the guy she's using for her alibi."

That got Lawlor's attention.

"How?"

Proctor leaned forward. "All right, listen. She's claiming she was with a guy named James Beck at the time of the murder. Before I came in, I was getting background on him. That's why I was late." Proctor didn't mention that Russell Hibbard had been the one gathering information on Beck.

"Okay."

"Her alibi, James Beck, is an ex-con. Served time on a manslaughter charge. Associate of known felons. Not a member of this community. I'm looking into him. I think he's good for the murder. I think they acted in concert."

"What's your proof?"

"Once I get the lab results back, I expect to find both their prints on the murder weapon."

"What?"

"His prints and the victim's blood on the knife used to kill Collins."

"Holy shit, Abel, that's game, set, match. Why haven't you arrested Beck?"

"I can't find him."

"Has he fled?"

"I don't think so."

"What does that mean? Is he here or not?"

"I have reason to believe he's still in the jurisdiction."

Lawlor grimaced and looked up. "Reason to believe? Are you shitting me? I don't want to hear lawyer-speak from you, Abel." Proctor didn't answer. Lawlor said, "Can you find this guy or not, Abel?"

"I can find him. If…"

Lawlor put his hands on the steel table and leaned over Proctor. "If what?"

Proctor looked up, meeting Lawlor's gaze, saying nothing.

Lawlor said, "Oh, no. No, no, no. Are you doing what I think you're doing?"

"What do you think I'm doing, Brian?"

Lawlor cursed quietly. "Fuck." He looked around the room. He spoke in a low voice. "There's nothing recording in here now, is there?"

Proctor said, "Absolutely not."

"You want her out so you can…"

Proctor held up a hand to stop Lawlor.

Lawlor said, "Fuck, you *are* doing what I think you're doing?"

Proctor answered with a shrug.

"How the hell do you think you can pull this off, Abel? Geller will go batshit. This is a murder charge."

"Listen, Brian, it's turning out this way whether I like it or not. It's not our fault that the goddamn state lab doesn't have results. Blame me. Say your hands are tied. Go for substantial bail. Irene Allen has no strong ties to the community. Only lived here for a couple of years or so. Only been employed for a short time."

"How short?"

"I don't know. I'm still looking into that. Go for a substantial bail. If she comes up with the money, that will be further confirmation."

"Of what?"

"A criminal conspiracy."

"The co-conspirator being Beck?"

"Yes."

"He's got money?"

"Looks like it."

"Looks like it how?"

"He owns property for starters."

"How'd he get his money?"

"Probably ill-gotten."

Lawlor stopped asking questions. The answers weren't helping him. He looked at his files. "Her lawyer isn't a fool."

"Morelli."

"Yeah. Morelli. I just told you his name."

Proctor said, "I don't know too much about him. He doesn't do that much criminal defense work in our court, does he?"

"Enough."

Proctor said, "Good. He should argue vigorously. That works in our favor."

Lawlor shook his head. "It'll just piss off Geller more."

"That will work in our favor, too."

"Because she'll use it as a chance to make me look like an idiot." Lawlor took a deep breath. "You really think this is the best way to go?"

Proctor answered succinctly. "I do."

"Our long-serving District Attorney Allen Grotowski is not going to like this."

"He'll like where it comes out. Two murder convictions instead of one. In fact, the only way this works is if we implicate both of them. If we don't bust her alibi, you'll never convict her."

Lawlor nodded. He could argue the point.

"All right, Abel. But I'm going to blame you as much as I can. You better be ready for a roasting. I'm not going to be the only one who looks incompetent."

"Do what you have to do. Trust me, she'll lead us to Beck. It's the fastest way to get everything you need to run a murder case across the finish line and put two people away."

Lawlor tried to look aggrieved, but Proctor knew Lawlor would take advantage of the opportunity to notch a victory in a murder trial. He would play ball.

They both checked their watches at the same time.

Proctor asked, "All set?"

"If that's what you call it."

"Good."

Lawlor looked around and lowered his voice. "You really think this woman will lead you to Beck?"

"It's my best shot. My only shot."

"All right. Don't fuck this up, Abel."

"I don't intend to."

Lawlor hurried out. Proctor sat back in the uncomfortable steel chair and folded his arms. He took a long breath and let it out slowly, letting his aggravation at Brian Lawlor seep out of him. He reviewed everything he had set in motion. He let out a short laugh. Brian Lawlor wouldn't be enhancing his status much by convicting two corpses.

25

Oscar Lund got more pissed off by the minute.

He sat in a beat-to-shit wheelchair outside the hospital entrance, bracing himself against freezing gusts of wind, wearing his dirty clothes from last night, wondering who and when somebody would pick him up and drive him home. A hospital orderly stood next to Lund comfortably bundled up in an enormous parka, acting like he had every right to ignore him. It didn't help Oscar's mood that the orderly was Black.

Finally, Lund saw his Jeep pull into the parking lot with Reid Vander driving. The deep dent in the front bumper added fuel to Lund's simmering rage.

Lund turned to the hospital orderly. "This is my ride."

"About time," said the orderly. He stared at Lund, daring him to complain.

Lund said, "Uppity asshole," but not to the man's face as he stood up out of the wheelchair. A wave of dizziness almost spoiled his tough guy act.

The orderly took back his wheelchair and walked away as if Oscar Lund might steal it.

Reid Vander pulled up to the curb and came out of the driver's seat, his right hand wrapped in a dirty Ace bandage. He opened the front passenger door for Lund with his left hand.

"Here you go, boss."

Lund said the same thing the orderly said to him. "About time."

"It took longer than I thought to get your car out of that mess. The damn tow truck had to back all the way in."

Lund struggled into the front seat.

"Just get me home, Reid."

"Okay. How'd they treat you in there?"

"All right, I guess. Didn't sleep much." Lund settled back after struggling to put on his seat belt.

Vander asked, "So what happened to you?"

Lund turned toward Vander and finally noticed his swollen nose, black eyes, and bandaged hand. "Shit, what happened to you?"

Vander shrugged. "Stopped a punch with my face." He lifted his right hand. "One of those pricks stomped on my hand." He wiggled his fingers but not much. "Something is definitely broke. I gotta get an x-ray after I drop you off. So, tell me."

Lund shifted in his seat, trying to ease the pain in his ribs.

"The fuckers tossed me in the back of a truck. Drove out near the end of Matteson Road. Worked me over with my bat. When I didn't tell them anything, they stuck me in my Jeep and shoved it into a tree. Had to crawl out of there. Ended up in the hospital. Almost froze to death."

"We shouldn't never have gone in there without knowing the score. It was supposed to be one guy."

"You can thank Abel Proctor for that."

Reid Vander nodded but said nothing. He'd been heading north but made an abrupt left turn heading west.

Lund said, "Which way are you going?"

Reid kept his eyes on the road. "Abel said I'm supposed to take you to a meeting."

"Now?"

"Yeah."

"I'm in no shape for a meeting."

"It's going to happen anyhow."

"Who's it with?"

Reid turned to Lund. "He didn't tell me, Oscar."

"Yes, he did. He told you."

Vander didn't answer.

Lund said, "Tell me."

Finally, Reid said, "You know who."

Lund nodded and smiled to himself, thinking, *good*. The man. The man whose name Reid Vander knew enough to keep out of his mouth. Camdyn Dent. This was going to be something. Oscar Lund took a deep breath. He felt like shit. He'd better get himself together. He was about to become one of the very few who'd actually laid eyes on Camdyn Dent. He wondered if Dent would be wearing a mask. Maybe a Covid mask. Lund suddenly felt like he had to take a piss. All those fluids they'd pumped into him. Should've pissed before he left. All the goddamn time sitting outside waiting for Vander. Fuck it. He'd take a piss before he met with the leader of the Kin. He had a right to piss, for chrissake.

The old Jeep bucked and jounced over the rough road that rose through a scrub forest. Every jolt caused a wave of pain through Lund's ribcage.

Lund had no idea where the hell Reid was taking him. He supposed that made sense. Someplace isolated. Someplace nobody knew about.

Vander turned abruptly onto what looked like a fire service road. There were fresh vehicle tracks through the snow, but the road was icy. Even with four-wheel drive, the Jeep had difficulty making it up the incline. Suddenly the road opened onto a property used to raise turkeys and rabbits. Off to the right were two hundred rabbit hutches, rough wooden boxes stacked ten high. It looked like at least a hundred rabbits were hunkered down in the hutches.

Reid stopped in front of a one-story, concrete-block building with a corrugated roof. An abattoir built for slaughtering the turkeys and rabbits.

Reid stared out the Jeep's windshield, avoiding eye contact with Lund.

"This is the place."

Before Lund could ask a question, his car door opened. A short, heavily bearded man wearing only a hooded sweatshirt against the cold motioned him out of the Jeep.

"Let's go."

Lund struggled out of his seat. Again, standing up made him dizzy.

"I gotta take a piss."

"Inside."

Lund looked at the man. Between the beard, long hair, and hood, there wasn't much of a face to look at. The man lifted his hand, and Lund saw the gun pointing at him. And a pillowcase extended toward him.

"What the fuck is this?"

"Put this over your head. Security protocol."

Shit, thought Lund, *I'm not going to be able to see him.* He pulled the pillowcase over his head.

The voice said, "Raise your hands."

Lund complied. He felt two hands start at the top of his shoulders and run down his back, arms, and sides. His legs. Pockets. Lund heard a door open. Then heard footsteps crunching in the snow. Hands grabbed both his arms, and two men led him into the building. Lund smelled the stench before he entered.

Lund felt himself pushed down into a chair. They were doing something with his hands. And securing his forearms to the chair's arms. And his ankles to the legs of the chair. Something was wrong. What was happening?

Somebody pulled off the pillowcase. Bright fluorescent light made him blink. And then he saw him. And Oscar Lund had to clench before he pissed himself. Too late. He felt the wetness.

Emmett Devereaux sat three feet in front of him, holding a plasma cutting torch.

Devereaux gave Lund a moment to look around. To take in the chair he sat on. Sturdy. Big. With wide arm rests. He looked down and saw that they had secured his right hand with two large U-bolts to a steel plate, one bolt at his wrist, one across his four fingers.

Devereaux watched the heavy-set man's eyes. A little more than three seconds to go from surprise and confusion to anger, and then to terror. Despair would come soon.

Lund had never seen Emmett Devereaux up close. He took in the dark hair and swarthy skin. Dark leather vest. Dark blue denim shirt. None of it darker than Devereaux's eyes. Black holes on a face with no expression. Not a shred of humanity in them.

Devereaux spoke softly.

"You know who I am?"

Oscar tried to speak. His mouth was dry. He had to clear his throat.

"Yes."

"Your name is Oscar?"

"Yes."

"So far, I believe you."

Oscar Lund opened his mouth to say something. Devereaux pressed his forefinger to his lips.

"Don't say nothing, Oscar. You don't want to cause yourself extra pain."

Lund followed Devereaux's eyes looking down to his hand secured to the metal plate.

Devereaux turned on the unit that powered the plasma cutting torch and attached a grounding clamp to the steel plate under Lund's hand. He leaned forward and cut a line into the metal. Sparks flew. Lund tried to pull his hand free. Impossible.

Devereaux looked at him with his dead eyes.

"Strange, huh? You'd think something that could cut through steel would cut through flesh and bone." Devereaux slowly shook his head. "Trust me, it don't. I've tried it. I can run this back and forth over your fingers; it won't cut through."

Lund felt his heart pounding. Sweat breaking out on his back and under his arms in the cold, unheated building.

"It'll burn, though. Burn like living hell. Maybe eventually burn through if I rig a piece of iron on top of your hand. I think a man your size and age, you look like your heart might give out first. But not right away."

Lund yelled out, "What do you want? Why are you doing this? I've been loyal. Done my duty for twenty-odd years. This isn't right."

"You let Joey Collins die on your watch. What the hell did you think would happen to you? A blood relative of a family loyal to Camdyn Dent. You've got one way out of this, Oscar. You tell me every damn thing that happened between the time you first saw Joey Collins last night and now."

Devereaux leaned forward and torched the fingernail on Lund's index finger. For two seconds. An eternity.

Devereaux waited for Lund to stop screaming and cursing. Then he said, "Talk."

Lund spoke nonstop, fighting the pain still burning on his fingernail. Devereaux didn't have to ask anything. When Lund finished, Devereaux said, "Repeat what you just said. But slower."

Lund did.

Devereaux nodded. He thought about using the plasma torch on Lund. He wanted to use it on Lund. He looked at his watch. It bothered him that he didn't have time, but just for the hell of it, he ran the torch back and forth across the top of Lund's hand. Lund screamed uncontrollably.

Devereaux yelled, "Shut him up!"

The bearded man in the sweatshirt shot Oscar Lund in the right temple.

Devereaux took out a folding knife and cut off the burned digit on Lund's finger. He had a small leather bag suspended on a leather thong around his neck. He pulled the bag out from under his denim shirt, placed the body part in the bag, and left.

The two men who brought Lund into the abattoir cut Lund's two-hundred-forty-pound body into smaller parts with circular saws and fed the bloody body parts into a well-used ProCut meat grinder, mixing in bags of turkey feed. It would take about a week for the 1,346 turkeys to consume the feed. Oscar Lund ended up much like the grubs, crickets, and other insects the fowl loved to eat.

26

Peter Morelli had made sure not to make any kind of guarantee to Beck that he could get Irene Allen released on bail. But that didn't mean he wouldn't go down without a fight. When the clerk of the court called the case, Morelli stood at the defendant's table taking on the game face of a determined advocate. Irene Allen sat in the chair next to Morelli, looking worn out and disheveled after a sleepless night in a holding cell.

After hearing the charges read and a pro forma not guilty from the defendant, Judge Geller turned to the Chief Assistant District Attorney, Brian Lawlor. It took a little over a minute for Judge Geller, a small elderly woman who favored out of fashion wire-rimmed glasses, to frown and stare daggers at the ADA. Instead of hearing evidence and a demand that the defendant be remanded into custody, Lawlor offered excuses and apologies. Morelli tried to keep a poker face. He took a quick look behind him to see if the sheriff's investigator Proctor was in the courtroom. He wasn't.

Finally, the judge interrupted. Eyes narrowed in anger, her voice tight with disdain, she asked, "Mr. Lawlor, what are you saying? This is a murder case. Remand should be practically a given, and you are tying my hands here."

"As are mine, your honor. The district attorney's office is hamstrung by the situation in the state forensics lab. Everything is backed up. There's a shortage of both testing materials and staff. Delays have put us in a position where we have to wait for the lab results to..."

Geller interrupted. "Then why aren't you requesting an extension of custody? You have forty-eight hours."

"Your honor…"

Morelli decided now was the time to take advantage of the situation. He interrupted Lawlor. "Your honor, pardon me. Is there any possibility that the test results will be here within twenty-four hours?"

Geller turned to Lawlor, "What's the answer, Mr. Lawlor?"

Lawlor spread his hands, shook his head, trying to look as frustrated and helpless as possible.

Geller turned back to Morelli. "Well, I guess that's your answer, counselor."

Morelli pressed his attack. "Your honor, there's no reason or basis for my client to remain in custody. There is absolutely no evidence…"

Geller interrupted Morelli.

"Save it, counselor. With zero substantial evidence remand is out. But I don't want to hear a long dissertation about releasing your client on recognizance. What's her situation?"

Morelli spoke fast and tried to be concise. He had a win here. Beck had agreed to finance bail. He wasn't going to push a judge who'd already made her position clear.

"Ms. Allen has no criminal history, never been arrested in this jurisdiction, resides in the community, is employed locally…" Morelli saw the judge already becoming impatient. He ended quickly. "Under the circumstances and because the defendant has limited means, we ask that bail should be reasonable."

Judge Geller didn't waste time.

"Bail is set at one hundred thousand dollars cash or two-fifty bond."

Morelli paused. He'd been juggling two interests in the case from the beginning. He had to tread carefully. Agreeing to cash bail would go against his claim that Irene Allen had limited resources. He had to take the bond. It would cost Beck $15,000 to remain in the shadows. Six percent of the two-fifty. So be it.

"We will arrange for bond, your honor. I assure you my client will make all appearances and comply with this court's demands."

Geller smacked her gavel down and said, "She had better. Good day."

Morelli sat down next to Irene and began talking before she could ask any questions.

"This is an incredibly good result, Irene. I've got to arrange for bond. It will take an hour, two at the most. They'll hold you here in the court's lockup during that time. Not in the sheriff's holding cell. I'll be back to file forms, and then they will release you to me."

Irene said, "How's the bond work? I don't have any collateral."

"Mr. Beck will take care of that. And cover the filing fee. You just hang in for a little while…wow, sorry. You look…"

"Like shit. I know. And I stink, too. They put a three-hundred-pound drunken woman in my cell at one in the morning. She puked all over herself. She was raving for hours. I can't get the smell of her out of my nose."

"Good lord. Okay, I'll move as fast as I can. Like I said, you'll stay in the courtroom holding cell."

"Fine. I just want to get home, shower, and burn these clothes. What about my car? I don't have any transportation."

"Your car is still at the state lab. I'll drive you home myself and arrange for a rental. Let me get to work. Sorry about last night."

Morelli stood and nodded for the bailiff to take Irene to the holding area and headed out to the privacy of his car to make phone calls. First to Beck. Then to a bail bondsman in Albany. As he walked to the car, he tried to figure out the simplest way to process the bond. Probably have Beck wire money to an escrow account he maintained and make the transaction with the bail bondsman from that account.

He started to call Beck but decided to text instead. He didn't feel like getting into a conversation. He paused a moment to figure out the text.

Got her bail. Big victory. Need to make financial arrangements.

27

With Oscar Lund taken care of, Irene Allen was next on Emmett Devereaux's list.

He checked the time. Another half hour before her arraignment started. He still made sure to drive past the address Abel Proctor had given him to confirm she wasn't home.

Devereaux slowed as he rolled by a small wooden house with weathered wood-shake siding and an eyebrow second floor. A brick chimney stood against the end of the house, rising above a roofline shaped like an old swayback horse. No lights were on in the house or cars parked on the property.

The day had turned overcast, the frigid moist air hinted of snow coming soon. Devereaux continued past the house around a slight curve in the road that gave him a view behind the house. No lights there either.

Devereaux made a Y-turn about five hundred yards farther on and cruised by Irene Allen's house from the other direction, confirming the address on a dilapidated mailbox mounted on a post pitched off-center. A quarter-mile ahead, Devereaux pulled off the road and drove his rusting Ford-150 4x4 into a clear space between a set of trees. Four-wheel drive and good snow tires on the old truck made the maneuver easy.

Devereaux walked back to Irene's house along the shoulder of the road, bare-headed, ignoring the wind and below freezing temperature. He wore a black utility coat lined in flannel. It had four pockets on the front. He didn't bother to zip up the coat.

No cars passed him before he veered off and headed to the back of the house. He circled the house once, again making sure nobody was home while he looked for a place to break in. He didn't need to look hard. In the back of the house, he spotted an unlocked Bilco door to the cellar. He let himself in, closed the door behind him, and stepped down a short flight of stairs into a space only five-and-a-half feet high. He found a pull cord and turned on a bare lightbulb illuminating a small furnace room. The foundation was rock rubble. Above him the original house beams held up a plank floor. Twenty feet past the furnace room were steps leading up into the house. The door at the top of the steps opened into the kitchen. Devereaux walked up the steps. The door handle turned, but a sliding barrel bolt on the other side kept the door shut.

Devereaux had lock picks, shims, and small screwdrivers with him. But a cheap, simple bolt lock couldn't be shimmed or picked. He could easily bust the lock off the frame, but that would alert the woman to a break-in.

From the inside front pocket of his coat, he pulled out two hacksaw blades joined together at one end with a nut and bolt, transforming the two blades into a kind of scissors. Like most doors in old houses, there was enough room to slide the two hacksaw blades between the frame and door, one blade above the bolt, the other below it. Devereaux squeezed the blades together, gripping the bolt between the teeth of the blades. He kept hold of the bolt and rotated the blades upward until the bolt lifted up from the notch that kept it in place. Holding the bolt in place, Devereaux had just enough room between door and frame to slide the bolt over so that it rested in the channel.

It took Devereaux ten moves to push the bolt over far enough to release the door.

During the four minutes of patient work, Devereaux occupied himself by thinking about what he would do to Irene Allen. He would be patient with that task, too. Slow and steady. Inflicting the pain necessary to find out the information Proctor needed to find someone named Beck. Devereaux thought about the parts of her body he would focus on to produce the right type of pain. And for how long. Devereaux had seen Irene Allen on one of the few occasions he went to the Field. He recalled that she was a small woman. He liked that. It should be interesting. Entertaining. He thought about what body part he would harvest after he killed her. Something feminine.

Once Devereaux had the basement door open, he moved quickly and efficiently throughout the house looking for weapons. He found two cans of Mace in a kitchen drawer. He turned on the water in the sink, took one of the canisters, draped a dish towel over his hand, and sprayed the contents down the drain. He did the same with the second canister. He left the water running, squeezed dish detergent into the drain, and washed his hand and the towel. He hung the towel to dry on the hook where he'd found it and replaced the empty mace canisters in the drawer.

He roamed through the rest of the house envisioning hiding places. He found a fully loaded Glock 19 with a bullet in the chamber stuck between the mattress and the box spring of a full-size bed on the second floor. He unloaded the gun, released the slide, and turned it over. Using one of his small screwdrivers, he pressed the release that allowed him to slide off the back plate. He pulled out the firing pin assembly and dropped the assembly and pin in his coat pocket. It took him two minutes to reassemble the gun without the firing mechanism, load it, and replace it under the mattress. The gun looked the same, but pulling the trigger would do nothing.

He found a baseball bat in the bedroom closet. He left it there and continued checking each room and all the closets, drawers, and cupboards. He walked carefully across the wood floors listening and feeling for any loose boards that might conceal hidey holes. He knew there were things around the house that she could use as weapons – kitchen knives, frying pans, a bike lock and chain hanging from a closet doorknob. None of that worried him. In fact, he wouldn't mind if the girl tried to defend herself with something in the house. Nothing like a fight to get the blood running.

He thought about the best place to hide and yet be comfortable while he waited for her to arrive home. He decided he could wait upstairs in her bedroom. There was an upholstered chair with a flowered print fabric small enough to fit into an alcove near a back window. He pulled out his cell phone to make sure he had a signal. Two bars. Good enough. Proctor would text him to confirm she was on her way to this house so that he'd have time to get out of sight before she walked in.

Emmett Devereaux settled into the chair. He sent text messages to a pair of his men. Hill people. Cousins. Men he could rely on.

He pocketed the phone and sat back in the chair. The house was dim and quiet. He relaxed and closed his eyes, letting his senses sharpen. He heard the furnace downstairs kick in and felt the warm air rise into the cramped bedroom. Eyes closed, Devereaux listened to the sounds of the old house heating up.

Soon she would be here. Tired. Anxious to shower. Change into clean clothes. Eat. Crawl into her warm bed.

Devereaux pictured it. She wouldn't see him or hear him until it was too late. And then he would have one, whole, entire, female body all to himself. To do whatever he wanted to.

A cancer had blossomed inside the Kin. It required a purge. A bloodletting. He would move from one person to another until Camdyn Dent was satisfied. It happened every so often. There would be collateral damage. Even among his hill people. Maybe even to himself. And then the Kin would go on. Until the next time.

Devereaux waited, falling into a trance of sorts, his mind floating free. Free of any sense of time. She would arrive soon enough.

28

After confronting Andy Miller, Beck and the others returned to Demarco's house. The predawn light filled the bedroom downstairs. It didn't stop Beck from settling into the bed and falling asleep until early afternoon. The others also slept.

One by one, each of the men appeared around Demarco's oval dining table. Demarco had finished a late breakfast of scrambled eggs and sausages prepared by Manny Guzman who had taken over Demarco's kitchen. Ciro sat down with coffee and a plate of food. Demarco filled him in on what happened with Andy Miller. Ciro nodded and asked a few questions between mouthfuls. Downstairs, Beck called the two hospitals in the area to locate Oscar Lund.

About the time Ciro finished eating, Beck came upstairs. Manny had come to the table with his second cup of coffee. Beck sat down and announced, "Oscar Lund made it. The hospital discharged him about an hour ago."

Ciro said, "Bad for him. Good for us. What's the plan?"

Beck said, "Same as last time but no more fucking around. We find out everything he knows about the Kin, everything he knows about the guy who got killed, why, and who did it."

Ciro said, "By any means necessary."

"Exactly."

Manny said, "What about the woman? We have to talk to her, too."

Beck looked at his watch. It was shortly after two o'clock.

"Her arraignment is happening soon. The lawyer said she'll most likely be held without bail. I can't set foot in that jailhouse."

Ciro said, "I'll talk to her."

"I'm sure she would be charmed by your suave charisma, Ciro, but I want Uncle Manny to talk to her. You, me, and Demarco are going to my place. I need to gather a few items. What kind of weapons do you have here, D?"

"Three more Glock Seventeens. A Mossberg Shockwave Five-Ninety in my truck. Couple thousand rounds of 9-millimeter ammo. And an assortment of 12-gauge shells."

Ciro asked, "That shotgun is the one with the short handle?"

"Yes. Shaped like a bird's head."

"Can you hit anything with that?"

"What do you think?"

Ciro said, "I think it's hard."

"For some."

Beck asked, "What about you, Ciro? I know you didn't leave the city with just your forty-five."

"No, I did not."

"So?"

"You know me, Jimmy. I'm a Smith and Wesson guy. Got a sweet SW M&P fifteen, twenty-two. Practically all polymer. Light, quiet as hell. Really fuckin' accurate. I can nail a baseball-size group from forty yards."

"How much ammo did you bring?"

"Three loaded twenty-five round magazines. And a couple of extra boxes."

Beck didn't bother to ask Manny if he'd brought any other weapons. He knew Manny had two revolvers. One long barrel, one short. Always had, always would.

Beck stood. "Okay, we've got Ciro's shotgun. My Beretta is in his truck. Ciro, bring your AR. D, might as well bring your extra Glocks. I've got my Browning. Ciro has his Smitty. We should be good for now."

Manny said, "Ten to one, they have your place staked out."

Beck leaned over and put both hands on the dining table. "I hope to God they do. Let 'em find out what happens if they trespass on my property."

Demarco said, "I don't mind giving them a fight if they want one."

Ciro said, "I don't mind seeing what these peckerwoods have got."

Manny drank his coffee and said nothing.

"I'm going back to my house," said Beck. "If it's now, it's now. While we do that, Manny, I'll check with the lawyer and see if you can speak to Irene this afternoon."

"Where will she be?"

"In the county jail in Belleville."

"All right."

"Same deal. No fucking around. Find out whatever she knows or thinks she knows. While you wait to hear from me, try to get some sleep. You have to go back to work tonight."

"You want me to keep working that slippery scarecrow."

"I do."

About a hundred yards from his driveway, Beck pulled the Honda Ridgeline over. Demarco stepped out of the Honda's crew cab seat and slipped into the forest bordering the north side of Beck's house. He quickly disappeared into the trees and undergrowth.

Beck continued down the road, turned into his driveway, and drove slowly toward his front door. In the passenger seat, Ciro had Demarco's pump-action shotgun laid across he knees, watching for signs of an ambush. When Beck stopped in front of his house, he saw that his caretaker had replaced the broken front door with a sheet of three-quarter-inch plywood attached to heavy-weight stainless steel hinges. Instead of a door lock, there was a steel shackle and hasp secured with a padlock. Beck found the key for the padlock bunked where he hid his old door keys.

The sight of the destroyed hallway made Beck wince. Dented walls, furniture destroyed, a lamp, pictures, a wall sconce all broken beyond repair. Blood stains on the walls would need a sealing primer and paint. His home. Desecrated. Beck's left eye twitched as he walked through the mess to get what he needed.

Ciro stood outside near Demarco's truck watching for enemies, one hand on the Mossberg's bird's-head grip, the other under the strap of the fore-end. He knew Demarco was around somewhere. He didn't even try looking for him.

Ten minutes later, Beck emerged from the house carrying a Tuffpak ammo box and a small overnight bag containing clothes. He had a pair of wool-lined, waterproof leather boots slung over his left shoulder. In the crook of his left arm, he held a Mossberg 590M mag-fed shotgun and a semi-auto Ruger PC Carbine that used 9-millimeter ammunition. He carried three lightweight Kevlar bulletproof vests over his right shoulder.

Ciro helped Beck place everything into the bed of Demarco's Honda. Beck went back into the house for more boxes of ammunition.

That's when Demarco appeared from the back of the house, holding a sheriff's deputy by the back of his neck while he pressed the muzzle of his Glock 17 firmly against the deputy's spine. Compared to Jones, the five-foot-nine captive looked like a cringing high school boy.

Demarco was not happy with his prisoner. He shoved him forward with enough force to send him sprawling face down on Beck's driveway.

Ciro stepped out from behind the truck door and firmly placed a foot on the deputy's back.

"What's this?"

"A moron."

"What'd he do?"

"Tried to shoot me."

Holding the shotgun's bird's-head handle with one hand, Ciro pointed the Mossberg at the deputy's head. "Why is he still alive?"

"He might have useful information."

Beck came out of his house, shut the padlock on the front door, and loaded two Sheffield ammunition boxes into the truck. He joined Demarco and Ciro. He looked down at the deputy and said, "Turn over."

Ciro kicked the man's right hip. "Turn over!"

The deputy rolled onto his back before Ciro kicked him again, his hands raised defensively. Ciro kicked his right arm out of the way and yelled, "Put your fucking hands down, moron. You think you can stop 12-gauge with your fucking hands?"

Beck stepped forward. He was beyond anger. His head and ear still hurt where Oscar Lund's fish bat had hit him. The pain just wouldn't ease off. He looked at the deputy. Twenties, out of shape, his hair cut short, fear twisting his face. He wore his deputy sheriff uniform and winter coat.

Beck said, "How the hell do you get to wear a uniform and carry a gun?"

The deputy had no answer.

"What's your name?"

"Holding."

"How long have you been watching my house?"

"I don't know."

Demarco fired a round from his Glock that hit the driveway three inches from Holding's left ear.

"Answer him!"

"Since eight. I got here at eight this morning."

Beck asked, "Who sent you here? Abel Proctor?"

After a moment, Holding said, "Yes."

"Did you call him when we arrived?"

Ciro knelt with one knee on Holding's chest, his weight crushing into the deputy. He pressed the shotgun barrel under the deputy's chin. "This one ain't going into the ground, pal."

Beck yelled, "Did you call him!?"

"I texted him."

Beck asked, "Are you part of the Kin?"

Holding struggled to speak with Ciro's weight crushing him. "No."

"Is Proctor?"

Holding hesitated. Ciro pushed the muzzle of the shotgun farther into the deputy's chin.

"Yes!"

Demarco said, "How long until more deputies get here?"

Beck answered before Holding could speak, "It won't be sheriff's deputies. It'll be Proctor and the Kin."

29

Morelli waited two minutes for Beck to return his text. He didn't. Morelli called Phineas Dunleavy and told him the situation. Dunleavy told Morelli someone would call who had access to Beck's funds. Morelli's phone rang two minutes later. Alex Liebowitz didn't identify himself. He told Morelli they would provide cash as collateral. He asked for a bank account and routing number where Morelli wanted the money. Leibowitz said, "Two-hundred-fifty thousand will arrive in that account before end of day. More likely within the next ten or fifteen minutes," and hung up.

Morelli called a bail bond agency he'd done business with. There were seven agents in the firm. The answering service connected him with one of the younger agents, an up-and-comer who wanted to make his mark with the firm and knew writing a bond for $250,000 would do just that. Before their conversation ended, the money was in Morelli's escrow account. He got the bond filed with the court in forty-two minutes. Finished the paperwork with the court clerk in fourteen. Sixty-eight minutes from start to finish. *That had to be a record*, thought Morelli as he escorted Irene Allen to his car and headed out of town.

The first thing Morelli said was, "I assume you've never been bailed out before."

"No."

"I want you to know that was unusually fast."

"Okay."

"And just so you know, that cost Mr. Beck fifteen thousand, and he's on the hook for two-hundred-fifty if you miss a court appointment."

Irene looked like she was trying to sleep while Morelli talked to her, but she had been listening.

"Understood, Mr. Morelli. You're driving me home now, right?"

"Yes. I have your address."

"Wake me if I fall asleep and you need directions. And thank you, Mr. Morelli. It's just that I'm wiped out."

"Sure. Fine. I'll get you home. My office is getting you a rental car. They'll deliver a car to your address."

"Thanks."

By the time Morelli stopped in front of Irene's house, she was snoring softly. Deep asleep. He spoke her name. There was no reaction. He took a moment to look at her.

Irene had reclined the seat a bit. Her face was relaxed. Her features were unmarred by movement or attitude. Her skin, even without makeup and even after a hard night, had a smooth luminosity.

Morelli reached over and touched her shoulder. She still didn't wake. He gripped her shoulder lightly and gently shook her.

In a split second, Irene sat upright, opened her eyes, and gripped Morelli's wrist.

Morelli said, "It's me. Just me. Your lawyer."

She came around quickly, cleared her throat, and said, "Oh. Yes. Sorry. Sorry."

She blinked and looked around. They were in front of her house. She seemed surprised.

"You found it."

"Yes. I didn't want to wake you. Are you okay?"

"Yeah." She cleared her throat again. "Sure."

"I'll walk you in."

"You don't have to."

"I do. Humor me."

Morelli walked next to her all the way to the front door. He'd returned Irene's belongings to her when they left the court. She dug out her keys and opened the front door. Morelli waited on the doorstep while she turned on the lights in the small foyer. The house felt warm. The lights made everything seem normal.

Morelli said, "All right. You're all set?"

"Yes. Thanks."

"You have anything to eat here?"

"Yes. I'm fine. Does Beck know I'm out?"

"Yes. You should contact him."

"I will."

"Okay then. I'll be in touch with you about next steps soon. Get some rest."

Irene had seemed like all she wanted to do was close the door and be on her own, but now she asked, "What are the next steps?"

"I start negotiating with the DA's office. I want the charges dropped. We'll see what happens. There's nothing for you to do. Just don't leave the area. If something comes up and you have to be somewhere, let me know and I'll petition the court." Morelli handed her his card.

"I will."

"There won't be anything you need to worry about for at least the next couple of days."

Impatient to be done with Morelli she said, "Okay. Great. Fine. Thanks."

Morelli said, "Call me with any questions."

"Sure. What day is it? Friday?"

"Yes. Don't think about this for the time being."

Irene nodded. She smiled and closed her front door feeling immense relief.

Upstairs, Emmett Devereaux stood in her bedroom closet. He smiled, too.

30

Beck squatted next to Deputy Holding, looking for his police radio. There was none. He checked the deputy's pockets and found a cell phone.

Beck checked the phone and said, "He told the truth. He used texts."

Demarco said, "Makes sense. No ringing. No need to talk. When was the last one?"

"Eight minutes ago. Put this dipshit somewhere out of sight. Make sure he can't make any noise." Ciro and Demarco each took an arm and lifted the deputy to his feet. Ciro smacked the side of the deputy's head.

"Walk."

Beck added to the text stream on the deputy's phone: *They're still in hse. What's ur ETA?*

The answer came back quickly. *15–20 m. Hold ur position.*

Beck went back into his house and came out the back door, also secured now with plywood like the front door. He had the key fob to his truck and a black Magic Marker. He found Ciro and Demarco. They'd handcuffed Deputy Holding to a sapling, his back against the tree. Ciro finished stuffing one of Holding's socks in his mouth, securing it with a shoelace.

Beck reached down and pulled out Holding's wallet, took a picture of his driver's license, then dropped it on the ground. He used the Magic Marker to write TRESPASSER across Holding's forehead.

Beck held up his phone and showed the picture of the driver's license to the deputy. "If I ever catch you on my property again, I promise you, I will go to your house and burn it to the fucking ground."

Beck checked his watch. Ten minutes had passed.

He waved for Ciro and Demarco to follow him and hustled to where they'd parked the trucks out front. He grabbed his mag-fed Mossberg 590M from the Honda's truck bed and tossed his key fob to Ciro. Demarco climbed into his truck.

Beck told Ciro, "Follow Demarco out the back way in my truck. Take a right, drive about fifty yards, and pull over. Wait for me."

Ciro asked, "What are you going to do?"

"See who shows up."

"Maybe we should all stay and whittle down the opposition."

"No. Not yet. Then we'd have to kill that dumbass deputy. He was just doing his job. Go on. I'll cut through the forest on foot and meet you."

Ciro wanted to argue with Beck, but he knew it wouldn't do any good. He headed toward the GMC while Beck ran behind the four-foot-high wood pile that walled off his parking area. He dropped behind the woodpile where he could see the front of his house. Two minutes after he got into position, a sheriff's patrol car flashing blue and red lights came up his driveway, followed by a truck and a Jeep. Abel Proctor jumped out of the sheriff's patrol car along with a deputy who was a Kin sympathizer. Five civilians jumped out of the other vehicles, all carrying long guns.

Clearly, this wasn't an official County Sheriff's Department action. Proctor hadn't come to arrest him. He'd come to kill him.

Proctor yelled orders sending two men to look for Deputy Holding. Staking out the house had paid off. Beck had come back. If he was still inside, he wouldn't need Irene Allen to lead him to Beck.

The other three Kin men took turns trying to kick open the plywood front door. Proctor's deputy looked in the front window.

Beck knew the replacement front door covered the entire door frame and opened out. Eventually, they would figure out the best move was to crowbar the hasp off. He pumped a shell into the Mossberg. It took every shred of his willpower to keep from stepping out and blasting them. They had no right to do this to his home. The place he'd come to escape from this kind of violence and violation. There were ten rounds in the shotgun's magazine. Enough to scatter them. Not enough to take them all out.

Beck told himself, *don't be stupid*. Now was not the time. Killing or wounding underlings wouldn't solve this problem. He'd gotten what he came for – weapons and ammunition. Forget about the damn house. It had already been desecrated. Forget about everything except one thing – a gang of criminals with the support of local law enforcement intent on killing him, the three men willing to die for him, and Irene Allen.

Beck forced himself to crouch down behind the firewood wall and head into the forest. He made it quickly into the cover of the trees and undergrowth. From back in the forest, Beck stopped to watch and listen to a pair of Kin thugs toting AR-15 rifles aimlessly walking around calling out Holding's name, a combination of stupidity and lethal force that made Beck want to shoot them. He might have taken the chance, but his cell phone began vibrating in his pocket. He dug it out and saw Peter Morelli's caller ID.

31

After she kicked her front door shut, the first thing Irene Allen wanted to do was strip off her clothes and get into a hot shower. But she was also ravenous. She'd hardly eaten anything since breakfast at Beck's house yesterday.

She couldn't believe that was only yesterday. It felt like three days ago. The food at the county jail was nearly inedible. Lunch was a white bread baloney sandwich, a small bag of stale potato chips, and a so-called fruit drink – six ounces of sugar water colored with red vegetable dye. Dinner was cold string beans and a blob of mystery meat covered in congealed barbeque sauce. And a carton of milk. Breakfast before court had been a doughy muffin with fake blueberries and lukewarm black coffee. She'd put the muffin in a napkin and squeezed it into a greasy ball, left it on the cardboard tray, and drank the tepid coffee.

Irene entered her kitchen. She took off her barn jacket and tossed it onto a kitchen chair. That got some of the jailhouse stench off her. She pulled open her refrigerator, hoping she still had at least a couple of eggs left, as she struggled out of her flannel shirt and tossed that on top of her jacket. She peered into her fridge. There were three large organic eggs and a block of parmesan cheese. She took the eggs and cheese out and set them on the counter. She opened the freezer. There was a half-loaf of Tuscan wholewheat bread.

Upstairs, Emmett Devereaux stepped out of Irene's bedroom closet. He walked slowly toward the open bedroom door, listening to Irene moving around in the kitchen. She was going to eat first before she came up to shower.

Irene reached for an iron skillet in the cabinet under the kitchen sink. She placed it on the stove and turned on a low flame. She heard something above her but dismissed it as the usual creaking and groaning of the old house.

The house felt cold. Irene rubbed her arms. She wore only her thermal top, t-shirt, and sports bra. She thought about going upstairs and taking a quick shower. Warm up and get the smell of that holding cell off her body. She would enjoy the meal more. She half turned toward the stairs and then told herself, *no, eat first. You want a hot shower, then sleep.*

Irene stepped over to the sink and turned on the faucet, waiting for the water to run hot. She wanted to thoroughly wash her hands.

Devereaux had moved to the top of the steps upstairs. He heard the water running in the kitchen sink. This was an opportunity. She'd never hear him coming. He moved carefully, stepping on the outside edges of each stair so the old wooden steps wouldn't creak.

Irene adjusted the temperature and pumped anti-bacterial foaming soap onto her hands. During Covid, she had fallen into the habit of scrubbing her hands for at least twenty seconds.

Devereaux stepped off the last stair, preparing for the final rush into the kitchen. She'd hear him then. Turn toward him. Terrified. And he would grab her by the throat, lift her, and slam her onto the floor. The rest would be easy.

Irene turned off the water.

Devereaux stopped just outside the doorway to the kitchen.

Irene reached for the kitchen towel hanging from a hook near the sink to dry her hands. She froze. For a second, everything went blank. The towel was damp. Someone had been here. Or *was* here!

Devereaux rushed into the kitchen as Irene turned to look behind her. She saw Devereaux coming at her. Without thinking, she grabbed the iron skillet and threw it at him as she bolted for the back door.

Devereaux ducked and turned. Too late. The hot, heavy iron skillet hit him in the side of the neck, dropping him to one knee.

Irene shoved a kitchen chair to the floor as she ran to the back door and turned open the deadbolt lock.

Devereaux was on his feet, holding the side of his neck, checking his throat, trying to ignore the pain. He was going to kill this bitch. Catch her. Beat her. Torture her. Hang her up like a piece of meat and make Beck come for her. And then kill both of them.

Irene wrenched the back door open and stumbled down the four stairs to her backyard. The freezing temperature made her upper body contract as the terror coursing through her gave her the strength to run. But where? Anywhere away from the man who had invaded her house and waited for her in the dark like an animal.

She ran across the snow-covered ground behind her house, trying to get out of sight behind a derelict tool shed fifty feet away. She didn't dare look back. The cold made it difficult to breathe. Difficult to do anything. At least she had her boots on. Once she got behind the shed, Irene forced herself to stop. To think. She dropped to one knee and peered out from behind the tool shed. She tried to slow her breathing. She began to shiver.

Behind her was an overgrown field that extended for at least a quarter-mile before it butted up against the narrow, paved road. The nearest house was about three hundred yards east on the road that ran in front of her house. It was fifty feet to the woods and another hundred feet through the forest to the road. If she made it, she'd still be far away from the neighboring house with no guarantee anyone would be home.

She reached for her cell phone in her back pocket. It wasn't there. It was in the Carhartt barn jacket she'd left in the kitchen. Shit!

And then he appeared. Devereaux. He stepped out of her back door and stood on the small porch scanning the area to see where Irene had run. He was wearing her barn jacket. Smiling.

Irene felt her throat constrict. She forced herself to take shallow breaths so Devereaux wouldn't see the plumes of condensation. The barn jacket was big on her and small on him. Why the fuck was he wearing it? To taunt her?

Irene looked to her right. The deer and invasive plants had stripped the understory of the woods down to a jumble of thin tree trunks, bare bushes, and fallen limbs. You could see through it all the way to the road.

She thought about weapons that might be in the toolshed. If he came for her, that's where she'd go. Get inside and barricade the door. Find a hoe. An ax. Something. Anything.

And then she heard a strange voice. "Ireeeene. Come on out, girl. You ain't had enough time to get far. And I don't see anything moving. Where you hiding?"

The voice had a relaxed twang to it. Not southern or western. What was it? Appalachian?

"I bet I know where you are, Irene Allen."

Did he really know?

The initial shock had subsided. Irene knew the temperature was below freezing. Eventually, the cold would incapacitate her, but for now her adrenaline was still pumping. She almost had control of her breathing.

Thinking about weapons brought to mind her gun. Maybe she could lure him to come after her. Run through the woods, then swing around to her front door. Get up the stairs. Get the gun. She wouldn't need that much of a lead. Ten, fifteen seconds. Pull the gun out from under her mattress, turn, and shoot.

She leaned back against the shed.

She hadn't heard him step down the wooden stairs. He was waiting for her to make a move, so he'd know which direction to run after her. Smart.

The gun. That was the move. Lure him into the forest. Then double-back to the house. He wouldn't expect that.

Everything came into focus for Irene. At least it would give her a chance. She had no chance of surviving if she stayed put.

"C'mon, girl. I ain't gonna hurt you. Just want to ask you a couple a questions."

Irene pulled the sleeves of her thermal top over her hands,

steeling herself against the brambles and branches in the forest that would tear at her.

Devereaux shouted out, "All right, bitch! Enough waiting."

All the sing-song playfulness disappeared. The man sounded murderous and evil.

Irene stood up and ran, completely focused on reaching the forest. She stumbled on the ice and snow but kept her balance. She didn't dare look back. She burst into a stand of buckthorn branches, shouldered past giant hogweed, and scrambled past a small stand of saplings, running and stumbling in between and past the undergrowth. The snow on top of a thick layer of leaves accumulated over the years hid the uneven ground, and she stepped into a depression that sent her sprawling. Her hands hit the cold snow. A jolt ran up her arms into her shoulders. Her right knee hit something hard. She couldn't get up.

Irene stayed down and looked behind her. She didn't see Devereaux. It gave her hope. She got up and ran, limping, fighting the pain, heading in the direction that would lead her to the road than ran past her house. She veered left, ducked under a cluster of Japanese barberry, and felt sharp thorns tear into her right arm and shoulder. She hissed at the pain and kept going. She saw an area free of trees, the ground mostly covered by stilt grass and ferns. She could see the edge of the road fifty feet away. She felt weak. Breathing in ragged breaths. No food, no sleep. The adrenaline had burned off. She had to keep going. She had to make it.

And then, out of nowhere, off to her right, fifteen, twenty yards, she saw him. Coming through the forest. How did he get around her like that? He didn't. It wasn't Devereaux. It was one of his men moving confidently and easily, loping along parallel to her like a wolf from a pack herding her toward the road. Toward death.

32

Beck let Morelli's call go to voicemail as he hustled out of the forest and scrambled up the roadside ditch. Both trucks were parked twenty feet ahead a few feet off the road.

Beck walked past Ciro in the GMC and headed for Demarco. Demarco powered down the passenger side window.

"D, we should get the guns and ammo in the truck beds out of sight. Divide it up and put it in the cabs. Put my Beretta in my truck."

"Got it."

Ciro and Demarco got to work transferring the munitions. There were three ammo boxes from Beck's house and two from Demarco's. They loaded those first and then set Beck's Beretta on top of the ammo boxes in his truck. They stashed the Ruger Carbine, Beck's 590 mag-fed Mossberg, and Ciro's Smith and Wesson M&P on top of the ammunition boxes in Demarco's truck.

While Demarco and Ciro took care of the guns and ammo, Beck stood in the road listening to Morelli's voicemail.

"Morelli here. We got lucky. She made bail. Whatever evidence the district attorney's office had got delayed at the state's lab. I jumped all over that. They didn't have anything else. The judge was pissed, but she didn't have much choice. She set the bail about as high as she could. I had to bond Irene out. Texted you but didn't hear back so I worked with your guy in New York to get funds. I drove her to her house. She had a bad night in the lockup, but she's fine. Call me when you can."

Beck saved the message. He went through the photos on his phone and pulled up Irene's driver's license. A vision of Proctor and his Kin goons roaming around and trashing his house distracted him. He forced himself to banish the images.

Demarco came over to Beck and said, "Everything's loaded up. Now what? Back to my place?"

Beck shook his head. "Not yet. Irene Allen is out of jail."

"She got bail?"

"The lawyer said they got lucky. Something happened with the evidence. She's home. I want to make sure she's safe. It's on the way to your place."

Demarco looked at Beck. He had seen Beck angry before. He knew the look. And he also knew the angrier Beck was, the less he talked. So instead of asking questions, he just said, "Lead the way."

Beck entered Irene's address in his map screen and drove alone in his GMC. He could tell by the map that Irene's house was in a rural area. He let his GPS guide him so that he didn't have to watch for every turn. It gave him time to think. He pulled out a bottle of ibuprofen from the truck's center console, picked up a bottle of water from his cup holder, and washed down six pills. He went through everything that had happened. Everything had escalated fast. That goddamn sheriff's investigator and his Kin stooges clearly thought they could do whatever they wanted. He couldn't let them get to Irene. He needed answers from her. She might not be in the mood for questioning after a night in jail, but that wasn't going to stop him.

Beck glanced at the GPS. They were approaching the last turn to Irene's house. This wasn't going to be an easy conversation. Arriving unexpectedly with Ciro Baldassare and Demarco Jones wasn't going to help. And then Beck heard two gunshots.

"Shit!"

Beck reached behind into the crew cab section, grabbed his Beretta tactical shotgun, and accelerated.

In the Honda Ridgeline, Ciro drew his Smith and Wesson .45 and handed the Mossberg 596 to Demarco.

Beck came around the bend and saw three figures on his side of the road. Nearest was a man holding a pistol aimed at Irene Allen about twenty yards away from him. She seemed paralyzed with fear. There was blood on her right shoulder and arm. Fifteen yards past Irene, another man stood in front of her house, also pointing a gun at her.

Beck accelerated, powered down his window, and hit the brakes. He brought his shotgun around and let go of the steering wheel. The man on the road turned and aimed his handgun at Beck. Beck fired a round of 12-gauge as he slid past the shooter.

Beck grabbed the steering wheel, straightened out the truck, and braked to a stop. He shoved the gear shift into park and jumped out of his truck as he heard more shots fired behind him.

The man in front of Irene's house fired at Beck. A bullet bounced off the asphalt two feet to Beck's right. Irene hit the ground. Beck raised the Beretta and fired a blast at Devereaux, still standing in front of him. Devereaux returned fire as Beck kept advancing and shooting, firing off rounds of 12-gauge with each step.

Devereaux turned away and dove through the open front door of Irene's house.

A third shooter appeared from behind the house and fired in Beck's direction.

As Beck turned to return fire, Demarco appeared in his peripheral vision. Both of them opened up with their shotguns at the third target. Devereaux's man went down in a hail of buckshot.

Suddenly, everything went quiet.

Beck turned to see if Irene was still alive. Ciro had helped her up and was holding her left forearm for support. The first shooter lay dead just off the road. Buckshot peppered his torso along with five .45 caliber bullets in his head and chest from Ciro's handgun. Blood from the corpse was turning the gray snow dark. The third shooter near the house was down, bleeding, and drawing his last breath. He'd been torn apart by six hits from Beck's and Demarco's shotguns.

Beck turned, about to run into Irene's house after the third man, then stopped when he saw Devereaux running into the field behind Irene's house. Demarco saw him, too. He ejected the remaining buckshot shells from his Mossberg Shockwave and quickly loaded it with three 12-gauge slugs. He lofted two shots into the air aimed at the fleeing figure. The deadly slugs just missed Devereaux as he turned for the cover of the forest.

Beck looked like he was about to chase after Devereaux. Demarco put a hand on his shoulder.

"We don't want to go chasing after him in there. The light's going out of the sky. It'll be too easy for him to take cover and shoot at us."

If it hadn't been for Demarco, Beck would have been running after Devereaux. He cursed, nodded, and then headed over to check on Irene.

Ciro had wrapped her in his dark wool herringbone overcoat. It covered her completely with a foot of coat on the ground. She couldn't stop shivering. Not just from the cold. From terror. Two minutes ago, Irene thought she was going to die.

Beck stood in front of her, put a hand on her forearm, and asked, "Were you hit?"

"No. No. I got scratched up in the forest."

"What happened?"

"I came home. Emmett Devereaux was waiting for me in the house. He was upstairs. I got out the back door just in time. I thought I might be able to outrun him. Swing around back to my house and get my gun, but there was another guy waiting outside. I got trapped between him and Devereaux."

"He had another man on the other side of your house, too. Doesn't matter. You're safe now. But we can't stay around here. That was Devereaux who got away?"

"Yes."

"Is there anything you need from the house?"

"Another coat. That son of a bitch took my barn jacket. And my cell phone. Where are we going?"

"Across the river to Demarco's house."

Irene said, "I don't think you'll make it across the bridge. Devereaux saw your trucks. He'll give Proctor a description. They'll catch you if you use the bridge."

Beck nodded. He knew Irene was right, but he didn't have any place else.

She said, "Don't worry. I have somewhere we can go."

"How far?"

"Twenty minutes."

"All right. Demarco and I will check your house with you. Make sure no one else is around. You get what you need, and we're out of here."

It took them five minutes to search every part of Irene's house while Irene grabbed clothes, her Glock 17 from under her mattress, her passport, and all the money she had in the house – six hundred and seventeen dollars. Devereaux had left her barn jacket on the kitchen floor and grabbed his coat when he cut through the house out to the road. Irene picked up her coat and looked for her cell phone. Gone.

While Demarco cleared the inside of the house, Beck checked the outside. He found the unlocked Bilco door. He used Irene's bike lock to secure it.

Beck put Irene in his truck and went back to talk to Ciro and Demarco who were standing near Demarco's truck.

"Irene said she has a house where she can hide out. I'll take her there and try to find out whatever I can." Beck pulled Oscar Lund's driver's license and handed it to Demarco. "Go find this asshole. Find out everything he knows about the Kin. We've killed two of them. No turning back now."

Ciro Baldassare had entered war mode. He met Beck's gaze but said nothing.

Demarco said, "Got it. Better you talk to her without us there. But like you said, James, fucking around time is over. Whatever these people know, we have to find out."

Beck nodded. He headed for his truck. Ciro and Demarco climbed into the Honda.

Emmett Devereaux watched them from fifty feet back in the forest. Two of his men lay dead. He had already tried to call Abel Proctor. Now he tried a second time. This time Proctor answered. Devereaux was terse.

"I got two dead. The girl is gone. This ends now, Abel. We need to meet with Camdyn. Tonight. Vic has to be there, too."

There was a slight pause and then Proctor said, "Agreed."

33

By the time Demarco and Ciro were nearing Oscar Lund's location, darkness had fallen. The GPS on the Honda Ridgeline showed that they were close to the address on Lund's license, but there was no sign of a house.

Demarco stopped his truck.

He asked Ciro, "Did we pass anything that looked like a road or driveway?"

"Hard to tell in this light. I didn't see anything on my side."

"Let's keep going. It has to be on my side. The drop off is too steep on your side."

Demarco edged forward. A minute later, he spotted a narrow, two-track road on his left. There was no mailbox. No posting. Nothing indicating there was a house at the end of the narrow road. Demarco turned left and edged up the path. Even though winter had diminished the foliage, his headlights illuminated shadbush, woodbine, and viburnum on both sides of the narrow road. Bare Virginia creeper vines encroached everywhere. It almost seemed like driving in a tunnel.

Demarco stopped and turned off his lights. Everything turned dark.

Ciro said, "Shit. You think we can see where we're going?"

"We'd better. If he's up there, he'll see the truck if we go any closer."

Demarco grabbed his Mossberg Shockwave and positioned his Glock in his waistband at his right hip. He handed Ciro the Ruger PC carbine.

"Take this. It's set up to take Glock magazines."

"Okay."

Ciro had his Smith & Wesson .45 under his belt in front where he could reach it. He'd fired the gun five times at Devereaux's man. He had five shots left. Demarco reached behind and opened one of the ammunition boxes on the back seat. He pulled out four magazines loaded with nine-millimeter ammunition. He handed two magazines to Ciro.

There was barely enough room to get out of the Honda and walk around to the front of the truck. Demarco's black Ridgeline blocked the only way in and out. Neither of them spoke as they picked their way along the snow covered path, their eyes slowly adjusting to the dark.

Demarco carried the shotgun by the bird's head stock. He'd moved away from Ciro to make it harder for anyone shooting at them.

Ciro's voice had dropped to a whisper. "If someone is up there, they'll have the high ground."

"It won't help them if they can't see us."

Ciro looked over at Demarco. All his clothes, from hat to boots, were dark. His skin tone was dark. He seemed to merge with the night. Ciro's dark overcoat and gray wool pants also made him difficult to see.

They trudged up fifty yards of hard going, then stepped into a cleared area. They were only ten yards from Oscar Lund's house when they could make out its shape. There were no lights burning anywhere on the property.

Ciro said, "Looks empty."

They stopped and stared at Oscar Lund's dark, rundown house. There were no vehicles in sight. Most of the trees around the property had been cut down, letting in a bit of moonlight. They could make out the shapes of other structures and assorted piles of junk on the property.

Ciro said, "There's nobody in there."

"Let's make sure."

As they stepped toward the house, they tripped a motion sensor, and spotlights flooded the area with blinding white light.

Ciro cursed. Both of them dropped down, expecting gunfire. Nothing happened.

Ciro looked for Demarco. There was a rusted snow plow off to his left. Somehow Demarco had been fast enough to get behind it. Ciro was flat on the ground, but there was nothing in front of him to stop a bullet.

Demarco had placed the barrel of his shotgun on top of the plow, his head just high enough to watch the house.

Ciro stood up, announced, "Fuck this," and headed for the house, holding the Ruger in his right hand. He walked two steps up onto the small porch and kicked in the front door. He stood in the doorway and yelled, "Knock, knock!" Then he found a light switch and turned on the inside lights.

Demarco came in behind him. He moved quickly into the house, his shotgun ready. They split up and checked all the rooms upstairs and down.

When they returned to the living room, Ciro dropped onto a couch covered in a threadbare plaid blanket.

"Tell me we have the right house."

"We have the right house. I saw mail with the guy's name on it."

"Where do they fucking deliver it?"

"It's addressed to a post office box."

Ciro made a face. "Okay. Now what?"

Suddenly, the security lights clicked off, turning everything outside black. Demarco walked over and maneuvered the broken front door shut.

Ciro said, "It's the same temperature in here as outside."

"What do you expect with no front door?"

Demarco walked over to an old Honeywell thermostat shaped like a clock. The temperature was set for fifty-five. He turned it to seventy-five degrees. A furnace kicked on. A blower pushed air into the room, first the cool air in the ducts and then warmer air.

Demarco curled his nose and said, "Smells like dead mice."

Ciro said, "Yeah. Well, better than a dead guy. You think what's-his-name is dead?"

"Probably. I think his Kin buddies figured he spilled since we let him live. They're cleaning house."

"They ought to actually clean this shithole while they're at it. Better yet, burn it down."

"Let's see what we find before they decide to do just that."

They started in the main room, looking under the filthy throw carpet, shoving everything off a long bookshelf, rifling through a breakfront cabinet. Demarco took out a tactical folding knife, sliced open the back of the couch, and stepped on the cushions. Ciro tossed the couch over and pulled off the fabric covering the frame. He stomped on the flooring, listening for hollow spots.

The kitchen took longer. They searched through cabinets, shelves, and drawers. Then moved on to a utility area off the kitchen with a second sink and more shelves. They found a Kimber Mako semi-auto in the refrigerator. Boxes of ammo in a large stoneware jug under a butcher block worktable in the kitchen. Ciro found a plastic grocery bag, and Demarco dropped the Kimber and ammunition into it. In the back of a typical junk drawer, Ciro found a three-inch roll of bills. He held it in the palm of his hand and got a sense of the weight.

"Three thousand. You want the over or under? Fifty bucks."

Demarco said, "Under. I can tell from here that's light on hundreds."

Ciro dropped the roll into the grocery bag. "We'll see about that, eagle eye."

In Lund's den, they pulled all the long guns off his gun rack and found more ammunition in his desk drawers. There was nothing else of value in the room.

Ciro said, "We're supposed to find out everything we can about the Kin. So far, we've got jack shit."

"What's next? Upstairs or downstairs?"

"Downstairs," said Ciro. "The good stuff is always hidden in the basement."

"I will defer to your greater experience."

The lighting in the basement came from bare bulbs screwed into overhead fixtures. Not enough to see clearly in the mix of different sections and levels. At the back of the basement, they found a safe behind a stack of old furniture and bundles of roofing shingles.

Ciro said, "What'd I tell you?"

Demarco looked at the safe and said, "Where are Ricky and Jonas when you need them?"

"We don't need the Bolo brothers for this tin can."

The safe was almost four feet tall by three feet wide. Ciro went back to a section of the basement where he'd seen an old workbench and tools scattered around. He returned with a four-pound sledgehammer, a twelve-inch cold chisel, and a five-foot crowbar. He used the chisel and the sledgehammer to pound open a section where the top of the door met the body of the safe. He did the same in the middle of the door. He inserted the head of the crowbar into the spaces and used his weight and strength to pry back and forth, using the leverage the five-foot crowbar gave him. He went back and forth between the top and side of the door opening the spaces wider and wider until the door popped free of the locking bars. He kicked the door wide open, revealing the contents.

Demarco clapped three times.

"Not bad. Less than five minutes. Didn't know you were so proficient in safe-cracking."

"More like safe-breaking. There was a time when I had to do whatever it took to make my nut."

"Old skills come in handy."

"Don't take much skill to open this piece of shit. The dumb fuck bolted it to the floor thinking that makes it more secure. It makes it easier to pry open."

Demarco shined his cell phone light into the interior of the safe. There were two shelves. Twelve ledger books filled the first shelf. On the second shelf were two aluminum ice cube trays holding 1-ounce gold Krugerrand coins. On the bottom of the safe were manila folders, a lockbox, and a small Trejo Model 1 machine pistol.

Ciro pulled out the lockbox and smacked it once with the small sledgehammer and chisel. It popped open, and thirty-five thousand in hundred-dollar bills spilled out.

"Not bad," said Ciro.

Demarco asked, "How much you think the gold is worth?"

"How many are there?"

Demarco counted them quickly, five at a time. "Eighty-four."

"All one ounce?"

"Yes."

As he bent over to rummage around the bottom of the safe, Ciro said, "They're each worth about two grand. A hundred-sixty-eight thousand in a six-hundred dollar safe. How stupid is that?"

"Don't discount that he lives in the middle of nowhere with his guns and security lights."

"All of which could work against him." Ciro stood up, holding the Trejo machine pistol. "Look at this little guy."

"What is it?"

"Fucking thing is a machine pistol. Fully automatic. I think it has eight rounds." He shoved it into the pocket of his overcoat.

Demarco said, "Interesting. I wonder if he buried more goodies around here someplace?"

"Probably. But there's no way to find it on a million acres covered with junk at night."

Demarco had been thumbing through one of the ledger books. He held one up. "These are worth something."

"Why?"

"They document a lot of transactions."

"What kind of transactions?"

"Extortion and drugs."

"What's the take?"

"First glance," Demarco scanned a few more pages. "Ballpark, maybe half a million a year. Probably more."

"Okay. We know the Kin is into crime. We kinda knew that before, didn't we?"

"Now we have an idea of how much crime. That's progress. And we didn't have to spend a couple of hours beating on Mr. Lund."

"Good point." Ciro kicked shut the safe door. "A half a million or more dollars for how long?"

Demarco closed one eye and thought about it. "I don't know. Based on the number of ledgers here, ten years. And Lund said he's one of eight district leaders."

"That's what they call 'em."

"Yes."

"That's a lot of money."

"Yes."

"So, where'd all that money go?"

Demarco said, "Good question."

34

Irene wrapped herself in a wool blanket Beck kept in his truck. She'd finally stopped shivering, but she looked wan and shell-shocked. Beck didn't bother her with questions. He sat silently and followed her directions leading him south toward the outskirts of Evans. The last turn took them into a dead-end street near the Hudson River. A row of small houses standing side by side filled the street. Beck felt increasingly trapped as he drove toward the dark cul-de-sac ahead of him.

"Where's the house?"

"We just passed it."

There was no room for driveways between the houses, so most residents had parked their cars and trucks on the street. There was a parking area just before the street ended on the left side with space for about ten cars. Beck backed in. Easier to get out and less chance of anyone connecting him to one of the houses.

Beck carried Irene's bag, his backpack, the Beretta shotgun, and one box of 12-gauge shells. He followed Irene as she led him to the fourth house from the end of the street. She disappeared around the side of the house and reappeared with a key. She had to jiggle the key to get the front door lock to turn. She pushed the door open with her shoulder. Clearly, she had done this before.

They entered a small hallway facing a set of stairs leading to the second floor. To their right was a living room, furnished comfortably – throw rugs, a long couch, coffee table, and inexpensive reproductions of two Florence Knoll armchairs. The kitchen was straight past the living room.

Beck stepped into the living room and set the bags and shotgun on the couch.

"Whose house is this?"

"A friend's. She's away. Her family is going to sell it. No one is using it for now."

The house brought up questions for Beck, along with others, but before he could ask Irene anything, she said, "Look, I just almost got killed and I watched you and two other guys shoot down two men, so I've got a lot of questions. But I have to shower. And eat. Maybe you can find enough food in the kitchen to make a meal. Then we can talk."

"Sure."

Irene grabbed her bag, turned up the thermostat in the hallway, and headed upstairs.

Irene went into a small bathroom on the second floor and turned on the space heater. While she waited for the bathroom to warm up, she went into the bedroom and dumped her bag on the bed. She picked up a pay-as-you-go cell phone she used as a backup that she'd brought from her house. She suspended service to the cell phone Devereaux took, then called Morelli's office and left her new number.

Twenty minutes later, Irene returned downstairs showered, hair washed, her cuts and scrapes cleaned and bandaged. She wore heavy wool socks, sweatpants, and a well-worn green plaid flannel shirt. While Beck stood in the kitchen with his back to Irene, she quietly slipped her Glock 17 between the couch cushions.

Beck had found waffles and sausages in the freezer and maple syrup in a cabinet. He used the oven to toast all the waffles and a frying pan to cook the sausages. There was also coffee in the fridge but no milk. He remembered that Irene drank hers black. By the time she appeared, he had a plate of food and a pot of coffee ready.

When Irene entered the kitchen, he turned to her and said, "You look a lot better."

"I feel better. I'm still so fucking tired I can't see straight, but if I get some food in me, I'll feel better."

Beck warmed up a small pitcher of maple syrup in the microwave. Irene sat at a drop-leaf table under a small window between the kitchen and living room. Beck brought over the food.

"You want coffee?"

"Yes."

"It won't keep you awake?"

"You could give me the whole pot and I'd sleep."

Beck watched Irene dig into the food. He stood near the sink eating a sausage. Lately, every meal was a breakfast.

Watching Irene eat reminded Beck of their night together. A mix of emotions hit him. He could tell Irene wasn't wearing anything under her flannel shirt. He felt a sexual attraction. He felt admiration for the way she'd stepped between him and Procter. He felt worried about her using a fake identity. All of it mixed with rage when he thought about how close Emmett Devereaux had come to killing Irene. He had no doubt that if they hadn't shown up, Devereaux meant to torture her for information. Use her as bait to get to him. And then kill her.

Morelli said Irene had been lucky to get bail. Bullshit. Luck had nothing to do with Morelli getting bail. The Kin had made that happen. They wanted Irene out of jail so Devereaux could kidnap her and use her to get to him. Camdyn Dent, or whoever was in charge, had ordered Procter to make that evidence disappear. Evidence he'd faked to begin with.

Once Irene had eaten something, Beck said, "How do you want to work this? Ask each other questions? You start? Should I?"

"I don't know. Let's just start. Who the hell are you and who were those two guys with you?"

Beck nodded, gathered his thoughts and said, "About fifteen years ago I got arrested, convicted for something that wasn't a crime, and sent to prison. I spent eight years inside before I got exonerated. I met a lot of bad people in prison. Those two men you saw were among the few that were good. The three of us, plus another convict, vowed to help each other survive after prison. The fact that I served time, guilty or not, makes me an ex-con. An outcast. The four of us rely on each other to stay out of prison and stay alive. Covid has kept us apart lately but hasn't changed anything. What about you? Why are you so set against the Kin?"

Irene finished the last bit of her meal and took a sip of coffee.

"Because they're assholes. Because they treat women like shit. Because they hurt people. They hurt someone I was close to. Very badly."

"Why? How?"

"It's complicated. I'm too tired to go into the details. I will, but right now I'd rather ask you what do you think is going to happen to us?"

"All right, but before I answer that, does the Kin know this person they hurt was close to you?"

"No. It happened three years ago. They don't know I was close to her. We kept our relationship private. I left the area before they found out I was part of her life. And I changed my identity. As far as the Kin is concerned, I'm a nobody. Another woman not even worth thinking about, particularly because they think I'm a lesbian."

Beck nodded, encouraged that Irene had admitted changing her identity.

He said, "All right, as far as what is going to happen to us, I think it's pretty clear the Kin wants to kill us. If not you, certainly me."

"Why?"

"Like you said before you took your shower, we shot two of their men. And without going into details, four goons showed up at my house last night looking to beat the shit out of me. The plan was for the sheriffs to take me off to jail after they tuned me up. Without going into details, the Kin assholes got the worst of it."

"You think Devereaux was at my house to kill me?"

"Most likely. After he tortured you and used you to find me."

"Shit, I thought they might pin Joey Collins's murder on me, us, but…"

"Oh, they'll do that for sure. But first they'll kill us. It'll be easier to convict us if we're dead. It takes law enforcement out of the picture. That gives them a free hand to do what they want about the murder. In my experience, that means killing anybody and everybody who had anything to do with it."

"How exactly are they going to convict us? We had nothing to do with it."

Beck began ticking off facts, keeping track with the fingers of his right hand.

"We were there the night of the murder. My bet is somebody used a knife on him. You were seen stabbing Elrod. Proctor found your knife. He had access to the victim's blood at the scene. Your prints are on the knife. So are mine. I moved it when I switched your clothes into my dryer. Proctor will come up with a bullshit motive. Case closed."

"Holy shit. I wonder if someone who wanted Collins dead saw us last night, saw me with the knife, and set up the whole thing."

"I'm wondering the same thing. I'm also pretty sure Proctor and the Kin engineered your release from jail. Not having the evidence for the arraignment, all of it. The ADA was probably in on it too. Devereaux knew you were coming home. How'd you escape?"

"I almost didn't. I wanted to make something to eat, so I washed my hands. When I grabbed the kitchen towel, it wasn't dry. For a second, maybe half a second, I was confused. Then I realized that couldn't be. I hadn't been in the house in like a day. Someone else used that towel. I turned to look around, and there he was, standing outside my kitchen. My goddamn heart stopped. I threw a skillet at him and ran out the back door. It didn't do me any good. Devereaux had guys outside, too. Why did you come to my house?"

"Morelli left me a voice message you got bail, and he took you home. I went over there to talk to you." Beck came over to the small table and sat across from Irene. He leaned across the table. "Irene, we're not going to survive this unless you tell me everything you know about the Kin. Any reason you can think of why someone wanted Joey Collins dead. Everything you know about Andy Miller. What happened with your friend. And what you want from me."

Irene frowned. She stared at Beck. She was about to say something but stopped when she heard tapping on the front door.

35

Outside the row house, Manny Guzman stood waiting. Beck had called him while Irene was in the shower and asked him to come to the Brick Row house. Manny heard footsteps inside. The door swung open. Beck reached out for the bag of groceries Manny was holding and stepped aside to let him enter.

"I hope you have something in here besides bacon and eggs."

"Frozen hamburgers and fries."

"Any chance of a vegetable?"

"Got some apples. Who picked this place, James? A dead-end street?"

"I know. Come in and meet my friend."

Irene had moved from the small dining table to the corner of the couch where she'd hidden the Glock.

Beck said, "Irene Allen, this is my good friend, Manny Guzman. I asked him to meet us here. Manny, Irene."

Manny nodded and smiled. Not something he usually did.

Irene said, "Hi."

"Hello."

Beck took the groceries and told Manny to have a seat. He brought the food to the kitchen. Manny took off his gray wool winter coat and sat in the chair opposite Irene, draping the coat over his knee as if he were only going to stay for a few minutes.

Manny said, "James told me what happened at your house."

Irene nodded. Manny nodded back without saying more.

Just then, Irene's cell phone rang. It startled her. She wasn't accustomed to the ringtone. She pulled it out of her sweatpants pocket. She assumed it was Morelli. Nobody else had the number.

"Hello?"

Manny could hear the voice of the caller. He listened carefully to the conversation.

"It's Morelli. I got your message about a new phone number. Is everything okay?"

"Not exactly. I lost my phone. This is another one."

"Why? What happened?"

Irene paused and then said, "I don't want to get into it right now."

"Why not? Where are you? Are you with Beck?"

"Listen, now isn't a great time. Do you need me to do anything, be somewhere for the court?"

"No. But as your lawyer I need to know where you are."

"I didn't leave town or anything. I'm close by."

Manny took it all in. Clearly, the girl didn't want to give out the location of the house.

Beck came back from the kitchen. He gave Irene a questioning look. She mouthed the word *Morelli*.

Beck motioned for Irene to give him the phone. Irene looked like it wasn't a good idea. Beck motioned again for her to hand him the phone. She did.

"Morelli."

"Beck?"

"Yeah."

"So, you're with Irene?"

"Yes."

"Where are you?"

"Someplace not suitable for our situation."

"What does that mean?"

"There was trouble at Irene's house. We need a place to stay. A place nobody knows about."

"What kind of trouble?"

"Peter, I don't have time for a cross-examination. Can you help me or not? I need a place big enough to sleep six. Something short-term. No more than a couple of weeks. Can you find that for me? If not, I'll figure something else out."

"All right, take it easy. I just don't like operating in the dark. When do you need this place?"

"Tonight."

"It's nearly six o'clock."

"I understand that. I'm hoping you might know somebody who does short-term rentals."

Morelli said, "Look, I know a couple of people. I try my best. But it'll have to be in the area. I can't do anything that would take Irene out of the court's jurisdiction."

"That's fine. I just need something nobody knows about except you and me."

"All right. Understood. Let me get on this and we'll talk later."

"Good."

"Not guaranteeing anything."

"I know. See what you can come up with. Just get back to me within a couple of hours either way."

"I won't need a couple of hours. There's only three people I know who might have something."

"I appreciate it. Call me as soon as you know."

Beck cut the call before Morelli could ask any more questions. Manny asked, "Who's that?"

"The lawyer Phineas recommended. I don't know anybody else who has contacts in the area."

Manny nodded. "Where're Demarco and Ciro?"

"Good question."

Beck dropped down on the couch near Irene. He had arrived at the point where his nagging pain and need for sleep were making him feel nauseated. He closed his eyes and forced himself to keep focused. To concentrate on what he had to do. He still needed answers from Irene. Now that Manny was in the room, it might be more difficult to question her. Then again, it might be to his advantage. The old gangster had a well-honed bullshit detector.

First things first.

He pulled out his phone and sent a text to Demarco. *ETA?*

The answer came back quickly. *Leaving now. Didn't find batboy. But useful info in hse. Where r u?*

Beck texted back the address of the house and: *Get here soon. Watch ur back.*

Beck looked at Irene. "Why'd Morelli call you?"

"I called him. Left my new phone number in case he had to reach me about court appearances or whatever. I didn't think he'd call me now. I didn't want to talk to him. I'm so damned tired I feel like I'm about to pass out."

Beck had no doubt after a night in a county lockup Irene needed sleep. He squinted, scratched his beard and his hair, and decided to ask one more question. "You said this is a friend's house. Is this the friend who had a problem with the Kin?"

Irene hesitated, then said, "Yes."

Beck gave her a questioning look. "What kind of friend was she?"

"A good friend." Beck waited for more. Irene said, "Not a girl-friend. Not a lover. Although that's the relationship she wanted. I wasn't so sure. But I did care about her. A lot. And she's gone now. Dead. She won't be returning to this house."

Beck nodded. There was more he wanted to ask, but he decided it could wait. The little bit Irene said explained a great deal.

36

When Devereaux told Proctor that Beck and his men had killed two of his men, Proctor knew he had lost control. Emmett Devereaux would not stop until Irene Allen and James Beck were dead. Even Camdyn Dent wouldn't be able to stop Devereaux. Not that he would want to. Dent had already made it clear that anyone who had anything to do with the death of Joey Collins had to answer for it.

Of course, Emmett wanted a meeting with Dent. No need to go off on his own when he knew Dent would agree with him.

A meeting with Camdyn Dent was also fine with Vic Myer, the last member of the triumvirate that ran the Kin. Myer relished any opportunity to endear himself to the supreme leader.

Proctor knew a meeting with Dent could bring problems. But it was unavoidable. Problems were already at hand. At least he would find out what Dent wanted done, which would give him a better chance to distance himself from the carnage.

Proctor pulled into the parking area near the red barn a little before seven. The meeting with Dent was scheduled for seven. Most customers didn't show up at the Field until nine or ten. If anyone happened by during the meeting, George Myer would make sure they didn't come near the barn.

As Proctor approached the back door to the barn, he saw George Myer sitting outside the entrance, his baseball bat laid across his lap. He nodded at Proctor as he entered the barn. Proctor saw Devereaux and Vic sitting at a table with four mismatched chairs.

It was quiet in the dilapidated barn. No one was preparing food yet. There was nothing competing with the barn smells.

Vic Myer and Emmett Devereaux sat across from each other. Proctor sat next to Vic, facing Devereaux.

Proctor felt a wave of fatigue come over him. He'd been running on too little sleep for too long. He checked his watch. One minute after seven. The back door opened. George Myer stepped in. All eyes turned to him. Big George had nothing to say. He looked around and stepped back outside.

Camdyn Dent pulled off Route 26 and onto a side road. He slowly drove into a small clearing on his right, pulled over, and parked. When he shut down his car and turned off the lights, the vehicle disappeared into the dark.

It took him five minutes to walk to the Field. He entered the barn in the front, not the back. Only he and the Myer brothers had a key to the padlock that secured the chain on the double doors out front.

For all of his life, even when he was too young to realize it, Camdyn Dent's future had been predetermined. At the age of sixteen, his father sat him down and told Dent that their family was one of four that provided the supreme leader for a secret organization known as the Kin. Camdyn had a general understanding of the Kin and knew his father had a leadership position; he did not know that his father held the position of supreme leader. Nor did he know that his father intended to do everything he could to ensure his son followed him into the leadership role. Camdyn's father explained to him that nothing would change until he finished his schooling and entered a career path. At that point, preparations for him to take on the leadership of the Kin would begin in earnest. Once he became supreme leader, Camdyn would hide his identity by living two lives. One in the public arena pursuing a typical career. The other life among the Kin. This was the way of the Kin.

Six years after that talk with his father, the son stepped into the role of supreme leader. His father died one year later. By then, Camdyn Dent had become accustomed to keeping his true identity secret, whether hiding in plain sight or hiding in the dark as he did this night, walking along a country road with the hood of his gray parka pulled over his head. Nobody saw him on the road. And nobody saw him enter the barn.

Vic Myer looked at his watch.

"He's a little late."

Peter Morelli stepped into the light and said, "Not really. I've been gathering my thoughts."

And listening to any comments, thought Proctor, happy that he'd kept his mouth shut.

Peter Morelli/Camdyn Dent slipped into the empty chair next to Emmett Devereaux, barely acknowledging the other men sitting at the table. He looked around at the interior of the old barn, saying nothing. Then he continued talking calmly, quietly, knowing they would listen carefully to every word.

"You know, I'm sure that at times we don't fully grasp how powerfully and efficiently our system works. Why our day-to-day operations carry on, almost on autopilot." Dent took a moment to look at the other three men at the table. "I'm not discounting all the work you three do. It's just that one could question why our system needs a man on top, hiding in the shadows, far above the fray. But let me remind you that we did not create our system. We did not create the Kin. There was a Kin long before any of us. Before our fathers and grandfathers and their fathers." Dent waved a hand as if to say that even speaking about this was irrelevant. "I've long ago stopped trying to parse out the wisdom of our ways. How can you describe something you can't really see? Yes, there is a structure. We have our working-class rural men and women. I think of them as the backbone of what we are. Victor's people." Dent paused to smile at Vic Myer. A smile that communicated his pleasure at how they extracted profit from dependency. Not just the dependency created by drug addiction but also a dependency on the tribal values that the Kin instilled in its followers.

He turned toward Devereaux. "Then we have Emmett and his people, those descended from the original stock. The tip of our spear, as they say." Dent took a moment to gaze into the dark eyes of Emmett Devereaux, nodding his approval of a psychopath unconstrained by normal human values.

"And, of course, there's Abel." Dent actually leaned across the table to pat Proctor's arm. "Our agent controlling the fools who think they are capable of enforcing society's rules on us."

Dent smiled, looking at the three men sitting with him.

"We have our structure and our roles within it. But don't confuse any of that with the true force behind the Kin." He held up both hands and formed them into fists. "The source of our strength, what makes what we do possible is who…we…are." Dent paused to let the words sink in. "We are the rightful leaders of this world we live in. Always have been. Always will be. It's our God-given right. We didn't choose it. It chose us. It's the underlying bedrock of reality that we cannot deny. As they say nowadays – it is, what it is. And always will be. You want to call it white supremacy, fine. You want to call it God's will. Fine. I don't care what you call it. *It* will prevail."

Dent relaxed his fists and said, "I've talked too much," and then continued right on talking, knowing his quiet, careful manner of speaking had captured them. "Enough of the history lesson. Remember what I'm telling you, but don't think we can be complacent. Right now, as we four sit here, the Kin is under attack. First, there's the murder of Joseph Collins. Descended from one of our leading families. Who would dare something like it? Have we become that weak?" Dent looked around the table for an answer to his questions. There were none. He shrugged imperceptibly and said, "The reality speaks for itself. The only question now is — what do we do about it?" Dent spoke more forcefully. "We make it clear that such a thing cannot stand. We cut out the cancer. Expunge anyone and everyone who had anything to do with it. We've started with Oscar Lund. Emmett, I take it you didn't get any information from him on who killed Joseph."

"No. He talked. Mostly a bunch of complaints and excuses. Nothing useful."

Dent nodded. "Abel told me he looked into Hamm Elrod. You believed his denials?"

"I did. But he's caused enough trouble on his own to justify his removal."

"I agree."

Devereaux said, "I can take care of him any time. He's not first on the list."

Dent nodded, "No he isn't. We know who is."

Devereaux said, "James Beck, Irene Allen, and Beck's men. They killed two of mine, sir."

Myer jumped in, "And crippled three of mine."

Dent turned his gaze toward Proctor.

"And tried to take me out, too. Yes. They must be dealt with."

Dent asked, "Dealt with how?"

Proctor measured his words carefully. He and Dent had already conspired to get Irene out of jail so they could find Beck. Somehow the timing hadn't worked. The ploy had turned disastrous. Or perhaps it had played out exactly the way Dent wanted with Beck showing up just in time to kill Devereaux's men. Proctor had long ago stopped trying to sort through Camdyn Dent's strategies. His objective was to go along with Dent while keeping open the possibility of achieving his own goals.

"I'll be brief. I agree Beck and the woman have to go. Even if they had nothing to do with the murder of Joey Collins. We've been looking into Beck. He's an ex-con. Served time for manslaughter. Irene Allen has been mouthing off about the Kin. She stabbed Hamm Elrod. I've got enough evidence to convict them. I say we kill them. Pin the Collins murder on them. Grotowski will agree to try them in absentia and he'll get a conviction. For all I know, they might have actually killed him. That takes law enforcement out of the picture. Frees us up to take whatever measures we need to make sure nobody ever even thinks about touching any man in the Kin."

Dent looked around the table for any reaction. There was none.

"I agree with you, Abel. And you, Emmett. Beck and the girl have to pay for the damage they have done to us. Along with the mongrel crew of criminals helping Beck."

Dent looked around the table to make sure he had everyone's attention.

"So far, we've underestimated Mr. Beck. I suppose that's understandable. He's a moderately intelligent white man with a decent amount of cunning who appears to have accumulated a certain amount of ill-gotten money." Dent flicked his hand dismissively. "Doesn't matter." Dent leaned forward. "I've already put into place a plan that will eliminate James Beck, Irene Allen, and his men, tonight."

Camdyn Dent paused to look into the eyes of the three men sitting with him. He looked for doubt in their eyes. He wanted to see skepticism. It would make him seem all the more powerful when he explained his plan. He waited, giving them a chance to voice doubt. None did. Dent continued.

"Here's what I need. Victor, you must provide a dozen reliable shooters. Men who will shoot to kill without hesitation." Dent checked his watch. "We have four hours to get them into position at a location forty minutes from here."

Myer responded, suddenly swept up by his supreme leader.

"A dozen shooters? Absolutely. No problem. I got ex-military who will answer the call. Damn good shooters. I've got my pick of experienced hunters who can put a bullet where they want it. More than enough to get a dozen. You gonna describe to me what they'll be doing?"

"I am." Dent turned to Devereaux. "Emmett, I'll need ten of your best men who can spot anyone moving through dark woods in a relatively small area. A couple of acres. In tonight's crescent-moon light. Men who are willing to take them out if they see them, without hesitation."

"Same time frame, I assume."

"Yes."

"I'll be there with ten of my best."

Everyone at the table felt the energy surging. The supreme leader actually had a plan. Their belief in him soared.

"Good. Abel, you're going to set up roadblocks for a half-mile-long section of Route 432 starting around midnight tonight. You'll be blocking off the entrance road to a house a half mile in. Your job is to ensure no one gets in or out until I give you the all-clear."

Proctor nodded, pleased that he wouldn't be part of the killing. Setting up the roadblock would be easy. He'd make it look like standard sobriety checkpoints.

"Yessir."

"Good. Now, here's what each of you and your men has to do." Dent took out a road map, opened it, and laid it on the table. Then he carefully explained how he planned on slaughtering James Beck, Irene Allen, and all of Beck's men. And how they should dispose of the bodies.

Dent folded up his map and ended his meeting by reaching into the breast pocket of his suit jacket and extracting a folded piece of paper. He slid the paper to Emmett Devereaux.

"When we complete tonight's action, we go to phase two. Emmett, I want you to make the people on this list disappear. Let me know if you need anything from Victor or Abel." Dent looked around the table one last time. "And then, my brothers, we will return to our normal operations."

37

Beck wasn't going to stop questioning Irene now. He sat in the Knoll knockoff chair next to Manny Guzman so he could look directly at Irene sitting opposite him on the couch.

"What happened to your friend, Irene?"

Irene Allen's face hardened. Her eyes narrowed. For a second, Beck thought she was trying to suppress tears. But it wasn't tears. It was anger. Irene took a deep breath and exhaled slowly. She looked away and retreated into herself, clearly reluctant to relive what had happened. Then she turned to Beck and said, "Back before I left for Maine, about three years ago, I found out that Deborah was dealing drugs for the Kin. I don't know how long she was doing it or at what level. All I know is she got arrested."

"Who arrested her?"

"The DEA. They sent her to the federal detention center in Brooklyn. They wouldn't let me see her. I talked to her on the phone twice. She said they were trying to get her to testify against the Kin."

Beck was surprised that a federal agency had been investigating the Kin. Clearly, they were selling significant quantities of drugs.

"They offered her a plea deal?"

"Yes."

"I presume she had a lawyer."

"Yes. Someone downstate. She didn't tell me much about him. The next thing I heard, one of the prisoners beat her up. I don't think it was too bad. Whoever did it told her to keep her mouth shut."

"How'd you hear that? From Deborah?"

"No. From a DEA agent who showed up at my apartment."

"What did he want?"

"He wanted me to tell Deborah she should take the plea deal and testify against the Kin. He told me about the assault. Said he wanted to get the plea deal done and get her out of the detention center and into a witness protection program."

"How did he know you were connected to Deborah?"

"I was with her when they arrested her. In this house."

"That's when you found out she was dealing drugs?"

"Yes."

"How'd you know it was for the Kin?"

"Because everybody knows they control the drug trade around here."

"What did you say to him when he asked you to convince Deborah to testify?"

"I said I would try."

"Did you talk to her?"

"No. I didn't get the chance. Deborah got attacked again. This time they had to send her to a hospital. She had a concussion, a broken nose, and a fractured eye socket. And something wrong with her neck."

"How did you find out about that?"

"Same DEA agent. He phoned me. By then, I was half out of my mind with worry. I was convinced that the Kin knew I was talking to the feds. I told that guy I wouldn't talk to him anymore until he got her out of the detention center and into witness protection. I hung up on him."

"Then what?"

"The hospital discharged Deborah, and those fucking assholes sent her back to the Brooklyn MDC. She committed suicide three days later. At least that's what the prison people called it."

"How?"

"I don't know exactly. I heard about it from Deborah's mother. She was too upset to give me any details."

"You don't think Deborah killed herself?"

"I don't know. Either the Kin drove her to it, or they had somebody do it. Either way, she died, and the Kin got what they wanted."

Beck nodded. Irene's story brought up questions.

"Do you think Deborah played a major role in the Kin's drug business?"

Irene didn't hesitate. She shook her head. "No. No way. First of all, she was a woman. The Kin doesn't put women in positions of power. She told me she just delivered drugs. She wasn't selling."

"What do you think she could have told the DEA?"

"I guess who was supplying her. Isn't that what they do? Start with the underlings and work their way up?"

Beck watched Irene closely. She looked at Beck and said, "The Kin is more ruthless than you can imagine."

Beck had no trouble at all imagining a drug gang being ruthless. He just hadn't imagined them operating in upstate New York. Or how they could have arranged a murder in a downstate federal detention center.

"What was Deborah's last name?"

"Ramirez."

"So you left after she died?"

"Yes. I didn't even go to her funeral. I called her mother, Marie, and asked when it would be. She told me not to come. She said two men showed up at her house asking about me."

"This house?"

"Yeah. Marie was still living here."

"Where's Marie now?"

"She's in a senior care place over near Philmont."

"Did these two men ask for you by name?"

"No. It was more general than that. They were asking for Deborah's girlfriend. I knew it wasn't the DEA. They knew how to find me. It had to be the Kin."

"What did Marie tell them?"

"She said she didn't know anything about Deborah's friends. Anyhow, with Deborah gone, I was already thinking about moving. Two Kin guys looking for me clinched it. I rented a van, packed up everything I could load in a day, left a note and the keys for my landlord, and headed for Maine."

"That's when you changed your name?"

Irene nodded. "Yes. Like I told you, I didn't think the Kin knew who I was, but I decided to make a change. I found this nerd who had a reputation as a hacker. Helped me put together a new identity. Enough to get a driver's license and a birth certificate. I worked off the books even after I got a social security number. Worked like a fucking immigrant. It sucked."

Beck nodded and said, "Why'd you come back?"

"I was living with someone I didn't want to be with. It was hard to get a job where I was. I figured enough time had passed. But most of all, I came back because I never forgot what happened to Deborah. I never stopped wanting to do something about it."

"Like what?"

This time it wasn't a gentle tapping on the door that interrupted Irene. It was a jaunty shave-and-a-haircut, two-bits knock.

Manny said, "Ciro."

Beck nodded and answered the door.

"Welcome," said Beck as he stood aside for Ciro Baldassare and Demarco Jones. The two men entered, nearly filling the living room. Ciro carried a large shopping bag. Demarco pulled a battered suitcase he'd found in Oscar Lund's basement.

"Home from the hunt," announced Ciro, holding up his bag of ledgers and folders. He was about to say more when he noticed Irene huddled on the couch and then downplayed it by saying, "A few mementos."

He turned to Irene and said, "Hello there, young lady. I'm Ciro." He pointed to Demarco, "And this gentleman is Demarco."

Irene stood up, introduced herself, and shook both their hands. Standing in front of the two men made her look tiny. And vulnerable.

Ciro turned to Guzman and said, "Emmanuel, what are you doing sittin' around? Why aren't you in the kitchen? Is there any food? I was thinking of shooting a deer on the way here."

Demarco took the bag from Ciro and set it on the small dining table near the kitchen. He parked the suitcase next to the table, hung his coat on the chair, and started unloading the ledgers and folders.

Manny and Ciro headed for the kitchen.

Irene remained standing. She said to Beck, "I'm sure you want to talk to your friends. Let me go upstairs and get some sleep."

Beck thought about going with her and finishing their conversation. He wanted an answer to his last question. But seeing how exhausted she looked, he let it go.

Irene retrieved her Glock from between the couch cushions. She held the gun pointed down and shrugged at Beck. "After what happened at my house, I decided to keep this with me."

"Understandable. When was the last time you fired that gun?"

Demarco looked up when he heard the word gun.

Irene said, "Five, six months ago."

"Where?"

"Behind my house."

"At what?"

"Bottles of soda."

"You hit anything?"

"Yes."

"Did you clean the gun after?"

"No."

"Do me a favor and let Demarco check your weapon. He's familiar with Glocks."

Demarco was already at Irene's side. He gently took the gun from her. He released the magazine. It was fully loaded. Then he ejected the round in the chamber, pulled off the slide, and took out the spring and barrel. As soon as he did that, he noticed the cover plate at the end of the slide was loose. He slipped off the plate with his thumb and said, "Well, you don't have to clean this gun. You don't have to do anything to it."

"Okay."

"No, not okay." Demarco held up the cover plate. "This isn't supposed to come off like that. Somebody took out the firing mechanism. You pull the trigger on this gun and nothing will happen." He handed back the disassembled gun to Irene. "I take it you don't keep your weapons locked up."

"I keep my gun under my mattress where I can get to it."

Demarco nodded. "I get that. But so can anybody else."

Irene grimaced. "Like the bastard who broke into my house."

"Was he one of those two pointing a gun at you?"

"Yeah. The one on my front porch. Emmett Devereaux."

Irene's expression tightened as she remembered her plan to get back into her house and get her gun. A gun Devereaux had made useless.

From the kitchen, Ciro said, "Don't worry, kid. Demarco will give you another Glock. One that works."

Irene left the gun parts on an end table and headed upstairs without another word.

Beck and the others waited until she closed the door to the bedroom, then they gathered in the kitchen, speaking softly so she wouldn't hear them.

Manny had been laying out food on the counter next to the refrigerator. He stopped and turned around. Ciro stood next to him, resting against the kitchen counter. Beck folded his arms and faced them, leaning against the counter that separated the kitchen from the main room. Demarco remained at the kitchen table.

Ciro said, "So what's with the broad, Jimmy? She's cute."

"She is." Beck looked at Manny. "What do you think, Manolito?"

Manny squinted one eye and tipped his head. Beck watched Manny thinking it through. He noticed his friend's hair and mustache had turned grayer during the months he hadn't seen him. He looked more tired. None of that mattered. Beck knew that Manny Guzman could size up devious, dangerous, lying criminals half asleep.

Manny said, "Maybe she's cute in a couple of ways. Obviously, she didn't tell you everything. Nobody does. I could guess at what she left out, but that's a waste of time. What she did tell you, she believes is true."

Beck said, "What did you think about her wanting to do something about what the Kin did to her friend?"

Manny said, "She didn't get a chance to answer your question. Don't matter. I don't think she has much of an idea how to get payback for her friend."

Ciro said, "Hey, we all know that little woman ain't going up against a local gang. She's trying to get you to help her, Jimmy. You got into a beef at that drinking hole. Sheriff guy tries to arrest you, she jumps in. Not to mention she jumped into your bed pretty quick."

Beck shook his head. "That doesn't quite make sense. She didn't know anything about me. Why would she think I'd help her get revenge on the Kin?"

Demarco said, "How much did she need to know? She sees you at that drinking hole looking like a surly bastard with your black beard and don't-fuck-with-me face. You put one of the Kin tough guys on his ass. That's enough for her to take a run at you."

Beck said, "I don't know. I'll press her on it when I get a chance. What did you find out at Lund's house?"

Ciro said, "Good stuff. Long guns. Small guns. Records. Money."

Beck said, "What records?"

From his chair at the table Demarco held up a ledger book. "Records of their take selling drugs and extorting dues. It looks like more money than you'd expect."

Beck said, "How much more?"

"According to these ledgers, Lund's take was taking in north of a half-million a year in payments from locals. I assume for protection or whatever. And assuming he told us the truth while you were tapping him on the head with that bat, he runs one of eight territories or districts, whatever they call it. So you can multiply what he took in by eight."

Ciro asked, "Adding up to what?"

Demarco tapped an open ledger on the table. "Skimming through this one ledger Lund was collecting a hundred and fifty bucks a month from two-hundred eighty-three families. Adds up to five hundred grand and change. Multiplied by eight is a little over four million."

Ciro said, "Shit. That's a nice little pile. Pays a lot of overhead."

Demarco opened the suitcase and lifted out more ledgers and folders, and the aluminum trays filled with gold Krugerrands. He placed everything on the table. Then he dropped four thick rolls of cash onto the table. "It took us fifteen minutes to find a couple hundred grand in gold and cash. Who knows how much more he buried around his property."

Beck said, "Gold? What is he? A pirate?"

"Gold is a favored asset of Nazis, conspiracy theorists, and a variety of criminals. And like Ciro said, the extortion money funds their operations. The big money is in the drug sales."

Ciro said, "Okay, this is getting interesting now. I was thinking the best move would be to just get the hell out of here. Hide out on a warm beach after humping around in this freezing weather. Take the little woman if you want, James. But maybe this could be good for us. D, what do those ledgers tell you about their drug operation?"

Demarco kept turning pages. "The bookkeeping is primitive. Lists and columns of numbers under abbreviations which I assume refer to oxy, heroin, fentanyl, and meth."

Ciro said, "That's classic, man. Start them on oxy, move on up from twenties to forties to sixties to eighties. Then when the pills don't work, shift to heroin. When that don't work, bump it with powdered fentanyl."

Manny said, "Squeeze every dime out of the poor bastards until they either OD or go to jail. What about the meth sales? That shit can be very profitable depending on supply."

Demarco had been making calculations on one of the folders.

Beck leaned back against the counter and listened to three life-long criminals piece together a picture of a drug trade and extortion that had gone on for years. They spoke of profit margins on the spectrum of drugs sold by the Kin. They discussed how financing their drug business with dues extorted from families enhanced the profit margins. Speculated on the number of people the Kin had addicted, factoring in that the Kin had trapped multiple generations in a single family.

Finally, Beck asked the question. "So, what's the net boys? Roughly."

Manny said, "We're working from one set of numbers, filling in gaps. Best guess, I'd say you're looking at a net profit of twenty million a year. But we don't know how it's divided. How many bosses are at the top?"

Beck said, "Based on what I know, I'd say it's Emmett Devereaux, their enforcer. Probably that sheriff's investigator, Abel Proctor, who's covering the law enforcement end. Maybe those two guys who run the Field. I'd say they're in charge of the day-to-day operations. They probably split a full share. And then the boss of bosses, someone named Camdyn Dent."

Ciro said, "That's a small group."

Manny said, "And we don't know how long they've been running this thing. We have twelve years of ledgers. Is that it?"

Beck said, "Based on what I've heard, the Kin has been in business for generations."

Ciro quietly said, "How long is a generation?"

Beck said, "Twenty or thirty years. I think this thing has been going on for easily a hundred years."

Ciro said, "That's a hell of a lot of money."

Beck said, "And a hell of a lot of misery."

Manny said, "It's an interesting situation. Has to involve a lot of close ties to operate that long. Their angle about protecting their way of life isn't all that new. Making it work with so many outside their gang is a hell of a trick."

Beck nodded. "They're more efficient at grooming a dependent population."

Demarco said, "They can't have been running a drug racket for generations. They'd have killed off their clientele years ago."

Beck asked, "What's the lifespan of an addict?"

Ciro said, "It ain't thirty years, that's for sure."

"I have the feeling the Kin started out differently and morphed into a horrifying enterprise. Life for these people has gone in one direction for decades. Downhill."

Demarco said, "Yes. Their schools are shit, their jobs are shit, their housing is shit, their healthcare is shit. It's no mystery they turn to cheap meth, bootleg oxy, Mexican heroin, and Chinese fentanyl."

Manny said, "And pay dues for the privilege. So, now what?"

Beck looked at each man. Ciro stood against the counter sipping coffee. His white shirt, dark blue cashmere sweater, and gray wool pants weren't as pressed and fresh as usual. A salt and pepper stubble darkened his face. None of it diminished his power.

Manny stood near Ciro, reserved and into himself, his workman's clothes the same as always, his arms crossed against his chest. Poker-faced.

Because he was sitting, Demarco didn't look as physically imposing as usual.

The three men were Beck's tribe. His crew. Partners. Outcasts. Brothers. Four men who would actually die for each other. That's what made Manny's question so important.

Beck repeated the question.

"Now what? We know where we came from and where we stand. Someone bumps into you out in the prison yard, looks at you sideways, you put him down. Hard. Otherwise, it never ends." Beck shrugged. "Whoever these guys are, they want me dead. And unfortunately, that includes you. Yeah, we could get the hell out of here. Take the girl with us if she wants to go. But running never solved anything. And these people seem to have a long reach. At least long enough to arrange a murder in a Brooklyn federal detention center. I don't want to look over my shoulder for the rest of my life any more than I already do.

"I gotta admit there's something about the way these pricks operate, the misery they're spreading, that pisses me off. But we're not thieves, and we're not social workers or cops. Whatever the fuck the Kin is – white supremacists, peckerwoods, fascists, citizen militia, a drug gang, whatever they are – we have to deal with them."

Beck paused, then repeated Manny's question. "So, now what? Now we take them down. Destroy their ability to hurt us. What does that mean? Take out their leaders. Kill enough of them so they wish they never tried to hurt us? How do we do that? I don't know. All I know right now is that I can't do it without you. And the next couple of steps. That's all I know."

The silence filling the kitchen lasted only four seconds before Ciro patted Beck on the shoulder and said, "You'll figure out the rest, Jimmy."

Manny Guzman nodded but said nothing.

Demarco stood up, rising to his full height, suddenly seeming like he had taken over a whole section of the kitchen area, and said, "So, what's the very next step, James?"

Beck said, "Getting the hell out of this little house on a dead-end street."

38

Beck was wrong about the very next step. There were several steps before they left the house on Brick Row.

Manny cooked hamburgers and fries. Beck and the others ate. They pulled up maps on their cell phones to check out the location of the safehouse Morelli had rented for them.

Ciro and Demarco decided to stop at the Walmart outside Belleville to get boots for Ciro. His black leather zip-up ankle boots weren't any good for tramping through the Hudson Valley in winter. Walmart was open until midnight, so they would be the first to leave.

Manny and Beck agreed on something Manny had to do before he headed for the safehouse.

While the others packed up, Beck walked quietly up the stairs, past the bedroom where he heard Irene's gentle snoring, and found a small room with a desk at the back of the house. Beck settled into a rickety Victorian-style swivel desk chair that creaked and wobbled under his weight. He put his feet up on a windowsill and called Alex Liebowitz.

The lanky hipster wasn't surprised when his phone rang, displaying Beck's caller ID. He was in front of his main computer station on the second floor of his renovated townhouse located on the waterfront in Greenpoint, Brooklyn. Two other computer workstations, servers, modems, routers, and LCD screens filled the space. Liebowitz put on his wireless headphones so he could enter information as Beck spoke.

"How are you feeling, Alex?"

Liebowitz answered, "Compared to what?"

"Compared to most days."

"I feel fine. It's been quiet lately. How are you?"

"In need of information."

Liebowitz flexed his fingers and said, "Talk."

"First up, I need to know about a woman who was in the Brooklyn MDC between two and three years back. Her name was Deborah Ramirez."

"Details?"

"Arrested in Cumberland County on a drug charge. I assume possession with intent to distribute."

Liebowitz asked, "Local law or federal?"

"Federal."

"Federal? Must've been a fairly large operation for upstate New York."

Beck said, "I think it's because they were dealing in drugs sourced from foreign suppliers, mostly Mexico."

"So who arrested her? DEA?"

"Yes. She died in custody. An apparent suicide."

"Ah, *that* kind of suicide?"

"Seems that way."

"Okay, she won't be hard to find with that piece of info. What do you need?"

Beck looked at the time. Almost eight o'clock.

"Everything you can get within an hour or so. Arrest records. Dates. The names of the DEA agents who arrested her, if possible. The attorney who represented her. Whatever you can find out about her and her incarceration you think would be useful to know."

Liebowitz had been typing almost fast enough to keep up with Beck.

"Got it. Anything else?"

"Yes. There's somebody up here named Andrew or Andy Miller." Beck recited from memory. "He resides at one-forty-seven Johnny Cake Lane. I need a workup on him. Background. Relatives. Arrest record. A quick first pass. Deeper later if I need it."

"Johnny Cake Lane? That's quaint. What town is that in?"

"I think it would be included as part of Coleville."

"Anything else?"

"Yes. This next part is a little nebulous."

"Nebulous, how?"

"Consider this. There are four men. All of them living in or around Cumberland County, New York dividing around twenty million in drug sales profits."

"Annually?"

"Yes."

"Dividing it equally?"

"Doubtful. Equally among three but probably a double share for the guy on top."

"And the twenty is net of expenses."

"Roughly. They cover their nut with an extortion racket and other crimes."

"How many years are we talking about?"

"This group has been in operation for decades. I don't know what the earlier years brought in."

Liebowitz said, "However you cut it, it's a good amount. You want to know – where's the money?"

"Yes."

"Names?"

"Abel Proctor, deputy on the Cumberland County Sheriff's Department bureau of investigations. Vic, I assume Victor, Myer and or his brother George Myer. Either of them could be listed as the owner of a property in the county about a quarter of a mile from Route 26 and Paradise Hill Road. Last one is Emmett Devereaux. Don't know much about him."

"Anything?"

"In his forties. I presume he lives in the area. Might have an arrest record."

"Well, at least you got a name that isn't so common. I'll start with the deputy sheriff. What's his age?"

"Late fifties, early sixties."

"Okay. What do you want first, the background checks or the suicide?"

"Deborah Ramirez."

"Assume you want this asap?"

"Feed me stuff as you get it. Stock up on the Red Bull."

"No need. We're talking hours, not days."

"So far," said Beck and hung up.

Beck's next call was to the Bolo brothers. He'd already sent them a text asking them to head up north.

Ricky Bolo answered on the second ring. It sounded like they were in traffic.

Beck said, "Are you driving?"

"Oh yeah."

Ricky's last name derived from the bolo ties he wore, often with western-style shirts featuring silver-tipped collars. Beck knew Ricky and his brother Jonas were Romanian but didn't know their real names. The brothers were master thieves, familiar with all types of safes, locks and locking mechanisms, and all the software supporting modern surveillance and security systems. They earned their living by helping high-end crews plan and execute takedowns and running their own long cons. Ricky never stopped talking or finding ways to enjoy himself. His brother Jonas observed, spoke little, and never tried to keep his brother from embodying the cliché of a wild and crazy guy.

Ricky Bolo said, "Speak to me, James."

"Where are you?"

"About an hour out."

"Okay, when you get near, find a motel, lay low. You still driving that step van tool truck thing?"

"No way, brother Beck. We got another rig. Less noticeable. Carries everything we need. And try this on for size, amigo – we won't need a motel."

"How so?"

"Picture it, my man. A customized motorhome. It's cool. You'll want to move in."

"Don't hold your breath. Hunker down close. I'll call you when I need you."

"You always need us, James. You know that."

"Of course I do. Stand by. Hi to Jonas."

Ricky Bolo made kissing sounds and hung up.

When Beck put down his phone, Irene appeared in the doorway. She tapped on the frame.

"Can I talk to you?"

"How long have you been standing there?"

"Not long. I wasn't really listening. I'm too nervous."

Beck said, "Why are you nervous?"

Irene gave him a look. "Are you serious?"

"Right. Forget it. Feeling better?"

"I didn't sleep long, but I feel much better. What's going on?"

"Downstairs you said you wanted to do something about what happened to your friend."

"Yes."

"I assume even more so since we know the Kin wants you dead."

"Are you trying to get me to run back to Maine?"

"Is that what you want to do?"

"I don't know. It's better than getting killed."

"You can still get killed in Maine."

"I'm not going anywhere. What can I do to get back at them for Deborah?"

"First, help us make sure the Kin can't hurt you."

"How?"

"What's your relationship with Andy Miller?"

Irene shrugged. "Co-conspirators? Bitch buddies. He doesn't like the Kin. He knows I don't. He lets me know what's going on."

"To what end?"

"Not much unfortunately."

"I want you to talk to Andy Miller."

"Why?"

"Because I think he wants to do something about the Kin. He obviously knows more about them than you or me. I want to know if he'll help us."

"Help us how?"

"By telling us everything he knows about the Kin. Who the leaders are. Where they live. How much influence they have in the sheriff's department. Anything and everything he knows. Why he's been hanging out at the Field watching and listening for eight months. You're smart, Irene. You know the Kin wants you dead. Find out from him how we can stop them. And don't tell me 'by killing them'. There are too many. We have to figure another way."

Irene leaned against the doorway, folded her arms, and nodded. "I don't know what that way is, but I'll talk to Andy. I suppose you want me to do that soon."

"I want you to do it now. Tonight."

Irene looked at her watch. "He'll be at the Field now. I'm not going back to the Field."

"Call him. Persuade him to take a break. Meet you somewhere close by. Manny will take you. Does Miller have a phone?"

"Yes. I know the number."

"Good. Call him. Convince him. Meet him nearby. He can go back to work after he talks to you."

"All right."

"You and Manny can stay here until Miller is ready to meet."

"Then what?"

"We're setting up in a new house. Someplace nobody knows about. Who knows about this place since Deborah's mother moved out?"

"Nobody really. Marie wants to sell the place. I think Deb's brother and sister have been haggling over the price."

"Do they know you use the house?"

"I don't use it." Irene pointed to her clothes. "These are Deborah's. They've been here for years. I wasn't even sure that bunked key would still be here."

"There's still a chance the Kin or Devereaux might connect this house to you. We need to get out of here. Talk to Miller. Persuade him to meet as soon as possible. After you meet with him, Manny will bring you to the new place."

"Okay."

Beck asked, "You still want a gun?"

"I already have one." She pulled a revolver out of the pocket of her sweatpants. "This one works."

Beck eyeballed the gun. It was a stainless-steel version of the classic Colt Cobra snub-nosed .38.

"That's a quality gun."

"It belonged to Deborah. She hid it under a floorboard in the closet."

"What's it loaded with?"

"Thirty-eight specials. Don't worry. I know how to use it. I did a lot of practicing in Maine."

39

Of course, Camdyn Dent didn't reveal to his Kin leaders why he knew where Beck, his men, and possibly Irene Allen would be hiding. Explaining how he had rented the house for Beck would detract from his mystique. However, he did stay in the barn with them to go over the details for the ambush that would wipe out their enemies.

He used a printout of a satellite image of the house and location in Winholm. He showed Vic Myer where he wanted him to set up a firing line hidden in the forest in front of the house. He wanted him in the center position on the firing line so he could keep his shooters disciplined and quiet. Myer nodded, asked no questions, and tried without success to turn down his maniacal grin.

Dent did the same with Emmett Devereaux showing him the area behind the house where he wanted Devereaux to position his men. Their job would be to make sure no one escaped the house when the shooting started. Devereaux nodded and said nothing.

Finally, Dent said, "Stay in position. Plan on attacking at two in the morning. That will give Beck and his friends time to arrive at the house. I will be there to make sure Beck and the others are in place."

Vic Myer asked, "What if all of them aren't in the house by two?"

"As long as James Beck is in that house, you attack, even if he's the only one. I don't think his mongrels will function well without him. If we have to, we'll hunt them down and deal with them later."

Devereaux said, "Every damn one of 'em."

Proctor said, "I'll keep getting information about them. We'll know how to find them."

Dent nodded. "Good."

Proctor asked, "Is there anybody close enough to the house who'll hear the gunfire?"

Dent said, "The closest dwelling is about a quarter mile away. That's the other reason we should hold off until two. Everyone in the area should be asleep by then. If Victor and his shooters do their job, every magazine should be empty in twenty or thirty seconds. No reason to reload. Even if someone in the area wakes up, if they don't hear anything more, they'll likely go back to sleep. If someone does call nine one one, it'll be your job, Abel, to intercept the call and make sure the call doesn't go to the state police. You handle it and keep the sheriff's people out of the area, too."

Proctor asked, "And after, what about the bodies and damage to property?"

"Emmett's men will dispose of the bodies. I'll deal with the property damage."

Proctor said, "Just to confirm one thing..."

Dent looked at his watch, anxious to end the meeting. "What?"

"We have to keep the bodies of Beck and the girl, assuming she comes with them. We can't have them disappearing. That'll make it nearly impossible to pin the Collins murder on them."

Dent nodded. "Yes. I presume you can explain why the corpses will have multiple gunshot wounds."

"I can make it look like somebody took retribution for killing an important member of the Kin. That sends the message we want. And it's the kind of case that'll go nowhere because there will be way too many avenues of investigation."

"Good. And if the girl isn't there, we'll have to locate her quickly and make sure she's dead." Dent turned to Devereaux. "Emmett, you keep the bodies somewhere convenient, and find that girl if she's not there tonight."

"I will."

"Abel, you let us know when and where you want the bodies found. Right now, we have much to do, gentlemen. This is a one-time opportunity. Get to work."

Dent stood up and left the barn by the same route he'd arrived.

On the walk back to his car, he reviewed his plan. He considered each of his top three leaders, what they needed to do, and how they would perform.

He had confidence in Proctor. Dent knew that Abel would always be balancing his best interests with the interests of the Kin. It didn't matter. Proctor had figured out the right moves to close the murder case and eliminate work for Irene Allen that Peter Morelli didn't want to do. Proctor's role in the massacre would be straightforward and limited.

Vic Myer should be able to execute a quick, bloody surprise attack. He would do his part. The men he'd pick would follow his lead.

Emmett Devereaux was another matter. He would be difficult to control. Dent understood that Devereaux had descended from primitive, violent people – among the original settlers in the Hudson Valley who lived near the western edge of the Berkshires. Hill people who many believed had descended from women fleeing the witch trials in Massachusetts. They had formed a matriarchal society. To gain leverage over the brutal, primitive men of that era, the women spread myths that they held powers men should fear. Supernatural powers that could affect how someone acted. Bring about illnesses. Make animals sick. Dent knew that Emmett Devereaux believed all of it. Dent assumed that Devereaux believed Irene Allen was a witch. How else could she have escaped from him? That's why Devereaux hadn't said anything about her during their meeting. The psycho was convinced uttering her name would add to her powers.

Dent slid behind the wheel of his Subaru Outback taking on the persona of Peter Morelli. He started the engine. Pulled a packet of lens cleaner out of the center console and cleaned his glasses slowly and methodically. He adjusted the climate control setting and turned on the Sirius XM classical music station. He thought about the short-term lease he would prepare for Beck's safehouse. Each thought, each action brought Camdyn Dent closer to the personality of Peter Morelli, closer to obscuring the venomous hatred and determination to kill that motivated Camdyn Dent. For Morelli, Camdyn Dent wasn't a person. It wasn't a name. It was a title bestowed on each successive leader of the Kin. A play on words based on German for Commander – Kommandant. Camdyn Dent. It always amused Morelli how few people picked up on that.

Morelli checked the time readout on his car's dashboard screen. 8:43 p.m. He texted the address of the house to Beck and told him to be there at midnight.

That would give him plenty of time to get to the location and ensure the death trap was set.

40

Morelli slowed down when he saw a derelict storage shed that marked the entrance to a one-lane dirt road. As he turned onto the narrow road, his headlights revealed the shed's rust-stained metal roof and weathered wood siding the color of gray slush on a city sidewalk.

The road to the house meandered through a quarter mile of forest typical for the area – mostly sugar maple, eastern hemlock, yellow birch, and scattered pine trees separated by sparse undergrowth because of poor soil and deer browse. Morelli drove slowly, noting that the forest wasn't dense enough to supply good cover for his shooters. They'd have to hunker down into dips and depressions in the uneven ground and depend on the forest's high canopy to shield them from the gauzy light of a crescent-moon hidden behind clouds. It didn't really matter. Nobody would be looking for them.

The road ended thirty feet from a ranch house fronted by a section of lawn now covered in snow and ice. There was a gravel parking area off to the left. It had been cleared of snow. There was room for at least six vehicles. Morelli parked his SUV there, as he was sure Beck and his men would. That would leave the front of the house free of anything obstructing the sightlines of Myer's shooters who would be ten or fifteen yards back in the woods. That would put them about thirty yards from their target, well within range to blow apart the front of the ranch house and every living thing inside it. The ammunition in their assault rifles could easily penetrate the house's wood siding, insulation board, and sheetrock walls.

As Morelli approached the front door, he took note of two picture windows on his left facing the forest and a series of three windows off to his right, one for each bedroom, all three facing in the same direction.

Morelli entered quickly. The ground floor was an open-plan living room, dining area, and kitchen. He walked around the space turning on overhead lights and lamps. He raised the thermostat to seventy degrees. The furnace kicked on, and forced hot air began flowing through the house.

Morelli stood in the middle of the main room facing the two picture windows. The first window revealed an area inside extending from the kitchen counter to a dining table that sat eight. The table ran parallel to the window. Anybody sitting at the counter, or the dining table would be an easy target. The second window supplied a clear view of the sitting area in front of the fireplace, including two couches forming an L around a large coffee table. Once Myer and his men opened fire, anyone sitting anywhere outside the kitchen would be torn to shreds in seconds.

Double sliding glass doors on the opposite wall made the kitchen and part of the sitting area visible to anyone in the back of the house. Off the kitchen, a hallway led to five bedrooms, three on one side, two on the other.

If by some miracle Beck or any of his men survived the first volley and managed to escape out the back, Emmett Devereaux and his men would quickly cut them down. Morelli walked over to the sliding glass doors and turned on two outdoor LED floodlights mounted over the doors. The fixtures produced 4,000 lumens of light. Enough to illuminate everything between the house and the forest twenty yards away.

Morelli took off his parka, laid it over one of the dining room chairs, and sat at the table facing the picture window. He pulled a short-term lease agreement from the inside pocket of his suit jacket and set it on the table. He stared out the window to see if he could spot any shooters taking up their positions in the forest. With the lights blazing in the house behind him and no lighting outside, the windows were an impenetrable black slab. He checked his watch. 12:16 a.m. Beck was late. Morelli smiled. Late for his own funeral.

41

Beck left the Brick Row house, leaving Manny and Irene to kill time until they could meet with Andy Miller. Irene seemed relaxed with Manny. Beck understood that. Manny Guzman exuded calm. A sometimes menacing calm but not so much with Irene. By the time Beck left, the kitchen was spotless, and the unlikely pair were sitting in the living room talking about the advantages of revolvers. Beck knew that Manny avoided semi-auto handguns. He always carried a short-barrel Charter Arms .44 Bulldog Special in one pocket of his work pants. And during troubled times like this, he carried a six-shot four-inch barrel Taurus 82 in his left pants pocket.

When Beck said goodbye, Manny was discussing the merits of Irene's stainless-steel version of the classic Colt Cobra snub-nosed .38 versus the original aluminum frame Colts.

Beck drove toward Morelli's safehouse in his GMC Denali, his Beretta 1301 Tactical shotgun wedged between the passenger seat and the console pointing up.

Fifteen minutes into the drive, Liebowitz called Beck. Beck took the call through his Apple CarPlay connection and listened while he drove.

First, Liebowitz told him, "Your friend's account about what happened to Deborah Ramirez was accurate as far as I can tell first pass."

Beck was pleased Irene had been truthful.

"Good."

"I'll keep going on it. There's more to find out."

"Okay. Did you get anything yet about the money trail with those guys?"

"Yes. We have a trail. I put Lucille on it. She started with Abel Proctor, like I said."

"Good."

"Took her only an hour to find two LLCs connected to Deputy Abel Proctor. She's really good at hacking into corporate filings, and these weren't too complicated. Those entities own real estate on both sides of the river up there."

Beck said, "So that's where his money is going?"

"At least a portion of it. Real estate in that part of the world isn't all that expensive. So far, we've found a storage facility occupying sixty-five acres off Route 23 near Belleville, a two-story standalone office building east of the river that houses a podiatrist's office and a real estate office, a car wash in Greenport, and three residential properties with rental tenants."

"That's a nice portfolio."

"We haven't got an accurate dollar value on it yet."

"Let that go for now."

"Okay. I'll finish up the Deborah Ramirez thing and tell Lucille to shift over to the next guy on your list. Victor Myer."

"Keep me posted."

Beck almost missed the turn from the two-lane road onto the dirt road leading to the safehouse. The black forest surrounding him absorbed the light from his hi-beams until he finally spotted house lights a quarter mile from the turn.

The Kin shooters had been in place for almost an hour. They saw Beck's headlights approaching from behind them and hunkered down flat on the ground, lying prone, becoming nothing more than unseen humps on the dark forest ground.

From inside the house, Morelli watched Beck pull in next to his Subaru. There was no sign of the others. When Beck got out of his GMC, Morelli uttered a quiet curse when he didn't see Irene Allen. He told himself the others would be here eventually. He'd kill time with Beck and see who else arrived. Myer had orders that nobody opened fire until he left, which would be no later than two o'clock.

Morelli stood up from the dining room table to greet Beck. He opened the front door wide and said, "Come in. I thought you'd be here sooner."

Beck ignored the comment and entered. He carried his backpack in one hand and the Beretta shotgun in the other.

Morelli said, "Just you?"

"At the moment."

"Where's Irene? I was hoping you'd keep an eye on her. You're on the hook for a quarter mill if she disappears."

"She'll be along."

Morelli smiled and nodded, pleased that they wouldn't have to go looking for Irene Allen.

Beck set his shotgun and backpack on the dining table. He looked around and nodded favorably.

"Looks good. How many bedrooms?"

Morelli stood next to Beck. He pointed to his right. "Five bedrooms, all down that hall. Master bed and bathroom at the end on the left. Another bedroom and bath on the same side. Three bedrooms across the hall." He pointed left and said, "A half bathroom over there past the seating area."

Beck took off his coat off laid it on the dining room table next to his backpack.

Morelli pointed back toward the front door. "Coat closets there, closets in all the bedrooms. There's another entrance on the other end of the house that opens onto an area where people leave their boots and skis."

Beck walked into the center of the seating area and then over to the sliding doors.

"What's out back?"

"A small yard. Then open space until you get to a wooded section. Behind that is a creek running along the back end of the property."

"How much land?"

"About sixty acres. The plot runs from the creek all the way back to where you came in."

Morelli took the lease out of the breast pocket of his suit coat and dropped it on the dining table. He pulled out a chair for Beck.

"We should fill this out and settle up."

Beck sat down and slid the lease in front of him. Morelli took the chair to Beck's right and explained the terms without referring to the pages of the lease.

Beck nodded, half-listened, and stared out the picture window. He looked around behind him. Beck realized that most of the ground floor was exposed to the outside. He wanted to get up and close the vertical blinds flanking the large picture window facing him but decided to take care of the lease first.

Morelli saw Beck turn and look through the sliding glass doors at the floodlit area behind the house.

"Who owns this place?"

"The owner lives in Boston. His family used this place as a ski house, but his kids have grown up. He and his wife don't ski anymore. He has a property management company book the place and run things. I've done work for the fellow who owns the management company. I contacted him directly. Don't worry, I didn't tell him who's renting it. I said it was a friend of mine."

Beck nodded. "Good. Thanks."

Morelli decided it was time to leave. Tell Myer to wait until two, and if nobody else showed up, kill Beck and call it a night.

Morelli said, "You'll notice I couldn't get the place for two weeks. But you have it until the eighteenth, with the option to extend until the twentieth. After that, another renter comes in on the twenty-second through New Year's Day. The property manager needs a day to clean." Beck wasn't listening closely to Morelli, but Morelli kept on talking, intent on making Beck feel he had provided him a safe place set up for short term rentals.

"So, Mr. Beck, it's five thousand for the week, plus twenty-nine hundred for the extra days and a security deposit of twenty-five hundred. I got him to include the cleaning fee in the twenty-nine. You'll get the security returned if there are no damages."

Beck finally turned to Morelli. "Is that what we agreed on? I forget."

"Yes. That's the price. I've got to charge you for the extra days whether you're here or not. You said you'd have cash."

Beck nodded. He was about to reach into his backpack for the cash when his cell phone rang. It was Alex Liebowitz calling. Beck was pleased to see he had three bars of reception in what seemed like an isolated area.

Beck said, "Can you hang on for a second?" He kept the phone in his hand and pulled out a stack of one-hundred-dollar bills from his backpack. He nodded for Morelli to count out the money as he stood up and walked toward the kitchen.

"What's up?"

Liebowitz said, "This'll be fast. Just a bit of information for whatever it's worth."

Beck said, "Okay," and watched Morelli count out piles of ten one-hundred-dollar bills.

Liebowitz said, "I got a copy of the BOP investigation into Deborah Ramirez's suicide at the Brooklyn MDC."

"Okay."

"A prison official by the name of Brett Sullivan ran the investigation. It reads sketchy to me."

Beck knew what Liebowitz meant by that. Alex didn't believe it was suicide.

"Did anybody raise a stink about it?"

"Not that I can tell."

"What about her defense lawyer? Any mention of him?"

"Not in the report. Let me see if they gave a copy of Sullivan's report to her lawyer."

Beck waited while Liebowitz scanned through an appendix. Beck glanced at Morelli. He counted out five one-thousand-dollar piles. He counted out four more bills and looked impatiently at his watch. Beck wasn't surprised that Morelli wanted to wrap this up and get home.

Liebowitz's voice came back on.

"Here it is. Name was Morelli. Peter Morelli. He had a law office on Rector Street in downtown Manhattan."

Beck said nothing for a moment, trying to control his reaction, and then said to Liebowitz, "Uh huh."

Morelli had been watching Beck. He thought the call had come from one of his men telling Beck when they would be arriving. But now he thought it was somebody else talking to Beck. Somebody who had caused a change in Beck's tone of voice.

Liebowitz noticed it too. He asked, "What's up, James? Does that name mean something to you?"

Beck tried to keep his voice neutral. He said, "Right."

Beck's mind raced. His first reaction was to explain it away. Morelli could have picked up Deborah Ramirez as a client through the ordinary course of his practice as a criminal defense attorney. He'd been with the Brooklyn District Attorney's office. His practice could easily have included defending federal prisoners. And then James Beck's second reaction kicked in with breathtaking effect.

It all made sense.

There was only one person who had the connections to enable the Kin to operate in so many realms. The man sitting no more than ten feet away from him. Peter Morelli was Camdyn Dent.

Liebowitz said, "You still there, James?"

"Yes."

"Can you talk?"

"No."

"Okay. I got it."

Beck saw Morelli watching him. He tried to smile apologetically and raised a finger to indicate *just a minute.*

Liebowitz said, "What do you want me to do?"

Beck tried to keep a matter-of-fact tone as he said, "A text?"

"A text? You want me to text the others and tell them what I told you?"

"No. Just, you know, something short."

"All right. I understand. I'll text them – *talked to James. Something is wrong.*"

"Right. Sounds good. Fine. I gotta go. Go ahead and do that. Now, please."

Beck cut the call. He returned to the dining table and sat down. He picked up the lease agreement and made believe he was reading through it.

Morelli said, "Don't worry about the lease, Mr. Beck. I drew it up. Just don't trash the place and be out on time." Morelli held up a set of keys. "Leave these on the dining table here. I'll make sure you get your security back. Scribble a signature on it so I can give it to the management guy, and I'll be on my way. It's getting late."

Beck picked up the pen Morelli had left on the table and said, "Sure." But he didn't sign. He was too preoccupied with what had been right before him. How Morelli had controlled everything. He had a criminal defense law firm in New York City that connected him to everything he needed to run his empire upstate – drug dealers, inmates in prisons, drug suppliers. He had a senior investigator in the Kin to help manipulate county law enforcement. He ordered Proctor to fix the arraignment so Irene got bail, so he could deliver her to Emmett Devereaux for slaughter.

And now Peter Morelli/Camdyn Dent had brought him to an isolated house, surrounded by woods, in the middle of the night. A place where every person he loved and cared about would join him. Not in a safehouse. In a deathtrap.

Beck swallowed, thinking furiously. To gain time, he flipped the pages of the lease to the signature page. He felt paralyzed. His only hope was that Alex would contact Ciro, Demarco, and Manny in time to head them off.

Beck scrawled his signature on the lease, put down the pen, but didn't hand the lease back to Morelli. He asked a question he didn't care about. "So, there's only two bathrooms in this place?"

Morelli was standing now, waiting for the lease. He'd already shoved the cash into his jacket pocket. He said, "Two and a half. There's a half bathroom off the sitting area."

Beck glanced out the front window into the darkness. He was pleased now that he hadn't closed the vertical blinds. The Kin ambushers had to see what he was about to do. He couldn't save himself. Maybe he still had a chance to save the others.

42

Vic Myer stood leaning against a tree. To hell with laying on the goddamn ground. The snow had soaked through his clothes. The wintry night air felt like it had penetrated into his bones. Standing also gave him a better view into the house. He could see the bearded asshole, Beck, sitting at the dining table with Camdyn Dent. They were looking at a document. Probably the lease. Myer's usual lunatic smile turned into a sneer. Dent was playing his Morelli lawyer role. Fine, but get on with it. This was not the time for the supreme leader of the Kin to be sitting next to someone in the crosshairs of eleven freezing, keyed-up, twitchy bastards holding long guns. Plus another six of his militia men hiding in the woods, huddled around trucks they'd parked in a clearing at the end of a fire trail. And another ten of Devereaux's dementos in back of the house.

Myer wanted to shoulder his assault weapon and empty a magazine into Beck right now. He was the principal target. Let it start and end now. Of course, Myer knew once he opened fire, the whole line of shooters would go off. No way would the Kommandant survive. Where the hell were the rest of Beck's pals? Apparently, coming from another location. More goddamn waiting.

Myer told himself to be patient. It was worth waiting if they could kill them all tonight. They'd destroy every living thing in that house as soon as Camdyn walked out and drove away. Myer checked his watch. He could barely see it in the dark forest. It said 12:52 a.m. *Well, fuck it.* Dent said the shooting should begin at two. He'd have to be out by then. The blood would be splattering soon. Even if the others never showed, getting black-beard Beck would be worth the wait.

Myer bent low and headed to his left, walking behind his row of shooters. As he passed each man, he told them to hang in, stand by, wait for his command. When he reached the end of the line, he could see Camdyn's Subaru and Beck's Denali. Myer recognized the GMC from the Field.

He still had a line of sight on Beck. And the shotgun next to him on the dining room table. The shotgun wouldn't do Beck any good. Once they opened fire, Beck would be twitching like a spastic puppet, all the bullets hitting him. They'd rip him apart. Dent had said thirty seconds of fire would do it. But Myer knew his men. All of them had extra magazines for their weapons. Once the shooting started, they'd reload and fire until he told them to stop, or they ran out of ammo. If anybody in the area called 911 about gunfire, tough shit. It was Abel Proctor's job to take care of that.

Even though only three of his men had combat experience, the others were competent enough to shoot at a target thirty yards away.

Myer picked his way between trees and undergrowth until he reached the end of the firing line. He dropped down on one knee next to Jefferson Baxter, one of the two vets on the firing line. Baxter sat on a shooting mat, his back against a dying ash tree, a Sig Sauer MCX Rattler resting across his knees. The weapon was lightweight, accurate at the short distance from the house, loaded with hollow point 300 blackout rounds, and equipped with a Sig suppressor on the barrel. Myer knew that, if necessary, Baxter would advance on his target, shooting until he had killed his enemy.

Myer put a hand on his shoulder and said, "Hanging in?"

"Roger that."

Myer turned toward the house. The forest at this end of his firing line was thicker. Baxter had moved closer to the house to get a clear shot. It also afforded him a partial view of the parking area.

Myer said, "When this pops off, whoever else is in the house, your primary target is the guy with the beard. You aim everything you have at him. Advance on him until you have a confirmed kill."

"Got it."

"Do not fire until the guy in glasses leaves the house, drives off, and you hear my command to shoot."

"Who is he?"

"A lawyer."

"He's going to hear the shooting."

"Don't worry about it. He's working with us."

Baxter nodded. He knew all he had to know.

Myer said, "Use the time it takes the lawyer to drive out to get into firing position for your shot."

"I've got that established."

"Good. How many mags you got?"

Baxter said, "Four. Thirty rounds each."

Myer's grimacing smile was nearly invisible in the dark as he said, "Once you take down your target, feel free to reload and strafe anything in there moving. There should be three or four others in there by two o'clock who need exterminating."

"We'll get it done."

Myer lightly punched Baxter on the upper arm and said, "Good. Standby. Be patient."

Myer slipped away and moved slowly along the firing line. As he passed each man he whispered, "Relax. Stay sharp." But each time he said, "Relax," Myer felt the tension rise.

43

Demarco and Ciro got the call from Alex Liebowitz about a mile from Morelli's safehouse. He put his phone on speaker and slowed down.

After they listened to Liebowitz, Demarco said, "So something is wrong, Alex, but James couldn't say what."

"Correct. He couldn't talk freely. When I said 'something is wrong', he said 'right'. Where the hell is he?"

"Supposedly, at a safehouse where we can hide out and regroup."

Liebowitz said, "No. I don't think it's safe."

"Okay. Did you call Manny?"

"He's not with you?"

"No."

"I'll call him now."

Demarco cut the call. Ciro turned to him. "Now what?"

Demarco said, "Let's find out."

Two minutes later, Demarco turned onto the dirt road leading to Morelli's safehouse and doused his headlights. They crept along until they saw a space on the right side of the road where there was room to park the Honda Ridgeline out of sight.

They got out of the truck cab and closed the doors as quietly as they could. Demarco slipped on his black Kangol wool hawker hat and zipped up his quilted Montcler leather down jacket.

He spoke quietly. "I'll see if I can find out what's wrong. Hang on while I take a look."

"Okay. Watch your ass."

"I'll have to move slowly. If you want something to do, load up extra clips for my Glock."

Demarco melted into the dark like a wraith, moving soundlessly along the edge of the road that led to the no longer safe safehouse, his Glock 17 ready in his right hand.

Ciro stood next to the truck. He looked around. With only a crescent moon hidden behind clouds, the night sky looked almost as black as the forest. He slipped back into the truck's cab. He opened the glove box to get a bit of light and started loading Glock magazines with 9-millimeter ammunition.

By the time he'd finished loading four mags, Ciro started worrying that something might have happened to Demarco. Two minutes later, the driver's side door opened, and Demarco slipped into the cab. He reached up and turned out the interior light.

"So?"

"It's a trap."

"Fuck. What did you see?"

"Let's sort out the guns and ammo while I explain."

As they transferred the weapons and boxes of ammunition from the cab to the tailgate of the truck, Demarco said, "This road leads to a ranch house about two hundred yards ahead. I picked out at least ten men. Most are on the ground in shooting positions in front of the house. They're spaced about six to ten feet apart. Most of 'em have ARs. There are two big picture windows on the side facing the shooters. House is all lit up. James is in there with one guy. I assume it's the lawyer Phineas got him."

"What the hell is the lawyer doing in there?"

"I don't know. Maybe he set up the trap."

Ciro considered that. "Okay. If he did, there won't be any shooting until he leaves. What are they doing?"

"Sitting on a couch talking. Somehow James figured out this is a trap. No way he's going to let the lawyer walk out of there."

Ciro said, "Right. We gotta move fast. Take out as many of these guys as we can so James has a chance to bust out of there. Any way we do that without getting shot?"

"Maybe."

Demarco had laid out the guns and ammunition he wanted. While he explained his plan to Ciro, he strapped on a Kevlar vest over his Montcler jacket. Ciro took off his wool overcoat to put on a vest, cursing the cold until he got his coat back on.

Demarco picked up Lund's Remington 10/22 loaded with ten bullets and slung it over his shoulder. He grabbed Beck's Mossberg 590M mag-fed shotgun loaded with ten rounds of 12-gauge buckshot and shoved a second magazine loaded with three-inch shotgun slugs into his coat pocket. He positioned his Glock in the front of his waistband and slipped four magazines loaded with 9-millimeter bullets into his back pockets.

Ciro had Oscar Lund's Trojan Arms AR slung over his shoulder and three magazines loaded with twenty-five rounds of ammunition in one pocket of his overcoat. He grabbed his S&W M&P 15 – 22 and three magazines holding thirty rounds of .22 caliber ammunition and stuck them in the other pocket. He shoved his Smith and Wesson .45 behind his vest.

Ciro said, "So you figure about a hundred feet from one end of the line to the other?"

"Yes. I'll let you get into place on the right end. I'll get on the left end and wait for you to open up. Don't rush into position. Walking through that forest is a bitch. Just go easy. Try not to let them hear you."

Ciro asked, "You think James knows what's out there?"

"He knows something."

Demarco returned to the truck, dug a Spyderco combat knife out of the center console, and clipped it to his belt. He came back and grabbed Ciro's shoulder.

"Listen, brother, they don't know we're coming. We goddamn hit them hard and fast and keep moving."

Ciro nodded. He didn't want to talk about anything. A dozen men with assault rifles meant hundreds of high-velocity rounds flying around. There was almost no way they wouldn't get hit. But Demarco's plan might work well enough to give James a chance to get out of the house. He concentrated on that. And on the image of Demarco Jones running and gunning in the dark. And on doing his part to take down his end of the firing line.

Ciro pulled on a black knit cap he'd bought at Walmart along with his new boots.

"Fuck it. Let's go."

44

Irene changed from her sweatpants into her jeans. She and Manny cleaned up the house and packed everything into Manny's Toyota 4Runner. Irene called Andy Miller. He answered on the first ring. Manny sat in his chair in the living room while she spoke in the kitchen. When Irene returned to the living room, she looked confused.

Manny asked, "What?"

"He agreed to leave the Field. He'll meet us at his house."

"You're surprised."

"Yes. I didn't think he would leave. But he said there's hardly anybody there tonight."

"Why?"

"He said something must be going on."

Manny stood up and grabbed the gray wool coat that had gotten him through so many New York City winters.

"The Kin must be gathering the troops. Let's go."

Irene went to the closet and took down a North Face jacket that had belonged to Deborah Ramirez. She left the barn jacket she'd retrieved from her house because Emmett Devereaux had worn it. She followed Manny out and locked the door behind them. She put the key back where she'd found it.

Thirty minutes later, as Manny approached Miller's house, he leaned forward and peered out the windshield of the 4Runner. He spotted Miller's SUV parked in front. Lights were on inside the house.

Irene said, "He must've left right away." Manny checked the time on the Toyota's dashboard. 11:50 p.m.

Manny nodded but didn't say anything.

"You think George and Vic are wondering why you didn't show up?"

"They already know why."

Irene led the way to Miller's front door. The door opened before she got close enough to knock. Andy Miller stood blocking the doorway. He wore his usual clothes – the stained coveralls, his orange knit cap, boots. But now that he was home, no eyeglasses and none of the village idiot servile act.

He peered over Irene's shoulder. "Where are the others?"

Irene said, "Let me in. It's goddamn cold out here."

Miller raised his right hand that had been down behind his leg, bringing his Glock into view.

"Don't come in if you or your friend the ex-con cook is lookin' to shoot me or threaten me. I'm not in the mood for it."

Irene stepped around Miller.

"What the hell's gotten into you?"

Manny stood at the doorway, holding out empty hands, waiting for Miller to step aside and let him in.

Miller did, just barely. Manny passed him and said, "You don't need the gun, hombre."

Miller's living room looked the same as the last time Manny had been there. Miller sat down in his fake leather chair, surrounded by books, magazines, and newspapers. Manny and Irene sat on his threadbare couch. The only lights burning were in the kitchen and the floor lamp next to Miller's chair.

Miller sat with the Glock in his lap.

"So?"

Irene said, "What's going on at the Field? You sounded worried."

Miller frowned. "I don't exactly know. Vic wasn't there. Hardly any of the Kin boys. Regular customers left early. So did I."

"What did George say about that?"

"Nothing."

Manny said, "What are you worried about?"

Miller gave Manny a blank stare. The kind of look he often gave people while he worked at the Field.

Manny said, "Hey. Knock that shit off. We don't have time for your act."

"Why not?"

Irene said, "Because Emmett Devereaux tried to kidnap me at my house. Beck got there in time to prevent it. There was a gunfight. He and his guys killed two of Devereaux's men. Devereaux got away. This shit is getting serious, Andy. It's time to tell us what you know."

"About what?"

Irene pitched forward on the couch. "About the fucking Kin, Andy! Why Vic and so many guys weren't there tonight!"

"All right, for chrissake, stop shouting at me. You should be able to figure it out for yourself. Whatever it is they're doing, it's pretty goddamn sure it has something to do with killing you, Beck, and everybody around him. You just said they tried to kill you. You think they gave up?"

"So what does that mean exactly? Vic Myer is out there gathering a bunch of his militia guys to go after Beck? He doesn't even know where Beck is."

Miller said, "Where is he?"

Irene said, "I don't know. Someplace that..."

Manny cut her off. "Hold on." Manny focused on Andy. "Do me a favor."

"What?"

"Put that gun down while you're talking to me. Go put it on the kitchen counter."

"Why, so you can pull out your gun and have the drop on me?"

Manny said, "I'll do the same." He took out the Taurus revolver from his right pocket and handed it to Irene, leaving the short-barreled Charter Arms revolver in his left pocket.

Irene took the gun from Manny and walked over to Miller. She said, "Come on, Andy, stop being an asshole. We're on the same side. Gimme the gun. We both know you haven't been hanging around the Field for the last eight months because you enjoy those Kin assholes treating you like an inbred piece of shit."

Miller looked up at Irene and smiled. He handed her his Glock and watched her put both guns on the kitchen counter. Irene sat down next to Manny.

"Okay," said Miller. "I've got no gun. I know damn well Irene has one. And I'd bet good money that ain't your only pistol, Mr. Eddie. But if either of you decides to shoot me, I guarantee you it will be the dumbest move you have ever made. Now stop fucking around and tell me where Beck is."

Irene looked at Manny. Manny looked back at her and turned to Miller.

"He's at a house near Winholm. Someplace his lawyer found for us. We're supposed to meet him there."

"You said near Winholm?"

"Yes."

"And what about his other two guys?"

"They're probably already there."

Miller slowly shook his head and muttered, "Good Lord almighty."

"What?" asked Manny.

Miller ignored the question and asked, "What's the exact location of that house?"

45

Beck handed the signed lease to Morelli and said, "Peter, I know it's late, but I wanted to talk to you about next steps with Irene Allen. Just a couple of minutes if you don't mind."

Morelli said, "Actually, I do mind. It's late. It's been a long day. I busted my hump to get you this place. I'm tired, and I'm going home."

Beck stood and pointed to the two couches in the seating area that formed an L in front of the fireplace. "Please, have a seat."

Morelli said, "We'll have to do this tomorrow, Mr. Beck. As it is, I won't get home until after two. I'm leaving."

Beck's voice hardened, "Hey, sit the fuck down. I'm tired, too. It won't take long."

Dent turned to look at Beck. Something had changed.

Beck pointed to the couch set parallel to the kitchen. Dent sat stiffly at the end of the couch. Beck sat at the end of couch facing the fireplace, his right knee was ten inches from Dent's left knee.

For the first time in a very long time, Peter Morelli felt fear. James Beck had turned dark and menacing and hostile.

And then Beck asked, "What do you know about Camdyn Dent, Peter?"

The sensation of alarm actually turned Morelli's stomach incapacitating him to the point where he couldn't come up with an answer.

Beck said, "Camdyn. It's an odd name. Where's that name come from?"

Something in Morelli kicked into gear. He took in a sharp breath, frowned, and said, "It's Celtic. Means winding valley."

Beck nodded. He reached around and pulled out his Browning Hi-Power from the holster clipped to his belt. He placed the gun on the seat cushion next to his right leg.

"This couch is too soft. Makes the butt of the gun press into me."

Morelli nodded, more to himself than to Beck. His plan had not gone as expected. Such is life. Time to deal with it. He reached around and pulled out a small Ruger LCP II .380 semi-auto he carried on his right hip and placed the gun on the seat cushion close to his right hand.

Morelli said, "Maybe you should carry a smaller gun."

The compact gun nearly fit in the palm of Morelli's hand, yet it held a magazine with six bullets plus one in the chamber, giving him seven chances to shoot Beck. He decided whatever was going to happen in the next minutes, he believed at such close range he could put enough bullets into Beck to kill him. He would aim for his face.

Beck smiled. "So, Camdyn, we find ourselves in an interesting situation."

Dent sat back, dropping the Peter Morelli façade. "When did you figure it out?"

Beck said, "About three minutes ago."

"Really?"

"Yes."

"What led you to it?"

"An accumulation of things. Particularly finding out you were the lawyer for Deborah Ramirez."

"The phone call?"

"Yes."

"From whom?"

"A colleague."

Dent nodded. "Your colleague must be good at what he does. That was quite some time ago. Deborah Ramirez. A foolish girl. Devolved." Dent shrugged and made a face like he'd smelled something bad, fully into the persona of Camdyn Dent.

"Devolved? What do you mean?"

"Reduced. Diminished to an inferior condition. In her case, losing her sense of gender, of morality. Devolving into a criminal dealing in drugs. A criminal stupid enough to get caught and worse, too stupid to keep her mouth shut."

Beck said, "Is that your way of justifying killing her?"

"There's no need to justify anything. She killed herself. We simply sped up an inevitable process."

Beck nodded. Dent's attitude brought into focus his monstrous view of humanity. Beck didn't bother disagreeing with Dent. Instead, he asked, "Did you know about her connection to Irene Allen?"

Dent answered with Beck a dismissive flick of his wrist. "No. What was the connection?"

"I guess it doesn't matter."

"Whatever it was, it's too far down on the list of my concerns to merit my attention."

"So what's on top on your list of concerns?"

Dent leaned forward slightly. "At the moment, killing you, your mongrel crew of followers, and Irene Allen. You and your men put three of mine in the hospital and nearly killed Abel Proctor. You did kill two of our men at Irene Allen's house. And for all I know, you and Irene Allen killed Joseph Collins. You are a very violent individual, Mr. Beck, and so are the mongrel criminals that do your bidding. The Kin is going to kill all of you. A fate you richly deserve."

Beck stared at Dent. He didn't even bother to tell him that everything he'd just said was a colossal load of horseshit. An insane justification for the violence he and his followers had done to Beck and his men and Irene Allen. And Deborah Ramirez and thousands of others. The man reeked of death and pathological narcissism. Suddenly, James Beck felt death descending on him. Everything slowed down. It became slightly more difficult to breathe. Nothing seemed more important than anything else as the moments fractured and concentrated so that each instant of his life seemed to blend with everything else. Nothing took precedence, not living or dying. Not the room surrounding them, or the guns on the couch, or the guns outside. Dent appeared to have merged with the air around him turning into something ephemeral.

Beck forced himself to take a deep breath, trying to return to the existent moment. He tried to figure out how he could avoid dying in the next few minutes. He was damned if he'd let this pathetic version of a human being occupy his attention, but he couldn't help but hear Morelli say, "I suppose you're sitting there thinking of shooting me. You do realize that two seconds after you fire your gun, a dozen men with military grade weapons will fire on you."

Beck focused on Morelli. He was asking him something.

"What?" said Beck.

Morelli leaned forward, "I said, wouldn't you prefer to continue living? Stand up. Leave our guns behind and walk out of here together. They won't shoot you as long as you're with me. We'll get in our cars and drive away. Live to fight another day. What do you say?"

Beck blinked, coming back to reality, but not as the same person he'd been just seconds ago, completely sure now of what he was going to do, and somehow okay with the idea it would kill him.

"I say that's an interesting question."

46

After talking to Jefferson Baxter at the far end of his firing line, Vic Myer made his way back to the center. He watched Beck and Dent sitting near the fireplace, talking. Why? Was Dent waiting for Beck's men and Irene Allen to show up? How long was he going to wait? Dent had been clear back at the Field. Beck was the primary target. If Beck ended up the only one in the house, that was enough. Wait for Dent to leave. Then open fire. Turn Beck into a pile of dead meat and splintered bones. Mission accomplished. End of story. But the Kommandant hadn't left. It was after one o'clock. Why keep waiting? Did Dent still think the rest would show up? Why push it?

Apparently the Kommandant had the patience to wait as long as possible to take down Beck's men and the woman. But this just didn't feel right.

Myer had been standing against a pine tree near the middle of his firing line. His shooters were almost evenly divided on either side of the dirt road cutting through the woods. Six on his side including him, five on the other. Myer wondered if he should send one of the men on his side back into the forest to see if they could spot any sign of Beck's men. The last thing Myer needed was armed men coming up behind them.

Myer pushed away from the pine tree and walked carefully behind the line, whispering as he passed each man, "Stay cool. Wait for the lawyer to leave. Fire only on my command."

When he reached the last man on the line, Myer crouched next to him. Seeing him jogged his memory. The guy wore black-framed glasses that reminded Vic of Buddy Holly. Holly was green. The guy's name was Greene. Dave Greene.

Greene turned toward Myer. He was a big man. Overweight. A man accustomed to using his size to intimidate people. And just in case that didn't work, Dave Greene always carried a gun.

Vic said, "Hey, Dave."

Greene awkwardly struggled up onto his knees.

"What's up?"

Myer put a hand on Greene's shoulder and said, "I want you to take a hike down the road. Move quietly. It's too dark to see real clear, so listen for any movement. Any sign of anybody else out there."

"You think there might be?"

"I doubt it. But there's no downside to checking."

Greene whispered, "Yeah. For sure. If I find somebody, what do you want me to do?"

"You have a handgun with you?"

Greene patted the butt of a .45 caliber Kimber MFG holstered at his hip.

"Always."

"Good. Have that weapon in your hand cocked and ready. You see someone, I don't give a shit who it is; you put them down. Try to keep it at a single shot. I'd prefer it doesn't set off the whole firing line. Then you high tail it back here."

Greene smiled. "You got it."

Greene hefted his 252 pounds up off his knees, brushed wet snow off his chest and pants, cradled his assault rifle in the crook of his left elbow, and headed out.

47

Demarco and Ciro walked on either side of the road. Demarco's skin tone and dark clothes made him nearly impossible to see. His relaxed stride made it difficult to hear him. After a minute, Ciro thought that Demarco had slipped into the forest. He tried to walk off the road but found himself losing his footing, making noise struggling across the uneven, snow-covered ground. He climbed back up onto the road's edge and stopped to catch his breath. He thought he heard something. Was it Demarco out in front of him? And then he heard a crunching sound coming toward him. The sound of boots on frozen snow.

Ciro stepped off the road and dropped down, lying flat in the ditch that ran alongside the dirt road. He watched a large shape come around a slight bend. He couldn't see him very well in the dark, but he was close enough to see the shape of the intruder's head. Ciro shouldered the Smith and Wesson MP 15-22. Although configured like an AR-15 rifle, the weapon was more accurately a pistol fitted out like an assault rifle. Ciro was certain he could put two rounds into the head of whoever was approaching in less than a second. Unfortunately, he wasn't sure the bad guys wouldn't hear the shots. And by now, Demarco might be close to their firing line. If the Kin shooters heard his twenty-two, Demarco would lose the advantage of surprise. He'd be cut down in the barrage they would unleash.

Ciro laid down his weapon. Lund's Trojan AR was already on the ground beside him. He'd have to wait until the asshole passed him, then grab him around the neck and yoke him until he died or passed out. Risky, but so be it.

The walk had relaxed Dave Greene. He still had his .45 Kimber in his hand. Surprising how heavy a gun could feel after holding it for only five minutes. Greene hadn't seen or heard a thing except his own footsteps. He wondered if he needed to go any farther.

He was about to turn around and head back when he heard a noise – Ciro Baldassare slipping as he tried to get on his feet and step onto the road. He'd landed flat on the ground, stifling the curse but not the grunt.

Greene turned and raised his gun but couldn't see anyone to shoot. Ciro was too low. Ciro saw Greene's gun. His first impulse was to reach for his own forty-five, but he was lying on top of it. He reached for the MP 15-22.

Greene saw him now. Raised his handgun, ready to unload the whole clip into whoever the fuck that was.

Ciro had the MP. He didn't try to get up. He pointed the weapon. Saw Greene's handgun rising. And then something moved behind Big Dave Greene. A dark hand whipped through the air, and a Spyderco combat knife blade slashed across the top of Greene's thumb. The razor-sharp blade cut through skin and tendons right down to the bone, rendering the hand useless. The next instant, Ciro saw the big man fly backward as Demarco Jones grabbed Greene's forehead from behind and slammed him onto the frozen ground. The back of Greene's head smacked into the icy road making a sickening, wet, cracking sound and David Greene fell into oblivion.

Ciro had come within a half-second of firing his twenty-two. He lowered the weapon and cursed at how close he had come to shooting Demarco.

"Fuck!"

Demarco and Ciro stood over the victim. Ciro said, "Let's drag this hump off the road and take anything we can use."

Within a minute, Ciro and Demarco had stripped Greene of his rifle, a Rock River Arms AR-15, his Kimber .45, plus two full magazines for the AR.

Ciro said, "Big boy has a lot of good stuff."

"Unfortunately, all his buddies probably do, too."

Ciro refused to think about the massive amount of firepower about to be unleased at them. Instead, he asked, "What do we do with this joker? Think he might try to crawl back where he came from?"

Demarco squatted down. He stuck a finger in David Greene's ear. It came out bloody.

"Skull is cracked."

Ciro said, "He still might make noise if he wakes up."

This wasn't the heat of battle. Demarco didn't feel like slitting the man's throat.

Ciro said, "Give me your knife. I'll do it."

Suddenly, Demarco snapped a swift, precise kick to Greene's jaw, dislocating it and breaking the left mandible.

Ciro said, "I don't know why you care if he lives, but okay. Even if he crawls back, he won't be able to talk much. You want his rifle?"

"No."

Ciro said, "I'll take it."

Demarco said, "I'll take his gun and one of the magazines."

"Help yourself. Take both magazines. I don't want to risk putting them in my Smitty."

They quickly squared away the weapons. Demarco said, "We should walk on this road until we get closer. It'll take us too long to get through all that mess in the forest."

"You mean for me to get through it."

"Uh huh."

48

Vic Myer couldn't stop shivering. His usual shit-eating grin had turned into a grimace. Partly because of the cold, partly because he couldn't move around. Mostly because of the unremitting tension caused by waiting for Camdyn Dent to leave that goddamn house. What was he waiting for? Myer realized that his men were getting restless. None of them knew the man inside the house with their target was actually the supreme leader of the Kin. Every minute that passed made it more likely that one of his men would say fuck that dumbass lawyer and start shooting.

Myer couldn't stand looking at Beck and Dent anymore. He could hear his men moving around. It was understandable. They'd been in position for over two hours. At least two of them were talking back and forth, which was plain stupid. And dangerous.

Myer looked at his watch. Dave Greene had been gone too long. Something was wrong. Still no sign of Beck's men. Myer had to admit the possibility that they figured out this was a trap. Well, so be it. Beck had three men. Three. He had eleven, well ten now, with Dave Greene missing. Plus, six more he'd left in a clearing a couple of hundred yards east of the house who were guarding the trucks and ATVs his men had used to get on site. Plus Devereaux's fighters behind the house.

Let Beck's men try something. Myer hoped they would try. It would be a slaughter. What difference did it make if they killed Beck's men in the house or out here? A few more casualties on their side. No big deal. All his men except for Jefferson Baxter had assault rifles and plenty of ammunition. Their weapons would shoot as fast as his men could pull the triggers. No way three of Beck's men could win against them.

Myer walked to the end of the shooting line on his side, telling everyone to sit tight, relax, wait until the lawyer left, and shoot on his command. Then he walked back across the road, doing the same on the other end of the line. He saw Jefferson Baxter sitting on his shooting mat, his back against a dying ash tree, the Sig Sauer MCX Rattler resting across his knees. He seemed completely relaxed. Why not? The guy had served two tours in Afghanistan.

Baxter stared at the house even though nothing inside had changed. It would have pleased Myer to know that the Army vet had been passing the time thinking about what he would do once the firing started. Baxter had rehearsed it in his mind over and over. Push off the tree. Pivot right while planting his right knee on the ground. Bring the left knee up. Prop his left elbow on his knee. Acquire the target. Commence firing. Baxter expected to kill the man within ten seconds max.

Myer thought about his shooter at the other end of the firing line, an ex-Marine sniper named Peter Felker. It had been six years since Felker served on active duty in Afghanistan, but he still trained with his weapons at least once a month. And Felker's ability to lie prone and remain ready for extended periods hadn't waned one bit. Or, at least, that's what Felker told himself. *It's just like riding a bike, Pete.* Over the last two hours, he'd hardly moved other than to occasionally secure the butt of his M40A5 rifle against his left shoulder and place the crosshairs of his Leopold scope over his target's head. The range was ridiculously close. Not more than fifty yards. The only thing between him and his target was the glass in the large front window. *No problemo. A 7.62 NATO round would go through that like it was nuthin'. Course, if the asshole moves off the couch and out of sight* ... Felker made a face and pulled back from the scope ... *just keep pumping rounds in there and let shit happen.*

Of the other nine men in Myer's shooting line, one was asleep, all were dealing with the frigid night air seeping into them, and not one of them anticipated what was about to happen.

49

Manny Guzman stared at Andy Miller and said, "Why do you want to know the exact address of that house?"

"Because I want to know how long it's going to take us to get there."

"Why?"

Miller looked down and rubbed the front of his forehead. Manny watched him struggle with something. He waited, giving Miller time to come to it. But Miller said nothing. Manny's patience with Miller ran out. His patience with everything ran out. Miller's dark, barely furnished house. Miller's clothes that never changed. His constant dissembling.

"Why?" Manny said. "Tell me."

Finally, Miller looked up.

"I don't even know if it will do any damn good." He looked at his watch. He turned to Irene. "Middle of the night." He looked back at Manny. "Your boys are probably dead by now."

"What?! What are you telling me?"

Miller muttered to himself. "I knew something was going down earlier tonight. I sure as hell didn't know where until you gave me that address. The Kin owns a ton of property around Winholm."

Manny stood up. He stormed over to the counter and picked up his gun. Miller followed him.

Manny asked, "How'd you know something was going down?"

Miller picked up his Glock and put it in the pocket of his coveralls. He headed for the hallway toward the back of his house. Manny and Irene followed close behind.

Miller said, "The supreme leader came down from on high to give orders. The Kin boys are going all in tonight. It might already be all over."

Miller led Manny and Irene to his bedroom. He pulled back a sliding closet door and stared at two long-guns propped against the back wall, boxes of ammunition and two bulletproof vests on the shelf. He quickly laid everything down on his neatly made bed.

"Tell me exactly what you saw."

"I saw Devereaux and Proctor go in the barn around seven. Vic was already in there. George was sitting in the back, making sure no one got close to the barn. I never seen all three of them in the same place at the same time. I thought, shit, wonder if the top dog will show. I knew he wouldn't go in the back door like the others. There's a front door to the barn shut with a lock and chain. So I slipped around the front. I missed the Kommandant coming in but not going out."

Irene asked, "The what?"

"The Kommandant. Camdyn Dent. The supreme commander."

Irene said, "Shit. Are you kidding? That's what Camdyn Dent stands for?"

"Yes. It's not a name. It's a title."

Manny shook his head and muttered, "Fuck."

Irene said. "Unbelievable."

"Believe it."

"So, who is he?"

"It was dark. He had a hood up when he snuck out. But I followed him. The slippery bastard had his car parked up the road. Not a big guy. About my height. When he got in, the interior lights went on. Dark hair. A little long. Glasses. Tie and shirt."

Irene had been standing just inside the bedroom door. She moved closer to Miller.

"What kind of car was he driving?"

"A Subaru. Outback. Too dark to make out the color. Tan or beige."

Irene said, "I don't believe it."

Miller stopped what he was doing.

"Don't believe what?"

For the first time in all the time Irene had known Andy Miller, he raised his voice.

"You know who he is?"

Just as she was about to answer, Manny's phone rang. He checked the caller ID and answered it.

"Alex, what's up?"

Irene and Miller watched Manny's eyes narrow. They only heard Manny's side of the conversation.

"Right. Yes. Seems like it. Where are Ciro and Demarco? Okay. Heading there now."

Irene and Miller looked at Manny. He said, "The safehouse is a trap. We have to go."

Miller said, "Who got the safehouse?"

Irene answered. "The lawyer Beck got for me. Peter Morelli. Camdyn Dent."

50

As soon as they saw the glow from the lights inside the house, Ciro and Demarco stepped off the road.

Demarco said, "Any closer, and they'll hear us." He nodded to his left. "I'll go in on this side and get behind them. You take the other side."

Ciro whispered, "Start with the twenty-twos. Less chance they'll hear them. Aim for their heads, switch to the heavy rounds when the shit kicks off."

Demarco held up Lund's Remington. "Right. I've got only ten rounds in this thing. I'll wait for you to start. There will be a hell of shot fired, Ciro, so find cover and keep moving."

Ciro said, "Fuck 'em." He pulled his knit cap down tight. He had Greene's Rock River AR-15 slung over his left shoulder, Lund's Trojan AR-15 over his right, and his .45 handgun in his waistband. He carried his Smith and Wesson MP 15-22 in his right hand. All the weapons were fully loaded, and he had extra magazines in every pocket. All the weapons and ammo added forty pounds. Ciro's Kevlar vest, overcoat, and boots added more weight. As strong as he was, Ciro Baldassare wasn't built to move easily under that weight through a snow-covered forest in the dark.

Demarco was nearly as strong as Ciro, and he carried a lighter load. Two long guns – Lund's Remington and Beck's Mossberg. He had a ten-round magazine for the shotgun in the pocket of his down jacket, four magazines for the two Glocks shoved into his waistband, and the Spyderco knife stuck clipped to his belt.

Demarco dropped a fist on Ciro's shoulder and turned into the forest. Neither man had anything to say. What could you say to someone who might be dead soon? Demarco disappeared before Ciro made it across the road and into the woods on his side.

Ciro's dark wool overcoat hanging past his knees made him difficult to spot in the dark forest, but the heavy overcoat soon picked up a coating of snow further weighing him down. Decades of piled leaves were under the snow and ice. With every sinking step, Ciro had to fight to keep his balance. He could make out the shapes of trees in the darkness, but he kept running into saplings, bushes, and hummocks of vegetation. Within three minutes, Ciro had to pause. The big man leaned against a red maple. He looked to his right, gauging his progress by where he stood opposite the house, more visible now with all the lights blazing inside. He'd come less than halfway to where he imagined the end of the firing line would be. He could see the clouds of water vapor he exhaled. He swallowed, tried to relax, went down on one knee. He peered into the dark where he thought the ambushers might be but couldn't see any clear targets.

Ciro knew Demarco would soon be in position. He'd been trying to match Demarco's speed. Stupid. He had to slow down, step more carefully and steadily, and angle toward the house until he could see his targets.

He stood and moved forward, pushing aside underbrush, climbing over fallen trees. He stopped, thinking he'd heard voices. He held his breath for a moment, listening. All he heard was a gust of wind blowing through the forest that made the trees above him creak and crack in the cold. Ciro shouldered past a stand of hobblebush and found himself in a small clearing. He peered around, worried that he might be visible. He took a step forward, slipped, and fell down on one knee. He stifled a curse. He saw the far end of the house. He had to be fairly close to the firing line, but he still couldn't make out the shooters. He wasn't sure he could get any closer without the enemy hearing him stumbling and struggling.

And then Ciro saw something he couldn't believe. Five feet in front of him and a couple of feet to his right, a crude wooden ladder stood propped against an oak tree with a double trunk. Hunters had made the ladder out of wood slats nailed to eight foot two-by-fours. A way out of the goddamn mess in this godforsaken shit-bag, freezing forest.

Ciro picked himself up and moved slowly toward the ladder. Looking up, he saw a crudely built deer blind about fifteen feet above him. It looked nearly derelict. The base was a platform made with three-quarter inch plywood nailed into the two main crooks of the oak tree. The sides of the blind were four by eight sheets of three-quarter inch plywood. There was an opening cut into the piece of plywood above the ladder to allow access to the blind. There was no overhang or roof.

Ciro had no idea if the wooden slats on the weathered ladder would hold his weight. He hiked the Trojan Firearms AR-15 more securely on his left shoulder, took the Rock River AR off his right shoulder, and replaced it with the MP 15-22. He propped the Rock River AR against the tree and placed a boot on the bottom rung of the ladder. He stepped up onto the rung, holding tightly to the two-by-four side rails, fully expecting the rung to break. It held. Slowly, carefully, he eased his right foot onto the next rung, grabbing the two-by-four rails of the ladder to transfer part of his weight off the rungs. He brought his left foot up to the next rung and slowly stepped up, pulling himself higher. He winced as he heard the rung creak under his weight. He muttered a curse, continued up, fearing that with each step the rung bearing all his weight would break, knowing that the higher he went, the worse the fall would be.

The terrain on Demarco's side of the forest was just as bad as on Ciro's, but he moved easily through the ice, snow, and undergrowth. He stayed relaxed and didn't rush. He moved steadily and quietly from tree to tree trying to spot his enemies.

The more Demarco saw, the more determined he became to even the odds. He passed three shooters lined up facing the house. A gap of about six feet separated them. He saw another shooter ten feet after that. That made four, one left at the end of the line. Five men, all of them presumably armed with military-style assault rifles designed to do one thing – kill human beings. Assault rifles fired small bullets with tremendous velocity. He and Ciro wore level 111A vests which could stop most of the rounds fired from assault rifles. The impact would incapacitate them, not kill them. If a high-velocity bullet hit an arm or leg, it would create a small entrance wound and then fragment and turn sideways inside the body, shattering bones and destroying massive amounts of soft tissue. If the bullet made it all the way through, it would tear open horrifying exit wounds.

Demarco stopped and closed his eyes to preserve as much of his night vision as possible. Most of the illumination in the forest came from the house. He hoped that once he reached the last man on the firing line there'd be enough light from the house to see his enemy.

Demarco stopped thinking about bullet wounds. About how James had discovered this was an ambush. Or if Ciro had gotten into position. He slipped away from behind the tree and kept going, intent on doing one thing – eliminate the first enemy. After that, and only after that, would he think about the next one. And the next. And the next until it was over, or he was dead.

51

Inside the rental house, Dent sneered at Beck and said, "So what's your answer, Beck? Or are you too dim to comprehend the question?"

Beck stared at Dent. He looked like a rational human with his professorial wire-rimmed glasses, lawyerly white shirt and suit, practical winter shoes. But the words coming out of his mouth made him look vicious, twisting his face with contempt.

Dent leaned forward, lost in his belief that he had a righteous argument and the power to persuade someone like James Beck. He went on about how the Kin was doing what the people of this great nation really wanted. What the people they elect year after year really wanted.

Beck finally said, "And what is it they really want?"

"They want the garbage removed from the system. The weak, the faithless, the degenerate, the mongrels and deviants."

Dent paused, waiting for a reaction from Beck. He got none. And for Camdyn Dent that was the most insulting reaction possible.

Rage raised Dent to another level of outrage.

"What is wrong with you, Beck? Do you think you can ignore me? I have more than twenty armed men out there. What have you got? What could you have? Three men? So your little phone conversation gave you a chance to get word to them. So what? So they're out there trying to figure out how to rescue you. I hope they try. They'll be slaughtered and so will you. Problem solved and the Kin will move on just as it has for decades, with or without me."

Beck nodded, staring at Dent, unmoving.

Dent slid toward the edge of the couch and leaned closer.

"Your only chance is to make a deal with me, Beck. Walk out of here with me. My man out there in charge knows who I am. He'll tell the others to stand down. You can drive out of here. If you want to keep up this fight, I'll accommodate you another time. But I wouldn't advise it. Your best option is to run far and fast."

Beck sat up a bit straighter.

Dent yelled, "Answer me, Beck!"

Ciro stepped up onto the deer blind. There was a moment of relief quickly replaced by dread when he realized he'd have to use the rickety ladder to get down.

He walked carefully toward the far side of the deer blind, the plywood platform sagging under his weight. He looked past the four-foot wall. From fifteen feet up, he could see from the right end of the firing line almost to the middle. The house was lit but didn't reveal much detail on the ground. He tried to spot the shooter at the end of the line. That's where he wanted to start, but he still couldn't clearly see a target visible on the dark forest floor.

That target was Peter Felker, the ex-Marine. Felker enjoyed preaching about the Marine Corp slogan – *Improvise, Adapt, Overcome*. Felker knew there would be nothing to eat out in the cold forest. He knew he'd be burning calories just to keep warm, so he decided to improvise, adapt, and overcome by stuffing his pockets with energy bars. He should have followed another slogan – Reduce, Reuse, Recycle.

Felker shoved the last half of his fourth energy bar into his mouth, crumpled the metallic wrapper, and tossed it near the other three wrappers piled near his right shoulder.

The crumpling sound caught Ciro Baldassare's attention. He looked in Felker's direction. Then he saw the light from the house reflecting off the pile of four energy bar wrappers. Now that he knew where to look, Ciro picked out Felker's shape lying on his shooting mat – his boots, legs, the mound of his back and shoulders. And Peter Felker's head positioned behind the scope on his M40A5 sniper rifle.

Ciro went down on one knee. He shouldered his S&W MP 15-22, gripped the rifle's polymer rail surrounding the barrel, and rested his left elbow on the edge of the plywood wall. There was just enough light for Ciro to place the rifle's Magpul sights a bit to the right of Felker's left ear. Just like he and Demarco had planned. Ciro breathed in and held his breath, ready to send a quiet stream of .22 caliber bullets out of the flash-suppressed muzzle of his MP 15 into Peter Felker's head.

Demarco Jones had been in position for three long minutes, patiently waiting for Ciro to start shooting. He'd spotted Jefferson Baxter sitting against a narrow hemlock tree, his back to Demarco, clearly silhouetted against the house's glowing picture window. Unfortunately, only about two inches of Baxter's head and ear were visible. His shoulder, part of his back, his hip, and leg were exposed, but a twenty-two in those parts of his body wouldn't kill him. It had to be a head shot, and there wasn't enough of a target. Demarco couldn't risk missing. Demarco waited for the sound of gunfire to make the shooter at his end of the firing line move away from that tree.

Dent yelled again, "Answer me, Beck!"

And finally, Beck did. He exploded off the couch. Before Dent could even react, Beck's right knee slammed into the underside of his jaw and neck, then dropped down crushing Dent's crotch with over two-hundred pounds as Beck smashed the butt of his Browning Hi-Power into Dent's face, shattering his nose and ripping a gash from the his forehead to his upper lip.

Dent had never experienced such pain in his entire life. He barely had time to flinch before the triple impact hit him, producing a wave of agony. He couldn't breathe, couldn't move, couldn't even think. In two seconds, the arrogant, entitled supreme Kommandant of the Kin ceased to exist leaving only a broken, disabled Peter Morelli.

Beck swept Morelli's compact Ruger away with his left hand as he pushed himself off Morelli and landed on the couch next to him. He wrapped his left arm around Morelli's neck, stood, and lifted the smaller man to his feet, holding the limp body in front of him. He turned sideways, jamming his left hip into Morelli as he pulled the shorter man's head back. Morelli gagged and flailed weakly at Beck's forearm. Beck raised his Browning and fired at the front window as fast as he could pull the trigger on his semi-auto handgun. The thermopane window exploded into a cascade of broken glass. Beck kept firing blindly at whoever was out there while he stepped back toward the fireplace, dragging Morelli along as a shield against the sporadic return fire from the Kin.

Beck's gunshots startled Jefferson Baxter. Instead of moving smoothly he lurched off the tree and still off balance tried to get into his shooting stance. Demarco waited as Baxter lifted his Sig into position, then calmly squeezed off four shots from Oscar Lund's Remington 10/22. Two shots went into the back of Baxter's head, making the would-be assassin bow. The next shot hit his neck. The last shot went into his spine at shoulder level. The Army vet died with his finger on the trigger of his Sig Sauer MCX Rattler, pulling off one shot as he hit the ground.

Ciro Baldassare's first shot came almost simultaneous with Beck's. His concentration was so intense, the MP 15 never wavered. He shot six bullets at the back of Peter Felker's head. All six hit within a three-inch space. Felker died with a mouth filled with a half-chewed dark chocolate, peanut butter energy bar.

None of the shooters on the firing line heard Demarco's or Ciro's twenty-twos. All they saw or heard were the shots from

Beck's 9-millimeter Browning blowing out the main window of the house and coming in their direction. It was the last thing any of them expected. Two shooters in the center of the line began to return fire. By the time Myer jumped up and yelled, "Cease fire! Cease fire!" all his men were shooting.

From his perch in the deer blind Ciro saw Myer waving his arms and yelling. Ciro shifted his aim to the left and opened fire, sending round after round at Myer's head, shooting ten rounds in rapid succession. Myer fell to the ground. Ciro kept shooting at the inert body until his weapon clicked empty. Ciro knew that with all the shooting, the flash suppressor on his MP 15 would make it unlikely for anyone to see him from fifteen feet below. Ciro ducked down and switched to the Trojan AR as he heard the booming explosions of Demarco Jones blasting the Mossberg shotgun.

Morelli had been right about one thing. The inside of the house exploded with automatic weapons fire. But it took longer than the two seconds he predicted. Between the initial shock and confusion, and Vic Myer yelling cease fire, it took nearly ten seconds for everyone on the firing line to open up.

Those ten seconds saved Beck from certain death. He kept Morelli's body in front of him and remained sideways as he stepped around the far end of the couch. He was almost into the kitchen area when the first bullet hit Morelli's left pelvis. The bullet fragmented and exited in pieces that cut into Beck's lower back. The second bullet to hit Morelli pierced his liver and kidney, exited his back after ricocheting off a rib and cut across Beck's stomach.

Worse than the bullets were the shattered pieces of glass spraying through the room along with chunks of sheet rock blown out of the front wall, pieces of the dining table, chairs, couches, and wood flooring.

Beck let go of Morelli's body and shoved it toward the empty window. He dove into the kitchen area as something cut into the right side of his face and arm. It stung like a razor slashing his face, but Beck ignored the wounds, and landed on the floor behind the end of the counter.

He stayed low, out of the lines of fire, and waited, trying to sense if the shooting might be subsiding. The opening to the hallway was six feet away. He had to make it into the hallway and try to reach the far end of the house to have any chance of escape.

Demarco was gone two seconds after Baxter hit the ground. He dropped the Remington even though he had six shots left and picked up Beck's mag-fed shotgun. He brought the shotgun up to hip level and moved quickly and steadily behind the line of Kin shooters, hustling across the uneven ground and underbrush back toward the dirt road. He didn't bother to aim through the shotgun's sights. He pointed the shotgun in the direction of the muzzle flashes in front of him. Each time he picked out a flash, he pumped two blasts of heavy 12-gauge buckshot at that area and moved on, keeping the shots low so he would hit flesh.

Ciro left his MP 15 behind and hustled over to the ladder. He gripped the wooden rails and held firm, going down fast, not caring if the slats broke. He hit the ground hard, jarring his repaired Achilles tendon.

He ignored the pain, crouched low, and picked up the Rock River Arms assault rifle he'd left at the base of the tree.

The booming shotgun kept blasting off to his left. Demarco doing his part.

The first volley of shots from the Kin shooters waned as several of them stopped to reload. Ciro knew he'd taken out two of them. From where he crouched, he counted three spots illuminated by muzzle flashes.

He checked the safety on the Rock River Arms assault rifle. Smacked the magazine to make sure it was securely in place and chambered a round.

Ciro moved to his left, out from behind cover of the oak tree's double trunk. He carried Lund's Trojan Firearms assault rifle in one hand and the Red Rock Arms rifle in the other. Ciro knew that once he started shooting the rifles, he'd give away his position, just like the flashes from Myer's shooters were giving away theirs. He knew he couldn't shoot and move through the forest like Demarco. He had to pick a spot and shoot to kill.

He moved closer to where he saw flashes, looking for cover. He was limping now. He thought about Beck inside the house. He didn't have much hope that his friend, the man who'd saved his life in a prison riot years ago, could have survived that first volley of gunfire. The thought enraged him, burning away his fatigue and pain. He saw a spot behind a large white pine that would give him enough cover. The Kin shooters were still shooting at the house. It seemed idiotic. They had already blown out all the windows, disintegrated parts of the wall facing them, and ripped apart the interior. He could make out three areas where muzzles flashed. All within range. He had two rifles and four extra magazines of ammunition.

Ciro Baldassare didn't care that this might be his last stand. He believed he could take out at least two of them before they took him down. The big pine was big enough cover him. He'd shoot from one side of the tree, then the other. Keep at it until he was dead, or they were.

The gunfire seemed more sporadic. Intermittent bursts of fire came into the house. Beck gathered himself for his last dash into the hallway. He reached up to his face and touched what felt like a piece of wood buried in his right cheek. A splinter of the floor stabbing his cheekbone. The pain was so intense it made his right eye water. He grabbed the splinter between his thumb and forefinger and pulled it out. Pain flashed through his face and blood flowed from the wound.

"Fuck!"

He quickly looked back into the open seating area. Peter Morelli / Camdyn Dent looked like a bloody, adult-size rag doll draped over the end of the couch. A bullet had entered his head while he lay on the couch, blasting out a chunk of his skull and brains. The entrance to the hallway was six feet away on a slight diagonal. There was a Viking stove in an alcove formed by what looked like two stone pillars. Beck figured that would give him cover and shorten the empty space he had to cross to about four feet.

Suddenly, a single shot cracked through one of the sliding glass doors that opened out to the back of the house. The bullet grazed Beck's upper arm and lodged into the base of the counter. There were more Kin shooters in back. Beck threw himself down to the floor as two more shots landed where he had been leaning against the counter base. Another volley of high-velocity ammunition ripped into the front room as Beck scrambled for the hallway.

As soon as he fired the last round in the Mossberg, Demarco hit the ground, turned over on his back, and became invisible. He popped out the empty magazine and shoved in the second mag filled with shells holding single slugs. Two shooters had figured out that someone was shooting at them from behind and were shooting back with round after round of supersonic ammunition. But that's all they were doing. Shooting back. Firing as fast as they could pull their triggers. They had no idea where their enemies were. Bullets were zinging above Demarco about four feet to his right, ripping through the forest, splintering trees, tearing up undergrowth and ground. And stupidly, giving away the shooters' positions.

Demarco rolled over onto one knee, fired two slugs at the closest muzzle flash, then two more at the shooter on the right. He dropped back down and crawled away. Even if Demarco hadn't hit the last two shooters, he'd achieved his goal. Anybody on his side of the road still shooting was aiming in his direction, not at the house.

And then Demarco heard bursts of gunfire from across the road.

Ciro Baldassare unleashed.

If James had survived the first barrages of deadly fire, he now had a chance to get out of the house, and they had a chance to get him out of the trap. Demarco stayed low, turned back where he'd come from, moving fast. He headed for the parking area past the left end of the house. When he reached the corpse of Jefferson Baxter, he picked up the short-barrel, compact Sig Sauer MCX Rattler.

Baxter had no use for it. Demarco Jones did.

52

There was no GPS in Manny's 4Runner. He wouldn't have looked at it anyway at the speed he drove. Irene tracked their position on her iPhone.

From the back seat, Andy Miller said, "Can't help anybody if we die before we get there, Mr. Eddie."

Manny said, "It's Manny. And drop the mister." He asked Irene, "How long?"

Irene looked up and down from her iPhone screen. They had just blasted through Freehold, Manny barely slowing down at a curve.

Irene said, "Maybe five, six minutes."

Manny and Irene were in the front seat, Miller in the back with the long guns.

Manny kept his eyes on the road and asked Miller, "What did you bring?"

"My Glock and two rifles. An M16, military issue that can shoot full auto. That's mine. You get an AR-15. Semi-auto with a thirty-round magazine. That's it for ammo."

"What about Irene?"

"I'm assuming Miss Irene has a gun. Should be enough. She's got one target."

"What?"

"Emmett Devereaux. The Kin is all in on this one, so he'll be there. Along with at least a few of his men."

"Anybody else?"

"Who else? Beck and your pals are supposed to be there, right?"

"Yes."

"Then Vic Myer will be there with a bunch of his militia fighters."

"Do you know the house?"

Miller said, "Never seen it but I heard talk about it. The place is out in the middle of nowhere. Shitbag scrub forest on all sides. Bad terrain. In the back, the woods don't go too far before they run into Belleville Creek. Might as well be a moat."

Irene stared out at the two-lane highway they were running on. They'd whipped past dense forest areas and open fields and had yet to see a car in either direction. Irene had been pressing her right foot against the floorboard as if there was a brake pedal there.

Irene said, "Figure Vic and his men will do the shooting. Devereaux will do the same thing he did at my house. He'll hide his men outside to prevent anybody in the house from getting away. Then they'll gather up the dead and wounded, and nobody will ever know they were there."

"That ain't all he'll do," said Miller. "He'll take body parts as souvenirs."

Irene said, "So he's not just a killer, he's also a pervert?" Suddenly, Irene said, "Shit! Stop, Manny."

She was the first to see the faint red and blue glow from lights flashing ahead somewhere around a curve in the road.

Manny braked hard.

Miller hissed, "Cut your headlights. Looks like that dogshit, son-of-a-bitch Abel Proctor is in this, too. The road we're on is the only way to get to the house. He must have roadblocks set up to keep anybody from goin' in or out until the slaughter is over. Well, if Proctor is still here, maybe it ain't over yet."

Manny peered over steering wheel.

"We can shoot our way past."

"Killin' sheriff's deputies ain't all that helpful. Plus, it'll let the Kin boys in there know we're comin'. Let's see if we can get around him. Go ahead slow."

"How far is it to the house?"

Irene checked her phone and said, "Quarter mile. Maybe a little more. We don't have time to walk it."

Manny eased forward.

"There," said Miller. "On your left. What's that? A driveway? A road?"

Manny didn't waste time answering. He made the left turn and followed a narrow asphalt lane as it rose up and away from Route 32. After a couple of hundred yards, Manny turned his headlights back on revealing an unsettling sight – an abandoned cemetery filled with tombstones and grave markers dating back to the seventeen hundreds. Forest litter and leaves covered the ground. The asphalt turned into a snow-covered path that rose deeper into the foreboding cemetery.

Irene followed a blue dot on her iPhone to track the direction they were heading. "Take a right when you can so we can move parallel to the two-lane down there and get past the roadblock."

Manny thought he saw a space between the crowded graves. Snow covered everything but not too deeply. He put the Toyota into four-wheel drive and edged into a left turn. His headlights illuminated gray slabs of tombstones leaning every which way, each one of them standing as a prophecy of death.

Miller said, "See if you can get by with just your running lights. If those bastards look up now, they might see us."

Again, Manny turned off his headlights. He picked his way forward mostly by feel, correcting his path when he heard the 4Runner bump into a tombstone. He thought about asking Irene or Andy to get out and guide him, but it wouldn't do any good without flashlights, which they didn't have.

On the right side of the Toyota, Irene and Miller could see the faint glow of red and blue lights flashing below them. They'd made it past the first roadblock.

Manny kept going through the cemetery. For some reason, he found the idea of being buried in a long-abandoned cemetery comforting. He strayed left and knocked down a tombstone. And then two more getting back in the right direction. He winced at the desecration.

The glow of the sheriffs' patrol car lights disappeared behind them.

Miller said, "We're passed the roadblock. Head right and see if we can find a way back down."

Manny turned right. There was no way forward except over graves and more tombstones. Out of the darkness a stone wall appeared blocking their progress. He braked suddenly, muttering a soft curse. "Shit."

Manny turned on his headlights. He got out of the Toyota and looked at the stone wall under the glare. It looked old. No longer sturdy and only about three feet high, but there was no way to get over it. Manny looked to his left and right and didn't see any breaks in the wall.

Andy Miller came out of the back seat, took one look, and said, "C'mon."

He strode toward the wall and without hesitation started lifting and pitching stones on the far side of the wall.

He said to Manny, "Don't just stand there, man. Do the same on your side. We got to make a ramp out of these stones, or we'll never get over."

Manny realized there was no mortar holding the stones together. He said, "Why don't I just knock it down with the car?"

"You need a ramp on this side. C'mon."

Manny jumped to the task, surprised at how strong the scarecrow Andy Miller was. It took an exhausting but surprisingly short amount of time to reconfigure the wall. Irene helped extend the ramp on their side.

By the time they finished, Manny had almost given up hope that they would get to the safehouse in time to help Beck. And then they heard the faint sounds of gunfire in the dead of night.

The three of them ran to the car. Manny tried to edge his front wheels onto the stones, but his back wheels spun uselessly on the snow and dead leaves. He put the Toyota in reverse and backed up slowly. When he was twenty feet from their improvised ramp, he reversed direction and moved forward. Slowly at first and then building speed. The gunfire below increased. Irene held onto the dashboard, cringing. Miller tightened his seat belt and grabbed the handle over the back door. There was no turning back now.

The front tires pitched up violently onto the stones. If it weren't for the seat belts, all three of them would have hit their heads on the car's roof. Manny kept his foot on the accelerator. They heard and felt an excruciating bang and then a grinding screech as the 4Runner's oil pan, transmission cover, and muffler scraped over the top of the wall and pitched downward like a roller coaster car.

Manny Guzman didn't hesitate or brake as the SUV headed downhill, bouncing and banging over the uneven ground. Everybody in the car felt like their backs might snap with each bone jarring impact. The 5,000-pound vehicle knocked down or flew over brush and saplings. Manny dodged past larger trees. A side view mirror ripped off. The right headlight disappeared. Luckily, the trees were sparse. Manny fought to keep the Toyota from turning over. As they approached the two-lane highway the ground levelled off. But now they had another problem. The drainage ditch on their side of the highway was too deep and too wide to cross. They'd survived the downhill death ride, but they wouldn't make it over the ditch.

Manny wrenched the steering wheel left and just missed crashing into the ditch. Irene let out a string of curses. Manny accelerated to keep from stalling. They picked up speed running alongside the drainage ditch heading toward a dense section of forest. It was either crash into the trees or turn right and take their chances. It was too late to stop.

Manny saw what looked like a mound of earth meeting the highway where the forest started. He took a chance and accelerated, made a hard right. The SUV hit the mound. The front wheels flew up off the ground. The left edge of the bumper banged into a tree. The impact sent the Toyota spinning toward the highway. The right front wheel hit the asphalt, breaking a strut, the left front came down hard with a loud bang. The four-wheel drive put enough power into the front wheels to drag the 4Runner onto the road. The car almost slid off the other side as Manny wrenched the wheel back left, then right to straighten the SUV out.

He accelerated along the narrow two-lane highway as oil and transmission fluid leaked and coolant spewed out of the cracked radiator. The remains of the muffler and tailpipe scraped over the road.

Nobody in the Toyota said a word.

Miller turned around to see if the sheriffs were coming after them. The road was dark. Manny saw the derelict shed that marked the road leading into the forest ahead.

Miller yelled, "This is it! Turn right!"

Manny turned in toward the sound of gunfire.

Something started grinding under the Toyota. Manny kept the accelerator down, but the car kept losing power. As they approached Demarco's Honda Ridgeline, the 4Runner died.

There was just enough momentum for Manny to steer the 4Runner off the dirt road. He turned off the ignition so he wouldn't start a fire.

Irene said, "I can't believe that happened."

Manny turned to Andy Miller and said, "Give me that rifle."

53

Abel Proctor spotted headlights moving on the rise high above him. The lights disappeared after about a minute. Seeing them up there concerned him, but he knew that homeowners used Route 62, about a half-mile on the other side of that ridge, to access their houses. He figured maybe somebody made a wrong turn or was taking a shortcut to their house. It didn't matter. There was no way anyone could get down onto Route 32 from there.

Before Proctor and his deputies set up the roadblocks, they had waited out of sight until Camdyn Dent arrived shortly after eleven. They kept out of sight when Beck arrived in his GMC shortly after midnight, and when Demarco and Ciro followed forty minutes later in the Honda Ridgeline. Proctor wasn't sure how many were in the two trucks. It didn't matter. Dent's plan seemed to be working. Whoever was in that house wasn't coming out alive.

Proctor closed off access to the house at 1:00 a.m. He set up sobriety checkpoints manned by himself and one deputy in a patrol car a quarter-mile east of the dirt road that led to the safehouse, and another a quarter-mile west of the road manned by two more deputies in a department patrol car.

It was 1:40 a.m. Getting close to the two o'clock deadline. Proctor rechecked his watch. The Kommandant should be driving out any time now. Suddenly, he heard a volley of shots. Then sporadic shooting. Then waves of gunfire.

The slaughter had begun. The James Beck problem would be over soon.

But where the hell was Camdyn Dent?

54

Ciro Baldassare stuck to his plan. Hunched over, kicking his way through the snow and foliage in the black forest toward the middle of the Kin firing line, he found a maple tree wide enough to supply cover.

From where he stood, he saw three areas where muzzle flashes revealed men still shooting sporadically at the house. He laid the Trojan Firearms AR-15 barrel up against the tree and took the Rock River Arms rifle off his shoulder. He found the safety on the left side above the pistol grip and flipped it into firing position. He chambered a round and leaned out from the right side of the tree. He was invisible. The shooters on the Kin line didn't even know he existed. Ciro breathed slowly, raised the rifle to his shoulder, firing quickly and steadily, spraying bullets around two areas, first around the muzzle flashes farthest right, then one shooter over to the left. Back and forth until his weapon clicked empty.

He spun back behind the tree, released the magazine, pulled another from his coat pocket, and reloaded. Somebody on the line had finally figured out shots were coming from behind them. Ciro saw low-hanging branches, bushes, and trees splintering and flying apart as high-velocity bullets hit them. None of the shots found his maple tree. When the shooting subsided, he leaned out the other side of the tree. He saw one muzzle flash. He got off six shots before return fire came in his direction. This time, bullets smacked into the maple tree. He got behind the tree, but not before a bullet clipped his right side. It pierced his wool overcoat, skimmed across the middle of his right side, and continued on, tearing the side of his bulletproof vest. Even so, the bullet had enough velocity to spin him around and down to his knees.

Down but not out. Ciro snarled and held the AR out from behind the tree. With one hand on the pistol grip and the other on the butt to steady it, he fired off a steady stream of bullets in a short arc and pulled the rifle back when it clicked empty for the second time.

The return fire came almost immediately. It came from two shooters in the area left of his tree. Ciro sat back against the tree. He laid down the empty Rock River Arms AR and grabbed the Trojan Arms rifle. He had whatever was in the second rifle and two more full magazines. Ciro struggled to his feet. He leaned out the left side of the tree and fired six quick shots. Same result. The return fire came quickly. Ciro barely made it safely behind the lifesaving maple tree.

"Fuck!"

They had him trapped.

Moving fast with the Mossberg in one hand and the Sig Rattler machine pistol in the other, Demarco made it unseen to the parking area in front of the west end of the house. Morelli had parked his Subaru nearest to the house. Beck's GMC next to it. Demarco positioned himself behind the Subaru where he could see what was left of the Kin firing line. Based on the muzzle flashes, Demarco figured there were three shooters still alive. One on his side of the dirt road and two on the other side. The shooter on his side kept firing sporadically into the house. The other two were shooting away from the house at Ciro.

Along with the muzzle flashes, the light from the house made the active shooters visible. Demarco also heard one Kin shooter screaming for help on his side of the road.

The two shooters farthest from Demarco had Ciro pinned down. The big man was holding his own. Returning fire in careful three-shot bursts, keeping his enemies also pinned down. Demarco figured Ciro didn't have much time before his ammunition ran out.

Demarco pulled out the sliding stock on the Rattler another notch and eased toward the front of Morelli's Outback. Demarco guessed the machine pistol had a thirty-round magazine. That meant he had twenty-nine shots. Demarco rested his left forearm on the left front fender of the Subaru and held the Rattler steady, aiming through the sights mounted on the Rattler's Picatinny rail. Demarco waited for the next muzzle flashes on his side of the road. He adjusted his aim slightly and fired off six rounds. The shooting on his side of the road stopped on the fourth shot. Two Kin shooters left, and one wounded and screaming.

Manny jumped out of the wrecked 4Runner and ran towards Demarco's truck. Andy Miller and Irene hurried after him. Miller caught up to Manny. He yelled, "Here!" and held out a Radical Firearms SOCOM AR-15. Manny grabbed the rifle and pulled open the truck door.

"Is the safety off?"

Miller said, "Yes. Round in the chamber."

Manny said, "We have to get James out of there. And Demarco and Ciro if they're still alive."

"Me and Miss Irene are going after Devereaux. The rest of 'em is cannon fodder."

Miller tightened the straps on his bulletproof vest tight and climbed into the truck bed. He stood behind the cab, grabbed onto the Honda's roof rail with his left hand and held his M16 with his right.

Manny and Irene climbed into Demarco's truck. Manny didn't bother to look for the key fob. He knew Demarco would have left it in the truck for a fast getaway. He was right. The engine fired up. He handed his rifle to Irene, maneuvered the Honda onto the narrow road, and roared off toward the battle.

Ciro saw the muzzle flashes and heard the shots coming from the parking area left of the house aimed at his enemies. Demarco had flanked them. He smiled and slammed his last magazine into the Trojan Arms AR. Once again, Ciro stepped out from the left side of the maple tree, but this time he walked toward the Kin firing line. He aimed at where he had last seen muzzle flashes and fired shot after shot, forgetting about taking cover, forgetting about everything except advancing toward his enemy until either he was dead, or they were.

Inside the house, Beck made it to the end of the hallway. He looked into the master bedroom on the left. There were two windows on the back wall and one window at the short end of the room. He turned and looked into the smaller bedroom across the hall. There was a window on the wall facing the front of the house and a short, four-foot door at the far corner of the room. He'd escaped death in the main room behind him, but he was still trapped in the house. There were men shooting out front. And someone had taken two shots at him from the back.

Beck headed for the small door in the corner. He tried to turn the doorknob. Locked. He stood to one side and kicked the doorknob until it broke and the shank flew off the door. He pushed the latch free of the faceplate and pulled open the door revealing a mechanical room, ten by ten and only six feet high. The walls and floors were made out of poured concrete. A small furnace, air handler, well pump, and circuit breaker boxes filled the space. A short set of stairs led down to the sub-ground room.

Beck stepped back. He said to himself, "Fuck that." No way he was going down into that room. And then he heard the sound of glass crunching underfoot out in the main room.

From his vantage point behind the house, Emmett Devereaux had seen Beck attack Camdyn Dent and use him for a shield. But he hadn't seen the result until he stepped through the empty frame of the sliding door and walked over the shattered thermopane glass. The sight of the bullet-ravaged corpse of the Kin's supreme leader paralyzed him for a moment. There was so much blood under the corpse it looked like someone had placed a red blanket on the couch and floor. Devereaux took a step toward the carnage and stopped. What had happened was unthinkable. How? This was supposed to have been a trap for their enemies. And then Devereaux saw the misshapen skull with a piece the size of a fist blown out. The startling whiteness of the bone against the bloody brain tissue. Something in his own head cracked open. A split between sorrow and rage. And then rage took over. Devereaux turned and fired two shots into the hallway, screaming, "You're dead! You're dead!" Repeating it twice more with two more shots. The noise deafened him, and the gun flash blinded him for a moment. He dropped to the floor, just before Beck leaned out the doorway on the end of the hallway and shot twice at him.

Beck spun back into the bedroom expecting Devereaux to return fire, but instead Devereaux crawled with the speed of a snake and made it into the first bedroom on the right side of the hall.

Beck stood next to the open bedroom door, his back flat against the wall, waiting, listening. He'd gotten enough of a glance to know it was Emmett Devereaux who had come into the house. The same man he'd seen at Irene Allen's house.

Devereaux did the same in the first bedroom, except that he was sitting with his back against the wall. He had six men outside stationed where they could see both the back of the house and the far end. Beck's only exit was out to the front. There were still guns firing out there which should discourage Beck from trying to escape that way. But Devereaux couldn't be sure how many of Vic Myer's militia were alive and able to take down Beck if he appeared. Clearly, Beck's men had engaged Myer's militia men. Devereaux couldn't let Beck escape the house. He had to make his move.

From his position in the parking area, Demarco could see Ciro firing at the last Kin shooters on the other side of the road. He angled out from behind the Subaru and did the same, advancing across the road and angling toward the forest where the last of the Kin shooters were hunkered down. Both men kept shooting until there was no return fire.

When the shooting stopped, Demarco veered to his right into the forest, moving fast toward Ciro. He saw Ciro at the edge of the woods, standing over the last of Vic Myer's shooters. He yelled, "It's me!"

Ciro turned and stepped toward Demarco. He was limping and bent over, holding his right side.

"You hit?"

"Got clipped. Didn't get through the vest. Cracked a rib or something. My fucking Achilles hurts, too. How about you?"

"I'm good."

Ciro wasn't surprised Demarco Jones had survived unscathed. The man was a nearly invisible angel of death. Both were half-deaf from shooting without any ear protection, but now that they were standing near the firing line, they heard cries of pain and calls for help from at least one injured man. They hadn't heard Devereaux yelling orders for his men to cover the east end of the house before he ran in looking for Beck.

Ciro said, "We should look for James."

Before Demarco could answer, two shots rang out, and he fell back.

Ciro Baldassare turned and fired shot after shot where he thought he'd seen a muzzle flash. His rifle clicked empty. Ciro dropped it, bent over, and grabbed the collar of Demarco's coat. He leaned back, using his legs and weight to drag his friend farther into the cover of the forest. With one last pull, he fell back, pulling Demarco with him. He heard the roaring engine of a truck and five seconds later saw Demarco's Honda Ridgeline blast into the opening in front of the house and slide to a halt near the front door.

The sudden shooting outside made Devereaux think Beck might have gone out the window in the bedroom at the end of the hall.

Devereaux scrambled out of his room heading toward the bathroom on the other side of the hall. He pegged three shots into the sheetrock wall next to the door of Beck's bedroom, hoping to hit Beck. But Beck was already in the doorway shooting back at Devereaux. He missed. Devereaux was too fast and had hunched over to make himself a small target.

Nobody was hit, but Devereaux had improved his position. He was closer to Beck and had a better angle on the bedroom where Beck was trapped.

Out in front of the house, both doors of Demarco's truck flew open.

When Devereaux ran into the house, all six of his men came out of cover in the forest to cover the house. One in back, and the rest covering the end of the house and heading around to the front. They all carried handguns except for the first one who made it past the far end of the house. He carried an AR-15. He was the one who had shot down Demarco.

Manny jumped down from the driver's seat holding the Radical Firearms AR-15. He opened fire from behind the left front fender of the Honda Ridgeline. Miller remained standing in the truck bed and sprayed Devereaux's men with his M16 on full auto.

Irene jumped out of the Honda, her revolver in hand, and ran toward the front door of the house.

Two of Devereaux's men went down. The remaining two retreated back around the corner of the house. Miller reloaded. He jumped down from the truck bed, advancing toward the corner, ready to open fire.

Suddenly, a phalanx of Kin shooters who had been guarding the vehicles hidden in the forest came running out to join the fight. They opened fire, mostly aiming at Andy Miller because they couldn't see Manny on the driver's side of the Honda Ridgeline. Manny adjusted his aim and shot back. Miller dropped to the ground and returned fire.

From his position back in the forest, Ciro saw the new wave of Kin shooters. He stepped forward, pulled his Smith and Wesson .45, and added to the barrage coming from Manny and Miller.

Suddenly, Demarco Jones jackknifed into a sitting position shouting the first curse Ciro had ever heard come out of his mouth.

"Fuck!"

Ciro yelled, "Holy shit!"

Demarco clutched his chest where his Kevlar vest had stopped the bullets. "Christ almighty. That was a hell of a punch."

Ciro said, "I thought he fucking killed you! You got any more ammunition?"

"Are there more?"

"Yeah, they got Manny and another guy pinned down."

"Manny!"

"Yeah. Manny, the girl, and another guy."

From his sitting position, Demarco pulled out two Glocks and opened fire at the new Kin attackers.

Miller's automatic fire from his M16 cut down one of the Kin shooters. He saw the flashes from Ciro's and Demarco's handguns off to his right. Manny fired the last bullet in his AR-15 taking out another Kin shooter, then opened fire with his long-barrel Taurus revolver. Two more Kin militia went down. Others tried to stumble or run back to the cover of the forest.

Miller jumped up and ran around toward the back of the house after Devereaux's men.

Inside the house, Irene heard Beck's gunshots in the hallway. She stopped and approached the opening, leaned forward. Devereaux popped out of the bathroom and fired three shots into the wall near where he thought Beck was standing, blowing holes in the sheetrock, but he missed Beck who had dropped down flat on the floor.

Irene Allen turned into the hallway with her Colt revolver in hand, the hammer cocked as Devereaux ducked back into the bathroom. She fired one shot that angled into the bathroom but missed Devereaux. Beck heard the shot and looked out and fired twice into the bathroom, but he, too, had a bad angle and missed. He yelled out, "Irene, is that you?"

"Yes!"

"Stay there. Keep him covered."

She stood next to the hallway opening and pointed the snub nosed Colt at the bathroom, determined to shoot Devereaux when he came out. But Devereaux knew he was trapped. He didn't hesitate. He made the decision to go after the weakest one – the woman.

He burst out of the bathroom firing shot after shot in Irene's direction. She fired once and missed. Devereaux was moving too fast. She panicked, pulled hard on the revolver, and fired. Devereaux fired back on the run. The bullet sliced across her left thigh, knocking her leg out from under her. She went down hard but held onto the Colt.

Beck burst into the hallway. He had four bullets left in his Hi-Power Browning. He fired one as Devereaux cleared the hallway, clipping him on the left shoulder. It spun him around and saved him from Irene's next shot. Still from a sitting position, she shot once more, missing. The .38 bullet cracked through the remaining sliding glass door, blowing apart the thermopane.

Beck ran toward the open sitting area, hunched over, hurting from his wounds, wiping blood away from his eyes, his Browning aimed in front of him, ready to shoot. He had wounds in his lower back, buttocks, and thighs, cheek, left arm, stomach, and left shoulder.

Irene had one bullet left. She had managed to scoot back on the floor, take cover behind the far end of the kitchen counter, and get up on her knees.

Devereaux's Glock 17 held seventeen rounds and one in the chamber. He figured he had four, maybe five shots left. He actually had six bullets left, more than Beck and Irene combined.

He was down on one knee using the end of the couch for cover from Irene who was saving her last shot, and from Beck who he knew was coming toward him from the hall. He looked back and forth intent on killing at least one of them, hopefully both. He decided to ignore Irene and shoot Beck.

Devereaux concentrated on the hallway. Beck stopped at the opening. All three were half-deaf from the gunfire inside the house.

Beck stood with his back pressed against the hallway wall. Everything slowed down. Even the gun smoke that filled the house seemed to drift slowly, wafting lazily in space. The last few gunshots outside ceased.

Beck slowly slid down the wall into a seated position. He figured he had one chance.

Devereaux slowly moved to his right, trying to get in front of the hallway opening. But that also brought him closer to the bloody mutilated body of Camdyn Dent. He tried not to look at what was left of the supreme leader of the Kin, but couldn't resist. The image seared into his brain. Beck had done this. Beck had to pay.

He knew Beck was in the hallway. He knew Beck didn't know where he was. He had the advantage. To hell with the girl. He jumped up to find Beck. He saw him, lower down on one knee. Lower than he expected. It took a second to adjust his aim. Beck was faster. He shot first. Missed, but before Devereaux fired, Manny Guzman burst through the front door, his long-barrel Taurus in hand.

Beck saw Devereaux turn and fire two rounds at Manny. Manny went down, firing one shot. Devereaux bolted left toward the sliding doors. Irene fired her last bullet. Beck fired twice at Devereaux, his second bullet ripping across the top of Devereaux's back. He kept moving. Beck kept moving.

Beck fired his last shot at Devereaux as he jumped out the empty sliding door frame. It missed.

Beck was out of ammunition. Irene was out. Manny was flat on his back. Beck screamed in frustration. And then he remembered Morelli's gun. He ran around the couch. Saw it on the floor. Grabbed the Ruger LCP II .380. Went to the sliding glass doors. Saw Devereaux running across the snow-covered ground heading for the cover of the forest.

Beck took the small gun in a two-handed grip. Raised it carefully. Devereaux was running twenty yards out. Beck fired. A puff of snow kicked up five feet short of Devereaux. In ten yards, Devereaux would be in the forest. Beck aimed higher where he thought Devereaux would be and fired three steady shots. The last shot caught Devereaux's right arm, knocking him down. He rolled over into a sitting position facing the house. Beck had a stationary target. Almost a hundred feet away, but stationary. He brought the gun sight into position. Beck felt like his whole body was shaking. He couldn't keep the small gun steady. And then, amazingly, from his sitting position Devereaux opened fire. The first bullet cracked into the house on Beck's left. He ignored it. A second shot hit the stone patio five feet in front of Beck. Beck fired. Devereaux fired back. The shot fell short. Both men kept pulling the triggers on their guns. Both guns were empty.

55

A strange silence fell over the area punctuated by screams and moans from three surviving Kin fighters. A seventy-five grain 5.56 bullet had shattered one man's femur four inches below his hip. The bullet had fragmented, shredded the femoral artery in his thigh, and tore out a one-inch exit wound. Another Kin shooter had the side of his head and ear torn off by 12-gauge buckshot. Devereaux's man caught a bullet where his right trapezius muscle met his neck while running from Andy Miller's M16, trying to take cover in the forest. The bullet had torn open a chunk of flesh and arteries. All three men would be dead in minutes.

Inside the house, Beck watched Emmett Devereaux standing up, staring at Beck. Beck turned away and ran toward Manny. As he passed Irene, he said, "Are you okay? Are you hit?"

"Yes. I don't think it's bad. The side of my leg."

"Stay there."

Beck hurried over to Manny, his heart pounding, thinking that a man he cared more about than himself had been wounded or shot dead. But Manny Guzman wasn't dead. He was trying to roll over, to stand, but he could barely move.

"Manny, Manny, are you hit?" Beck saw that Manny had on a bullet-proof vest. He ran his hands over the vest. His hopes soared. There was no sign that Manny had been hit.

Manny said. "It's my goddamn back. Fuck! Something seized up on me. Hurts like hell. Something got fucked when I drove down a hill out there."

"All right, all right, it's okay. Just stay down."

"No. I gotta get up. We gotta get out of here."

Beck helped Manny rollover and get to his hands and knees, then to his feet. Demarco appeared at the front door.

Beck said, "D! You're alive."

"So far. You, too, I see." Demarco had dropped the Sig Sauer Rattler and retrieved Beck's Mossberg shotgun. He asked Manny, "You okay, partner?"

"Yeah, yeah. My back went out. What about you?"

"I'm fine." He stepped forward and wrapped his long arm around Manny's upper back to help him stand. Manny wrapped his hand around Demarco's shoulders.

Beck noticed a cut on Demarco's forehead where a splinter from a tree had hit him and blood where a bullet had ripped out a chunk of flesh out of his trapezius muscle about two inches from his neck. Three inches and the big man would have died. None of it seemed to bother Demarco.

Ciro appeared in the doorway, his .45 in hand and helped Demarco walk Manny out the front door. Beck had run into the house to check on Irene. Demarco and Ciro walked Manny toward Beck's truck.

Beck came out of the front door holding Irene Allen by the waist, her arm over his shoulder. The blood on his face had dried. He'd retrieved his Burberry coat, so the blood on his arm, shoulder, and stomach weren't visible. Nobody noticed the blood on his lower back and pants, most of it Peter Morelli's.

Beck and Irene followed Demarco and Ciro. The five of them gathered near Demarco's truck.

Beck asked Ciro, "You okay? Did you get hit?"

"Not really. Just nicked on the side. Didn't penetrate the vest."

"How about you, D?"

"My vest took two center hits. The ceramic plates shattered, but nothing went through. But I'm going to have trouble taking a deep breath for a while." Demarco asked Manny, "How about you, old man?"

"Just my back. We had to go around a roadblock. Getting back on the road was a downhill run. And my damn shoes didn't keep out the snow. My feet are freezing."

Beck said, "What roadblock?"

"The sheriffs had the road leading to this place blocked about a quarter-mile from the road that leads in here. Probably the same at the other end."

Irene asked, "What happened to Andy?"

Manny said, "Last I saw him, he ran around back."

Irene asked, "Going after Devereaux?"

"I guess."

Suddenly, five rapid gunshots sounded behind the house. Everyone ducked. Demarco shouldered the Mossberg, aiming at the corner of the house. Ciro pointed his .45 in the same direction. For twenty long seconds nothing happened. Then Andy Miller called out. "Don't shoot. I'm comin' round."

Irene yelled, "Did you get him?"

Miller appeared. "If I did, it woulda been just luck. I saw that murdering bastard run out of the house. I staked out a spot in the woods." Miller looked at Beck. "You two had a little exchange. Then he got up and strolled away. I opened up on him with my Glock, but he saw me and jack-rabbited into the undergrowth. If I hit him, it was just dumb luck."

Beck said, "The hell with him. The hell with all of them. Let's get out of here before any more of these assholes show up. We'll have to deal with a roadblock. What kind of ammunition do we have left?"

Demarco said, "There's plenty of 9-millimeter for the handguns. And slugs for the shotguns."

Andy Miller hurried off.

Beck yelled, "Where you going?"

"Harvest some firepower off the dead."

In two minutes, Beck and Irene were in his truck with Ciro in the truck bed holding the mag-fed Mossberg 590 reloaded with twelve-gauge shells. Beck had retrieved his backpack and Beretta shotgun from the house and re-loaded his Browning. Demarco sat behind the wheel of his truck with Manny in the passenger seat holding a loaded Glock and Andy Miller standing in the truck bed with a fully loaded AR-15 he'd scavenged from one of the dead Kin shooters. His empty M16 laid at his feet.

Beck got out and walked back to Demarco, "We're heading south. Follow me."

"Where exactly?"

"I'm still figuring out the sequence. Anybody gets in our way, shoot until they aren't."

Demarco looked at his watch. 3:27 a.m. "Sun should be up in a couple of hours."

Manny asked, "What's next?"

Beck said, "Finishing this."

56

It had been fifteen minutes since Proctor heard any gunshots. Even though the battle had gone on for much too long, only one 911 call had come into the sheriff's department substation in Cairo. When dispatch called for a deputy in the area to investigate, Proctor had told the deputy with him, "Take the call. Tell them you're in the area and you'll investigate. Wait twenty minutes, call back, and say that some assholes were shooting at speed limit signs but are no longer on the scene."

The call hadn't escalated to the state police, but that didn't solve Proctor's real problem. Camdyn Dent had never left the house. Nor had he called Proctor. For the first time in his life, Abel Proctor felt paralyzed with indecision brought on by the realization that something he had spent his entire life building and protecting was crumbling to pieces.

He was about to go against instructions and call Dent when he heard the sound of a shotgun booming a half mile down the road. It had to be Beck and his men. How could any of them have possibly survived?

The two deputies motioned for Beck to slow down and stop his GMC Denali. Beck didn't stop but slowed enough so that Ciro Baldassare, standing in the truck bed, had time to fire two blasts of 12-gauge at their flashing light bar, blowing it to pieces. As Beck rolled slowly by, Ciro continued pumping round after round of 12-gauge into the patrol car. Windows, tires, headlights, and the radiator all exploded while Beck powered down his window and fired his Browning above the heads of the deputies, forcing them to run for cover on the other side of the two-lane highway.

And that was just the beginning. Demarco Jones followed close behind. As Beck pulled away, he yelled out his window to Andy Miller, "Hold on!" Then he accelerated and rammed his Steelcraft heavy-duty bumper and brush guard into the front fender of the ravaged patrol car. Miller held onto the rail bar on the top of the Honda, rested the barrel of his assault rifle across his forearm, and shot above the heads of the deputies as fast as he could pull the trigger.

The impact sounded like a small bomb. The patrol car spun across the road and ended up in the drainage ditch on the other side of the highway. Demarco accelerated after Beck, leaving behind one destroyed patrol car and two terrorized deputies. Andy Miller slid down in the truck bed and kept his AR trained on the deputies just in case one of them might be stupid enough to stand up and shoot back.

Up ahead, Beck heard the impact and smiled. He glanced at the wreckage in his rearview mirror. He handed his cell phone to Irene and recited a number for her to dial.

At the other end of the roadblock, Abel Proctor heard the gunfire punctuated by the bang when Demarco's truck hit the patrol car. If he'd had any question about the failure of Camdyn Dent's plan to kill Beck and his men, he didn't now. Nor did he have any doubt about his next move.

57

After they shot their way through Proctor's roadblock, Miller and Ciro transferred everything from the truck beds into the crew-cab seats of their respective trucks. Miller rode with Demarco and Manny saying nothing. Ciro helped Irene into the GMC's crew cab seat so he could sit next to Beck.

By the time Beck parked in front of Andy Miller's house, the pre-dawn light had dispelled some of the cold December night's darkness.

Beck had seen how Miller helped them get through the roadblock. And Irene had filled him in on how Miller had helped with the battle at Morelli's safehouse. Beck accepted that the enemy of his enemy had been his friend. But Beck still didn't know how far Miller's support extended or his motives. Beck would have to find out, but now was not the time.

Miller jumped out of Demarco's truck with his empty M16, left the Kin AR, and retrieved the Radical Firearms AR-15 he had given Manny. Beck stepped out of his truck and met Miller at his front door.

Beck said, "Thanks."

"I didn't do it to save your skin."

"Why then?"

"I got my reasons. As far as you're concerned, Mr. James, my advice is that you and your friends leave this area and don't look back."

"Wouldn't that be nice," said Beck. He didn't offer his hand to Andy Miller. Miller opened his front door, stepped inside, and shut the door.

Beck looked at the closed door for a second, then turned around and got back in his truck. Demarco followed as Beck led the way to the Walmart Supercenter outside Belleville. With Miller out of the truck, Manny talked to Beck about something he'd seen at Andy Miller's house. When he finished, Beck turned to him and smiled. "That's pretty goddamn interesting, amigo."

"I thought so, too. Figured you'd know what it means better than me."

"And all of it right there in plain sight."

"Yep."

Beck drove through the sprawling Walmart parking lot and continued around behind the superstore where he found a forty-foot Tiffin Phaeton motorhome painted in a color called fire opal parked at the edge of the asphalt strip that ran past the store's loading docks.

Beck pulled in next to the motorhome. Demarco parked his Honda alongside Beck's GMC. All the vehicles were out of sight from both the roads surrounding the Walmart and the parking lot on the other side of the building. Everyone except for Irene got out of the trucks and stood staring at the Bolo brothers' motorhome.

Ciro said, "What have these maniacs done now?"

Demarco said, "Apparently, they've scammed somebody out of a motorhome."

Beck said, "You think this qualifies as hiding in plain sight?"

Nobody answered.

Suddenly the door to the motorhome swung open. Ricky Bolo stood at the top step with his arms wide open. He wore a pair of German corduroy carpenter's pants, a vintage Hudson Bay wool blanket jacket with wide stripes in green, red, yellow and black, UGG high fur work boots, and an oversize orange Peruvian Vicuna scarf, no hat.

"Welcome aboard, gents."

Beck let the others go in first. He went back to the GMC and helped Irene out. The bullet wound on her left upper thigh made it difficult to put weight on that leg.

He asked, "You okay?"

"I'd feel better if I knew Devereaux was dead."

Again, she put one arm around Beck's shoulders, and he held her by the waist as he helped her walk slowly to the motorhome. Beck knew Irene was in pain. He didn't want to take advantage of her situation, but he enjoyed having her weight on his shoulders and her body next to his.

When they reached the mobile home, Beck helped her up the first three steps. She pulled herself up the last step using the handrail and quickly sat in the oversized front passenger chair. Beck followed her and closed the door behind him. He swiveled Irene's captain's chair so that she faced the inside of the mobile home. Beck stood next to her in the driver's chair, taking in the scene. The interior *looked* like a home. There were wood floors, plush leather sofas that turned into beds, overhead recessed ceiling lights, an eating nook, LCD screens, cabinets, closets, hidden storage spaces, a bedroom, even an ersatz fireplace that displayed a flickering flame on another LCD screen. All of it in soothing beige and cream colors. But all of it crammed into a long narrow space now filled with too many large, disheveled, tired, injured men reminded Beck of his days in prison where every space seemed to be filled with men always on the verge of violence.

Muddy boots and shoes covered the floor in the front of the Tiffin. Demarco stood at the breakfast nook table, picking out a fresh t-shirt, shorts, and socks from a pile of XL underwear newly purchased by Ricky Bolo at Walmart.

Manny had already put on a new pair of socks. He stood in the kitchen area, bent over trying to brace himself with one hand on the counter as he assembled the ingredients for breakfast and setting up frying pans on the electric induction stove. There were two cartons of eggs and three packages of pork sausages on the counter next to the stove and a pot of coffee.

In the bedroom area, bulletproof vests and coats filled the floor of the largest closet. Ricky Bolo stood next to a half-dressed Ciro

Baldassare, telling him how to take a Navy shower so the hot water wouldn't run out. An ugly purplish bruise had already formed on Ciro's right side where a high-velocity bullet had clipped his vest.

Beck stayed back from the activity with Irene and leaned back into the driver's chair thinking about the steps he would go through to treat his wounds and alleviate his pain. His remembrances of prison brought to mind the mounting odds that all of them would end up incarcerated. How many men had they just killed or injured? Getting framed for killing Joey Collins had fallen to a minor annoyance by comparison.

Beck considered telling Ricky Bolo to fire up his massive, rolling hideout and head for the Canadian border. They had certainly pushed back the Kin's ability to hurt them. Beck had his passport in his go bag. If Demarco didn't have his with him, they could stop by his house in Ghent and get it. Alex or Phineas could gather Manny's and Ciro's passports and meet them somewhere. Once in Canada, they could buy whatever they needed and fly out of Montreal-Pierre Elliott Trudeau International airport to anywhere they wanted. Beck knew that Irene had her passport jammed into the back pocket of her jeans.

Beck didn't spend much time thinking about that option. He knew it would only be a temporary solution. At least half the Kin leaders were alive – Devereaux, Proctor, and George Myer who would certainly take the place of his brother. From all he'd heard, the Kin still had plenty of followers. Beck had an idea about how to end the war against the Kin, but he still needed information to know if it had a chance of working. They had been lucky to survive Morelli's attempt to kill them. Beck knew that as things stood, their chances of surviving against the remains of the Kin were low. Even so, Beck was sure that to a man, Demarco, Manny, and Ciro would stick with him to the end.

But first things first.

Beck sat in the driver's seat. He figured out how to swivel the chair so he could face Irene. Her eyes were closed. Beck lightly tapped her on the knee. She looked at Beck.

"We should get your wound treated."

Irene widened her eyes and said, "Anything to get my pants off, huh?"

Beck smiled. "Absolutely. But I want Demarco to do the honors. He's better at it than me. C'mon, let's get you set up on that couch."

Irene stood up with difficulty. She limped over to the couch with Beck's help. She held onto Beck with one arm as she peeled off her jeans. He lowered her onto the couch. Devereaux's bullet had cut a four-and-a-half-inch furrow through her skin a little higher than midway across the outside of her thigh. The wound angled up slightly toward her hip. She kept her North Face jacket on, but only blue cotton panties for her bottom half.

The combination of Irene in her underwear and the ugly bullet wound caused a weird combination of feelings in Beck. He felt both attracted and deeply concerned for her. Luckily, the bullet hadn't penetrated deep enough to destroy underlying muscle. Beck had seen too many gunshot injuries that split open all the layers of skin down through fat and muscle, turning the injuries into gaping wounds. Irene would end up with a scar that would permanently mar her beautiful skin but not much else. Beck hoped the scar wouldn't mar her psychologically.

Her wound made Beck think of his wounds. He had yet to look at the cut on his face. There were three bullet wounds under his clothes: his left shoulder, the side of his left arm, and his stomach. Plus, a cluster of small wounds on his backside and legs from the bullet that went through Morelli. The hydrogel dressing Demarco had used to seal the long slice on his forearm had stayed intact, but the wound still ached a bit. The injury on the side of his head and ear still plagued him. He knew he would be recuperating for weeks. None of that concerned him. The fatigue setting in did. Beck hoped enough coffee would counter the exhaustion. He had to keep going. He banished any thoughts about for how long.

Irene looked down at her wound. There was little bleeding. The hot bullet had partially cauterized the wound.

"Not too bad, huh?"

Beck said, "Just a small souvenir of your latest adventure."

"A souvenir that fucking hurts."

"That'll go away when we get it closed and bandaged. Somewhat."

Ricky Jonas appeared holding a white terry cloth robe. He helped her stand up and draped the robe over her shoulders. She worked her arms into the robe. It was much too big for her. She pulled the terry cloth around her, leaving the injured leg exposed. Ricky Bolo couldn't resist the impulse to joke around. He patted Irene's shoulder and pointed to the bullet wound. "It's beautiful, baby. Be a nice conversation starter whenever you hop into bed with someone."

Irene gave him a veiled smile and said, "Yeah, talking about getting shot should be a turn-on."

Ricky smiled and said to Beck, "My kind of woman. By the way, Jonas is on top of that thing you wanted him to do. He should be calling in soon."

"Good. Thanks."

Beck set up two chairs next to the sofa. Demarco approached Irene. He'd already washed and disinfected his hands. He slipped on a pair of sterile latex gloves.

Beck helped Irene lie back on the couch. "You know Demarco, right?"

"Kind of. Have you done this before?"

Demarco slipped on a surgical mask. It dawned on Irene that none of them bothered to wear masks indoors. Not so surprising. Surviving a murderous gunfight in the woods made the latest Covid variant seem irrelevant.

Demarco said, "I've treated wounds like this a couple of times. Seen it done a lot more." He pointed to his face. "Try to relax. This isn't a big deal, but it will take a little time. I've got to clean it. Sterilize the skin around it. And then I'm going to staple it. Stitches will take too long. And I'm not good enough at stitching it the right way."

"What's the right way?"

Demarco motioned as if he were holding the needle and said, "Stitching under the top layer of skin. Internally so you don't get those crosshatch marks on the surface. It takes practice. And takes longer. The staples will be fine. The worst part is putting in the lidocaine. But that I'm good at. A doctor friend taught me how. Two pokes on either side of the wound, and then fan the needle around as I inject. It'll numb everything."

"Whatever *fan* means."

"You'll see if you want to watch."

"No thanks."

Beck sat next to Demarco. He had a box of supplies on his lap. Demarco folded back the terry cloth robe from Irene's leg and started to work. Beck handed Demarco what he needed as the process unfolded. A towel and small bedpan that Demarco slipped under Irene's thigh. A gauze pad and antibacterial soap to clean the wound. An irrigation syringe filled with saline solution to rinse out everything. Betadine to sterilize the skin around the wound. A small syringe loaded with lidocaine.

Demarco said, "What do they always say when they numb it?"

Beck answered, "A little pinch now and some burning."

Demarco repeated the words as he injected the lidocaine. He put in four shots along the length of the wound, two on each side.

Demarco kept up the small talk to distract Irene. She was a good patient. Stoic and silent, staring up at the ceiling. The lidocaine did its job. The wound was clean. Demarco started carefully closing the wound.

Beck had nothing more to do. He sat and listened to the surgical wound stapler. Click, click, click. It sounded to Beck like a clock ticking away time. Time he did not have.

58

Abel Proctor felt his world collapsing around him, along with his physical ability to keep going. It felt like days since he'd slept. It took more and more effort for him to concentrate. And more caffeine. He'd downed two coffee drinks to get him to his office where he wrote up a bullshit report blaming the destruction of a patrol car and shots fired at two deputies on a drunk with a shotgun who'd crashed into a sheriff's patrol car running their sobriety roadblock. Proctor provided a vague description of the vehicle stipulating that there had been no time to catch a license plate. He made sure there was nothing in the report that could connect James Beck to the scene.

He left headquarters, drove his Nissan truck to his storage unit on Route 8, and called George Myer, despite his reluctance to speak to a man Procter knew would be in a murderous rage. George Myer looked like a big, slow-witted, violent man. The big and violent parts were true. The slow-witted part wasn't.

"It's me."

George Myer's deep voice rumbled, "What the hell happened?"

"All I know is the Kommandant's trap didn't go as planned. Me and my deputies were out on the two-lane leading making sure nobody got in or out of that house. And monitoring nine one one calls so they wouldn't go to the state police. I thought the ambush would take thirty seconds, maybe a minute, like Camdyn said. The damn thing went on for nearly forty minutes. George, I didn't see any of our men come out of there in my direction. Not Camdyn. Not anybody. Then about fifteen minutes after the gunfire stopped, two trucks shot their way past my roadblock at the other end."

"Beck?"

"Him or some of his men. Although I can't figure out how anybody survived all that shooting. Have you heard from our people?"

"Did you go in there to look?"

"Hell no. I went back to my office and filed reports covering up the calls about shots fired in the area and how a patrol car got shot to shit and shoved off the road. Have Emmett or Vic called you?"

"No."

Proctor waited for Myer to say more, but he didn't.

"You'd better send people in there, George. Find out the damage. Beck and his men could be dead for all we know. If we have survivors, we have to get them out of there. And the dead."

Again, Myer didn't respond to that. Proctor asked, "Have you heard from Camdyn?"

Myer said, "I haven't heard from anybody but you. We need to meet. Now."

Proctor looked at his watch. He needed more time. He needed to sleep. He asked, "Where? The barn?"

"Yes."

Proctor said, "Okay, but I just submitted my reports. Sheriff Ciccone is going to want to talk to me about them. And I need to get home and change my clothes and grab some sleep. Get your people in there now, George. Find out what happened. Clean it up. I'll meet with you at noon."

Myer said, "The hell with that. Get here now."

Proctor exploded. "Goddamn it, George, did you or did you not hear what I just said? I need sleep. Last I looked, I'm still part of the ruling three. And you're still just Vic Myer's brother until we find out otherwise. You do not fucking give me orders. I just spent hours covering up a colossal fuck up which I had zero part in planning. Like I been doing for the Kin every damn day of my life for twenty odd years. And every time risking imprisonment for it. So don't give me any orders. You have no fucking clue how much shit I've done to keep the Kin operating. I'll be at the barn at noon."

Proctor hung up before George could respond. He felt his heart pounding. He was short of breath. He jumped out of his truck, opened the rolling door to his storage unit, and stepped inside. He had no intention of meeting with George Myer at noon or any other time.

Beck's phone rang two seconds after Demarco clicked the last staple into Irene's wound. He walked to the front of the mobile home and answered the call.

"What's up?"

"I got him," said Jonas Bolo. "Just like you predicted. He showed up at the storage facility about ten minutes ago."

"Alone?"

"Yeah. I couldn't follow him in, or he would've spotted me. I'm watching him from the parking lot outside."

"What's he doing?"

"Made a phone call then went into his storage unit."

"How many units are in that place?"

"There's one heated building near the office. Maybe fifty units in there. Outside there are six buildings with unheated storage units. Each of those buildings is about thirty yards long. They house back-to-back storage units except for the last row. So about four-hundred units."

"Surveillance?"

"Minimal. Cameras on light poles at the west end. I'll take care of them. Nobody's on site tomorrow, Sunday, to even check them. You said it's gold bullion?"

Beck said, "Yes. I put Alex on trying to find where the Kin profits end up. He found records of armored truck shipments delivering gold bullion to that facility for years."

"What quantities?"

"I don't have the final numbers from him. I think most of the shipments were hundred-gram bars."

"You can fit one of those in the palm of your hand. Around six grand per bar. Any idea how much is in there?"

Beck said, "Millions."

"Well, that's a start," said Jonas, "Unfortunately, we only know the location of one out of nearly four hundred units."

Beck said, "I think there might be three more units with bullion."

"Okay. So how are we going to find them?"

"I don't know yet."

"Uh huh. Well, we need those locations. And we need to know how they're storing the bullion. They can't be just sticking it in cardboard boxes and dumping them in storage units closed with padlocks."

"They have gates and those cameras, too, right?"

Jonas made a dismissive sound. "Baby stuff. Who's even watching the cameras? The entrance gate is pretty sturdy, but the fences are only five-feet high."

"So what do you think? Safes?"

"Yes."

"These yokels won't have safes you and Ricky can't break into."

"No. But we'll need time for even basic units. And you're talking about four of them."

Beck said, "You've got one night. Tonight."

"Are you serious?"

"Yes."

"James, we have to know the brand and model of the safes so we can prep the right tools and methods. Without that, breaking four safes in one night is not possible."

Beck said, "Jonas, the only shot we have is to move fast. The guy you followed could be cleaning out his unit as we speak."

Jonas said, "Good. Let him. Easier to take the gold from him instead of pulling it out of a locked safe."

"Good point. Is he still in there?"

"Yes."

"If he starts taking gold out of his unit, try to estimate how much."

"Sure. I can make an estimate based what I see. A million dollars in gold is about thirty-eight pounds."

"Good. Then after he leaves, you get into that facility and see what kind of safe he has, assuming you're right about them using safes. That will let you know what you're up against. Maybe we'll get lucky and they're all using the same type of safe."

"Don't count on it, James. I need to see into all three units."

"Fine. Start with Proctor's storage unit. See what's in there."

"Okay. The office here closes at two on Saturday. Why don't I follow this mark and see where he ends up? Then I'll head back here after they close and see what's in his unit. That'll give you time to hopefully locate the other storage units."

"Okay. You think they might have guards patrolling or checking the place?"

"I don't think so. If they do, I'll deal with it."

"Good. Stay in touch, Jonas. We have to get this done tonight."

"Hey, one more thing, James. You think any of the other bad guys will be showing up to move their bullion?"

"Not right away. We hurt them last night. Whoever is left leading the Kin will concentrate on killing us when they find out we're still alive."

Jonas said, "Don't get killed before you figure out who else has gold in that storage facility."

"I'll try not to."

Beck hung up. He felt too claustrophobic to stay in the mobile home. He stepped outside, breathing in the frigid air while he called Alex Liebowitz and Phineas Dunleavy. He kept the calls short. He went back in and stood with Manny in the kitchen. Beck gave Manny a summary of his plans and what he needed Manny to do. Manny listened, made a few comments. Beck listened. The exchange didn't take much time.

59

Abel Proctor loaded a little over four million dollars in gold bullion from his storage unit along with two file-storage boxes filled with documents, and three pieces of furniture he wanted for a two-bedroom log home outside of Lander, Wyoming. He'd purchased the house eighteen months earlier using the same LLC that owned several of his properties in the Hudson Valley. He had another six million in bullion in a storage facility vault in Casper, Wyoming. Money that he'd been accumulating from his share of Kin profits over the course of twenty-three years.

Next on his list – mail the nine-by-twelve envelope containing his retirement forms. He'd mail them on his way out of town. They would arrive on Sheriff's Ciccone's desk in three or four days. By then, a law firm in Albany would have started liquidating his properties, and Proctor would be watching the sunset from the porch of a house 2,060 miles away owned by William T. Balog. Proctor had spent five years making transactions and filing taxes to establish the new identity.

Proctor checked his watch. Not even nine o'clock. Time enough to grab a couple of hours of sleep and leave town before the noon meeting called by George Myer. Chug a couple energy drinks and keep going until he hit Ohio. Grab a night's sleep and be in Wyoming tomorrow night.

He'd done his bit for the Kin. He had no desire to cover up the carnage at Dent's safehouse or the killing that was coming. Time to go.

Proctor closed the tri-fold Tonneau cover on his truck bed and closed up his storage unit. He'd emptied the safe and left it open along with furniture and a bag of old tools. Whoever bought the storage facility could have it.

Jonas Bolo remained parked amidst the cars in the Applebee's lot, watching Proctor through his trusty Bushnell Ultra HD monocular scope. He watched the mark snap shut the padlock on the storage unit rolling door and get into his truck. Jonas expected him to head for the exit. Instead, Proctor turned in the opposite direction and drove to the last row of storage units at the south end of the facility. Jonas lost sight of the red Nissan Frontier as it passed behind the three remaining buildings. He had to get out of his van and run to the far end of the parking lot to see that Proctor had stopped in front of a storage unit near the west end of the last row. Proctor stayed in his truck for about a minute, then pulled away and drove straight toward the exit.

Jonas made it back to his van just in time to see Proctor exit and turn left on Route 8. Jonas Bolo followed just close enough to keep Proctor's truck in sight. Proctor was too tired and focused on his escape plans to notice the nondescript white rental van following him. Jonas stopped well behind Proctor when he saw the Nissan turn into the driveway of a modest ranch house, one of many like it in the residential neighborhood. Proctor's house sat on a quarter acre lot, bordered by a privet hedge, now just a jumble of bare branches in the dead of winter.

Jonas watched Proctor get out and unlock a side door at the far end of the ranch house. He left the door open and began bringing in the items from his storage unit. First, he carried in five PAMP Suisse bullion storage boxes holding the gold. By the size of the boxes and how Proctor carried them, Jonas figured each box held about a million in gold bullion. Four million dollars and change, assuming all the boxes were full. Four million. Easily transportable. In a ranch house in a quiet neighborhood. Guarded by one guy who had to pause and catch his breath before he could carry in the last box.

Jonas smiled. He wanted to go back to the storage facility like Beck said. But he couldn't. Not with four million in gold bullion sitting right there.

Jonas slipped out of his van and walked away from Proctor's house. He walked to the end of the block, cut over one block, and walked back in the direction of Proctor's house. When he came opposite Proctor's house, he walked quietly between two houses until he could see Proctor's backyard. Jonas quickly peered through his monocular to check the back of Proctor's house. There was no garage. No security cameras mounted in back of the house. No lawn furniture. There was a small toolshed and a barbeque grill under a tarp. He took note of a back door, two steps up from the ground.

The area was quiet. The mid-morning hour and cold had kept everyone inside. There were no dog walkers. Nobody heading out for Saturday morning errands. Jonas eased forward to get a better view. Maybe see in through Proctor's back windows. Jonas stepped carefully so his boots wouldn't squeak on the frozen snow. He stopped, not wanting to test his luck that someone would see him. Or a dog would hear him and start barking. He was about to lift the monocular to look into Proctor's windows when he saw something in his peripheral vision. It was off to the right on the other side of an above-ground swimming pool drained and shut down for the winter. Small clouds of breath condensing in the freezing air. He lifted the monocular. If it hadn't been so cold, he would have never seen him. A figure dressed in camouflage, hunkered down leaning against an above-ground pool, watching the back of Abel Proctor's house.

Jonas could only see the profile of the watcher. That was enough. He eased back out onto the street. He wasn't the only one interested in Proctor. Luckily, from his vantage point the watcher hadn't seen him hauling in boxes of gold.

He continued around the block and walked to where Proctor's street intersected with the street running north. He paused long enough to scope out the cars parked near Proctor's house. Sure enough, there was one car with its engine running parked where the two men sitting in the front seat could see whoever went in or out of Proctor's house. Unfortunately, they had seen Proctor transferring boxes into his house. Although he doubted they knew what a PAMP Suisse box looked like. Or that PAMP stood for Produits Artistiques Métaux Précieux, a precious metals refining and fabricating company.

    Jonas continued on and started the long walk back to his van via the next block over. He used the time to call Beck.

60

Beck came out of the motorhome's bathroom looking quite a bit different. The beard was gone. Mostly so he could clean and bandage the gash in his cheek. But also because he was sick of the damn thing. The beard reminded him that he was in a place he no longer wanted to be. A place that had turned dangerous and foreign to him. He'd also did his best to clean whatever wounds he could reach. They were all fairly superficial, although the one on his shoulder would need some attention from Demarco.

Irene was asleep on the couch where they'd tended to her wound. Ciro stood next to Manny in the kitchen area eating yet another breakfast. Demarco sat at the dining nook with an array of Ricky Bolo's medical supplies waiting to treat Beck's wounds.

Manny headed to the bathroom for his turn to clean up, walking a little better after taking 20 milligrams of oxycodone, also supplied by Ricky Bolo.

Beck sat at the small table opposite Demarco and extended his left arm for Demarco to work on. Between the lidocaine, disinfectant, stapling or closing with butterfly bandages, Demarco methodically tended to all of Beck's wounds. When it came to the cut on his face, he said, "It's not that big. Let's glue it so you don't end up looking like Frankenstein."

"Yes, let's."

Just then Beck's phone rang. He talked out of the side of his mouth as Demarco squeezed the wound together and applied surgical glue.

"Jonas. What's up?"

"We have an opportunity."

"I'm listening."

Before Jonas finished talking, Beck interrupted and said, "I agree. Wait in your van. We're on the way. Let me know if anything changes."

Beck didn't waste time asking Demarco and Ciro if they were up for more trouble. He made a sandwich of scrambled eggs and sausage on rye toast, filled a cup with black coffee, and told his partners to grab their vests and guns and follow him.

Ciro and Demarco wolfed down the last bites of food on their plates. On the way out, Beck asked them, "How are you two holding up?"

Ciro said, "I got at least one broken rib, so I am not moving with my usual alacrity."

Beck said, "Your what?!"

"You heard me, dipshit. It means…"

"I know what it means."

Ciro pointed a thumb at Demarco. "Killer here is being stoic. He took two shots dead center on his vest. Good thing the bullets didn't hit the same spot. Tell him how you fixed up that little chunk a bullet took out of your trapezius using a mirror."

"It'll do for now."

"I duct-taped his fancy winter coat."

"You guys are a hell of a team."

Ciro said, "Those bullets from an AR hit hard, man. D's alacrity is fucked, too."

Beck looked at Demarco. "How bad is it?"

As the three climbed into Beck's truck, Demarco said, "My brisk and cheerful readiness is somewhat diminished. Where're we going?"

Beck pulled out a bottle of Ibuprofen from the center console and downed four of them with coffee. He bit off a third of his egg and sausage sandwich and answered Demarco with his mouth full.

"To start the end game. You two Florence Nightingales can nap on the way."

61

Normal human emotions like fear, amusement, relief, guilt, or shame barely made a blip in George Myer's narrow spectrum of feelings. Except for anger. Anger verging on rage pulsed hard in him.

George sat in the barn at the Field, listening to Emmett Devereaux confirming the death of the supreme leader of the Kin, Camdyn Dent, and most likely all of Devereaux's fighters, all of the militia men on Vic's firing line, and an unknown number of their men guarding the trucks who got into the fight late. And worst of all, most of all, the near-certainty that George's brother Vic was dead, too.

While Devereaux spoke, he saw confusion, disbelief, and rage rising in George Myer. He saw it twisting George's face. Making George clench his fists in frustration. He looked like a human pressure cooker with no way to release the building forces. There were no heads within reach of George Myer's baseball bat that he could pound into a bloody pulp of brains and bone.

Devereaux wore the same clothes he'd worn during the battle. His coat, vest, and denim shirt torn and bloody across his back, ripped near his shoulder. His way of proving to big George that he had barely escaped with his life. That didn't mean Myer wouldn't explode and strike out at him. Devereaux couldn't let that happen. He needed to stay alive. He needed George Myer.

Under the table, Devereaux slowly gripped the Glock he'd shoved in the front of his waistband when he'd entered the barn.

He looked at Myer with his dead black eyes and said quietly, "George, you got to focus. We got killing to do now, George. There can't be any more mistakes. Just listen to me for a minute."

Devereaux's words didn't lessen George's rage, but they did get his attention. He met Devereaux's gaze. Devereaux could feel Myer's need to kill infecting the space between them. Fine. He needed that rage. He felt the need to kill as much or more than George Myer.

Myer said, "I'm listening." The two words heavy with threat.

Devereaux kept his hand on his gun and his eyes on George Myer.

"First, we got to get our people up to that house. Find out if any of ours survived. Find out if we killed any of Beck's. Bring the bodies out. Prepare ours for burial. Burn our enemies."

Myer listened.

"Based on what you say Abel told you, we got to assume Beck, at least some of his men, and probably that witch Irene Allen survived. We got to send men to Beck's house and her house. Put the word out everywhere. We got hundreds of eyes out there. Everyone's got to be searching. Check the hospitals. Anywhere they could get medical help. Urgent Care places. Anywhere they could get food, gas, or clothes.

"As soon as Abel gets here, we got to have him alert his people. Every deputy out there with the Kin has got to be looking. We know the trucks they're driving. Every deputy with us has to be on the lookout."

Devereaux could see that George was listening. He kept on.

"George, you got to start gathering your militia men. I'm calling in more of my people. It's up to us now to protect the Kin. To protect our operations. To protect our holdings. When we find these bastards, we got to be ready for a fight. I want to find them. Kill 'em or capture 'em if we can. I want Beck and every damn one of them to die a long, long, death with as much pain as possible. I want everyone to know what happens to anyone who dares to go against the Kin."

Myer nodded but said nothing.

Devereaux leaned forward. "We got to finish them off. They're hurting. I shot that girl and saw her go down, but she could be alive. I shot one of Beck's men. He went down. I shot Beck. Hit him at least twice, but he was still standing, shooting at me when I ran out of ammo. This is it, George. Don't worry about Abel. Let him sleep. I'll make sure he does his part."

Myer said, "I'm already on it. I got three men watching his house right now. They sent me a text. His truck is parked outside his house. They'll be pounding on his door at eleven to make sure he's on his way."

"Good. Let's get to work."

Devereaux took his hand off his gun and walked away from the table to make calls. George sat at the table and started making calls.

Devereaux hadn't mentioned Andy Miller. He knew it was Miller firing at him when he ran into the forest. If George knew about Miller, a traitor in their midst, it would send him over the edge. Or about how Miller and the witch were working together. Devereaux wanted their blood, their suffering, and their body parts for himself.

62

Beck followed the truck's GPS map to the address Jonas had given him. The readout said their arrival time was in seven minutes. Ciro insisted that Demarco take the front passenger seat in Beck's GMC since he had the longest legs, but only because he wanted to sprawl out across both back seats in the crew cab. He settled in and sipped from a large Styrofoam cup of Manny Guzman's coffee.

Beck sniffed the air.

"How much Scotch did you put in that coffee?"

"Enough to sweeten that motor oil Manny calls coffee. Ricky had a bottle of Macallan in a hidden cabinet over the sink."

"Everything in that rolling clown house is hidden. Drawers, cabinets, couches."

Ciro tapped his Romanesque nose. "Not from this bloodhound."

All three men had caught a second wind. Their clothes were still stained with mud, blood, and sweat, but they had showered, picked out fresh underwear and dry socks from Ricky Bolo's supply, and eaten. They'd swallowed enough painkillers to take the edge off their aches and downed enough coffee to stave off their fatigue.

As Beck drove, he thought about their injuries. Traumatic bruising to Demarco's chest. A bullet wound to his trapezius. Cracked ribs on Ciro and a possible injury of a repaired Achilles tendon. Manny's back problem. And a list of injuries to him that kept getting longer.

One thing Beck knew for sure, Demarco Jones, Ciro Baldassare, and Manny Guzman injured were better than ninety-nine percent of men healthy.

Ciro interrupted Beck's thoughts.

"So, what now, Jimmy? What are we doing?"

Beck thought about explaining what they had to do and why. But the readout on his map screen said they were two minutes from Abel Proctor's house, so he just said, "We're going to take out three bad guys and take control of four million dollars in gold bullion."

"What?"

"We're going to…"

Ciro said, "I heard what you said. What do you mean by *take control*?"

Demarco said, "And by *take out*?"

Beck paused, then said, "There are three guys watching a sheriff's investigator's house. We don't want them to see what we're about to do or get in our way, so we have to make sure they don't. A bullet in their heads would be the simplest thing to do, but they're in a residential neighborhood. Shooting might attract too much attention. We'll have to figure it out.

"The sheriff's guy has four million in gold bullion. I need it to run out the rest of my plan. So…"

Ciro said, "What the hell, guys? Get our hands on it means we're stealing this gold, right?"

"Yes. What happens after that is a little complicated. Let's just take it step by step."

Beck pulled in front of Jonas's rented van. The quieter, more studious Bolo brother joined them in Beck's truck. Ciro sat up so that Jonas could sit in the other passenger seat in the crew cab.

Beck turned and said, "What have we got here, Jonas?"

Jonas explained everything quickly and succinctly.

Beck listened and then asked, "Okay. Demarco, how about you take care of the guy in the backyard?"

Demarco nodded and slipped out of the truck.

"Ciro, we'll deal with the two in the car. I'll drive past them. Park on the opposite side of the street. We'll cross over and walk up behind them."

"And then shoot them?"

"If we have to." Beck said to Jonas, "Gather what you need to break into that house. Quietly. And then wait in your van for us to give you the all clear."

"Got it."

Beck pulled out and parked his truck far enough away so the two watchers in the Jeep wouldn't see his truck in their side view mirror.

Ciro said, "So, you don't want to walk up and shoot these jokers."

"No. It could make Demarco's job harder if he hasn't already taken the third guy out. And I don't want Proctor to hear gunshots."

"He's the guy in the house?"

"Yeah."

Ciro nodded. "Okay."

When they reached the other side of the street, they stopped. Ciro knew by the look on Beck's face he was figuring out a way to take out the watchers. He asked Ciro, "How many guns do you have?"

"One. My forty-five. You?"

"One. My Browning."

Beck's face scrunched with concentration. "Shit."

Suddenly, Ciro said, "Wait." He patted the pockets of his overcoat. "I got two. I forgot I have a little machine pistol I found at that house up in the hills." He pulled it out and showed it to Beck. "Made in Mexico. If it works, it'll spit out eight shots in a couple of seconds. Twenty-twos. Nice and quiet, James."

"Good enough. Give me your .45. Hang onto that toy and hope it works if you have to use it." Beck walked over to a walkway leading to a house nearby. A stone border ran along the edge. He kicked loose a stone about the size of his fist.

Ciro said, "What's this for?"

Beck told him his plan. Ciro shrugged and followed him toward the tan Jeep.

Having decided on a plan, Beck did not hesitate. Did not worry about Ciro. He focused only on what he intended to do. His Browning and Ciro's Smith and Wesson were both stuck in the front of his waistband. With the rock in his right hand, Beck quickly walked to the Jeep's back door on the driver's side and pulled on the door handle. The door opened. He didn't need the rock. He dropped it, pulled out both guns, and quickly slid to the center of the back seat. Only one of the Kin watchers turned around. The other looked in his rearview mirror. They thought it was the third watcher coming in out of the cold. Beck jammed a gun barrel under the base of each man's skull. He pressed hard and said, "Mouths shut. Put your hands on the dashboard. Slowly."

They hesitated.

Beck pressed the muzzles into their skulls and said, "Now."

Beck didn't recognize the man in the passenger side seat, but he did recognize the driver – Hamm Elrod with his thumb in a cast.

Beck said, "How's your thumb, asshole?"

Elrod hadn't recognized Beck without his beard. He stared in the rearview.

"You!"

"Yeah, me. Keep your hands on the dash and don't move."

"We shoulda just shot you and been done with it."

"I'm thinking the same thing. Don't give me a reason."

The driver's side door opened. Ciro pointed his twenty-two at Elrod.

"Out. Hands on your head."

When Elrod turned toward Ciro, the back of his head moved away from the muzzle of Beck's Browning. Beck thought, maybe his plan would work. And then it didn't.

Maybe Elrod saw how small Ciro's gun was. Or maybe he decided he wouldn't take this shit from Beck. Whatever the reason, he lunged at Ciro.

Ciro fired a quick burst of twenty-twos into Hamm Elrod's forehead. And, without even a second's hesitation, fired the rest of his bullets into the passenger's head.

It ended so fast, Beck had no time to react. The gunfire from the Trejo made a ripping crackling sound. Nothing like the bangs their handguns would have made.

Ciro quickly shut the driver's side door as if to contain the sound that had already disappeared. He slid into the backseat next to Beck.

"Well, we tried."

Beck nodded. "You did the right thing."

He held up the Trejo. "Pretty quiet, right?"

"Yes. I think we're all right. Not much blood."

"Those little bullets stayed inside their heads. Now what?"

"Might as well make it a little harder for someone to notice this. Get behind the wheel, drive over to my truck, and follow me."

Ciro got out and shoved Elrod's dead body on top of the dead passenger. He drove the Jeep back to Beck's truck. Beck got out, opened the Jeep's passenger side door, and took a picture of the dead bodies with his phone. He slammed the door and got into his truck. Ciro followed Beck out of the neighborhood. While they drove, Beck called Demarco.

"You take care of your guy?"

"Yes."

Beck didn't ask how. He asked, "Where are you?"

"With Jonas in the van."

"Did you hear any gunshots a few minutes ago?"

"No."

"Good. We'll be back to Jonas's van in ten minutes."

"Okay."

Beck found a parking lot outside a nursing home four blocks from Proctor's house. He led Ciro into a section of the lot that was about half full. He motioned for Ciro to park two slots away from the nearest car. Ciro locked up the Jeep and joined Beck.

A light flurry of snow began to fall. Beck hoped there would be more to come.

Ciro asked, "What do you want me to do with the keys?"

Beck said, "Keep them. We're going to leave them in Abel Proctor's house."

63

Beck and the others stood behind Jonas Bolo as he cut a hole in one of the glass panels on the side door of Proctor's house. It made a slight scraping noise. Not enough to alert anybody inside. He managed to pop out the glass, unlock the door, and step aside for Beck, Ciro, and Demarco to enter.

The house was quiet. Beck motioned for Ciro and Demarco to look around, He headed toward the back of the house for Proctor. He found the investigator snoring soundly in a room darkened by blackout shades and a bedside white noise machine pumping out a soothing low hum. Clearly, a bedroom designed for a man who slept at odd hours. Beck took a chair from a small desk opposite Proctor's bed and rolled it to the head of the bed.

From his seat next to the bed, Beck watched the son of a bitch who had caused him so much trouble sleeping peacefully. Another of the many men in law enforcement who had made Beck's life hell. Egotists who wielded enormous power, including deadly force, with hardly any concern about using that power. Macho assholes who made a point of their contempt for anyone or anything that tried to control them. But this guy Proctor had taken abuse of power to a whole different level. Watching someone like Proctor sleeping comfortably and soundly while he had to fight pain and fatigue every moment made Beck want to shoot a bullet in Proctor's ear.

Instead, he smacked the barrel of his Browning on Proctor's nose.

"Wake up, shithead."

Proctor bolted upright. Beck punched him in the chest and sent him back down on his bed.

"I said wake up, not sit up."

Beck pressed the barrel of his gun under Proctor's chin.

"Your worst nightmare, huh? Except it's not a nightmare."

Demarco entered the room and pulled open the blackout shades.

Ciro stood at the doorway and said, "As real as that urge to shit yourself."

Proctor blinked. Fully awake. Staring up at Beck.

"What do you want?"

"You mean in addition to what I've already got?"

Ciro said, "Should I start loading that gold, James?"

"Bring it into his living room. I want to count it." Beck pulled the Browning away from Proctor's chin and said, "Get up. Let's go."

Beck backed away, giving Proctor room to get off the bed. Proctor swung his bare feet onto the floor. He wore a baggy, white tank top and green boxer shorts.

Proctor cleared his voice. "Let me get some clothes on."

Demarco Jones suddenly appeared next to Proctor, moving so fast that Proctor didn't see where he'd come from. Jones grabbed Proctor's right ear and lifted him to his feet, tearing the top of his ear. Then he grabbed Proctor's head and shoved him to the floor. He kicked Proctor until he scrambled out of his bedroom door, screaming at Demarco to stop. Demarco let Proctor get to his feet. Then he shoved him down the short hall into the living room.

The flurry of terrifying violence stopped when Demarco pushed Proctor onto the couch in his living room with enough force that the couch tipped back onto two legs.

Proctor pressed his hand against his bleeding ear, bent over making an unintelligible combination of curses and grunts. He began to shake.

Beck took a seat in a discount-store reclining chair facing the couch. He pointed his Browning at Abel Proctor. Demarco sat on the couch next to Proctor, turned toward the sheriff's investigator, crowding into his space.

Beck, too, stared at Proctor until the deputy investigator looked up at him.

Beck raised a forefinger to his lips. "Unless you want my friend Mr. Jones to splatter your nose all over your face, and break half the teeth in your head, don't say anything until I ask you to." Beck paused as if picturing it. "Keep in mind, I won't be able to stop him if he starts in on that. Not that I'd want to stop him."

Ciro appeared easily carrying two of the PAMP Suisse storage boxes of gold bullion and dropped them near where Beck sat.

Nobody said anything as Ciro brought in three more boxes. Two filled with gold bullion and one with documents that Proctor had taken from his storage unit. He dragged a small coffee table with one foot over to a wingback chair. Then he picked up the box of documents and sat with the box on his lap. He tossed aside the lid and started looking at the contents. Nobody said anything during all this. Ciro glanced through the first folder of papers and dropped it on the floor. He continued tossing aside anything that didn't interest him. Commenting and placing documents that did interest him on the coffee table.

"Bullshit. Bullshit. Interesting. Your cholesterol is even higher than mine. Lookie here, a passport. And guess what?" Ciro looked up at Proctor. "Another passport! Same picture. Different name. William T. Balog. You're a shifty bastard, aren't you?"

Jonas Bolo entered the living room carrying Proctor's laptop. There wasn't any place to sit in the living room, so Jonas sat at a small oval dining table between the living room and kitchen. He opened the laptop and turned it on.

Beck looked at Jonas Bolo, then turned back to Proctor.

"Just when you thought it couldn't get any worse."

When the home screen appeared on Proctor's laptop, Jonas said, "You want to tell me the password that unlocks this piece of shit?"

Beck looked at Proctor and said, "Now you can talk. What's the password?"

Proctor stared defiantly at Beck.

Beck looked at his watch and said, "Listen to me. My friend there can go into your operating system and override the password in ten minutes."

Jonas said, "Five minutes. Plus, I opened up the stupid little floor safe in your closet. I have your master password. I can open all your files. I can get into all your accounts. Even if you have two-factor authentication. I got your phone, email passwords, and computer, pal. Last chance to save us five minutes."

Beck said to Proctor, "We're criminals, Mr. Proctor. We'll find out everything anyhow. What's your password?"

Finally, Proctor spoke.

"You think I don't know that you're going to kill me as soon as you get what you want?"

"Wrong. I don't want to kill you. I want the State of New York to lock you away for the rest of your life. I can absolutely guarantee you from experience that's worse than me putting you out of your misery." Beck pulled out his cell phone and brought up the photo of the dead men who had been watching Proctor. "How am I going to do that? Let's start with these two dead guys you killed. We'll let the state police know where they are. And where they can find the gun you used. And the keys to their car. Plus, a motive for you to kill them. They were spying on you. Guess your Kin pals know you're a sneaky fuck. Oh, and there's another body." Beck looked at Demarco. "You have any idea where that body is, D?"

"I'm betting it's in this fellow's backyard. Covered with snow. Not so much that it would be hard to find."

Beck nodded toward Ciro looking through documents and Jonas overriding the password on Proctor's computer. He said, "And if three murders aren't enough to put you away, I'm pretty sure we'll find evidence documenting a zillion crimes that will send you away for a couple of hundred years."

Ciro announced, "Hey, look at this? A deed! Where the fuck? Lander, Wyoming? That ain't exactly around the corner."

Jonas said, "Yeah, but it's not that far from a precious metals depository in Casper. And guess who has a storage space there."

Beck said, "God damn, Proctor, these two guys aren't even my best at this. Imagine what we'll find out in a couple of days."

Suddenly, Proctor reached down between the seat cushion and the end of his couch. Beck and the others watched Proctor madly digging around and finding nothing.

Jonas said, "I found it. And the one in the holster under your bed. And the one in the kitchen drawer." He dug the guns out of his coat pockets and laid them on the dining table. "

Beck turned back to Proctor and said, "So, about us killing you after we have what we want. We going to have everything we need to take everything you own and send you to prison for the rest of your life, and yet, there you sit, still alive. You're supposed to be a detective, draw a conclusion."

Proctor defiantly stared back at Beck.

"Don't strain your brain, Proctor. We need you alive so you can do something for us. It won't take more than a few hours. If you do, we'll let you scamper off into the Wyoming sunset with a chunk of the bullion you took out of your storage unit. We'll let you keep all of your bullion in Casper, your house in Lander, and your properties around here. We won't turn over evidence of crimes you've committed to law enforcement. And cross my heart I swear we won't kill you. Unless you double-cross us, in which case, we'll take everything, turn over evidence, and if the good guys don't send you to prison, we will kill you. So, what's it going to be?"

"You want me to turn against the Kin."

Beck nodded. "Bingo. Which isn't asking that much, Proctor. You were already turning against the Kin with your little escape plan."

"It's not the same thing."

Beck said, "No, it's even better. You work with us and your chances of actually getting away from the Kin go way up."

Proctor said, "You'll never take down the Kin. There's too many of them."

Beck leaned forward and said, "You better hope we do."

After a pause, Proctor said, "And I'll be able to go when?"

"Before dawn tomorrow."

Proctor looked down, shook his head, and then looked at Beck. "Fuck it. It's not like I have a choice."

"Brilliant deduction."

"Okay," said Proctor. "What do you want from me?"

64

Manny Guzman finally laid down on the bed at the back of the Tiffin mobile home. He'd finished cleaning up the breakfast dishes and putting the compact kitchen in order. He had to lower himself down in stages. Forcing himself to move around hadn't helped his back. He tried to relax. Tried to release the pain, even though he knew it was futile. He didn't know if it was a muscle pull, a herniated disc, something broken, or all of the above. Whatever it was, he knew it was going make it more difficult to do his part in Beck's plan. He set his phone alarm for one hour. Just in case he fell asleep.

Irene Allen slept soundly on the couch near the front of the mobile home. Ten milligrams of hydrocodone and the Lidocaine Demarco injected around her wound continued to keep the pain down. Ricky Bolo was out walking around the parking lots surrounding Walmart stealing a car for Manny. The soft rumble of the Tiffin's big diesel engine combined with the gently falling snow outside created a cocoon of soft sounds that muffled everything around Irene. She didn't even hear Ricky Bolo return. Or Manny leave with him.

Ricky stood outside with Manny next to a late model Kia Telluride, its engine running.

Manny asked, "How'd you get this?"

"You wouldn't believe how many morons leave their key fobs in cup holders. I actually found two cars in my walkaround. This is my top pick. Drive it like you own it, man. How long you going to be gone?"

In the short time Manny had been standing with Ricky, there was already a dusting of snow on his shoulders. "I don't know. Is this thing good in the snow?"

"Should be. It's got all-wheel drive." Ricky waved a hand to his left. "When you come back, park it over in that direction. They'll think they misremembered where they parked it."

Manny climbed in the Kia and looked over the instrument panel. He didn't know how to enter a destination in the vehicle's GPS. Nor did he want to leave Miller's address in the system, so he used his phone to find Andy Miller's house.

By the time he parked in the open space in front of Miller's house, a half-inch of snow had turned the gravel into a clean white patch. Manny didn't think Miller would shoot him, but just in case, he had his Charter Arms Bulldog revolver in his hand when he knocked on the front door.

Miller opened the door with his Glock in hand.

"You again?"

Manny said, "Me again. Did you get any sleep?"

"A little. You?"

"Not much."

Miller opened just wide enough to let Manny in. Manny brushed the snow off his wool coat and stepped in. Miller had been sitting in his faux-leather chair. He returned to his seat. Manny sat on the couch, trying to find a comfortable position for his aching back. The only light in the room came from the lamp next to Miller's chair and whatever daylight made it through the snow clouds outside.

Miller asked, "So what do you want, Mr. Manny?"

Manny left his coat on and his revolver in the pocket as he pulled his hand out and rested it on the arm of the couch.

"I want to know what you want."

Miller stared at the stolid man across the room, looking for any sign that Manny was trying to bully him. Manny's gaze gave away nothing. Finally, Miller said, "Why do you give a shit about what I want?"

"Because you went to war with us. You helped us get out of that fight alive. People don't risk their lives for no reason. Makes me want to know why."

Miller responded with a shrug.

Manny nodded, conceding that Miller wasn't going to answer him. So, he said, "Okay. Let me put it this way. I think I know why you grabbed your rifles and helped us get James out of that trap. And why you been hanging around out in the cold in the shithole finding out about the Kin. I'd like to know if I'm right."

"So, you want me to confirm something you think you already know."

"Correct."

"Okay, Mr. Manny, I'm all ears."

"Part of it is because you hate the Kin. I suspect they're hurting people you don't want hurt. But that's not the main reason."

"What's the main reason?"

Guzman met Miller's defiant gaze, the painfully thin man, still wearing his same dirty coveralls to hide his scarecrow frame and bowlegs.

Manny said, "You want the girl, Mr. Miller. More than anything else, you want Irene Allen."

Manny waited a moment to see if Miller would protest. He didn't. Manny continued.

"She's against the Kin, too. Mostly because of what they did to her friend, Deborah Ramirez. You talked about it with her out at the Field. Plenty of dark, quiet spots where you two could commiserate and make plans with nobody seeing you. It was your way to get close with her. It's the girl you want, Mr. Andy."

"You think so, huh?"

"I do."

"More than anything else."

"Correct. More than anything else. You got other reasons, but that's the main one. In fact, I think you killed Joey Collins for her."

"Why would I do that?"

"To start a war inside the Kin so she would see her enemies suffer, and you could take advantage of the chaos that would follow."

"Well, Mr. Manny, that might be something *you'd* do, but not me."

"Then who did?" Miller shrugged. "Either way, I still think it's the girl you want. I don't see you risking your life to fight the Kin. But you would definitely risk your life for that girl."

Manny saw Miller's façade of stubborn anger and opposition waver. He stared at Manny and then admitted the truth.

"I would."

Manny nodded. "That girl might actually be worth it."

"How'd you figure it out, old man?"

"Same way *you* figure out shit. Kept my mouth shut and eyes open."

Miller nodded, conceding the point. Then he said, "Well, be that as it may, Mr. Manny, we both know it ain't ever going to happen."

Manny shrugged and tipped his head.

Miller said, "What's that mean? Don't try to con me, old man. No way I'm gonna mean much of anything to Irene Allen. She's all over her big hero, Mr. James Beck. He's the one she wants, not me. Not me in a million years."

Again, Manny shrugged.

Miller said, "Stop with that bullshit. Say somethin' that convinces me I ain't wrong or you can get the hell out of my shitbox house right now."

Manny struggled against the nagging pain in his back and leaned forward, his elbows on his knees.

"Listen to me, hermano. I don't think that young lady knows what she wants. And don't ever think you know what James Beck wants. That man is no less than three steps ahead of most everybody on most everything. You ask me, Beck would never let that girl get involved with him."

"What does that mean? You trying to tell me he hasn't fucked her?"

Manny gave Miller a look. "Did she fuck him, or did he fuck her? And why? Who gives a shit? This ain't high school, man. You think she and Beck are into a big romance? Whatever they did three days ago or why they did it has been left far behind, my friend. The only one who's had a long relationship with Irene Allen is you, not James Beck."

Manny sat back on the well-worn couch and waved a hand like he was brushing away a fly. "You used Irene's hatred for the Kin as a way to build a relationship with her. She used Beck's fight with one of the Kin assholes to get a relationship with him. You and Beck both ended up fighting the Kin. Tell me I'm wrong."

Miller was silent.

Manny said, "The question is, now what happens?"

"With who?"

"We're talking about you and Irene Allen. With you two."

"What's there to talk about, Mr. Manny? Irene got her revenge. Or enough of it to satisfy her."

"Maybe. Maybe she got her fill of payback last night along with a bullet wound to remind her what it cost. Beck got out of that trap alive, barely. We took out their leader and some of their men, but you know damn well this ain't over. Irene Allen ain't walking away from this mess. And neither are you if Emmett Devereaux is still alive, which I'll assume he is until I see his dead body. The big cabron George Myer is alive, and he's just as dangerous as his dead brother. Probably more so. And Abel Proctor is still alive. They got plenty of followers left. They're coming after us and won't stop until we're all dead. Then they'll put the whole thing back together only worse than ever."

Miller said, "That's why I told your pal Beck he should get the hell out of here and take all of you with him."

"We don't intend to run from people who tried to kill us and will keep on trying. If we stop now, we're all gonna have to look over our shoulders for a long time. That includes Irene."

"So what do you want to do? Wipe out the rest of the leadership?"

"Yes. But we want to do more."

"More? What more?"

"Answer me something and I'll tell you."

"What?"

Manny spoke slowly, carefully laying out his case in a way he wouldn't lose Andy Miller. Ready now to play his last card.

"The Kin has been around for a long time. Right?"

"Generations."

"It couldn't have lasted that long if the whole thing was based on extorting and addicting people to drugs. Right?"

"No. There was always a strict leadership at the top. And a certain amount of crime so people could make ends meet. But these last ten, twenty years it's gone way off in another direction. The Myer brothers are thugs. Emmett Devereaux is a sick sadist who gets off on maiming and killing. Abel Proctor is the greediest bastard among them. And the most corrupt."

"So what did the Kin do for people before those bastards took over?"

Now it was Miller who leaned forward. "You gotta understand, Mr. Manny. There's always been people around here under the thumb of the upper class. Startin' way back when landowners ran this part of the state like a feudal empire. They had people indentured. Close to bein' slaves. It took violent opposition to put a stop to it." Miller sat back. "I ain't interested in givin' you a history lesson, but if you don't understand by now this country is built on exploiting the weak, you never will. There are still folks who need what the old Kin provided. I got aunts and uncles and cousins all around here who've been losing the fight to keep rich assholes from chipping away at whatever little we got left. Buildin' huge fuckin' houses on forty, fifty acres, then buying up another hundred to keep the local riffraff away. And we end up with fuck all. Shit schools, shit health care, shit jobs. The Kin is using our misery to take what they want, too. You trying to tell me a bunch of criminals like you and James Beck give a damn about any of that."

Manny Guzman had a naturally menacing presence. He didn't have to raise his voice to make a point and didn't raise it now.

"You don't know what we do or don't give a damn about. Spend a month in a maximum-security prison and I guarantee you'll know more about exploitation than you do now." Manny pointed to the books and papers around Miller's chair and then to his right eye. "I know you understand a lot more about how it all came about. I got good eyes, my friend. I may not know what the titles of those books and papers that you're reading mean, but my brother James does. Hell, I can't even be sure I'm pronouncing 'em right." Manny squinted at one of the books on the floor. "*The Anti-Oligarchy Constitution. Reconstructing the Economic Foundations of American Democracy*? What's the title on that brown cover? *The Populist Moment. A Short History of* what?"

Miller smiled and said, "*Of the Agrarian Revolt in America*."

"I bet you got more of that stuff on your little iPad there. And I'm damn sure all those magazines piled up on the floor ain't *Guns and Ammo*. You know it your way. We know it ours. But we both know killing more of the Kin sons-a-bitches ain't enough. We have to take away their power. We have to change everything."

"And you really think you can do that?"

"We have to do it. Odds are against us, but we have a shot if you do what I think you can."

During the entire conversation, Miller had been holding his Glock. He put it on the side table and said, "Which is what?"

Manny nodded. Andy Miller was ready to hear Beck's plan.

65

The first thing Beck did after Proctor agreed to work with him was grill the deputy about the Kin gold and the storage center. Beck and the others listened carefully to his answers then left him with Demarco and went to Proctor's bedroom.

Beck shut the door behind them. Ciro sprawled out on the bed, unconcerned that his new boots were soiling Proctor's blankets and sheets. Jonas sat in the desk chair. Beck leaned against the door.

Beck asked, "How much do you think what he told us is true?"

Jonas said, "Around fifty percent."

Ciro said, "A hundred percent that fuck hasn't told anybody the whole truth in his entire worthless life."

Beck said, "Nobody tells the whole truth."

Jonas said, "We have to assume he only told us the truth about stuff he knows we can verify. Then decide if that gives us enough to pull this off."

"Okay. What stuff is that?"

"He told us the four storage units with gold in them. Once we break into them, we'll know if he lied."

"What else?"

"He told the truth that he stored his bullion in a Bischoff safe. We can verify that once we open his storage unit. Wouldn't be my choice, but amateurs may think they're good because they're expensive. And it's plausible he doesn't know the serial number."

Beck said, "What about the other safes?"

Ciro said, "He lied. He said he doesn't know what safes the others used, but we can't prove he lied."

Beck said, "What else?"

Jonas said, "He says he doesn't know how much gold the others have. But it doesn't matter. He had four million stashed here, and the records on his computer show another six in a storage facility in Casper, Wyoming. That's enough to push forward. Odds are way in our favor the main storage unit has more than sixteen."

"Agreed," said Ciro. "We have a good idea based on what he ended up with, but I guarantee you all those bastards skimmed and lied to each other about what they took."

Jonas said, "And remember, their holdings were accruing before any of the current leaders came on the scene. The guy who knows how much that is, is dead."

"What about his answers regarding security?"

Jonas said, "It squares with my first take on the place."

"Okay, so do you have enough to go on, Jonas?"

"Yes. Don't get me wrong, we got our work cut out for us. The Bischoffs are lock key safes. We have to get through a combination lock, then open the key lock."

"You can figure out the combination?"

"Yes."

"What about the key lock?"

"We can drill out the locks, which is time-consuming, and we'd have to build a drill rig which we don't have time to do. Or, we fabricate picks based on schematics we can access using the make, model, and serial numbers, which I still need to find."

"And your picks will work?"

"It's not just the picks. It's the lock picker. Bischoffs are old safes. Everything is moving to digital. Years ago, you could find a bunch of guys who could pick those locks. Nowadays, maybe five guys in the world can do it."

Beck said, "And you're one of them, right?"

"Yes," said Jonas. "But I haven't picked locks like these in years. Normally I'd train for three or four days to get up to speed."

Beck said, "You'll practice on the job. You'll get better with each safe."

"Assuming they're all Bischoffs."

Ciro said, "Two to one, the main safe ain't a Bischoff."

Jonas said, "I'd say a hundred to one. I'm going to have to find out what's in that storage unit, then we can put together what we need."

Beck asked, "How much equipment do you have with you?"

"A lot. Torching rods, electronics, magnets, pullers, fiber optics, a bunch of stuff you don't need to hear about. That Tiffin motorhome is nuts, but Ricky was right about one thing. There's a ton of storage space in the bins under the living space, so we brought a full arsenal. We also have to track down diagrams and schematics on the Bischoff so we can fabricate the lock picks."

Beck looked at his watch. "Can you start now?"

"We have to. It's nearly one. I need to swing by the motorhome to pick up two pieces of equipment. Then get over to that facility and find out what we need to know."

Ciro asked, "You need someone to watch your back over there in case someone sees you?"

"Thanks, Ciro, but I think I can move around without being noticed. But you can do one thing before I go."

"What?"

"Get Proctor's padlock key to his unit. It'll save me time drilling out his lock. And since he owns the place, keys to the office and his pass card to the front gate."

Beck asked, "You think the office might have keys for the other units?"

"No. People put their own locks on. I want to get in the office to fiddle with the CCTV cameras."

Ciro jumped up from the bed and left to get Jonas what he needed from Proctor. Beck said, "Ciro, remember I want him to be able to walk and talk."

Ciro mumbled something and headed to the living room. Jonas called his brother. Beck sat on the edge of the bed fighting the urge to lay back and sleep.

Beck heard muffled noises from the living room and then the side door opening and closing. Ciro returned. He dropped a set of keys and a plain white plastic RFID card on the desk next to Jonas.

"Those are the keys to his truck and the heated storage building. The little one opens the padlock on his unit. Key card opens the front gate. The office lock is a keypad. The code is five-seven-eleven-ten. Same code to turn off the alarm in the office."

Jonas said, "Like the stores."

"Huh?"

"Five-and-ten. Seven-Eleven."

"Oh. Right. Genius."

Jonas thanked Ciro, pocketed the items, and left for the storage center.

Ciro asked Beck, "What now?"

"Now we get our asses out of here. When those guys we took care of don't call in and Proctor doesn't show up, this place will be crawling with Kin."

Ten minutes later, Abel Proctor's house was empty. The only evidence left behind was a hole in one windowpane on Proctor's front door.

66

By the time Jonas Bolo pulled up to the security gate at Proctor's storage facility, the snow was falling fast. He had to run his rented van's windshield wipers at full speed. Jonas didn't mind. The more snow, the harder it would be for the CCTV cameras to pick him out.

Proctor's pass card opened the sliding security gate to the facility. Up close, the gate looked more substantial than Jonas had previously thought. He decided to avoid going into the office. The possibility that Proctor had lied about the alarm code outweighed the possibility of finding useful information or the need to sabotage the CCTV cameras. He couldn't risk setting off a silent alarm now.

He parked behind the office and loaded his equipment into a black canvas tool bag. He'd memorized the unit numbers where Proctor claimed the other Kin leaders stored their gold bullion. Before he checked them, he wanted to look into Proctor's unit. He had the key to Proctor's padlock, so it wouldn't take much time. Jonas left his van and walked. Although midday Saturday was a good time for other renters to be at the facility, the cold weather and snow had discouraged visitors. There weren't any other cars or renters in the facility.

Jonas walked past the row of light poles along the west side of the storage facility. The poles had CCTV cameras mounted on top, but Jonas wasn't worried about being seen. When he reached Proctor's unit in the middle row, he set down the toolbag, brushed the snow away from the All-Weather padlock, opened it with Proctor's key, and lifted the rolling door. He unzipped his bag and pulled out an LED work light powerful enough to illuminate the inside of the nearly empty storage unit. A safe stood in the middle of the unit, its door wide open, revealing a prominent diamond-shaped black and yellow logo displaying the silhouette of an armored knight with a pole ax and a large B. Underneath the logo appeared the word Bischoff.

Jonas shined his light on the model number plate – a Summit TRTL model 6021. He already knew the dimensions: outside 68 5/16 inches x 28 5/16 inches x 32 11/16 inches deep. Inside dimensions. 60 x 21 x 21 inches. Jonas took photos on his cellphone and texted them to his brother.

He was about to leave when he spotted something. A ten-foot, fiberglass folding ladder. Jonas made a quick decision and grabbed the ladder.

He closed Proctor's unit, locked the rolling door, and walked with his ladder to the storage unit behind Vic Myer's unit. He set up the ladder and climbed to the roof with his tool bag. He crouched low and walked to the center of Myer's unit. He dropped flat onto the snow and ice and cleared away a four-inch spot. His gray insulated bib overalls and black water-repellant insulated jacket kept him dry. He ignored the cold, the falling snow, and concerns about someone seeing his ladder. He pulled out a black plastic box from his bag. The box held a piece of equipment used by military and law enforcement anti-terrorist teams – a nearly silent drilling system that could open a 5-millimeter hole in the roof. Drilling through the roof would be faster than drilling through the corrugated steel rolling doors and give him a 360-degree view of the unit's contents from above.

Jonas drilled slowly and steadily. It took eighteen seconds to cut a hole through the roof. He lifted out the drill bit and pulled an A/V microprobe from his canvas bag. He slid the probe through the hole and into the unit. The probe was attached to a small monitor in the canvas bag. The probe produced enough light to provide a view inside the unit. Unlike Proctor's unit, this one was nearly filled with cardboard boxes, plastic bins, old furniture, tools, hunting gear, and spare tires, all neatly stacked against the three walls of the unit or on metal shelving. Jonas rotated his probe until he saw what he had hoped for. Another Bischoff Summit TRTL.

Next was Emmett Devereaux's unit. He used the same procedure. Up to the roof, drill a hole, and look in from above. This time it didn't work. The unit was packed with mounds of random junk that nearly reached the ceiling. If there was a safe in the unit, it was buried under the mess.

Jonas Bolo's gut told him there was a safe in that unit. But he would have to drill open the padlock holding the rolling door shut and empty out the storage unit until he found the safe and then put everything back. Even if the safe was near the front, it would take too long. Better to spend his time finding the safe that held the main stash of bullion.

Jonas carried his ladder and duffel bag to the last row of storage units. Unlike the other buildings that held two back-to-back units, this one held only a single row of units.

Jonas believed Proctor's warning that there were additional security cameras focused on Dent's unit, so he carefully made his way to the southeast corner of Dent's single-row building. He peered around the corner. He saw a CCTV with a 360-degree fish-eye lens mounted above him. He pulled out his trusty monocular, dropped down onto the snow, and crawled around the corner just enough to scope out on the full length of the building. There was another fish-eye lens mounted on the wall at the far end. Dent's unit was in the middle of the row in range of both CCTVs. This was definitely the main storage unit for the Kin gold hoard.

CCTV cameras were also mounted on the light pole at the west end of the facility, providing yet another view of Dent's row. Jonas decided to check the camera views in the office before he left. Right now, he had to see inside Dent's unit and find out what he'd be dealing with.

The snow fall seemed to have increased a bit. Jonas carried his toolbag and ladder to the back wall of the single-row building. This time, instead of climbing onto the roof, Jonas positioned his ladder so that he could drill into the top of the back wall. He knew the wall was concrete block, so he switched to a small but powerful rotary hammer drill with a carbide-tipped masonry bit. The bit churned slowly through the concrete block and hit another surface. The bit stopped cutting. He pulled out the drill and switched to a bit made with cobalt that could cut through metal. Jonas sensed the drill bit grinding through what felt like a steel plate reinforcing the back wall, which didn't surprise him. He pulled out the tip, oiled it, and went at it again. He kept the speed moderate and steady. Suddenly, the resistance ended as the drill pushed through. He hurried now, curious to see inside the storage unit. He slipped in his A/V microprobe. For a moment, he thought there wasn't enough light coming through the probe. He had the canvas bag and monitor on top of the stepladder. He turned the light source on full and aimed the probe right, left, up and down. The light seemed to be absorbed by the darkness inside. He pulled the probe out, checked it, and repeated the procedure. There was nothing in the storage unit. Absolutely nothing. Not a box. Not a piece of furniture. Not a safe.

Jonas packed up his equipment and stepped off the ladder. It didn't make sense. Why the reinforced wall and extra CCTV cameras? Jonas looked up to check the number on the back wall. According to Proctor's information, this was the right storage unit. He stood for a moment, considering his next move. There seemed little point to risk checking for alarms or motion detectors on an empty storage unit. He decided to find out what he could discover in the office.

He headed along the east side of the facility, keeping away from the light pole cameras on the west side. He carried the step ladder past four rows and laid it on the ground near the wrought iron fence that bordered the property. Then he continued to the office, all the while considering explanations for why the Dent storage unit was empty.

Jonas entered the 571110 code on the door lock and alarm pad. Both worked. Proctor had told the truth.

The office was set up as expected. There was a reception counter facing the front door with a gray metal desk behind it so that whoever sat at the desk could greet customers entering the office. Behind the desk there was a long table holding a pair of twenty-two-inch monitors and two video recording decks. Each monitor displayed sixteen images in real-time. Two walls in the office had windows with Venetian blinds. The blinds on the window facing the security gate were open.

Jonas rolled the swivel desk chair to the table holding the monitors. Both monitors were displaying the camera feeds. He quickly identified eight images as long shots of the rows between storage buildings. Other images showed the inside of the heated units, the entrance to the office, and the front gate. That's when Jonas saw a pickup truck pulling up to the main gate. He wasn't overly concerned. The driver opened the sliding gate with a pass card. But his concern escalated as two more pickup trucks and two cars also entered the facility with pass cards. These weren't storage unit customers. His luck had run out. The Kin had sent men to guard their bullion.

Jonas quickly took off his jacket and draped over the back of the desk chair. He stuffed his tool bag under the desk and flipped on the desk lamp. He turned his back on the entrance and used the mouse to open the software program that controlled the cameras. Bolo was familiar with the software running the system. He pulled up the settings and began reconfiguring the camera feeds. First, he disconnected the camera mounted over the office door and erased the entire day's recordings. Then he checked the vehicles that had just entered to see where they ended up. The pickup truck and one of the cars stopped in front of Camdyn Dent's storage unit.

Proctor had given him the correct unit number. The other three vehicles ended up in front of Myer's, Devereaux's, and Proctor's units. Whoever sent these men didn't know that Proctor had moved his stash of gold and that Dent's storage unit was empty. Jonas was about to grab his jacket and tool bag and leave when he saw one of the two vehicles in front of Dent's unit drive away. It was the first pickup truck that had entered – a well-maintained Chevy Silverado pickup. Jonas sat back down and continued fiddling with the images on the monitors. The office was the safest place for him now. He'd have to brazen it out.

When the front door popped open behind him, Jonas wasn't surprised. He swiveled around and said, "You ever hear of knocking?"

One of Devereaux's men stepped in and closed the door behind him like he owned the place. Jonas clocked him for a familiar criminal type. Charles Manson size. Hair grown past his ears and a scraggly beard. The kind who compensated for his slight stature with meanness and treachery. He wore a stained down jacket over a mechanic's shirt.

Instead of answering, the man said, "Who are you?"

Jonas didn't respond right away, as if he had a choice in the matter, even though Jonas knew he didn't because he was one-hundred percent sure that the man in front of him had a gun and would shoot him without a drop of remorse.

Jonas said, "My name is Warren Pierce. I'm with the company that services this facility's closed-circuit TV system." He nodded toward the computer screens. "CCS."

"Uh, huh. What does CCS stand for?"

"Complete Commercial Security. Who are you?"

The man ignored Jonas's question.

"You got any ID?"

"Yes, I have ID." Jonas reached behind to take out his wallet. The intruder pulled aside his coat revealing an embroidered name patch on the pocket that said Dewey and pulled a six-shot revolver from his waistband.

"Slowly, pal."

Jonas pushed back farther from the desk and said, "What the fuck are you doing? You can't come in here and pull a gun on me?"

"I just did. Show me some ID before I shoot your ass."

The back of Jonas's chair bumped into the table with the monitors. He slowly reached back and took out his wallet. He thumbed through the contents and pulled out an ID for Warren Pierce employed by Complete Commercial Security. His picture was on the ID along with a company logo, 800 number, and a QR code. No address. He also pulled out a business card that looked like the employee ID along with a title: Chief Technician. He was about to hand over the fake ID, when he spotted a gun holstered under the desk behind the reception counter.

Jonas slowly wheeled himself forward holding out the identification with his left hand while he placed his wallet on the desk to free his right hand. As Dewey reached out for the identification, Jonas took hold of the revolver under the desk, slipped it out of the holster, and rested the gun on his thigh. If the peckerwood with the gun asked to see any other ID from his wallet, Jonas knew he would have to shoot him.

Jonas watched Dewey study his identification. He said, "I service this place every other Saturday. After two o'clock when the manager closes the office."

Dewey ignored Jonas and looked back and forth at him and the picture on the ID. Jonas had the feeling he couldn't read. Good thing he had a picture ID.

He asked, "Is that your van out back?"

Jonas ran his index finger over the gun. It was a revolver.

"Yes. Why?"

"I didn't see no sign on it."

Jonas looked the gunman in the eye. One more question, one movement of the hand holding the gun, and he would shoot fucking Dewey Dipshit.

Jonas said, "That's because the company is too damn cheap to provide me with a vehicle. Half of the equipment I use is mine, too. I gotta freelance with other jobs to make ends meet. Trust me, they don't pay me enough to worry about someone pointing a gun at me. And guess what?"

This caught Dewey's attention. This time he responded to Jonas's question.

"What?"

"My damn boss is an Africoon who sits on his Black ass in an office all day while I'm out in a goddamn snowstorm doing all the work."

Dewey gave Jonas a knowing smirk. "Probably gets paid more'n you, too."

"Damn right, and he doesn't know half of what I know about these systems."

Dewey handed back Jonas's fake ID.

"There's things you can do about that."

Jonas said, "I prefer not to go to jail. My wife and kids wouldn't like that too much."

Jonas watched the intruder slip his revolver into his waistband. He said, "Yeah, well, a new day is comin', my friend. How much longer you gonna be here?"

Jonas turned to look at the monitors behind him as if they would give him the answer.

"Shit, two more damn minutes. I'm declaring work is over for the day. I'm headin' home."

"Good idea." Dewey Newsome turned and left the office. He had no idea how close he'd come to dying.

67

Pain woke Irene. But not completely. She was trapped in a nightmare that put her back in the safehouse with Emmett Devereaux turning to shoot at her, a maniacal grin twisting his face, as Irene desperately tried to pull the trigger on her revolver but couldn't because the trigger wouldn't move.

Finally, with a gasp, Irene sat up. She tried to swing her legs off the couch, which unleashed more than enough pain to jolt her awake, so much so that she made a choking sound that prompted Ricky Bolo to look up from his computer.

"Don't worry, kid. That right there is about the worst it's going to get."

Irene turned toward Ricky. He sat at the small dining table researching diagrams of Bischoff safe locks.

Irene slowly swung her feet onto the floor. She felt faint. Ricky moved fast, getting to her quickly, one hand on her arm the other on her back.

"Bend over. Head between your knees. It'll pass. Just breathe."

"Jeesus."

"It's the painkillers and the shock." He gently patted her back. "You'll be fine. You should eat something. Soup. I have tomato soup."

Irene slowly sat up. The thought of red tomato soup made her feel sicker. She took a deep breath and exhaled.

"No soup."

Ricky said, "Then juice. I got apple juice."

"Where is everybody?"

"Busy. James has everybody doing something. Not sure what exactly."

"What does he want me to do?"

"I don't know. I'll text him and tell him you're awake and getting yourself together."

Ricky went to the kitchen area and brought Irene a glass of apple juice. He watched her drink it.

She said, "God, I feel gross. Can I take a shower?"

"Sure. We'll cover your bandage with a couple of layers of Saran Wrap. Keep that leg clear of the shower stream, and you'll be fine. I got clothes that should fit you. Crap from Walmart, but good enough for now."

Irene handed him the empty glass and nodded. "Okay. Thanks."

She stood up from the couch, the too-large robe Ricky had given her covering her thermal top and blue cotton panties. She pulled the robe back from her leg so Ricky could cover her bandage with plastic wrap. He helped her walk to the bathroom.

"You got about five minutes of hot water."

He left a towel and new clothes on the top of the toilet seat. Irene saw Ricky pause at the door.

"I'm fine," she said.

"You sure?"

"Yes."

Ricky hesitated.

"What?" said Irene.

"I was thinking I could give you a little step ladder you could sit on."

Irene smiled at Ricky's kindness.

"I don't need to sit. I got too much hate in me to fall down."

Ricky smiled back. "Good."

He headed back to the small dining table and sent a text to Beck.

The little miss is up and about. I'll get some liquids and food in her.

Ricky checked the time. 2:03 p.m. He looked out the small window near the table. The gloomy daylight seemed in sync with the fast-falling snow.

Irene came out of the bathroom dressed in the Walmart clothes: jeans, and a plain black long-sleeve T-shirt under a black and red checked flannel shirt. Fresh white socks and Hanes white cotton panties. She handed all her old clothes to Ricky, including her sports bra. He dumped everything in a white kitchen garbage bag and told her to sit at the smalling dining table.

"You should eat. How about scrambled eggs and bacon?"

"I can't take another breakfast meal. What else you got?"

"Frozen pizza. Frozen fettuccine alfredo with chicken and broccoli. Frozen beef and broccoli over rice."

"Beef and broccoli. And coffee. Black. Please."

68

Beck and Ciro walked into Proctor's living room. Jonas was already gone. Demarco sat on the couch still glaring at Proctor.

Beck said, "Get dressed, Deputy. You've got five minutes to load two boxes of your bullion into your truck. We're taking the other half. Take whatever documents you want and anything else. We're keeping your laptop." Beck held up the key to Proctor's truck. "Don't bother looking for this."

Proctor stared at Beck for a moment. The fact that he was actually leaving his home and the life he'd lived for decades suddenly hit him. It made him feel sick to his stomach.

Beck yelled at him, "Go!"

Proctor flinched and headed to his bedroom to dress.

Beck turned to Ciro and Demarco. "You guys make yourself scarce for about an hour. There'll be a lot of assholes looking for us and our trucks. When I hear from Jonas, I'll call you and tell you the plan, and you can head over to the storage facility."

Demarco and Ciro nodded. There was no point in asking questions.

Beck said, "Ciro, you take my truck. I had Jonas put half of Proctor's bullion in the crew cab."

Ciro said, "Why only half?"

"I want Proctor to think he has the other half."

Ciro almost pointed out that Proctor did have the other half but dropped it. He could see that Beck was on a roll. This wasn't the time to slow things down with questions or comments.

Beck got a text. He told Ciro and Demarco, "I'll see you later," and turned away to read it.

It was from Ricky Bolo. *The little miss is up and about. I'll get some liquids and food in her.*

Beck texted back. *Good. Hang in there. I'll need her functioning.*

Ciro and Demarco headed out. Ciro asked Demarco, "What're the odds Jimmy's plan is going to work?"

Demarco smiled. "I'll answer that when I know what the hell the plan is. What do you want to do for an hour?"

"How about skiing?"

"How about finding some coffee?"

"Okay."

Jonas found himself slightly out of breath, mostly from hurrying through the snow to get to his van parked behind the storage facility office. He speed-dialed Beck as he drove out of the storage facility.

Beck answered on the first ring. "What's up, Jonas?"

"It's a mix."

"Let's have it."

Beck stood outside Proctor's front door watching him load bullion, documents, and a small backpack into the cab section of his Nissan while he listened to Jonas. After Jonas finished, Beck said, "Okay, you know the storage units with gold, and you didn't have to shoot that peckerwood who barged in on you."

"That's for sure. Turns out that gun under the desk was a Smith and Wesson Governor loaded with four-ten shotgun shells. Would've made a mess I didn't have time to clean up."

"And a hell of a bang. Probably would have brought in the others."

"Yep."

"So we have two guards in front of each storage unit."

"Right. A total of eight."

"And they're not within sight of each other."

"Correct."

"What's next for you?"

"I'm headed back to hook up with Ricky. Pull together what we need and pack up."

"How long will that take?"

"It shouldn't be long. Ricky has the schematics. He's working on adjusting our lock picks."

"Let me know when you're ready to head back to the storage facility. Sooner the better."

"I will. See you."

Proctor came over to Beck asked, "What now?"

Beck said, "We drive to sheriff's headquarters, you get whatever evidence you have on the Joey Collins murder, and hand it to me."

Although Beck hadn't mentioned this before, it didn't surprise Proctor.

"After that?"

"I'll let you know. Sit in the truck. I have a couple of calls to make."

When Proctor got into the Nissan, Beck called Manny.

"Where are you?"

"With our friend. We're heading out to do that first thing."

"So he's in."

"Yes. In his way."

"Still the cagey bastard."

"Of course."

"But he understands what we want to do?"

"He does."

"All right. I'm going to loop in Irene now. She's got to handle him from this point."

"That's what he wants, James."

"Good. Hang on a sec." Beck walked to Proctor's truck and motioned for him to get in the driver's seat. He was anxious to leave. He climbed into the passenger seat, "Drive."

"Where to?"

"Sheriff's headquarters." Proctor gave Beck a quizzical look. Beck waved him off. Beck spoke into his phone. "I'm going to call her now and fill her in." Beck checked his watch. 12:47 p.m. "Let me know how your thing works out."

"I will. Then what?"

"Miller has to work on the rest of it. I'll text you the address where you should meet us. It's a storage facility."

"That makes sense."

"By the way, what are you driving?"

"Something Ricky stole for me. It's nice."

"Good luck. See you soon."

69

The Kin men were filtering into the Field, naturally dividing into two groups. The majority were members of the militia wing now controlled by George Myer. The other group, about half as many, were Emmett Devereaux's men. The militia guards were generally large, beefy men wearing outdoor clothing suitable for hunting. Parkas, heavy boots, insulated bib overalls. In addition to handguns, almost all of them carried assault rifles slung across their backs, the weapons resting on their bellies. Very few of Devereaux's men had long guns. All of them had one or two handguns holstered out of sight, along with knives, blackjacks, straight razors, anything that could kill or maim. They wore the same clothes they wore every day.

Most of the men stood around their vehicles in the parking area. Smaller groups were out in the field stacking firewood in the pits until the flames rose high into the snow-filled air. The word spread quickly about the deaths of Vic Myer and their Kommandant. A belligerent anger pulsed through the groups that grew with each passing minute while they waited for George Myer and Emmett Devereaux to come out of the barn and tell them how to take revenge on their enemies.

Inside the barn, Emmett Devereaux and George Myer sat at separate tables making phone calls to gather men and arms; alert everybody to find Beck, his men, and Irene Allen; and to locate Proctor so he could get his deputies involved.

Devereaux spent a good deal of his phone time trying to find anybody who knew where Andy Miller lived. He became increasingly frustrated that everyone he talked to couldn't even understand why he was asking about the skinny retard with the thick glasses.

Suddenly, George Myer slammed his fist down on his table. Devereaux asked, "What?"

"The boys I had on lookout at Proctor's aren't answering! They're dead, Emmett. I can feel it. They're dead. They killed them. And probably got Proctor, too." Myer slammed his fist on the table again. Devereaux thought he might actually break it. He hurried over and sat across from George.

Myer said, "I've called those boys on lookout twice. Three different phones. No answer. Beck and his bastards killed them. And most likely Abel."

"All right. All right. If that's true, it means Beck and his mongrels are still in the area. Good. We'll find them and finish them once and for all. If they're insane enough to come after us, they'll have to come here, and we'll slaughter them. And don't count Abel out just yet. We need to find out if Abel's dead or alive."

"With or without Abel, we need his deputies out there looking for Beck and his killers."

"Call any deputies you know who will help us."

Myer nodded, calming down. "All right. We can't wait for Abel. Assuming he's even alive."

"Assume he's alive until we hear different. Abel has always done things his way. Track down some deputies. And find out if any word has leaked out about what happened at the safe house."

Myer said, "Okay."

Devereaux stood up and pulled on his winter coat with difficulty. "We should send more men to the storage facility."

Myer said, "You think they know we store our gold there?"

"No. Dewey Newsome called me. He said everything was quiet at the storage facility. We should still send more men."

Myer said, "Time to relieve them guys anyhow."

"Right."

For the first time, George Myer thought of something other than killing. He asked Devereaux, "You get your wounds looked at?"

"When it's over. I'll pair up two of mine with two of yours like before?"

Myer said, "Okay. And I'm going to station men around our perimeter. I don't like all these guys standing around doing nothing. You want some of your fighters with mine?"

"Definitely."

Myer and Devereaux left the barn, each heading in a different direction to select men. Fifty feet from the barn a figure sat in one of the old Adirondack chairs scattered around the Field. Snow swirled around him He wore a hooded sweatshirt, dark coat. and flannel-lined jeans, the hood pulled low. He wore a wool scarf tied around his neck. Nobody paid him much notice or would've recognized Andy Miller if they did. Miller watched Myer and Devereaux until they were out of sight. Then he walked through the swirling snow and slipped into the barn.

After Manny Guzman had explained Beck's plan to Andy Miller, they quickly agreed on Miller's first task. Miller walked straight to the side wall of the barn and found the bright yellow plastic line that connected the two-hundred-gallon propane tank to the oven. He knelt down, took out a Swiss Army knife, and opened the punch awl. He twisted the awl into the side of the hose until he had opened a small hole. Propane gas hissed out of the opening. Miller took a device out of his pocket that Ricky Bolo had assembled using a lithium battery charger, a flip phone, and a small piece of white phosphorus wrapped in a thin piece of plastic wrap. Miller placed Ricky's device under the propane hose near where he had made the hole, then covered everything with loose straw on the dirt floor of the old barn. Miller checked his watch. It had taken him eight minutes to turn the dilapidated red barn into a time bomb.

He slipped out the back door, walked around the side of the barn, and up onto the road. It took him another eight minutes to walk to where he and Manny had parked their cars. He slipped into Manny's stolen Kia Telluride.

Manny asked, "All set?"

"Yep."

"How long has the propane been leaking?"

"About ten minutes."

"Anyone in the barn?"

"Not when I left."

Manny nodded. Ten minutes was more than enough time. At sea level propane was fifty-percent heavier than air. By now, it would have covered the ground around the leak, and the cold temperature would have prevented most of it from evaporating.

Manny pulled out his cell phone and dialed the number of the phone attached to Ricky Bolo's device. It took thirty seconds to produce enough heat to melt the thin layer of plastic wrap covering the white phosphorous which caused air to hit the white phosphorus, which caused it to spontaneously burst into a searing, inextinguishable flame.

Thirty-seven seconds after Manny's call, they heard the first explosion—a dull whump as ninety-eight gallons of propane burst into a fireball that filled the inside of the barn, along with a ten-foot flame spewing out of the flailing propane tank hose.

Manny turned to Andy Miller.

"That should keep them busy."

Miller nodded. He said, "When will she be there?"

"She's probably there now. You can call her, or she can call you. We should get out of here."

Miller got out of Manny's car and into his Subaru Forester. Neither of them spoke. They were past that now. As Miller closed the door to his SUV, he heard the propane tank outside the barn explode. The Field was dead now. Andy Miller didn't care one bit. He was past that, too.

70

Proctor stopped his Nissan at the intersection of Routes Eight and Twenty-nine. Beck sat in the passenger seat next to him with his Browning pointed at Proctor's ribs. Proctor signaled for a left turn. Beck said, "Change of plans. Turn right. We're going to the storage facility."

Proctor made the turn and said, "How do we get in? Your man has my pass card."

"Don't worry about it. Listen to what I tell you to do. Don't ask questions. Don't double-cross me. Don't give me any reasons to shoot you. I already have plenty."

Abel Proctor remained quiet, concentrating on his driving. He leaned toward the windshield, both hands on the wheel, staring out at the falling snow. Beck made a quick call to Demarco.

"You in position where Jonas told you?"

"Yep."

"I'll be there in a few minutes."

"Got it."

After three miles of silence, Proctor said, "You know, there's not that much difference between us."

"How so?"

"We both take care of our own by whatever means necessary."

"And this from the guy who's packing up his shit and leaving for Wyoming without a goddamn thought about taking care of anybody but himself. You can shove that false equivalency bullshit right up your ass, pal."

Ten minutes later, Beck saw the entrance to the storage facility, "Turn into the entrance. When the gate opens, drive to the office."

Proctor followed instructions. Jonas Bolo stepped out of the office and handed Proctor's storage unit key to Beck.

Beck handed Proctor the key and pointed to the path along the west of the storage center.

"Drive to your storage unit on that path. Stop before you turn into your row. Let me out. When I tap on your tailgate, make the turn, and drive slowly to your unit. Slowly. Let the Kin boys guarding your unit know it's you, so they don't shoot you. Park in front of your unit, tell them you need something. Then get out and open the door."

"Then what?"

"Pretend you're looking for something inside. And do not fucking turn around."

Proctor did as instructed. When he stopped to let Beck out, he saw that Ciro and Demarco were already waiting, hidden from sight behind the corner of the storage building. They joined Beck and followed behind Proctor's Nissan as he turned into his row. Proctor lowered his window and waved at two men in a Toyota Tacoma pickup parked in front of his storage unit.

Beck, Ciro, and Demarco walked behind the truck, staying out of sight. The two guards got out of their pickup to see what Proctor wanted. Both had AR-15 rifles. One of them motioned for Proctor to stop. The guards looked like brothers, two locals wearing almost identical camouflage parkas and ski pants. One had a knit cap; the other was bareheaded.

Proctor got out of his truck.

"I need something from my unit."

One of the guards said, "I thought that was you, Mr. Proctor."

Both of them followed Proctor as he went to unlock his storage unit. Ciro moved around to the front of the truck.

All three came out from behind the truck with their guns drawn. The guards had their backs to them. Beck and Demarco stepped into the into the glare of Proctor's headlights. Beck called out, "Hey there."

Both guards turned to Beck and Demarco pointing their handguns at them. For a moment, it looked like the guard in the knit cap might raise his rifle. And then Ciro Baldassare stepped out of the dark on their right side. His Smith and Wesson .45 made it three guns pointing at them.

"Hands on your heads," said Beck.

The guard with the knit cap hesitated. Ciro Baldassare didn't. He stepped forward, smacked the barrel of his .45 against the guard's head, and kicked the man's legs out from under him. Then he kicked the guard's ribs and said, "Get up. Put your fucking hands on your head." He didn't need to kick him again.

Proctor pulled open the door to his storage unit.

Ciro kept his gun on the guards as Beck and Demarco took their weapons – two assault rifles, two handguns, two hunting knives – and tossed them in Proctor's truck bed.

Beck asked, "Do you guys do all your shopping together?"

They didn't answer.

Beck told them, "Yeah, you probably should keep your mouths shut."

Beck pushed one of the guards into the storage unit and over to the wall on the left. Demarco led the second guard to the wall on the right. It took three minutes for Beck and Demarco to hogtie the guards' hands and feet with yellow polyethylene packing rope they found in Proctor's storage unit. Ciro stood back with his handgun ready just in case either of the prisoners decided to do something stupid.

Beck pointed to Ciro. "Either of you makes a sound, and my friend will come back and shoot you. Trust me when I say he really wants to shoot you."

Taking out the guards in front of Emmett Devereaux's storage unit was a little more complicated. These two were clearly Devereaux's men – smaller, suspicious of Proctor, less heavily armed. Proctor said he was checking up on them and that men would come to relieve them in a couple of hours. This time, because

Devereaux's unit was in a building near the east end of the row, Beck, Demarco, and Ciro came around the corner behind the guards. One of them had an old Weatherby bolt action hunting rifle. The other a shotgun.

Beck didn't take any chances they might hear them approaching. From twenty feet away, he yelled, "Hands up!"

Beck, Demarco, and Ciro spread out so the guards couldn't easily shoot all three of them quickly, but they still raised their guns.

Proctor yelled, "Don't be stupid. Drop your weapons!" Not because he cared about the guards. Because he might get shot if Beck and his men opened fire.

They walked the captives back to Proctor's storage unit and tied them up. They tossed the Weatherby and shotgun into Proctor's truck bed along with knives, one handgun, straight razors, and a small fighting stick.

The next two guards in front of Vic Myer's unit were easier to take down. They were sleeping in their car, an old Ford Taurus station wagon. Beck and Demarco pulled them out of their car at gunpoint while they were half asleep. They gave up without a fight. Same drill – weapons into Proctor's truck bed, tie them up in Proctor's unit.

It was clear to Beck that the Kin had sent guards from both Devereaux's hill people and Myer's militia. On the walk to Proctor's unit, the snowstorm had increased. They had to lean into the wind to keep going. Ciro muttered, "Fucking cold. Fucking snow." He said, "You know how much easier and faster this would all be if we just shot these assholes?"

Beck said, "I need these bums for something."

"What?"

"You'll see. How're your boots holding up?"

Ciro said, "I'm still breaking them in. They feel cheap."

"Don't worry, big guy. This won't be much longer. I'm going to speed things up."

Beck called Jonas Bolo. He and Ricky were waiting in the office. Beck told him to get to work on the first safe.

Jonas said, "We'll do Myer's Bischoff first."

"Makes sense. While you do that, we'll unload the other unit. You brought Irene, right?"

"Yes. She's gonna stay in the office watching the monitors. If she sees anything, she'll call you."

"Good. Is she okay?"

"Pretty much. Hang on." Beck waited. Jonas came back on the phone. "Manny just drove in. He's driving a brand new Kia Telluride Ricky found for him."

Beck said, "He deserves it. Send the old hombre over to Proctor's unit. I'll meet him there."

While Ciro and Demarco tied up the two new prisoners, Beck told them, "When you're done with them, get my truck and transfer the weapons from Proctor's truck into mine."

Beck took Proctor aside and said, "It's time we took care of our last bit of business together."

"What's that?"

"You're going to go to headquarters and get the evidence you have on me for the Joey Collins murder."

"You mean the murder weapon?"

Beck said, "Which is Irene Allen's knife."

"Yeah. With her prints and yours on it. Along with Joey Collins's blood."

"How'd you verify they're my prints?"

"New York Department of Corrections records."

Beck nodded. "So you put some of Collins's blood from the murder scene on the knife and turned it into the murder weapon."

"You figured it out."

"Pretty much."

"Classic, right? The murderers returned to the scene of the crime. Tried to get rid of the weapon while I was in pursuit."

Beck frowned. He imagined Proctor supplying a motive and opportunity to go with the murder weapon that would convince a local jury.

"You have anything else?"

"Besides the weapon?"

"Yes."

"DOC reports on your criminal history, forensics on the prints, lab reports on the blood, and a preliminary autopsy on the victim."

Manny Guzman appeared out of the swirling snow. He'd parked the Kia near where Beck and Proctor stood.

Beck pointed to Manny. "My friend Mr. Guzman will drive you to the sheriff's office. He'll sit in your truck. You bring out everything you have. Hand it over to Mr. Guzman. We left two million in your truck bed. If my associate sees anybody except you come out of that office, if he sees anybody following him after you drive away, he'll shoot you, and we get the two million. If you come back here and give me your evidence, you get the two mil, everything else we agreed to, and you're free to go."

"Or you're free to shoot me."

"Hey, I could shoot you right now and save all the risk to Mr. Guzman. Take my chances that your bullshit evidence won't hold up after my lawyers destroy your reputation with the proof we have of your crimes. But you've cooperated so far. Do this last thing and I'll keep my end of the bargain. Refuse, and I'll put a bullet between your eyes. Your call."

Proctor hesitated.

Beck asked, "Are you actually thinking this over?"

Proctor said, "Follow me."

Proctor walked Beck to his truck. He opened the rear door of the extended cab and folded up the jump seat. Taped to the bottom was the sealed evidence bag holding the doctored knife and all the reports. He pulled off the tape and handed the evidence to Beck.

Proctor said, "How about I give you this now, you give me the envelope that was on the seat of my truck, and let me be on my way?"

Beck said, "One of my guys already dropped it in a mailbox."

"Those were my resignation papers."

"I know. I looked inside and resealed it."

"Good move. If you kill me, that will buy you time before they start looking for me."

"Yep."

Proctor nodded and handed Beck the sealed evidence bag.

"Then I'll be on my way?"

"When you leave, don't call any of your Kin pals."

Proctor said, "I'm surprised reinforcements aren't here already."

Beck gave a small shrug. "I might have delayed that a bit." Beck pointed to Proctor's storage unit. "By the way, do any of these morons know what they're guarding?"

Proctor smirked. "Hell no. They think it's guns or drugs. Or maybe cash."

Beck nodded. He said, "Stick around until we take down the last two guards watching Morelli's unit. Once they're locked up with the others, you can go."

"You need me to come with you?"

"No. I'm going to drive over in that station wagon that belongs to one of the guards. Get their attention while my partners do the old sneak up from behind bit."

Proctor said, "You think that's going to work?"

"I got a secret weapon."

"What's that?"

"There's an empty pizza box in that station wagon. I'm gonna hold it out the window."

Proctor smirked. He knew the pizza box would work.

"Hang in here with Mr. Guzman."

Proctor looked over at Manny. He wondered if the stolid-looking ex-con was going to shoot him as soon as Beck left. He certainly looked capable of it.

Beck saw Proctor staring at Manny.

"He won't shoot you as long as you don't do anything stupid."

Proctor nodded.

Beck turned to leave and then turned back.

"By the way. Any idea who killed Joey Collins?"

Proctor frowned. "Not really. It could've been anyone who was there that night. Or hiding out in the dark. Could have been you and Irene Allen. Look at the evidence. Maybe you can figure it out."

71

There were three explosions at the Field. The propane gas in the barn. The propane tank outside the barn. And George Myer.

Emmett Devereaux had to fight the urge to shoot the raging bully in the head and be done with him. The sound of approaching fire engines stopped him. Sheriff's deputies and state police wouldn't be far behind. He stood back as Myer stormed around, pushing and shoving men. Yelling at them to ready their weapons, form into a line surrounding the property, and prepare for an attack that Devereaux figured would have already happened if the explosion in the barn had been the first strike.

Devereaux watched the flames eat through the barn's roof. Smoke poured out of every opening. The exploding propane tank had set fire to half the wall on the right side of the barn. Devereaux saw no point in staying until fire and police vehicles blocked the only road out. He headed for his Ford F-150, telling as many of his men he spotted to get their vehicles and follow him. Devereaux was sick of trying to keep George Myer in line. He knew if Myer saw him leaving, he would accuse him of running away from the fight. Devereaux pulled out his knife. If George Myer tried to stop him, he would stab him as many times as it took to send that big, crazy bastard to hell where he could join his smirking asshole brother.

Next stop, get his holdings at the storage center and head for the hills. Literally.

Jonas Bolo and his brother Ricky had spent years using automated dialers to help decipher combinations on various safes. As the automated dialers became more sophisticated, so too did their skills. The dialers accelerated their understanding of combination dial mechanisms. Training with them helped the Bolos discern the subtle variations between each number on a combination dial, hearing and feeling with increasing accuracy when the locking mechanisms dropped down ever so slightly after each successive correct number. They could also do what no dialer could. Research the construction of safe dials. They knew exactly what the internal mechanisms of various combination dials looked like, how they were built, tooled, and fit together.

Drilling out the padlock on Myer's storage door, setting up their lights and a mini iPad, taping reference pictures to the safe, and laying out the key picks Ricky had refined took fourteen minutes.

The brothers' plan from the beginning was to team up on the Bischoff. The safe had two combination dials, each with a lock. Plus a third lock on the door. The Bolos closed themselves in the storage unit and went to work. Ricky worked alone on the first combination dial. Jonas recorded the numbers Ricky recited on a custom spreadsheet using a mini iPad. While Ricky worked the dial, Jonas laid out his customized lock picks. The best automatic dialers could have done the job in a few hours. The Bolos figured out the first combination in forty-two minutes.

Ricky switched to the second dial, tracking his own numbers while Jonas worked the picks to open the first lock. Twice, Jonas used a tiny file to hone the notches on the lock picks. Jonas felt awkward at first. But with each passing minute, as he worked, he fell into a deeper connection with the hidden parts of the lock that he pictured in his mind. It became like a blind man forming an image by feel.

Jonas took sixteen minutes, forty-two seconds to unlock the first lock.

He switched back to tracking numbers. Defeating the combination dial and picking the second lock took a total of twenty-two minutes and twelve seconds.

The last lock on the door took two minutes. In just under one hour, Ricky Bolo pulled open the Bischoff revealing one shelf holding hundred-gram bars of gold bullion stacked five inches high and seven inches deep, nearly filling the twenty-one-inch-wide space.

Ricky had wrapped his Vicuna scarf around his head and under his chin to keep his ears warm. He let out a soft whistle. Jonas had already done the math: 1,900 grams. Depending on the price of gold, it amounted to somewhere in the neighborhood of eleven million dollars.

But that wasn't all. The Myer brothers had diversified. The bottom two-thirds of the Bischoff contained neat stacks of currency in various denominations of U.S. dollars, Canadian dollars, and Euro notes. The Bolos didn't have time to count it. Jonas figured out a number estimating that fifty was the likely average denomination and then eyeballing how high the currency was stacked. Rough estimate, at least another five million.

While Jonas did his calculations, Ricky pulled open the storage unit door. Beck, Demarco, and Ciro were standing outside Myer's unit waiting. They'd finished taking down the last two guards using the pizza ploy and pulling out all the junk blocking the safe in Devereaux's storage unit. Ricky motioned toward the open Bischoff.

"Ta da!"

"Congratulations. How much?"

Jonas came out to join them. "Sixteen million. Or thereabouts."

They knew Proctor had taken four million in bullion from his unit. He had six more in Wyoming. Beck didn't think he owned six million in property, but the amount was close enough to what the Myer brothers had accrued.

Beck didn't waste time thinking about it. He told the Bolos, "We uncovered the safe in Devereaux's unit. It looks different from this one. Newer. Maybe better? If you two can't open it quickly, best move on to Dent's storage unit. Try to figure out what's going on with it."

Without another word, Ricky and Jonas got in their van and headed over to tackle Devereaux's safe. They arrived to find the contents of Devereaux's storage unit scattered around out front, already covered in a coating of snow.

As the Bolos drove off, Beck backed his truck into the Myer's unit. Demarco and Ciro helped him load the gold bullion and cash into his truck bed.

As soon as they finished loading the gold, Beck, Ciro, and Demarco drove to Devereaux's unit. Ricky and Jonas had drilled out the padlock, opened the storage unit, and unloaded equipment from their van. Jonas had just finished setting up a work light trained on the safe. Beck had been correct. It wasn't a Bischoff.

Beck walked into the unit.

"So?"

Ricky responded. "This is a little unique. It's a high-end safe. Custom made from something that started out as a rifle safe. You're right. It's a better safe. It's made with a high-density compressed concrete material encased in magnesium steel plates. The concrete is reinforced with a matrix of carbon filters. Can't cut it. Can't blow it open without destroying whatever is inside. You can't drill out the dials or pick the locks because it has a shitload of re-lockers that kick in if you fuck with them."

Ricky was delivering bad news but with a smile.

"So what's the answer?"

Ricky tapped his head with a forefinger. "Information will kill this beast." He turned to his brother. "Has to be on the back, right?"

"If it's anywhere."

"What?" asked Beck.

Jonas walked behind the safe and said, "The serial number plate. It's here, back left corner."

The brothers retired to their van and powered up a high-end laptop running two monitors to hack into the safe manufacturer's website. They used the serial number of the safe to obtain a copy of the original purchase invoice that showed the buyer, date of purchase, order number, and warranty numbers. Next, they set up an account using credentials from a legitimate locksmith license and submitted all that information which started the process that would provide them the safe's combination. Forty-seven minutes later, after going through all the double-authentication processes, they had the combination.

Jonas said, "Hope nobody reset the combination after they bought the safe."

Ricky smacked his brother's shoulder and said, "Don't put a Kenny O'Hara on it."

Everyone gathered around the safe. For some reason Ricky unwrapped the scarf around his head before he spun the dial and entered the combination. He turned the handle. The safe door opened.

There were no shelves inside the safe. There was, however, a stack of 100-gram gold bars formed into a golden chimney. And also a pungent smell.

Beck asked, "What the hell is that smell?"

All three men sniffed the air. Finally, Jonas said, "It smells like insecticide. Bug spray."

Ricky stepped forward and wiped his finger on the side wall of the safe. He sniffed at the tip of his finger.

"I think you're right."

Beck said, "Why use that?"

"Because he's bat shit crazy?"

Beck said, "Well, some kind of crazy for sure. How much gold is there?"

Again, Jonas did a rough estimate.

"About the same as Myer's. Another eleven or twelve million. But no cash."

Beck, Ciro, and Demarco formed a relay line and began transferring the gold into Beck's truck bed.

As they took apart the gold chimney, they found another surprise — a pile of shriveled body parts. There were pieces of fingers, ears, what looked like the tips of noses, teeth, and other dried-up things no one wanted to guess at.

Ricky gave voice to what others were thinking. "Sick fuck."

"Forget it. Time is short. You two have to figure out what's with that last unit."

When all the gold bullion was removed, Jonas Bolo stood staring at the inside of the safe. He didn't move. The others thought he was looking at Devereaux's grisly souvenirs. He wasn't. Something else had attracted his attention.

He said, "Wait."

Beck asked, "Why?"

"Something is off."

Jonas hurried to his van and quickly returned with a Vevor eight-inch suction cup glass lifter capable of holding a 220-pound sheet of glass. He attached the suction cup to the bottom of the safe, gripped the handle, squatted, and lifted up using his back and legs. Beck helped Jonas raise a two-inch piece of steel and move it out of the safe. Under the false bottom was a five-inch stack of hundred-dollar bills in banded bundles, each worth $10,000. The total was almost two million dollars.

Jonas said, "The framing on the bottom didn't match the top. Even if you count a little more room for the bolts to secure the safe to the floor."

Ricky patted Jonas on the back. "Good goin', bro."

"Well done," said Beck. "Now, go see if you can solve the mystery of the last unit while we load this up."

Everyone jumped to it.

Ciro finished loading the contents of Devereaux's safe into Beck's truck.

The Bolo brothers headed for Dent/Morelli's storage unit.

Demarco went to get his truck to join Ricky and Jonas at Dent's storage unit.

Beck drove Manny's Kia to the office.

When Beck walked into the office, he saw Irene watching the CCTV images on the two monitors. She turned to look at Beck.

Beck asked, "How're you feeling?"

"Weird. Kind of weak. Looks like this snowstorm is keeping everyone away."

"Did you eat anything?"

"Yes. A crappy frozen dinner. Ricky also gave me some energy bars. I just ate one. Tasted like sawdust. Had a bottle of water with it."

Beck walked over next to Irene and looked at the images on the screen. The snow swirling around in the bright glare of the light poles made the images almost useless. The fisheye lenses at each end of Camdyn Dent's storage unit showed clearer images of Demarco and the Bolos standing in front of Dent's unit. Ricky had parked the rented van so that the headlights illuminated the front of the storage unit.

Irene asked, "You finding anything?"

"Yep." Beck pointed at the images of Dent's storage. "That's the big mystery, though. That's where the main holdings should be. But Jonas said it looked empty inside."

"Have you figured it out?"

"Not yet. Have you talked to Andy Miller?"

"Twice."

"What's he saying?"

"After the explosion, he hid in the woods across the road from the barn. He saw Devereaux and a bunch of his men heading out. Driving across the field behind the barn. There's a service road that runs through the forest and hooks up with the road out front."

"Sneaking out like the rat he is."

"You think he's coming here?"

"I'm doing what I can to make sure of it. What about Myer?"

"Andy said Myer is still reacting to his barn blowing up."

"Where's Andy now?"

"He's not big on explaining things. He told me you have to buy him some time.'"

Beck grimaced. Checked his watch yet again. He didn't have much time to buy. His odds of winning the endgame were evaporating. Worse, he could not stop a deeply embedded fear from rising up in him. Fear that he was leading his partners, and Irene, into a battle they could not possibly win. A fear worse than all his pain and exhaustion. A fear that created an overpowering urge to gather up everybody and flee.

And then Irene said, "Did you hear me?"

Beck turned to her. "What?"

"The last thing Andy said was you have to buy him more time."

At that moment, Beck knew that every moment he wasted, paralyzed by fear or doubt, made the next moment more dangerous. Forward. He had to go forward to the end.

"Yes. I heard you. How long ago did Devereaux leave?"

Irene checked her watch. "I don't know. Forty-five minutes? An hour?"

Beck nodded. It was going to be close. Very close. "All right, I'm letting Proctor go in a couple of minutes."

"The red Nissan?"

"Yes. Open the gate for him. Close it after he leaves."

Beck dashed out into the cold and snow and raced back to Proctor's storage unit. He slid to a stop and yelled out to Proctor, "Time for you to go!"

He waved for Manny to jump in the Kia and drove to Dent's storage unit. When he arrived, the Bolos, Ciro, and Demarco were standing in front of Dent's unit.

The rolling steel door was open, revealing what looked like a giant safe with two doors. It filled the entire opening.

Beck and Manny got out and joined the others.

Beck asked, "What's going on?"

Ricky answered while Jonas kept staring at the safe.

"Well, what you're looking at is a custom-built walk-in vault. It looks like it fills the interior of the unit. It's a box inside a box. Not as strong as the last two safes, but it's pretty secure. I haven't ever seen one this big. Jonas drilled through the back of it, thinking he was going through a steel plate put in to reinforce the back wall. He was actually drilling into the back of this vault. Problem is, based on what he saw, the whole damn thing is empty. It's a goddamn mystery."

"Can you open it?"

"Sure, but Jonas is still trying to figure something out."

Beck said, "We don't have time. Just open it."

Jonas turned to Beck. "Don't do anything yet. I think I know what's going on. While I find out, Ricky, get one of the guard's trucks. The biggest you can find."

Ricky said, "Really?"

"Yes."

Ricky said, "Yahoo," and ran off.

Jonas ran to his van and returned with his drill, the A/V microprobe, and a fifty-six-inch molding pry bar that weighed almost sixteen pounds. He handed the all-steel bar to Demarco and said, "Stand by."

Within two minutes, Jonas had drilled a hole in the three-foot section of concrete block wall next to the rolling steel door. He inserted the probe, checked the AV screen, and turned to Beck as Ricky drove up in a Dodge Ram 1500. Ricky lined up the rear bumper with the center of the vault's door. Because Dent's unit was in the last row, Ricky had plenty of room in front. He stopped twenty feet away from the door.

Beck said, "Now what?"

Jonas said, "Now I know where the gold is."

He showed Beck, Ciro, and Demarco the faint image on the A/V microprobe screen. It revealed a line of neatly stacked gold bullion between the wall of the huge vault and storage unit wall.

"Somebody had a clever idea. The vault fills most the storage unit, but not all of it. There's about two-and-a-half feet of space on both sides between the vault and the walls. That adds up to about a thousand square feet of hidden storage space."

"Great. Good job. How do we get it?" asked Beck.

"Stand back."

Jonas waved at Ricky. Ricky pulled his seatbelt tight, revved the truck engine, and backed up. First slowly, then with increasing speed until he slammed into the vault doors at 25 mph. The collision was impressive. The vault doors broke open. The truck's back bumper broke off, the truck bed buckled, and the back axle and frame cracked.

Ricky managed to pull away even though both back wheels scraped the compressed wheel wells.

Jonas said, "Crude, but quick." He turned to Demarco still holding the pry bar. "I'm sure there are removable panels on the side walls, but they've buckled. You should be able to pop them off with that bar."

"Happy to," said Demarco.

Ricky joined them carrying a Lylting 160,000-lumen LED flashlight.

Beck said, "Nice job, boys. Now, don't bother loading the bullion. Toss everything you find into the center of the vault. Ciro and Manny, help build the gold into a nice pile, then unload all the weapons in my truck bed and put them with the gold. Then take a few bundles of cash from my truck and spread it around."

Ciro asked, "Then what?"

Before Beck could answer, his phone rang. It was Irene. He listened for a moment and said, "All right." On his way out of the vault, he yelled to them, "I'll be back as quick as I can and let you know what's next."

Beck ran to the Kia parked nearby. Demarco, Manny, Ciro and the Bolo brothers stood in the middle of the vault looking confused.

Ciro said, "Is he going to leave all this gold in here?"

Demarco had figured out Beck's plan, but he didn't take the time to explain it. He said, "Not exactly." He lifted the pry bar onto his shoulder and headed to side wall of the vault saying, "Tick, tock, boys. Tick tock."

72

Watching his red barn collapse in a ball of flames had a strangely mesmerizing effect on George Myer. He felt released from playing the role he'd been relegated to while his brother took center stage.

The local volunteer firefighters hadn't even tried to fight the blaze. They had three hoses unreeled but used only one of them to spray down the smoldering propane tank. George Myer watched along with the others, his rage settling into a simmering core of hate focused on James Beck, the bearded outsider who came from nowhere and threatened everything. Myer turned away from the fire when one of his militia men approached.

Myer barked, "What?"

"Devereaux ain't here."

"Where is he?"

"Seems like he left with a bunch of his men."

"When?"

The man shrugged.

"How?"

"I think they drove out through the field. Not all of them. Some vehicles are still here."

Myer was about to grab the man and tell him to find where Devereaux went when his phone rang. It was Proctor.

"George!"

"Where are you?"

"Doing what I do. Get over to the storage place. They're stealing the gold."

"Who!?"

"Beck and his men, for god's sake. Get over there! Tell Emmett. Bring everyone you got. This is your chance to kill them all!"

Proctor cut the call before George Myer could yell questions at him.

He'd called Myer with his last burner phone, hidden under the front seat of his truck. Proctor powered down the driver's side window and threw the phone out as he headed toward the Thruway. He would have enjoyed seeing the Kin militia boys slaughter Beck and his men, but it wasn't worth the risk. He'd done his last bit for the Kin.

Proctor realized his heart was pounding a bit. Was it because he feared what would happen to him when the Kin figured out he'd disappeared? Maybe they'd assume he was dead. Maybe they wouldn't. Fuck it. They'd have to find him first. He was now William T. Balog. Soon to be in a small town in Wyoming. Free and clear. Proctor vowed to put in a hundred miles before he stopped for coffee.

Proctor's phone call released George Myer. He finally had a target. A chance to kill James Beck and every one of his goddamn criminal mongrels, proving to all that he was now the true Kommandant of the Kin. The new Camdyn Dent. The gold was secondary. Killing Beck, shooting him, running his truck over the body, cutting it to pieces, and burning the remains was all Myer could think about.

He moved quickly among the men, issuing orders, organizing them into groups, assigning them to vehicles, making sure their weapons were ready. He hurried to his truck, a brand new, pine green Ford F-350 King Ranch 4WD crew cab. There was a heavy-duty truck box mounted in the bed packed with two assault rifles, a Remington shotgun, boxes of ammunition, two baseball bats, and outdoor gear.

George bulled his way through the emergency vehicles to the dirt road. He was alone in the truck, muttering to himself, checking his rearview mirror, making sure other trucks and vehicles were lining up behind him. He tried to breathe deeply and slowly. His time had come. Time to destroy his enemies. And everyone who stood between him and his right to lead the Kin.

While everyone worked on stacking gold in the big vault, Beck raced through the falling snow to the office. He fought the Kia's steering wheel to try to keep the SUV from sliding out of control. He forced himself to stop looking at his watch. They would either have enough time, or they wouldn't. When he turned into the row where the office was located, the Kia slid out from under him. He let up on the gas and straightened it out just before his back end smashed into the side of the office.

He slid to a halt and beeped his horn. Inside the office, Irene followed Beck's instructions and opened the sliding security gate the entrance. She came out of the office wearing the North Face jacket she'd taken from Deborah Ramirez's house and a knit hat Ricky Bolo had given her. She got into the Kia as the front gate rolled wide open. Beck noticed she was only limping slightly.

Beck drove off and turned onto the asphalt path, again staying on the west side of the storage facility, heading for Camdyn Dent's unit. He slid to a halt in front of the open storage unit. The interior of the vault was ablaze with work lights. Demarco had pried off three large panels on the left wall of the vault and two on the right side. There was a four-foot pile of gold bullion in the middle of the vault, some of it in boxes, much of it scattered loosely. Manny was tossing handfuls of hundred-dollar bills around the gold. Ciro was bringing in all the weapons they'd taken from the Kin guards.

Beck and Irene got out of the SUV and walked into the vault. Irene stood mesmerized by the sight.

Beck asked Ricky, "Is this all of it?"

"All of it from the left side, about half from the right."

"Any cash?"

"Maybe farther back."

Demarco approached the pile carrying six canvas bags filled with gold Krugerrands. Beck grabbed two bags and poured a trail of gold coins from the pile to the outside while Demarco dumped the rest of the gold coins on the pile.

Both Ricky and Jonas dumped another armful of bullion on the floor. Beck shouted, "How much do you think is here?"

Jonas asked, "Including what's still between the walls?"

"Yeah."

"At least two hundred million. Bullion in various sizes from multiple refineries. Krugerrands that go back years. This stash has been building a long time."

Everyone had gathered around the pile. Manny helped Ciro prop the Kin rifles on the pile with all the other weapons.

Beck announced, "Time to get out of here. Ricky, Jonas, take what you think is right to compensate you from behind the wall, then pack up and get the hell out. Leave your work lights on in here. You can try to go out the front gate or drive out where you cut open the iron fence if you think your van can make it. Up to you."

Ricky and Jonas looked at each other. Ricky said, "Five million?"

Jonas said, "Fine."

As the Bolos retrieved their cut, Beck motioned for the others to follow him out. They gathered near Beck's GMC and Demarco's Honda. Irene took one more look at the Kin treasure. It seemed unreal.

Beck spoke quietly. "Let's divide up what we took between the two trucks. Quick as you can. Demarco, you and Ciro leave in Demarco's Honda. Manny, Irene, you take my truck. I'll drive the Kia out. Let's go."

With five people working, it took less than three minutes to move half the gold and cash into Demarco's Honda.

Everyone boarded the vehicles. Ciro and Demarco in his truck. Manny behind the wheel of Beck's truck with Irene next to him. When Irene turned to watch Beck get into the Kia, she noticed the gold bullion and bundles of cash behind her. It didn't seem like much compared to what Beck had left behind. Manny saw her expression.

He said, "If we wanted their money, we'd have taken all of it."

"Why only this much?"

"Finder's fee. Covers expenses with something for pain and damage. Time and the risk. A portion of that is yours, too."

Manny followed Demarco and Ciro toward the west end of the facility. Irene turned to watch Beck fall in behind them. But as they drove into the darkness past the glare of the outdoor lights, Beck turned east.

Irene said, "Where's he going?"

Manny said, "To start a fight."

73

As the two trucks drove off into the dark, Beck headed toward Proctor's storage unit, got out, and pulled up the rolling door. Eight men turned to look at Beck, all still hogtied, hands and ankles bound and joined together with short lengths of rope. The Kia's headlights revealed that two men had made their way next to each other. One of them was trying to untie the rope binding the other man's wrists. He hadn't succeeded.

Beck walked to the nearest man. He pulled out a folding knife and cut the rope between the man's wrists and ankles, then did the same for two others and dropped his knife on the ground. He stood back and pointed a thumb over his shoulder. "Your guns are inside a unit in the last row. Cut yourselves loose and get the fuck out of here."

With that, Beck hustled to the Kia and drove back to the west end of the storage facility. He kept going past all the buildings and turned north into the empty field, heading for the seven-foot wrought iron fence that bordered the facility. The fence was about fifty yards away. Most of the distance was open ground. A border of bushes and saplings stood in front of the fence. The Bolos had used acetylene torches to cut out a section. Beck didn't have to look for the opening. He followed the tracks in the snow left by the Honda Ridgeline and his GMC.

The Kia's all-wheel drive kept the SUV going over the uneven terrain and crushed undergrowth. Beck stopped just before the opening in the fence. Past the fence was a service road built on top of an abandoned railroad line. Beck's headlights made the road look like a big white stripe cutting through the dark. That was his way out. But Beck didn't take it. He shut down the SUV and jumped out.

The wind-driven swirling snow felt like tiny bits of ice hitting his face. Beck pulled his watch cap lower and walked back toward the storage facility. The first prisoners from Proctor's storage unit were already arriving at the gold stash. Beck heard shouts. He kept going, moving steadily, trying not to lose his footing on the uneven, snow-covered ground, but he found himself stumbling, as much from exhaustion as anything else.

By the time Beck got within twenty yards of the gold vault all eight of the Kin guards had arrived at Morelli's storage unit. Some were scrambling to retrieve their weapons. Others were stuffing their pockets with cash and gold. All of them were arguing. Beck stood in the snow covered field watching and waiting. He'd lit the fuse. There was nothing more he could do but watch and wait.

There was more yelling. A fight broke out inside the vault. One of the guards from Myer's militia ran out of the vault. A gunshot sounded inside. Then a flurry of shots.

Three more of Myer's militia men ran out of the storage unit. One joined the guard on the right of the open door, the other two took cover on the left side. The guard on the left leaned in and fired a burst of shots into the vault. Return fire from Devereaux's men inside came quickly. The shooter on the right joined the fight, firing blindly into the vault.

Beck saw headlights at the east end of the storage facility. Three pickup trucks barreled through the open gate. He caught glimpses of the trucks as they passed between buildings. All three trucks were filled with men hunkered down in the beds.

When the trucks turned into the last row, the militia fighters outside the vault turned. The two nearest to the oncoming trucks pointed their rifles at them. Someone in the lead truck stuck a hand out of the driver's side window and shot at the militia guards. They both returned fire. The two guards on the other side of the storage unit door continued exchanging rounds with Devereaux's men inside the vault.

All three trucks slid to a halt forming a perpendicular line ten yards from the storage unit. Emmett Devereaux jumped out of the first truck holding his Glock. He took cover behind his door. His men jumped out of the truck beds, some of them exchanging shots with Myer's militia men outside the vault. One went down. The surviving three turned and dashed back into the vault, shooting at whoever was still alive inside.

Devereaux tried to stop the chaos. He came out from behind his truck door firing his Glock into the air, shouting orders for everyone to, "Cease fire! Cease fire!"

For a moment, it looked like Devereaux was going to succeed. Beck stood alone in the dark watching his plan fail. Devereaux's men came out from behind their trucks, slowly approaching the open vault. But then the power of a two-hundred million pile of gold took over. Seeing the gleaming pile of gold, one of Devereaux's men ran toward the open vault doors. Rifle shots cut him down before he made it inside. The battle erupted with more force and brutality. All of Devereaux's men opened fire.

Beck kept looking east. In moments this would all be over. Where the hell was George Myer? He couldn't believe that Proctor hadn't double-crossed him and called Myer. Had he just called Devereaux and *not* Myer? And then, movement from the east end caught Beck's attention. Another group of trucks and cars came tearing through the open entrance led by a green Ford F-350. Was there still time for this to work? The shooting from Devereaux's men began to fade. There was no return fire from inside the vault.

But then George Myer's battle rage dispelled any doubt that this was over. He drove his 6,000-pound Ford F-350 into the line of Devereaux's trucks, smashing through and plowing into a clump of Devereaux's men moving toward the vault.

Devereaux opened fire with his Glock, shooting at the driver's side window of Myer's truck. Too late; Myer had come out the passenger side with a Remington ARC-18 to join the battle. His men poured out of the trucks opening fire on Devereaux's men who were taking cover wherever they could find it – inside the vault, in the doorways of other storage units, behind their trucks.

Myer stood near his truck surveying the battle ignoring the carnage around him. He didn't care that Kin men were dying. He only cared about one man – James Beck. Where was he? Was he in the vault? Was he already dead?

Myer walked toward the vault opening as if he were bullet proof.

Devereaux was still near his truck ten yards to the right of the vault. He saw Myer walking forward. That big fucking maniac had ruined everything. Devereaux snarled in frustration. He had almost stopped the chaos when that idiot showed up. Clearly the man had lost his mind. He watched Myer walk into the vault as if he were the new Camdyn Dent. He wanted Beck. He wanted the gold. Emmett Devereaux's black eyes darkened with murderous intent. Hunched over, moving quickly in the swirling snow, Devereaux headed for the vault, his Glock in hand.

Out in the empty field, Beck started to back away into the darkness. A feeling of defeat and exhaustion overwhelmed him. He saw Myer's men slowly wiping out their opposition. He saw Myer disappear into the vault. He didn't see Emmett Devereaux weaving his way between vehicles and dead men heading for the vault. He assumed Devereaux had been shot. Beck's plan had half-worked, but ultimately failed. Now there would be one leader of the Kin – George Myer, the most brutal and inhuman of them all.

Devereaux edged around the smashed open vault door. He peered in. The hulking mass of George Myer stood in front of the gleaming gold, unmoving, surrounded by blood and torn apart bodies.

Devereaux didn't have an easy shot. He edged around the door, almost directly behind Myer. Crouched low, he raised his Glock, ecstatic at the prospect of shooting George Myer in the back. He had him. He forced himself to exhale before he squeezed the trigger. He knew he would need to shoot Myer more than once. But as he applied pressure to the trigger, a massive volley of gunfire erupted outside. Bullets hit everywhere. On the walls outside, the trucks, steel doors, and inside the vault.

George Myer dropped. Devereaux's shot went high. He kept firing, but he couldn't see Myer down on the ground. The Glock clicked empty. Devereaux dropped the Glock and pulled his knife. He screamed in rage and frustration as he scrambled forward to make sure George Myer was dead. He was going to stab Myer on every part of his body that was lethal. He was going to break his blade in Myer's skull.

Myer was on the ground struggling to get up. A high-velocity 5.56 had clipped his shoulder and spun him around. Devereaux leapt high, his knife positioned for an overhand stab. George Myer seemed defenseless. He wasn't. The sixteen-pound steel pry bar that Demarco Jones had used lay under Myer's hand. He grabbed it and swung the steel bar with adrenaline fueled force at Emmett Devereaux. The chiseled end of the pry bar hit the side of Emmett Devereaux's head while he was in midair. The force of it shattered his skull, broke Devereaux's neck, and killed him before the feared Kin enforcer landed amidst the gold Krugerrands, dead bodies, and hundred dollar bills.

Outside, Andy Miller's forces were advancing on the storage unit. He and his clan had come out of the scrub forest. Miller had his military issue M16 on full auto, loaded with two taped-together magazines. He and his people fired volleys, but not at the remaining Kin fighters. They fired over their heads until the few survivors dropped their weapons.

Beck watched Miller and a phalanx of men and women walking slowly like wraiths emerging from the darkness into the light. It was over. Finally. Andy Miller had carefully calculated when to make his move. Now he and his people were taking control. What that would mean in the end, Beck didn't know. He didn't care. It wasn't up to him anymore. There was nothing more he could do.

Beck turned to head back to the Kia, so drained by his wounds and weary from struggling so long without sleep he wasn't sure he could make it. He put everything out of his mind except taking the next step. And the next. And then, his peripheral vision caught something moving off to his right. A figure moving fast north and east away from the scene.

"No. No, no, no."

There could only be one man that size. George Myer running into the dark, running so he could fight another day.

A burst of rage hit Beck like an electric shock. This couldn't happen. Not after everything they'd done, everything they'd risked. Not after so many had died. Beck ran full out, angling toward Myer, closing the distance between them. Beck reached for his Browning, pulling it half out of his holster until he realized there was no time to stop, aim, and shoot at a running target. Before he even got his footing Myer would be gone into the dark. Beck stumbled, recovered, pushed his Browning back in the holster and strained for one more burst of speed. He closed the distance and dove at Myer in one last desperate attempt to stop him.

The impact shook them both. Myer had more mass. Beck had more speed. They both went down. Beck recovered first, rolling past Myer, and almost getting to his feet. But Myer reacted quickly. He didn't try to stand. He grabbed Beck's ankle and pulled him to the ground, then scrambled to get on top of Beck. Beck smashed an elbow into Myer's face. Myer straddled Beck. Before Myer could get his balance, Beck drove a fist into the side of Myer's head and shoved him off with his arms and hips.

Beck struggled onto his feet, reaching for his Browning. The gun wasn't there, knocked loose from the holster. Beck stepped back as Myer got to his feet, shaking his head, taking deep breaths.

The two men stood facing each other.

In the faint glow of light from the storage facility's light poles, it took a moment for Myer to recognize Beck without his beard. Myer growled, "You."

Beck nodded. He didn't dare take his eyes off Myer to look for his gun. He hadn't shoved it into the holster far enough. It was gone.

Myer balled his fists, stomped toward Beck, intent on murder.

Beck had fought big men before. But never in a snowstorm on an uneven field, injured and exhausted. Beck stepped farther back, testing the ground under his boots. His right foot went into a depression. He almost lost his balance. Beck couldn't backpedal and wait for an opening. This would be a stand-up punch-out. The odds were horribly in George Myer's favor.

Beck crouched low as the big man closed the distance between them. If Myer dove in for a takedown, Beck knew he didn't have the footing to counter him. Or the strength and leverage to stop Myer from beating him to death once Myer got him down. So Beck struck first. He leaped forward out of his crouching position, aiming a straight left fist at Myer's throat. Myer saw it coming and turned his shoulder, blocking the punch. He swung a roundhouse left at Beck's head. Too slow. Beck turned and ducked under the roundhouse, then twisted a right hook aimed at Myer's liver, but he couldn't shift his weight quickly enough on the snow-covered ground. The punch landed above Myer's left hip. Myer slammed both his forearms down on Beck's shoulders as if he could pound Beck into the ground. Beck went down onto his knees. Myer tried to ram his knee into Beck's face, but Beck blocked it with both arms. It still knocked him over. Beck rolled into the momentum and staggered to his feet.

His arms and shoulders felt paralyzed from Myer's blows. Myer smiled at him, unhurt, unfazed by the bleeding from the bullet that had grazed his left shoulder. Completely confident. He wanted to beat Beck down to the ground so he could stomp him to death.

Beck widened his stance. Myer stepped toward Beck. Again, Beck crouched low, forcing the taller man to punch down. Beck ducked and slipped the first four punches, took one that glanced off his injured ear. The pain infuriated Beck. He banged his head into Myer's chin, ducked, and came up again, landing a hard right into Myer's jaw. Beck knew he had connected. He ducked and dodged left away from a weak swing and banged a left hook to the other side of Myer's jaw. Myer grabbed at Beck, trying to get his arms around Beck's shoulders, but Beck dropped down again, twisted, turned, and pounded a left and a right hook into Myer's ribs. Myer grabbed him again. Beck dropped almost to his knees, breaking Myer's grip, punching Myer's midsection with his last bit of strength. It was like hitting a heavy bag that wouldn't move.

Myer managed to get one arm around Beck's neck, holding him in place. He punched Beck's head with blow after blow. The punches hurt, but they weren't knockout punches, landing mostly on the top and side of Beck's skull. Myer held on. Squeezing Beck's neck harder, twisting as if he could rip Beck's head off his shoulders. Beck couldn't breathe; the pain was paralyzing. He managed to turn his right shoulder into Myer's side, creating just enough room to backhand the side of his right fist between Myer's legs, again and again, until Myer finally gave up his grip.

Both men staggered back, gasping. Myer screamed at Beck. Head lowered, arms out, he lunged at Beck, determined to knock him down and get his hands around Beck's neck.

Beck had one move, one chance. His arms were gone. His fists battered. He launched a straight right kick, the same move he had used against Hamm Elrod when this insanity started. He didn't aim. He concentrated on meeting the force coming at him with as much force as he could muster.

It wasn't nearly enough to stop George Myer. He landed a heel into the left side of George Myer's snarling face. The big man's momentum carried him forward. Myer's head and shoulder smashed into Beck, knocking him back five feet. It felt like a car had hit him. Beck landed on something hard. A rock? An exposed root? Beck could barely breathe. He rolled over onto his hands and knees, facing Myer. He watched Myer force himself into a standing position.

Beck couldn't move. He knew it was over. He was done. He dropped his head. And then saw what he had landed on. It wasn't a rock. It was his gun.

Beck grabbed for the Browning, desperately trying to pull it out of the snow. Myer staggered forward. Beck had the gun in an icy grip. He rose up on his knees and pulled the slide back, chambering a round. Myer took a step and rushed at Beck coming at him like an avalanche. Beck fired three shots. Not enough to counter the momentum propelling the 272-pound man. George Myer's body crashed into Beck, knocking him back, falling on top of him, pinning the gun between them. Before Beck recovered from the impact, with his life draining out of him, Myer grabbed Beck's throat, intent on crushing Beck's windpipe as he was dying. Beck thrashed under the massive body. With his last bit of strength he pulled the gun out from between them, jammed it into Myer's left side, and pulled the trigger until the grip on his neck finally let up.

Beck was alive. Myer was dead. But Beck didn't have the strength to push the huge bleeding body off him. Beck could barely breathe. He felt the warm blood soaking into his clothes. He thought to himself, "What a strange, ridiculous way to die."

74

Beck was gone. Unconscious. And then he heard, as if in a distance, Irene Allen yelling at him. And then he felt released back into life as Manny Guzman and Irene managed to roll George Myer's dead body off him.

Beck gasped for breath and struggled to sit up but couldn't. Demarco and Ciro arrived and lifted him to his feet. Irene grabbed his bloody coat and yelled, "You were supposed to follow us!"

Beck coughed. Took a breath and said, "I was following you."

Ciro steadied Beck. Demarco took the Browning from Beck's hand slipped it into his pocket, already thinking about disassembling the parts and tossing the pieces into places they'd never be found.

Ciro said, "What were you doing under that fucking stronzo? Taking a nap?"

"Yeah, I figured I'd use him for a blanket."

Manny said, "C'mon, let's get out of here before the cops come."

Irene said, "They're already here. Andy has the undersheriff Bruno Cole and Russell Hibbard closing off the entrance until he and his people secure everything."

Beck took that in, once again he realizing there was much he didn't know about Andy Miller.

Irene turned to the others and said, "Can I talk to James for a minute?"

Beck nodded at his partners, and they headed for the trucks they'd left out of sight about twenty yards back in the dark.

Irene said to Beck, "I guess it's over."

"Is it?"

"What's left?"

Beck said, "Maybe figuring out who killed Joey Collins."

"Does it really matter?"

Beck said, "Maybe not. I wasn't thinking about it until a little while ago."

"Why then?"

"These last hours were insane, but for about a half hour I couldn't do anything until Jonas and Ricky opened the first safe. So I read the autopsy report on Joey Collins."

"How'd you get that?"

"From Proctor."

"What did you find out?"

"Collins had two wounds. A puncture wound to his throat. And a deep slash across his neck. Seemed like someone stabbed him from in front, and someone else slashed his throat from behind."

"I guess it was Vic and George. Vic in front, George from behind."

"Or was it you and Miller? And don't tell me you were with me when it happened."

Irene took that in. "What makes you say that?"

"Your clothes."

"What?"

"That night, at my house, before we got into bed, you went to put your clothes in my washing machine because they smelled of smoke from the fires. You turned on the machine, but you didn't put your clothes in. You did that later when you came back."

"From where?"

"I'm assuming the Field. That morning, I got up before you. I took your clothes out of my washing machine and put them in the dryer. There was something about your clothes that I noticed. It was in the back of my mind until now."

"What?"

"They were too wet. The spin cycle on my washing machine is set to high. If your clothes had been sitting in the washing machine for three or four hours, they would've been a lot dryer. You washed your clothes when you returned. Maybe to get the blood off them."

"You concluded all that from wet clothes?"

"And the fact that you didn't want to go back and get your car that morning. You asked me to drive you to work. You only agreed after I pointed out you wouldn't have a car to drive home after work. The closer we got to the Field, the quieter you got."

Irene nodded. "Okay, Sherlock. I did go back. I took your truck. The key was in it. But I didn't go back to kill Joey Collins. I went back to talk to him."

"About what?"

"Helping me and Andy do something about the Kin. We didn't think Collins agreed with the way the Kin operated. Plus, Collins was pissed off about what happened during that robbery. And the way Hamm Elrod was blaming him. Andy figured it was a good time to feel him out. Andy said Oscar Lund told Joey and Hamm to stay at the Field until closing to establish an alibi. So I took a shot. I went there to recruit him. I had no reason to kill him."

Beck said, "I could come up with a few reasons."

"Like what?"

"His family supported the Kin for generations. Maybe he still did. Maybe your conversation didn't go so well, and he threatened to rat you out, so you and Miller had to prevent that. Or maybe you knew that killing him would start a war in the Kin that you could use to your advantage."

Irene said, "Or maybe Joey thought the Kin his family supported way back when had changed for the worse. Maybe Dent-Morelli found out Joey wasn't buying into all the Kin's Nazi heritage and white supremacy shit. Maybe he didn't want Joey competing for leadership. Maybe he considered Joey a weakling and decided to kill him and use his murder as an excuse to clean house. Maybe Dent engineered the whole robbery thing and made sure Joey was at the Field so George and Vic could kill him."

Beck said, "That's a lot of maybes."

"And maybe that's exactly how it went. I can see you suspecting me because I snuck out on you and made you suspicious about the way I acted in the morning. But when I got back to the Field, I parked your truck off the road and walked in. I saw Joey Collins dead in the parking area near the fence. His blood was all over the snow and ice. It scared the shit out of me. I raced back to your place. When I got back, I took another shower. Like I was freshening up after our…time together. And you're right. That's when I washed my clothes."

"And yet you told me that you let Proctor arrest you because you didn't know Collins was dead. You said you thought he was arresting you for stabbing Hamm Elrod."

"Chrissake Beck, that was the best I could come up with. You think I believed all those deputies and state police were at the Field because fat-ass Hamm Elrod got poked in the arm?"

"So why did you let him arrest you?"

"Because I knew I didn't kill Joey and figured they'd have no case. And because I couldn't let you knock out Proctor and take his gun. Or whatever you were going to do. Like I told you, we would've had the whole sheriff's department after us. And the state police."

Beck nodded. He turned and started walking toward where he'd left the Kia SUV.

"Well, there's no case against you now. I've got all the evidence Proctor faked. And Proctor won't be around to do anything. You confirmed that with Andy, right?"

Irene walked next to him. "I did. He had two of his people follow Proctor when he left. They were going to take care of him as soon as he pulled into the first rest stop. And bring back the gold you gave him."

"Good."

She asked, "So what now?"

Beck said, "Time to disappear."

"Where're you going?"

"Someplace warm."

"How?"

"One of my guys chartered a jet. It's waiting in Albany. He said we got one just before the Christmas vacation rush."

"You are goddamn rich, aren't you?"

"Yes."

They walked a few more steps. Irene waited for Beck to say more, but he didn't.

She pulled her passport out of her back pocket and said, "You know, I went to a lot of trouble to get this and hang onto it."

"I know."

"If you're not going to ask me to come with you, why'd you let me drive out of there with your guys?"

"Because I had no guarantee my plan was going to work. Or that Miller would show up. And I didn't know he had the fix in with the sheriff's department. Are you sure you want to leave with us?"

Irene grimaced. Finally, she said, "Actually, no. I'm not."

Beck nodded and said, "For what it's worth, I think you should stay here. I know Miller is counting on you. You two could make sure the fight was worth it. There's at least two hundred million dollars you and Miller can put to use alleviating some of the misery the Kin has caused over the years."

A noise behind them made Beck and Irene stop and look back at the storage facility. Someone had slammed shut the door of Dent's storage unit hiding the gold and the damaged walk-in vault. He bent over to padlock the door.

Miller's people were fading away into the forest. The few surviving Kin fighters who could walk went with them. The wounded and dead had been loaded into trucks and driven toward the office. There was no trace of the final battle in front of Dent's storage unit. Soon the sheriff's deputies would be streaming in to clean up after an internecine war between factions of the Kin, presumably over the contents of safes that were now empty.

Irene said, "I don't suppose you'd consider coming back at some point and helping us."

"No. It's not my fight now, Irene. It never really was."

Irene nodded and said, "One last question, James Beck."

"What?"

"How did you know you'd win?"

Beck looked at Irene. "I didn't."

"Then why'd you do it?"

"In my world, if someone does what they did to me, to my guys, to you, it's not even a question."

Irene nodded. "But did you actually believe you could win?"

"I knew we were united, and they were divided. We were fighting for our lives; they were fighting for a bullshit fantasy. That's not good enough when someone actually starts shooting back."

Irene nodded again.

Beck said, "I also figured you and Miller had something going on against the Kin. So, it wasn't just our fight."

"Right."

"Hey, I have to get out of here before I fall down."

"Yes. Sure."

"I can't drive. I'll go with Manny in my truck. If you need a car, there's a nice Kia out there you could use for a few days. The fob is in the cup holder."

"Still considerate to the end, huh?"

"Sure."

"I think I'll leave it there. I'll come up with something."

"That's probably smart."

Suddenly, Irene stepped forward and kissed Beck on the lips, lightly and tenderly. She stepped back and said, "Goodbye, James Beck. Take care of yourself." Then Irene Allen turned and walked away.

Beck watched her head for the storage facility. She seemed more diminutive than ever, but somehow now walking with more purpose than ever.

He turned and trudged toward Manny, Demarco, and Ciro who were waiting near the back of Beck's black truck, the red tail lights illuminating them. He wasn't far from them. Only about fifteen yards to go. But it seemed very long.

None of the three moved forward to help him. They wouldn't take away his dignity. Beck walked slowly realizing he'd never really understood Irene Allen. He had been almost certain that she had killed Joey Collins. Even now, he could picture it. She would have had no trouble approaching Collins without alarming him. At least not at first. And then when he became suspicious, or heard someone approaching from behind, stab him. Beck wondered if a detailed autopsy report would show that the knife entered on an upward angle. He had little doubt that Andy Miller had the wherewithal to come out of the dark behind Collins and render the terrible wound that had started a war.

Beck smiled. He'd never really know. And he was fine with that.

As he approached his truck, Manny climbed behind the wheel. Beck struggled into the passenger seat. Ciro and Demarco headed for the Honda Ridgeline to lead the way out.

Manny turned to Beck. "You good?"

Beck said, "Are we all alive?"

"Yep."

"Then I'm good."

AUTHOR'S NOTE:

There are hundreds of extremist groups in the U.S. They run the gamut from white supremacists to anti-government to Neo-Nazi to general hate groups. It's not uncommon for some of these groups to finance their operations through crime and pursue their goals through violence and, in some cases, murder. Nor is it surprising that some collude with sympathizers in law enforcement.

The Kin, of course, doesn't exist. It is a fictionalized amalgam of these groups created to dramatize an underlying reality. Although I set the story in upstate New York, it's not meant to convey that rural New York is specifically a home for extremist groups that are a danger to America's multi-racial democracy. These groups exist in all fifty states. That being the case, I've used made-up names for the area in which the action takes place. There is no Cumberland County in New York State. Most of the names of towns are also made up.

ACKNOWLEDGEMENTS:

I am deeply thankful to Brooks McMullin, Dermott Ryan, Howard Shultz, Pavel Alexandrov, Joe Hartlaub, and Nick Utton who were generous enough to read an Advanced Copy of *Tribes* and offer their immensely helpful reactions, corrections, and advice. *Tribes* became a much better book because of them. Also, thanks to retired New York State trooper Captain Tony Miserendino who early on helped me to understand how state and county law enforcement agencies interact in N.Y. State and how they share resources. Any inaccuracies on how things work are mine, not his. And of course, thank you Ellen for all your help and support. Not to mention how wonderful it is to have another writer across the hall to accompany me on the long journey it takes (for me) to write a novel.

AND A REQUEST:

If you enjoyed *Tribes*, it would mean the world to me if you would share your opinion with others by posting a review. Amazon, for better or worse, is the place where many readers turn to for reviews. It's easy to post a review there. A rating and a few words are all that's needed, but feel free to go into detail. I appreciate knowing what readers think of my work. It is extremely helpful to me.

Thanks.

For more information on my other books, reviews, publishing schedule, blog posts and more, visit www.johnclarkson.com

Made in the USA
Las Vegas, NV
03 March 2025

18975325R00246